THE

Complete Tales

OF

Nikolai Gogol

Volume I

THE

Complete Tales

OF

Nikolai Gogol

Volume I

*Edited, with an introduction
and notes, by*

LEONARD J. KENT

❖❔❖❔❖❔❖❔❖

*The Constance Garnett translation has been
revised throughout by the editor*

THE UNIVERSITY OF CHICAGO PRESS

Chicago and London

Published by arrangement with Chatto & Windus Ltd. — The Hogarth Press Ltd., London and A. P. Watt Ltd.

Portions of this book are adapted from the following translations of Nikolai Gogol by Constance Garnett: *Evenings on a Farm near Dikanka* © 1926 by Constance Garnett, renewed 1954: *The Overcoat and Other Stories* © 1923 by Constance Garnett, renewed 1950.

The University of Chicago Press, Chicago 60637
The University of Chicago Press, Ltd. London

02 01 00 99 98 97 96 95 94 93   5 6 7 8 9 10

Library of Congress Cataloging in Publication Data

Gogol' , Nikolaĭ Vasil'evich, 1809–1852.
 The complete tales of Nikolai Gogol.

 "The Constance Garnett translation has been revised throughout by the editor."
 Bibliography: p.
 I. Kent, Leonard J., 1930-   II. Title.
PG3333.A15   1985   891.73′3   84-16221
ISBN 0-226-30068-4 (vol. 1)
    0-226-30069-2 (vol. 2)

For VALERIE

CONTENTS of Volume 2

CONTENTS

PREFACE

When *The Collected Tales and Plays of Nikolai Gogol* was published by Pantheon in 1964, and then by Modern Library in 1969, I included in those editions some prefatory remarks about the world needing a collected Gogol, some forty years having elapsed since Constance Garnett's five-volume translation—long out of print and extremely difficult to find—had appeared. I noted that only Gogol's novel, *Dead Souls*, and one of his three completed plays, *The Inspector General*, had been rendered into English with considerable success, by B. G. Guerney. I grumbled about the stories having been dealt with shabbily, if at all, almost always appearing in mediocre translations, in slender, garish paperbacks, each containing several tales flung together haphazardly, as if Gogol had no organizational principles in mind! Then, too, these mishmashes were perversely free of even the most basic annotation. Perhaps Everyman would simply intuit what he needed to know about these pieces. For example, opening the pages of Gogol's first story, *The Fair at Sorochintsy*, would it not be immediately clear that the peasants climbing atop blazing stoves were not simply masochists, that Little Russia was not another of those adorable Russian diminutives, that girls with black eyebrows had neither Latin fathers nor baleful souls, and so on?

In terms of these earlier complaints, I stand about where I stood, with one happy exception: Milton Ehre and Fruma Gottschalk have translated the plays in a manner superior to all earlier efforts (including Garnett's, for her version of the plays is most uncharacteristically subdued, even flat). On the other hand, the Guerney *Dead Souls*—which first appeared at its best in 1948—is now out of print. It remains a first-rate translation, always spirited, often eloquent, sometimes absolutely inspired (despite a pervasive whimsicality). Bookstores now carry three other versions: the Magarshack is easily the best of these, being "accurate" and "readable" even as it is sometimes inelegant and a bit precious; the Reavey seems merely conscientious and plodding; the MacAndrew—and original lines simply vanish in many of his efforts!—should be read only *in extremis*. As for the tales, some of them are still available in motley: disconnected and discontinuous as ever.

This said, it is gratifying and salutary to note that the quality of Gogol studies these past twenty years has been exceptional. Among other wholly admirable achievements are those of Victor Erlich, Simon Karlinsky, Robert Maguire, and Donald Fanger. *Spasibo!*

This edition of all the tales—as Gogol organized them—reproduces the apparatus of the earlier editions: an introduction and footnotes intended to inform, a chart describing the Russian civil service ranks of Gogol's day, a chronological list of all his writings. The bibliography, expanded and updated, is the most ample available. (The reader new to Gogol criticism might do well to begin by reading in the dozens of works published these last twenty or so years—*after* reading Gogol, of course.) There are a number of corrections and new revisions, the result of time, distance, and criticism.

For his generous assistance in proofing these volumes, thanks to my dear friend and colleague, Oscar José Santucho.

It is a pleasure again to invite you to partake of Gogol's inimitable feast. He was the most wonderfully original and delightfully, maddeningly, idiosyncratic of them all: a virtuoso who better than anyone else knew how to tiptoe through the world upside down.

LEONARD J. KENT

Cheshire, Connecticut 06410
August, 1984

ABOUT THE TRANSLATION

The decision made twenty years ago to use the Constance Garnett translation as the basic text for a collected edition seems now even more obvious and correct than it did then. Despite an infrequent misreading or Victorianism, her work remains remarkable; indeed, in the context of almost all subsequent efforts, her grace, eloquence, and verve now seem even closer to the tone and letter, the very spirit of Gogol. Then, too, did she not have the marvelous good sense and rare taste to preserve the interrelated thematic cycles without which others "make mincemeat of the author's intentions"?

The thousands of revisions made earlier have been augmented by a far more modest number of new ones. The effort to keep faith with the soul of the original continues. To this end, among other things, Cossacks have still not learned to say "Hi!" All the Agafyas and Matveys have refused to become Agathas and Matthews. The medium of exchange remains kopeks and rubles. (Indeed, could one ever again sleep the sleep of the truly innocent if Akaky Akakyevich—in a Penguin edition, almost certainly—was but once to shriek, "Sixteen quid for an overcoat!"?)

L. J. K.

INTRODUCTION

All of Gogol's tales are in these two volumes. He wrote far less than any other major Russian and yet what he wrote is not of whole cloth. We have here the romantic, fantastic, Gothic, as well as the realistic and satiric; there is the sentimental, and yet there is the grotesque, too; we have here singular examples of Russian humor, but so too do we have extraordinary examples of Russian horror; we have writing that is brilliantly imaginative and highly original, but also that which is strongly derivative; there is the inimitable Gogol prose—coarse, dense, nervous, exuberant, hyperbolic, and there is another kind of prose—dignified and eloquent. Can we find a common denominator?

Ever since the publication of *The Overcoat* in 1842, Nikolai Vasilievich Gogol has generally been viewed from one of two extreme positions. Motivated more by subjectively created points of view (including those born of public and political pressures) than by objective analysis of textual, historical, and biographical evidence, many critics have approached Gogol with specific critical apparatus that is so strictured that it almost always precludes appreciation of diverse or inconsistent or contradictory or paradoxical elements within the works. By striving too hard to shove Gogol into a carefully labeled drawer—a convenient but hardly enlightened arrangement—these critics make simple that which is never so simple, even when dealing with a far less complex subject.

It was the very important Russian critic Vissarion Belinsky, an outspoken leader of the liberal wing, who created and championed one of the extreme points of view. Belinsky interpreted Gogol to serve his ends; he insisted that Gogol was a naturalist, a realist; life was in his works; he was a depictor of what was, a staunch benefactor of the much-abused "little man," the insulted and the injured; he was an apostle of progress (and this about an amazingly consistent archconservative who accepted even serfdom as a necessary and desirable condition of life). Belinsky fed Gogol's ravenous ego, and Gogol too much needed and enjoyed the accolades to correct the faulty premises on which Belinsky had based his arguments. Gogol awoke one morning to find himself a founder and inspirer of the Russian realistic movement. Even Dostoevsky (who certainly knew better, for his *Poor Folk*, so deeply indebted to Gogol's *The Overcoat*, is yet so imbued with genuine compassion for the downtrodden and the humiliated that it is an implicit criticism of the lack of sympathy Dostoevsky found in Gogol's treatment of the "little man") allegedly added to Gogol's stature as a realist by noting that "We all come from under Gogol's *Overcoat*." [1] If so, was it realism per se that Dostoevsky was referring to or, rather, the vistas that Gogol had helped open up, the subject matter with which he dealt that helped irreversibly broaden the horizon and scope of the literature which was to follow?

It remained for Dmitry Merezhkovsky, a leader of the Russian symbolist movement which flourished during the last years of the nineteenth and the first and second decades of the twentieth century, to break away from Belinsky's point of view. By the time of the emergence of the symbolist movement the pendulum of taste had swung to the opposite end of its arc. Gogol, the symbolists now proclaimed, cared nothing for "reality." He neither revealed nor exposed; he merely created fantasies, imaginative, distorted fantasies that had no relationship to reality; he projected himself, his own very marked neuroses; he was, they insisted, a creator and not a reflector. And it is not without irony that the Soviets, almost one hundred years after Belinsky's appraisal of Gogol, joined forces with the great liberal and pushed the pendulum back to its original position, and once more Gogol became "an apostle of enlightenment."

And what of Gogol's originality? Is he a phenomenon seemingly without roots and obligations? One might be led to such a conclusion after noticing that the question of his indebtedness to ante-

---

[1] Scholarly tradition has long insisted that Dostoevsky made this comment and we therefore include it; however, no one, to my knowledge, has ever been able to find this very famous line in any of Dostoevsky's writings. Melchior de Vogué is often thought to have attributed the statement to Dostoevsky, but he attributes it only to a Russian "very much involved in the literary history of the last forty years [1846-86]" (*Le Roman russe*, Paris, 1897, p. 96).

cedent literary history is usually ignored or mishandled, or paid such scant attention to that the implication of total originality is quite impossible to avoid. Or, as others insist, is he merely a reflection of the writers who had preceded him?

What of his influence? Is it true that among the great Russian writers only the young Dostoevsky learned from him, that Turgenev and Goncharov and Tolstoy, true realists, owe him nothing?

Nikolai Gogol contains multitudes. We cannot ignore historical and textual and, in Gogol's case especially, biographical data in trying to determine what he was, how he became what he was, how important he was, and the heritage he left behind.

There were at least five powerful literary influences operating in Russia at the time of Gogol's birth; these were assimilated and used to direct and shape the efforts of this most essentially original of all the great Russians: the sentimental novel, the fantastic (Gothic) novel, the historical novel, Ukrainian folklore, and the Russian literary tradition.

The sentimental novel, its obvious excesses aside (and who can forget Richardson's virtuous and nonvirtuous heroes, *les rakes*, his tightly corseted and forever-fainting heroines?), must be appreciated as much more than merely a framework for the expression of sentimentality which Meredith called "fiddling harmonics on the string of sensualism." It made profound contributions to the genres which were to supersede it.

Rousseauistic in origin and in philosophy, devised mainly to illustrate innocence and inherent human goodness, the sentimental novel had no choice (if its obvious didacticism was to be effective, if it was to depict positive characteristics) but to complement the goodness of its characters; and to accomplish this, stressful settings were created to show characters to have not merely, in Milton's terms, "blank virtue" (cloistered goodness), but "pure virtue" (experience-born goodness). The characters who peopled these books, therefore, were not at all unlike those we usually accept as being essentially naturalistic. The sentimental novel redefined the hero image. Social position and knowledgeability per se were no longer considered adequate or indispensable requisites. Virtue, moral fiber, became the essential criterion. The pathetic situation, in turn, to be artistically conveyed, demanded a setting that was immediately recognizable to the reader, hence realistic. Indeed, and this is not con-

tradictory, much of sentimental literature was pervaded by a genuinely realistic tone, atmosphere, and framework. Its people, again
despite their excess of sensibility, were identifiable human beings.
The *Luftmensch* had settled to earth. Further, though it is generally
agreed that "The great wave of the international romantic movement had spent its force in the fourth decade of the nineteenth century" (the exact decade during which both *The Overcoat* and *Dead
Souls* saw life), we hold that it was this very movement that supplied the sentimental philosophy which enabled Gogol to use for
major characters the insignificant, the iconoclast, the pariah, the
lunatic, and the rogue (who owes much to the picaresque tradition,
too). The earlier movement established the attitude that enabled the
likes of Akaky Akakievich and Chichikov to serve as central characters. The new hero, the humbled, humiliated, insulted, injured,
and his foils, the rogue, rascal, cheat, were born of a pathetic rather
than an ethical attitude toward life. Not only was the seed that
was to sprout into the naturalistic tree present in the sentimental
novel, but, in the later genres, unmistakable vestiges of both Rous-
seauism and sentimentality remain. The influence of the sentimental
novel was impossible to avoid in Gogol's Russia; indeed, Gogol
often refers to such novels in his letters (he knew them in either
Russian or German translations).

The sentimental novel, then, supplied Gogol with a general type
of protagonist and the pathetic milieu and attitude within which he
would function.

The fantastic school, essentially romantic to its shuddering core,
supplied less clear but equally vital ingredients. Generally, "mood"
best describes the contribution.

The relative neglect of this latter influence probably stems from a
contemporary revaluation of its material. The works of Ann Rad-
cliffe and even those of the much superior E. T. A. Hoffmann—
enormously appreciated in Gogol's Russia—are sometimes considered crude and inept, somehow inferior art because tastes have
changed. But in nineteenth-century Russia, Gothic writings were as
popular as they were in Western Europe. The influence of Hoffmann was all-pervasive. The impact in Russia of this genre, perhaps
out of all proportion to its inherent merit, was possible because of
Russia's attachment to things Western, but was not a concomitant
of general sophistication. The Russian public generally depended on
foreign taste without having reached the level of foreign sophistica-

tion that would have enabled it to accept such material with more detachment, reserve, and critical insight. The public overreacted to it; it too avidly accepted this fresh import and established it, on the conscious level, as a standard to be imitated (and when Pushkin—with Hoffmann in mind—wrote *The Queen of Spades* the effect must have been staggering).

The popularity of the Gothic novel was such that it is impossible to avoid the conclusion that Gogol knew many of them at first hand, many more by reputation.

In brief, Gogol fell heir to the glorification of the supernatural. The symbolic dream had been born (or, rather, reborn) in Hoffmann. The irrational and incomprehensible world that lurks behind visible activity was lighted up. The spiritual and mystical became prominent. The dark corner became more important than the sun-drenched field. The shadows grew more central than the subjects that cast them. This view of life, focusing on the small, cramped, closed, struggling section of humanity, discovered man inextricably bound in a tightly constructed and airless room. Melancholia bathed the setting and its people, a melancholia intimately interwoven with sentimentality, yet expressing the "brooding" rather than the "aching" heart.

Certainly a great deal of Gogol's art may be viewed as a reaction against the sentimental and fantastic schools, but even this very reaction owed much to its precursors.

As for the historical novel, it had long been imported from the Western world, and novels of adventure were eagerly devoured. Walter Scott's romances were enormously popular; indeed, imitations were much in vogue years before Gogol wrote *Taras Bulba*. Even if we find it difficult to discover Scott reflected in *Bulba*, we must yet admit that the historical novel of the West was not only responsible, in great measure, for the inspiration and birth of *Bulba*, but, indeed, had for a long time been preparing an audience for its reception. *Bulba*, after all, essentially a highly romanticized recreation of the tone and quality of an historical period written in the epic tradition, had no direct Russian antecedents.

Ukrainian folklore and its tradition (for details of which Gogol incessantly pestered his mother) permeate the two volumes of *Evenings on a Farm near Dikanka*. With the exception of *Ivan Fiodorovich Shponka and His Aunt*, a highly realistic story with grotesque elements in it, *Evenings* consists of imaginative, escapist,

fantastic, romantic stories which combine eloquent passages of de-
scriptive narrative, realistic elements, coarseness, earthy humor, and
gruesomeness. Much of the thematic material stems directly from
the folklore tradition (that included the enormously popular puppet
theater, of which Gogol was so fond that he included it in the setting of several of the stories). Gogol's early characters are drawn
from this tradition (if inimitably shaped by him): sorcerers, de-
mons, water spirits, and a peculiar kind of Russian devil who is at
once earthy (e.g., he's not above trying to seduce a married woman
—who is not above being seduced) and frightening (but vulnera-
ble); as well as superstition-motivated peasants almost always in
pursuit of riotous and fleshy pleasures, intrepid and reckless Cossacks, boys with flashing eyes and pounding hearts, and the dark-
browed beauties who dream of them. What Gogol drew from the
Ukraine served him far beyond his earliest volumes. The coarseness,
the densely textured prose, the search for the detail that strips away
pretension, the sheer exuberance—all were qualities early learned
and long retained.

There is the matter of Gogol's language. The tradition of re-
strictive pseudoclassical taste had been chipped away by many of
Gogol's precursors (Karamzin, Krylov, and Zhukovsky, for example). The Russian tongue had been revivified, put to uses which
were once imagined beyond its potential. Pushkin, more admired as
a poet than as a writer of fiction, wrote prose that was measured
and reserved. His success in disciplining Russian and making it
highly functional was important to Gogol.

We have barely touched the list of influences (D. S. Mirsky, for
example, has compiled his own list: "the numerous mixed traditions
of comic writing from Molière to the vaudevillists of the twenties,
[and] Sterne, chiefly through the medium of German romanti-
cism," etc.), but perhaps we have made our point. The stage has
been set. We focus on April 1, 1809,[2] the Ukrainian market town of
Sorochintsy, where "our hero" is about to be born.

Nikolai Vasilievich Gogol was the third of twelve children born
to Maria Ivanovna and Vasily Gogol and the first to survive in-
fancy. His mother, eighteen years old at the time of his birth, also

---

[2] New Style. The Russians used the Julian calendar (Old Style) until 1917 and,
in the nineteenth century, were twelve days behind the Gregorian calendar
used in the West. Dates have been converted to correspond to Western practice.

contained multitudes: she was at once deeply pious and superstitious, a fervent believer in omens, premonitions, and dreams; she was incredibly naïve, and, to judge from her letters, was never more than semiliterate. It was not without difficulty that she distinguished between the actual and the fanciful, and she never quite reconciled her professed morality with a sense of ethics (she was, for example, eager for her son to supplement his income in the civil service by taking bribes! Wasn't everyone?). The extent of her sophistication can be garnered from material collected by her biographer, which includes, in her own words, the story of how the Queen of Heaven graciously appeared to her in a dream and indicated who her future husband would be. And much later, in an autobiographical sketch (which she knew would be read), there is a comment to the effect that she was so inordinately fond of her husband at the time of their marriage that she almost believed, though she could never quite decide, that she preferred him to her favorite old aunt.

Gogol's father, a small landowner, like his wife was one of those countless members of the petty gentry, but infinitely more worldly than she. An amateur playwright who even had one of his plays published, he was gregarious and apparently outgoing, but he was pathologically tainted. He suffered from two diseases: manic-depression and hypochondria; and worse, from a chronic Russian illness, lack of funds. We can well appreciate this comment by Janko Lavrin (a native Yugoslav with a penchant for British understatement): "The offspring of such a couple could hardly boast of overflowing vitality, energy, and health."

Nikolai Gogol, almost dead at birth, somehow survived. His mother lavished all she had on her sickly child. She smothered him with concern. His ego grew immense from such nourishment; the mother inculcated in him her own peculiarities, imbued him not only with her own mysticism, but, perhaps more important, with a totally unrealistic and debilitating sense of self-worth and self-esteem. And there was other "nourishment" too, which was to haunt him to his death: tales of the devil and of the eternal fires blazing in hell, the torment inflicted upon sinners which his mother, he wrote in a letter, "described so strikingly, in such a horrifying way." And from the same letter, recalling his childhood:

I felt nothing passionately; everything seemed created solely to gratify me. I loved only you, and I only loved you because Nature herself had inspired this feeling in me. I viewed everything with indifference. I attended church because I was ordered to go, or because I was carried there. . . . I crossed myself only because I saw others doing it.

In such a setting, with his own intrinsic nervousness serving as catalyst, early in life he began to withdraw from the threatening world of reality into the much more comfortable world of fantasy. He defended himself by becoming introverted, and he fed his ego with his vibrant imagination. But under such circumstances the personality is warped. Spontaneity is destroyed. And it is not difficult to understand complementary causes of his incipient psychosis when we cull from letters and reminiscences of his contemporaries descriptions of him as he attended school in Nyezhin, which he entered at twelve, during May 1821, and which he left not before the middle of 1828: his face "seemed to be transparent"; he had a persistent skin disease which caused him great discomfort; his shoulders were already stooped, and he was thin and short (with the unkindness common to young people, his schoolmates soon dubbed him "the mysterious dwarf"). He was nearsighted and, by his own admission, his nose was an enormous if not unfaithful beast. His Latin teacher described him as "always taciturn, as if there was something he was hiding in his soul; he had an indolent look and he walked with a shuffling motion." That he had an exceedingly difficult time of it at school is obvious. But he fought back. His wit was his only weapon, and he used it to destroy others. By shifting the focus of the coarse laughter he was able to succor himself. He was very capable of laughing, but only at the expense of others.

Reading the letters he wrote home from Nyezhin, one begins to appreciate his agony. Everywhere are to be seen the defensive forces that he mustered. He is overwhelmingly precious and melodramatic. The letters are a riot of pretentiousness. When he is involved with his favorite subject, "Me," he grows hyperbolic and delusional.

In two letters he wrote in October 1827, we can see the quality of his thought. The first is to one of his few friends; the second to his uncle:

> I do not know if my plans will come true, whether I too will live in that heavenly spot [St. Petersburg] or whether the wheel of fate will heartlessly cast me with the crowds of the self-contented mob

(what a horrible thought!) into the world of nonentities, consigning me to the dismal quarter of obscurity.

Cold sweat drenches my face at the thought that I may perish in dust without becoming famous for any extraordinary accomplishment. Living in this world would be terrible if I failed to make my being beneficial.

Gogol insisted that he had learned very little from that "stupid institution," but he had read. He knew something of Pushkin, and in letters to his mother he often requested literary magazines. Then, too, he had already begun work on a long poem inspired by Voss's *Luise*.

It is not surprising that Gogol was successful as an actor while at school (he had always been a good mimic, and he needed a place in the spotlight) and that, further, he was singularly effective in female parts.

Gogol's sexuality, or lack of it, has long been subjected to lively if not always enlightened debate. In letters to his father, there are several references to the fact that he had improved his state of morality while at Nyezhin, the implication being, of course, that while at home, perhaps on vacation, he had been sexually involved with one or more of the serf girls, but that he had since seen the light. We know of no other possible sexual experience he might have had throughout the course of his life, but even a not very close reading of his works strongly points to the sexual abnormality of their author.

Gogol's women are either highly idealized (there is a parade of alabaster-breasted heroines) or threatening or destructive: in *Ivan Shponka*, they appear in frightening numbers with goose faces; in *Taras Bulba*, it is the bloodless heroine who destroys Andrei; in *Viy*, the female is a fiendish ghoul; in *The Marriage*, the hero leaps from a window lest he be forced to give up his bachelorhood. In *The Nose*, there is obvious material available for a Freudian interpretation of a castration complex; in *Nevsky Prospekt*, we detect Gogol's deep revulsion toward the sensuous, and so on. Only Gogol's very coarse women contain the sparks of life.

It is possible that if Gogol did indeed have an affair on his father's estate, his sense of guilt caused him to overreact and destroyed his future capacity to love; but it seems more consistent, in the light of what we know of him and his situation, to believe that he created a sexual fantasy with which to torment his parents and titillate himself. He was able, using this fantasy, to create an opportunity to pat himself on the back for no longer doing what he had not done.

In an essay called *Woman*, Gogol's intrinsic make-up is manifest: "What is woman? The language of the Gods! She is poetry. . . ." One must give to love. Gogol had long been conditioned to receive.

Evidence of compulsive autoeroticism is consistent with our point of view. In the Russian edition of Gogol's collected works, there is a highly revealing autobiographical piece in diary form, *Nights in a Villa*. In it, Gogol describes his friendship with a young man, Iosif Vielhorsky, in surprisingly brazen physical terms, something he could never accomplish when writing of or describing a woman. He may have been a discreet homosexual; there is no doubt of such fantasies. (See S. Karlinsky's provocative *The Sexual Labyrinth of Nikolai Gogol* [Cambridge, 1976]).

Late in 1828, at nineteen, this very complex human being left for St. Petersburg to make his mark. In letters home, he wrote of devoting himself to humanity, of "taking up jurisprudence." Perhaps he really went there to publish the long poem he had been working on even while at school. Most probably, Gogol left for St. Petersburg with little idea of what he was going to do there, knowing only that he had to do something.

St. Petersburg welcomed him coldly and cruelly—especially his nose—and this confused young man found himself in bed for days, his nose frostbitten and his eyes running from a severe cold. Wracked with depression, he wrote his mother that he was "sitting around and doing nothing . . . the [favorable] rumors spread about it [St. Petersburg] are nothing but lies. . . ." But something had to be done.

Whether he tried to get a job in the civil service at this time is moot. He wrote his mother that this was the case, but what Gogol wrote her sometimes bore no relationship to truth (he often fed her the pap on which she thrived). We know he did apply for a job in the theater, stammered his way through an excruciating interview, but his effeminate voice and a totally indifferent reading precluded success on the stage. The situation was desperate when he wrote his mother asking for information about the Ukraine, its traditions, and its dress ("to the last ribbon"). In cold St. Petersburg, stories of the warm and sunny Ukraine were very much appreciated, and

Gogol hoped that writing tales of the Ukraine would bring commercial success, or at least a respite from his poverty.

Maria Ivanovna answered. Information was supplied; money and the inevitable bits of tidy morality were furnished too. But even before this support arrived from home, Gogol had published (at expense he could ill afford) the poem he had brought with him from Nyezhin, *Hanz [sic] Küchelgarten,* under the pseudonym V. Alov. In the introduction to the poem, Gogol, in need of a heavy pat on the back, blew his own horn (even as Chartkov will later blow his in *The Portrait*):

> . . . we are proud to have been instrumental in acquainting the world with the creative work of a young man of talent. . . .

But Gogol had misjudged the world's eagerness to meet him. The reviews that appeared were fair: that is, they found nothing singular about it, and ridiculed its pretentiousness. Gogol was devastated, especially because it becomes increasingly clear that his intense desire to succeed, to serve as benefactor, to rise above the mass of mediocrity, grew from an ever-increasing conviction that the world was really no more than a haven for what he later called *poshlost,* that is, banality and tawdriness, triviality, pretentiousness, petty conceits; that he wanted to escape surrendering to a totally negative vision of humanity.

The poem is very long, without distinction, and derivative; Gogol burned all the copies he could get his hands on after its poor reception. Not translated into English, its primary interest lies in offering us an insight into the ambivalent forces within him, the contradiction between what was expected of him (what he feared he would yield to) and what he expected of himself. The hero (Hans-Gogol) is a restless romantic who leaves both home and sweetheart (and in letters to his mother Gogol had often mentioned some vague dream about sacrificing himself for humanity in some distant land) to travel the world and search for answers to the eternal enigmas of life, only to return to home and sweetheart and spend the rest of his days in comfort and joy, in *poshlost.* And this, in relative terms, was one of the choices open to Gogol: the civil service and a measure of respectability, some money and the creature comforts of a steaming samovar—a full belly and a dead soul. But Gogol himself was too disturbed and agitated to settle for this. He did what he had to do: he ran, but he could not enjoy running away. There was too much guilt (disappointing his mother, absconding with a sizable sum of her money) attached to preclude the need to rationalize. A proficient liar, he invented three excuses: it was God's will (and his mother saw everything in this light); he was in physical distress (not at all unusual); he had had a shattering love affair with an angel ("She was a divinity") who turned out to be more than slightly fallen (and some critics also believe this).

"Lacerated soul" and all, Gogol boarded a steamer, noting that he was going to America, where, theoretically, neurotic geniuses were more warmly welcomed, but the ship stopped in Lübeck, Germany, and so too did Gogol (though he did do some wandering through the Continent). He returned to St. Petersburg after several weeks, and surrendered to the civil service (taking a job that rivaled the triviality of Akaky's in *The Overcoat*); but in 1830, while he was still in the service, *St. John's Eve,* one of the stories to appear the following year in *Evenings on a Farm near Dikanka,* was published in a St. Petersburg magazine. It was the beginning of his literary career.

By the end of the same year, a number of his stories and articles saw print. He met Zhukovsky, a foremost romantic poet and translator, and Pletniov, poet, critic, and professor of Russian literature at the University of St. Petersburg. But money was still hard to come by, and though Pletniov got Gogol a teaching position in a school that catered to the daughters of noblemen, he had to take a job as a tutor as well (to a moron, to judge by the *Reminiscences* of Count Sollogub, whose relative was being tutored: ". . . and this is a cow, you know, cow, moo, moo . . ."). In 1831 things brightened considerably. He met the great Pushkin, whom he had long and sensitively admired, and somehow these two very different people became friends. That same year stories that Gogol had long been writing appeared in the first volume of *Dikanka,* and the next year the second volume of *Dikanka* appeared. Their success was immediate and profound. Nikolai Gogol found himself a famous man in a city that was no longer so cold and hostile.

Sandwiched between the eight stories which comprise these first two volumes is *Ivan Fiodorovich Shponka and His Aunt.* It is so different from the others, is so clearly an anticipation of the more mature works, that we need to discuss it separately, and at some length.

The other tales of these volumes, heavily saturated with folklore elements, are essentially romantic, escapist-motivated stories. Here there is already the curious Gogol mingling, e.g., the use of a preface which precedes each volume in which there appears the homely personal comment by a very earthy beekeeper, Rudy Panko, who, in quite matter-of-fact terms, guarantees the validity of the stories. These prefaces somehow add an aura of "factualness" even to the outlandish, somehow root even the most flagrantly romantic elements of the stories in the earth. The setting, the Ukraine about which Gogol waxes so eloquent, precludes a totally negative vision. If, for example, there is a devil who needs to be feared, he is at the same time to be ridiculed because he is a peculiarly Ukrainian devil, endowed with the same mentality as the very peasants he would outfox and destroy. Typically, many elements are combined in these seven stories. There is gaiety:

> She [Panko's grandfather's aunt] used to say that his father . . . had been taken prisoner by the Turks and suffered goodness knows what tortures, and that in some miraculous way he had escaped, disguised as a eunuch.

there is warmth and comfort:

> I remember as though it were today . . . my [Panko's] mother . . . on a long winter evening when frost crackled outside and sealed up the narrow window of our hut . . . would sit with her spindle pulling out a long thread with one hand, rocking the cradle with her foot, and singing a song which I can hear now.

there is coarseness:

> "What's lying there, Vlas?"
> "Why it looks like two men: one on top, the other under. Which of them is the devil I can't make out yet!"
> "Why, who is on top?"
> "A woman!"
> "Oh, well, then that's the devil!"
> . . . .
> "A woman straddling a man! I suppose she knows how to ride!"

the Gothic:

> A cross on one of the graves tottered and a withered corpse rose slowly up out of the earth. Its beard reached to its waist; the nails on its fingers were longer than the fingers themselves. It slowly raised its hands upwards. Its face was all twisted and distorted.

and the eloquent:

How intoxicating, how magnificent is a summer day in Little Russia [the Ukraine]! How luxuriously warm the hours when midday glitters in stillness and sultry heat and the blue fathomless ocean covering the plain like a dome seems to be slumbering, bathed in languor, clasping the fair earth and holding it close in its ethereal embrace!

There is indeed "the charm of wild flowers about them," a charm born of Gogol's extraordinary gift with language, its rich texture and exuberant expression. But *Shponka* is very different. The Ukrainian sun is less brilliant. Coarseness, the Gothic, gaiety, eloquence disappear. The romantic world disappears and is replaced by a world in which *poshlost* thrives (a "real" world which is not quite real because of the intensity of its reality). For the first time an element of sadness is introduced, and we sense the Gogolian *smekh skvoz sliozy* (laughter through tears). We laugh at the grotesqueness of Ivan Fiodorovich, but there are "tears" because he is a victim of a world perhaps no less ugly than our own.

Beginning with a middle-aged, not-too-bright bachelor (of course) placed in a realistic (identifiable) setting, in a realistic (recognizable) situation, Gogol begins the process of intensification that is so typical of almost all his later works: detail is heaped upon detail, minute observation upon minute observation, until the wholly mediocre and originally sympathy-provoking Shponka begins to lose our sympathy because he begins to lose his identity as a recognizable human being. We find ourselves roaring at the monster Gogol has created. He becomes what all Gogol's grotesque heroes become, *too* much: *too* naïve, *too* stupid, *too* complacent, *too* mediocre. He swims in a sea of *poshlost* and he finally drowns in trivia. Yet there is an aura of reality. Of what is it compounded?

Gogol's vocabulary, syntax, and verbal inventiveness drive many Russians to distraction, and even in English the amazingly full-bodied texture of his work is apparent. It is this very density that begins to supply an answer. The sheer collection and intensification of detail (e.g., the fact that a turnip is not merely large, but "more like a potato than a turnip") forces the reader to conclude that such a minutely detailed world must, in a sense, be real. After all, the author seems to know it so well, so intimately. But surely D. S. Mirsky is correct when he notes that Gogol's reality only *seems* real. It seems real because it is packed and stuffed and highly idiosyncratic reality. There are other factors accounting for this aura of reality.

His characters (and we exclude only the grossly romantic and Gothic) are, despite their excesses, identifiable and recognizable, too. His "little man," his coarse man, his rogue, his marvelous "vegetable man," his drunkard, his fool, his mediocrity—all are part of the real world, much more a part of it than the soulful romantic hero or the fiendish Gothic creation can ever be. And their motivation is real, their reaction to stimuli is real because it is predictable, and the code by which they govern themselves is also real. Despite all this, his characters are primarily caricatures. On occasion they are symbols of almost mythical dimension.

The frame of reference within which these characters move and function is very real indeed. *Poshlost* is real; so is corruption; so is injustice; so is selfishness. Gogol's intensive detailing accounts for its recognizability, and even his hyperbolic distortion of it cannot mask it. Need we be surprised to read of the bureaucrat who squirmed through a performance of *The Inspector General* or of the serf owner who was tortured by feelings of guilt (though such reactions are self-imposed)? Laugh as we will at Ivan Fiodorovich or Akaky Akakievich or the two old-world landowners or the two Ivans, the meanness of the world that reduced them to what they are is disturbing.

Stylistically, we understand how Gogol accomplished his grotesque. But what motivated him, what kind of personality can work in this genre with such unerring brilliance? We quote two of the many comments Gogol offered retrospectively:

> All is disorganized within me. I see, for example, that somebody has stumbled; my imagination immediately grasps the situation and begins to develop it into the shape of most terrible apparitions which torture me so much that I cannot sleep and am losing all my strength.

His deep-rooted neurosis explains not only the choice of subject, but explains its treatment, its density, its forcefulness, its microscopic vision.

> . . . in order to get rid of them [fits of melancholy] I invented the funniest things I could think of. I invented funny characters in the funniest situations imaginable.

It is easy to appreciate the cathartic function of his fiction. What is "funny" to a psychopathic personality may be viewed as grotesque by others. We may laugh when a fat man slips and lands in a puddle of water, but our normalcy insists we stop laughing when we realize that he may, after all, have hurt himself; but to laugh, as Gogol does, despite the fact that he may be in pain, or to laugh precisely because he is in pain, is something else again. It is the world of the grotesque.

Gogol accepted fame in a manner thoroughly consistent with his personality: he overreacted. He became a boor and something of a dandy (as grotesque a creature as he ever created), but because imaginary pain had become a necessary expiatory mechanism, he regaled his friends with stories of the incurable illnesses that ravaged him. In 1834, so few years after the publication of *Dikanka*, Gogol had influence enough to wangle a professorship of history from the University of St. Petersburg, no minor accomplishment considering the fact that his idea of the general subject was vague. It was a fiasco. Ivan Turgenev, soon to become the famous writer, was one of Gogol's students:

> We [the students] were all convinced . . . that he knew nothing of history. . . . At the final examination . . . he sat with a handkerchief wrapped around his head, feigning a toothache. There was an expression of extreme pain on his face, and he never opened his mouth. . . . I see . . . Gogol's lean figure, with a long nose and the two ends of his black handkerchief surging above his head like two ears.

Gogol soon left the school. During the next four years he devoted himself almost exclusively to writing, and the bulk of what he was to write throughout his life took shape during this period.

In 1835 the two volumes of *Mirgorod* were published, the first containing *Old-World Landowners* and *Taras Bulba* (which was to be thoroughly revised before its republication in a collected edition of his works in 1842), the second containing *Viy* and the altogether remarkable *The Tale of How Ivan Ivanovich Quarreled with Ivan Nikiforovich*. Of these, two stories, *Bulba* and *Viy*, belong to the earlier romantic Gogol tradition; the other two belong to the *Shponka* tradition, and stand as direct anticipations of Gogol's later works.

Taras Bulba, Gogol's longest tale, seems much less impressive now than it must have been to a contemporary reader. Without precedent in Russian literature, cast in the epic tradition, boisterous and romantic, peopled by nongrotesque characters who are led by a hero of classical strength and determination, rich in detailed scenes of battles and hand-to-hand combat, containing traditional comic elements—the sly Jew, for example—and a love affair, pervaded by the masculine odor of sweating men and their horses and their campfires and their strong drink, laced with eloquent passages and supported by some resemblance to historical fact, strongly anti-Polish (as were its readers on the date of its initial publication), it is not difficult to appreciate reasons for its popularity. But it now seems inferior to any of Gogol's nonromantic works. It suffers from a very poorly handled and totally unconvincing love affair. The Polish girl is, typically, less flesh than marble, and with the exception of Taras and his long-suffering wife, all the characters are highly contrived and artificial. Debilitating as these weaknesses are, there is a gusto about the work, a verve, that makes it at once vivid and exciting; and there is, on occasion, that peculiarly Gogolian touch:

> . . . but the majority [of the Poles] were the sort of people who look at the whole world and everything that happens in it and go on picking their noses.

and the deft realistic detail:

> . . . and at that moment [he] stumbled over something lying at his feet. It was the dead body of a woman, apparently a Jewess. She seemed to be young, though there was no trace of youth in her distorted and emaciated features. . . . Beside her lay a baby convulsively clutching her thin breast and pinching it with his fingers in unconscious anger at finding no milk.

Viy, which also belongs to the earlier Gogol tradition, to quote from Gogol's footnote, "is a colossal creation of the popular imagination." It is basically a horror story infused with humorous elements, the prosaic, and the realistic. That the story is at all successful bespeaks the singular ability of the author to mingle such diverse elements into something of a cohesive whole. At times the story seems to be melodramatic Poe that frightens less than it irritates. The realistic and comic descriptions of the seminary and its students are superior to the Gothic framework. But Viy and his ghoulish cohorts are so horrible that they cease being monsters; they are made of pasteboard.

xxx   *Introduction*

As no discovery has ever been made of the alleged folklore source of this "colossal creation of the popular imagination," it is a fascinating document, and close examination of text reveals how many of Gogol's fears are here projected: demoniac woman, the threatened church (his soul), what the psychoanalyst would refer to as the imago (the unconscious infantile conception of parents).

Old-World Landowners and *The Tale of How Ivan Ivanovich Quarreled with Ivan Nikiforovich* are wonderfully successful stories which stem from the *Shponka* tradition and are representative of the mature Gogol, but they differ from each other, especially in tone.

Old-World Landowners is at once realistic and grotesque, but its grotesqueness is mitigated by the absence of overt hostility, by the presence of something idyllic. It concerns a symphony of digestion orchestrated by a couple who love and thoroughly enjoy their totally vegetable existence, their *poshlost*, their absolute Philistinism. Almost all of their lives is devoted to oral activity: they eat or they anticipate eating, or they prepare what is soon to be eaten. And during the small portion of each day when they are not so engaged, they warm their bellies on the stove. They are literature's most contented creatures, and Gogol cannot help but treat them with some measure of warmth and tolerance. If they are grotesque because they function on a totally animal level, they are yet sentimentally depicted because the "cage" in which they find themselves is both self-imposed and totally adequate to their needs. It is their complete lack of pretentiousness which dulls the barb of Gogol's pen, and at most, Gogol's outrage is cooled to diluted satire.

The Tale of How Ivan Ivanovich Quarreled with Ivan Nikiforovich is one of the most outrageously funny stories in print, but at its conclusion a very powerful element of depression, gloom, and hopelessness is introduced and alters the tone of all that preceded it, making it deeply ironic. Also told in a realistic manner, totally non-Gothic, it is an example of grotesque realism. The disastrous effects of *poshlost* are never clearer, and the story ends with the famous *"Skuchno na etom svete, gospoda!"* (It is a dreary world, gentlemen!)

The characterization, always Gogol's major strength, is superb. Gogol's art is never stronger, more sure, more controlled. A genius is at work, and his touch is everywhere ("Ivan Ivanovich's head is like a radish, tail downwards; Ivan Nikiforovich's head is like a radish, tail upwards."). Character is developed by focusing on mannerisms, on snuffboxes, on how often one shaves, on how one walks, eats, sleeps—and always with great precision. And what people we have here! The boy "who stood very tranquilly picking his nose" (and notice the effect of the Gogolian "very"), Agafya Fedoseevna who had *exactly* "three warts on her nose," the quite remarkable judge whose "upper lip served him instead of a snuffbox," and so on.

In 1835, under the title *Arabesques,* Gogol published what he himself called a "mishmash" of articles and stories. In the first part we find the first version of *The Portrait,* in the second part, *Nevsky Prospekt* and *Diary of a Madman.*

The Portrait is Gogol's least representative story, closer (but not very close) to *Viy* and *A Terrible Vengeance* than to anything else he ever wrote; especially in the earliest version. It is a German romance which happens to be written in Russian and, in its final version, suggests that Gogol is the author only because of the unmistakable didacticism infused in it. It is devoid of the grotesque and of Gogol's intense realism. It combines the Gothic, romantic, and didactic, and it is peopled with fleshless allegorical symbols: the hero (Vanity), the mother and daughter (*Poshlost*), the old man in the portrait (Devil), the professor (Reason), the artist who had painted the portrait (Sinner-Expiator). In its final version (1842) its didacticism offers us insight into Gogol's ever-increasing preoccupation with religion, morality, and the horrible wages of sin.

Nevsky Prospekt is essentially romantic, but it blends the tragic and the comic, and there are very full passages which are totally realistic. Nevsky Prospekt (the most important street in St. Petersburg) is described in great realistic detail. It comes alive, and the reader senses, alternately, its excitement and its early-morning sadness. One of the story's heroes, Piskariov, a disillusioned romantic who kills himself, almost certainly represents Gogol, and Piskariov's experience (except for his suicide for which Gogol substituted flight) closely parallels the mythical adventure about which Gogol once wrote his mother. Pirogov, the other hero, Piskariov's foil, is a realist. Disappointed if not disillusioned, the would-be lover goes not to kill himself but, rather, to a party (after calmly eating two creampuffs) where "he spent a very pleasant evening, and so distinguished himself in the mazurka that not only the ladies but even their partners were moved to admiration." Obviously, in Gogol's world, it is the romantic who fares poorly.

In *Diary of a Madman* another dreamer finds reality impossible and withdraws to the comfort of madness. The grotesque, the tragic, and the comic are mingled with eminent success. The tragic is born of the one lucid moment when the madman recognizes his desperate plight and would soar from his predicament, only to realize that flight is impossible. He utters the absurd (and considering the situation, grotesquely irrelevant) "And do you know that the Dey of Algiers has a boil under his nose?"

Gogol's sexual abnormality is again expressed with blatant clarity. The symbols might have been drawn from a Freudian primer. Here is part of an entry in the diary:

> Tomorrow . . . the earth will sit on the moon . . . I must confess that I experience a tremor at my heart when I reflect on the extreme softness and fragility of the moon. . . . there is such a fearful stench all over the world that one has to stop up one's nose. And that's how it is that the moon is such a soft globe that man cannot live on it and that nothing lives there but noses. And it is for that very reason that we can't see our noses, because they are all in the moon.

In a story written at about the same time, *The Nose*, once more a nose disappears, but this time it walks the streets of St. Petersburg in full dress and is not *in* the moon. Published in 1836, in the third issue of Pushkin's *The Contemporary*, *The Nose* is absolute nonsense, but, as Mirsky notes, "in it more than anywhere else Gogol displays his extraordinary magic power of making great comic art out of nothing."

There is wonderful satire here (the nose itself "is driving around town, calling itself a civil councilor"): the gray-headed clerk in the newspaper office who refuses to take an advertisement asking for information about the nose (because "the newspaper might lose its reputation"); the efficient policeman who finds the nose ("And the strange thing is that I myself took him for a gentleman at first, but fortunately I had my spectacles with me and I soon saw it was a nose"); the doctor (who "was a handsome man . . . magnificent pitch-black whiskers, a fresh and healthy wife, ate fresh apples in the morning, and kept his mouth extraordinarily clean, rinsing it out for nearly three-quarters of an hour every morning and cleaning his teeth with five different sorts of brushes").

The Nose is Gogol's final major effort in the realm of the fantastic (Akaky's corpse, in *The Overcoat*, is the only trace of it to appear again). Strongly reminiscent of Sterne (whose *Tristram Shandy* appeared in Russian during the first decade of the nineteenth century), it also owes part of its birth to a flood of literature and anecdotes concerned with noses. Gogol first called it *Son (Dream)*, and some critics suggest that Gogol playfully reversed the letters of his title and arrived at *Nos (The Nose)*. As ingenious as we admit this to be, it seems more likely that Gogol was probably dissatisfied with working *merely* on the dream level, and by transposing the dream to St. Petersburg reality, caused what was fantastic to become, in its realistic frame of reference, grotesque and satiric as well.

The Coach, published in the same issue of *The Contemporary*, is much more than an anecdote in which a pretentious humbug and liar is unmasked. It is a brilliant technical display; there is a gaiety about it, life about it: the odor of vodka, leather, and the hilarious exposure of the philistines.

The last of the Petersburg stories and the greatest and most influential is *The Overcoat*. Begun in 1839 (then called *The Official Who Stole Overcoats*), redrafted until 1841, it made its appearance in 1842, in the third volume of Gogol's collected works.

We have already noted its reception by liberals (and by persistent contemporary critics) as an example of "critical realism," and the spurious impression such an interpretation gives of its content and its author. Such interpretation refuses to recognize the grotesque nature of our hemorrhoidal hero (who so delights in his copying work that he even brings it home for amusement), and the grotesque quality of his existence which is so reminiscent of *Shponka*. Here we have again the grotesque-creating "*too* much": Akaky Akakievich is *too* content dealing in trivia; he has *too* much garbage resting on his hat, *too* many flies in his soup, tries to save money *too* carefully (by tiptoeing on the cobblestones to prevent wearing out his shoes); the tailor's toenail is *too* much like a turtle's shell and his shop stinks *too* much. Somehow, those who insist on seeing this as critical realism ignore the conclusion of the story when Akaky comes back to haunt St. Petersburg, and comes back not as a ghost but as a totally fantastic corpse. It is not easy to find in the text the compassion and humor with which Akaky is allegedly treated. At most there are only minor traces of social sympathy.

But we must not overstate the case. If Gogol despised Akaky and what he represented, at the same time he may have felt sympathy for him because his grotesquely cruel, dreary, "real" world made him, at least in part, the monster that he is and, being more guilty than he, suffers the return of the corpse.

Gogol's last story, *The Overcoat*, strongly reflects his increasingly moralistic point of view. Akaky is subject to his derision not because of his dire poverty, not because he accepts his situation without struggling against it, but because there is in him a total absence of spiritual values, because he functions only on the level of an automaton. From Gogol's point of view, the overcoat is meaningless, as is the short-lived improvement in Akaky's social situation. It causes no spiritual change in Akaky; the inner man is still dead, only the surface has been altered, only trivialities are involved. The coat is the façade behind which Akaky hides his spiritual nakedness, and it is this, of course, that leads to his pitiless destruction.

The plot is slight, but the characters are remarkably vivid. Only in *The Tale of How Ivan Ivanovich Quarreled with Ivan Nikiforovich*, in *Dead Souls*, and in *The Inspector General* do we find creatures created with such consummate brilliance. Once met, Akaky Akakievich is unforgettable, as are the Person of Consequence, the tailor, his wife, the sneezing corpse; even the cockroaches, the stench, and the unbelievably shabby "dressing gown" come alive.

Gogol had long been interested in writing for the stage and, as early as 1832, only a year after the first volume of *Dikanka* brought him fame, he had already written two plays, *The Suitors* (later to become *The Marriage*, published in 1842) and *The Order of Vladimir of the Third Class* (whose theme—a frustrated official gone insane—reappears in *Diary of a Madman*). Of *The Order of Vladimir*, only four scenes survive, and these four have been translated by Mrs. Garnett: "A Lawsuit," "The Servant's Hall," "An Official's Morning," and "A Fragment."

The Inspector General (*Revizor*), the greatest of Gogol's three serious attempts at play-writing and the greatest comedy Russia has ever produced, begun during October 1835, was completed in only two months, performed for the first time on the first of May 1836, published the same year, and revised for the 1842 edition of Gogol's collected works.

Using the ancient literary device of mistaken identity for his plot,

Gogol peopled the play with as motley and vulgar a crew as he could create; even his hero, like all his heroes, functions on the same low plane. It is a delightful and outrageous caricature, although Gogol himself, already obsessed by religious mania, insisted that the arrival of the real Inspector General at the conclusion of the play is the call to the Last Judgment. It is a singular play in that it is devoid of love interest and functions beautifully without a single sympathetic character. It is one of the great ironies that this play written by a conservative who cared nothing for reform should be seen as a satire on social corruption. Like *The Overcoat*, it is very much concerned with the absence of moral fiber. It is the nakedness of the soul that is here mercilessly and hilariously exposed.

Densely textured, enormously imaginative, it contains incredibly funny dialogue. Gogol's feverish imagination found even the rich Russian language inadequate to his needs; he molded it, changed it, added to it. This makes much of the play almost completely untranslatable (for example, no dictionary can begin to meet the needs of Osip's long speech).

The characters, though nothing more than puppets, are vigorous and energetic puppets, recognizable as grotesque symbols of real counterparts. The hero is a fool (and a scoundrel), the mayor is a fool (and a crook), the mayor's wife is a fool (obsessed with delusions of grandeur), his daughter is a fool (too silly to be obsessed with anything)—fools, fools, fools, and how glorious it is to watch them function in Gogol's fool's paradise: a nonspiritual and godless world!

The Marriage, one of the remaining two genuine plays, is less great. It is less satiric, much more relaxed. It aims at being great fun and it is. It is very reminiscent of *Shponka* both because its hero is very much like Shponka, and because once more there is evidence of Gogol's castration complex. Contemplating marriage, Shponka is haunted by an endless array of imaginary wives, all with goose faces; Podkoliosin, about to be married, being less introspective than Shponka and a firm believer in direct action, does what any good Gogol character would do under the circumstances: he leaps from a window and makes his escape.

There is little action in the play and the characters dominate it. To complement them, Gogol reverts to an ancient (strongly antirealistic) tradition and makes rather full use of comic names. It is a device that made its first appearance in *Dikanka* and again appears very strongly in *Dead Souls.* There is Yaichnitsa (Omelet—who thinks of changing his name to Yaichnitsyn but hesitates because it sounds too much like *sobachiy syn,* "son of a bitch"), Pomoikin (Slop Pail), Perepreev (Overripe), Dyrka (Hole), and so forth.

It is a coarse play on a coarse theme played by coarse people, but Gogol accepts the situation without enmity, and what could have been biting satire is pleasant diversion.

The Gamblers, also published in 1842, is no more than a neatly constructed little play in which a cardsharp becomes himself the victim of cardsharps. It is inferior Gogol because it is devoid of Gogol's greatest gifts, comedy and exuberance. Eric Bentley's free translation of the play (*The Modern Theatre,* III, New York, 1957) is a valiant attempt to make it actable, but the play was stillborn.

There are three other completed dramatic pieces, all of them slight, all of them concerned with *The Inspector General. Homegoing from the Theater* (1836) is involved with fictional spectators who have just seen a performance of *The Inspector General* (an idea borrowed from Molière); *The Dénouement of the Inspector General* (1846); *Addition to The Dénouement of the Inspector General* (1847).

Gogol left for Lübeck, Germany, in a cold sweat, in June 1836. He was to remain away from Russia, excepting two eight-month visits, for twelve years. Various reasons are given for his departure, but it seems clear that he was bitterly disappointed by the staging of *The Inspector General* and in its misinterpretation. His vehemence can be clearly seen in a letter he wrote to a friend three months after leaving Russia:

> There are so many detestable faces in Russia that I couldn't stand looking at them. I still feel like spitting when I remember them.

With this taste in his mouth, Gogol wandered through Europe, often in ill health, running from himself. He found Rome an absolute delight, and he continued the work on *Dead Souls,* which he had begun in Paris and Vevey, but it came hard, so hard in fact that he asked a friend to get him a wig so that he could open the pores of his scalp because his inspiration was getting "clogged." The frail little genius almost completely toppled out of the real world. His hemorrhoids, it seems, "were spreading to [his] stomach!" In Paris, during September of 1838, he went through a new mental crisis, and by 1840 he was so overtly psychotic, so obsessed with the fear of death (which to Gogol always represented hell) that he often found it impossible to sleep alone in his room. He was tortured by imaginary illnesses and nearly drained of strength, but he managed, by the end of 1841, not only to complete *The Overcoat*, but to complete the first part of *Dead Souls*. Only sections of the second volume remain, for just before his death Gogol threw the manuscript of the second part into the fire, a masochistic ritual he engaged in at least three times during his life.

But there is no reason to treat the first part as anything less than a cohesive whole. Gogol had envisioned what Dante's *Divine Comedy* had accomplished: a three-part work involved with sin, expiation, and salvation. It is the first volume, the "sin" volume, that is brilliant; what remains of the second is not very good, primarily because Gogol's distorted vision could hardly portray positive virtues successfully, and it is not surprising that only the grotesque creation in the volume, Petukh, is well drawn. By the time of writing the second volume, Gogol was burning up with religious fever and consumed by a messianic complex. He believed that he was to serve, as Christ had served, to save the world.

Dead Souls, published in 1842, owes much to the picaresque tradition, to Sterne, and to Vasily Narezhny, an early-nineteenth-century Ukrainian novelist who worked in the genre. It was from him that Gogol borrowed for his story of the two Ivans.

Chichikov, another virtueless hero, is the personification of *poshlost*. Drab, vulgar, dishonest, Chichikov travels through Russia in quest of satisfying an outrageous scheme to buy dead souls (serfs) who are still registered (before a new census takes place) and therefore technically alive and of value. The title, however, serves another function. Gogol is very much occupied with the thought that the souls, literally, are dead too.

The greatness of the novel, typically, rests on its wonderful characters, those remarkably spirited caricatures that symbolize the vices of man. As always in the mature works, Gogol's pen is deft and the work is deeply grained and densely textured. Once more that famous everything-as-it-should-be world the Russians are so fond of is not really as it is supposed to be at all: flies are almost human; frock coats are alive; clocks are snakes; animals and furniture are reflections of their owners. Everywhere there is the distortion of reality.

The characters are masterpieces of comic creation: Sobakevich (*sobaka* means "dog") is a brute; Nozdrev ("nostril") is a braggart; Manilov (*manit* is "to lure") is nauseatingly sweet; Korobochka ("little box") is grossly stupid and a hoarder; Plyushkin (*pliushka* means "pancake," a coarse one, and Plyushkin suggests a soft, moist slap) is the most grotesque miser in literature.

The conclusion is eloquent. An exposed but hardly repentant Chichikov soars over the Russian roads, the *troika* becoming a symbol of all Russia: "Whither art thou soaring away, Russia?"

Pushkin is reported to have sighed a famous sigh upon reading it: "How gloomy is our Russia!" and Gogol is reported to have uttered a famous reply to Pushkin's famous sigh: "It is all nothing but caricature and mere fancy." We have tried to indicate that in Gogol there is no reason why the two points of view cannot be seen to live side by side.

In 1847 Gogol published his infamous *Selected Passages from a Correspondence with Friends*, a classic of reaction, a sermon on the wages of sin, in which Gogol and God stood hand in hand. Gogol played Christ and he offered heaven to the sinners if they would repent, but instead of gaining disciples he found himself mercilessly chastised by liberals *and* conservatives, who refused to recognize the "preacher of the knout, apostle of ignorance" as a messiah. The self-deluded Gogol was startled at the venom spit at him. It was the beginning of the end. The next five years, his last five, were the most excruciatingly painful of a life that had been full of pain. Thoughts of sin and suffering took full possession of him and, the flames of hell already licking at him, his creative power, already noticeably weak when he wrote the second part of *Dead Souls*, utterly deserted him.

In 1848, desperately ill and frightened, Gogol returned to Russia from a trip to the Holy Land. He grew increasingly frail, and in February 1852, he began a Lenten fast that he was never to break. Tortured by physicians who did not understand the nature of his disease, leeches sucking blood from his nostrils, totally exhausted, he wasted away.

On the morning of the fourth of March, not yet forty-three years old, Nikolai Vasilievich Gogol sacrificed himself for having failed to deliver God's message to the heathens of Russia, and literature lost a consummate artist.

Gogol's influence, in general, has been grossly exaggerated. Russian realism, we have pointed out, owes him a debt, but not one involving his "creation" of the first "little man," [3] his "creation" of the coarse and vulgar setting, or his "critical realism." Rather, the debt involves his apotheosis of the insignificant man and his dismal world, an apotheosis which helped lift taboos, which helped make such figures and such complementary settings subjects fit for competent and respectable literary treatment. In fact, as the Russian critic Vasily Rosanov pointed out, Russian literature following Gogol generally tapped a different vein, tended to move away from his work. A fresh reading of the mature Dostoevsky, of Turgenev, of Goncharov, of Tolstoy, seems to validate this point. Much that is basic to Gogol's art is absent in his followers.

We have noted some of Gogol's literary antecedents. We view him primarily as an intermediary who expresses ideas and uses techniques which existed in embryonic or relatively full-grown shape before his appearance in the world of letters, yet we do not deny that he is perhaps the most genuinely original of writers; indeed, it is his singular originality that precludes him from being an important literary influence. If there is a common denominator in Gogol, it consists of his verve, his exuberance, his linguistic intensity and skill, his great density and texture, his distorted vision of a world he felt destined for hell. All of these are the inimitable features of his art.

The best of Gogol can stand comparison with the best in literature. We need not tremble at putting him in the select company of Rabelais and Cervantes and Swift and Sterne and the others "who knew how to walk upside down in our valley of sorrows so as to make it a merry place." If Nikolai Vasilievich Gogol was hardly of this world at all, his works remain a brilliant and integral part of it.

Leonard J. Kent

Quinnipiac College
Hamden, Connecticut

---

[3] The prototype of the "little man" in Russian literature seems to be the much-abused father in Pushkin's *The Postmaster,* completed in 1830 and published as one of the works of the "late Ivan Petrovich Belkin."

Nineteenth-Century Russian Civil, Military, and Court Ranks*

CIVIL RANKS	CORRESPONDING RANKS		
	ARMY	NAVY	COURT
1 Chancellor (of the Empire)	Commander in Chief	Admiral in Chief	. . . .
2 Actual Privy Councilor	General of Cavalry General of Infantry General of Artillery	Admiral	Chief Chamberlain Chief Marshal Chief Equerry Chief Huntsman Chief Steward Chief Cup-bearer Chief Master of Ceremonies** Chief Carver**
3 Privy Councilor	Lieutenant General	Vice Admiral	Marshal Equerry Huntsman Steward Chief Master of Ceremonies** Chief Carver**
4 Actual Councilor of State Attorney-general Master of Heraldry	Major General	Rear Admiral	Chamberlain (ranks 3, 4)
5 Councilor of State	. . . .	. . . .	Master of Ceremonies
6 Collegiate Councilor Military Councilor	Colonel	Captain (1st class)	Gentleman of the Bedchamber (ranks 5-8)
7 Court Councilor	Lieutenant Colonel	Captain (2nd class)	
8 Collegiate Assessor	Major (Captain or Cavalry Captain)	. . . .	
9 Titular Councilor	Staff Captain Staff Cavalry Captain	Lieutenant	. . . .
10 Collegiate Secretary	Lieutenant	Midshipman	. . . .
11 Naval Secretary	. . . .	. . . .	. . . .
12 County Secretary	2nd Lieutenant Cornet	. . . .	. . . .
13 Provincial Secretary Senate, Synod, and Cabinet Registrar	Ensign	. . . .	. . . .
14 Collegiate Registrar	. . . .	. . . .	. . . .

* According to Peter the Great's Table of Ranks, civilians held military titles which corresponded with the grade they had achieved in the civil service. Such titles were rarely used, except by those in the upper grades, the "generals."
** The titles of Chief Master of Ceremonies and Chief Carver could belong to persons of either the second or third class.

THE

Complete Tales

OF

Nikolai Gogol

Volume 1

EVENINGS ON
A FARM
NEAR DIKANKA, I

Preface

"What oddity is this: *Evenings on a Farm near Dikanka*? What sort of *Evenings* have we here? And thrust into the world by a bee-keeper! God protect us! As though geese enough had not been plucked for pens and rags turned into paper! As though folks enough of all classes had not covered their fingers with inkstains! The whim must take a beekeeper to follow their example! Really, there is such a lot of paper nowadays that it takes time to think what to wrap in it."

I had a premonition of all this talk a month ago. In fact, for a villager like me to poke his nose out of his hole into the great world is —merciful heavens!—just like what happens if you go into the apartments of some fine gentleman: they all come around you and make you feel like a fool; it would not matter so much if it were only the important servants, but no, some wretched little snotnose loitering in the backyard pesters you too; and on all sides they begin prancing around you and asking: "Where are you going? Where? What for? Get out, peasant, out you go!" I can tell you . . . But what's the use of talking! I would rather go twice a year into Mirgorod, where the district court assessor and the reverend Father have not seen me for the last five years, than show myself in the great world; still, if you do it, whether you regret it or not, you must face the consequences.

At home, dear readers—no offense meant (you may be annoyed at a beekeeper like me addressing you so plainly, as though I were speaking to some old friend or crony)—at home in the village it has always been the peasants' habit, as soon as the work in the fields is over, to climb up on the stove[1] and rest there all winter, and we beekeepers put our bees away in a dark cellar. At the season when you see no cranes in the sky or pears on the trees, there is sure to be a light burning somewhere at the end of the village as soon as evening comes on, laughter and singing are heard in the distance, there is the twang of the balalaika and at times of the fiddle, talk and noise . . . Those are our *evening parties!* As you see, they are like your balls, though not altogether so, I must say. If you go to balls, it is to move your legs and yawn with your hand over your mouth; while with us the girls gather together in one hut, not for a ball, but with their spindle and carding comb. And at first one may say they do work; the spindles hum, there is a constant flow of song, and no one looks up from her work; but as soon as the young men burst into the hut with the fiddler, there is an uproar, fun begins, they start dancing, and I could not tell you all the pranks that are played.

But best of all is when they crowd together and begin guessing riddles or simply babble. Goodness, what stories they tell! What tales of old times they dig up! What frightening things they describe! But nowhere are such stories told as in the hut of the beekeeper Rudy[2] Panko. Why the villagers call me Rudy Panko, I really cannot say. My hair, I think, is more gray nowadays than red. But think what you like of it, it is our habit: when a nickname has once been given, it sticks to a man all his life. Good people get together at the beekeeper's on the eve of a holiday, sit down to the table—and then you only have to listen! And, I may say, the guests

---

[1] The stoves referred to throughout these stories were very large, two-level affairs made of brick. The top of each level was covered with clay or tile. Children and pets often napped on the lower level, and adults warmed themselves by sitting on it. The upper level—about one yard from the ceiling of the hut—was often utilized by all the members of a family, sometimes simultaneously, as they stretched out on it to enjoy its warmth. (ed.)

[2] "Red" in Ukrainian, i.e., "redhead." (ed.)

are by no means of the humbler sort, mere peasants; their visit would be an honor for someone of more consequence than a bee-keeper. For instance, do you know the sexton of the Dikanka church, Foma Grigorievich?[3] Ah, he has a head! What stories he can reel off! You will find two of them in this book. He never wears one of those coarse dressing gowns that you so often see on village sex-tons; no, if you go to see him, even on working days, he will al-ways receive you in a gaberdine of fine cloth of the color of cold potato mash, for which he paid almost six rubles a yard at Poltava. As for his high boots, no one in the village has ever said that they smelled of tar; everyone knows that he rubs them with the very best fat, such as I believe many a peasant would be glad to put in his porridge. Nor would anyone ever say that he wipes his nose on the skirt of his gaberdine, as many men of his calling do; no, he takes from his bosom a clean, neatly folded white handkerchief embroidered on the hem with red cotton, and after putting it to its proper use, folds it up in twelve as his habit is, and puts it back in his bosom.

And one of the visitors . . . Well, he is such a fine young gentle-man that you might any minute take him for an assessor or a high officer of the court.[4] Sometimes he will hold up his finger, and looking at the tip of it, begin telling a story—as choicely and clev-erly as though it were printed in a book! Sometimes you listen and listen and begin to be puzzled. You can't make head or tail of it, not if you were to hang for it. Where did he pick up such words? Foma Grigorievich once told him a funny story satirizing this. He told him how a student who had been getting lessons from a deacon came back to his father such a Latin scholar that he had forgotten our language: he put *us* on the end of all the words; a spade was *spadus*, a female was *femalus*. It happened one day that he went with his father in the fields. The Latin scholar saw a rake and asked his father: "What do you call that, Father?" And, without looking at what he was doing, he stepped on the teeth of the rake. Before the father had time to answer, the handle flew up and hit the boy on

---

[3] Grigorievich is not Foma's surname. The second of the three names which Russians and Ukrainians possess is the patronymic (*otchestvo*). It is formed by adding *-ovich* or *-evich* (sometimes contracted into *-ich*) to the father's given name in the case of males, and *-ovna* or *-evna* in the case of females. The family name is used but rarely, usually on formal occasions or for official business. (ed.)

[4] A chart listing civil, military, and court ranks appears on p. xli. (ed.)

the head. "The damned rake!" he cried, putting his hand to his forehead and jumping half a yard into the air, "may the devil shove its father off a bridge, how it can hit!" So he remembered the name, you see, poor fellow!

Such a tale was not to the taste of our ingenious storyteller. He rose from his seat without speaking, stood in the middle of the room with his legs apart, craned his neck forward a little, thrust his hand into the back pocket of his pea-green coat, took out his round lacquered snuffbox, flicked his finger on the mug of some Mussulman[5] general, and, taking a good pinch of snuff powdered with wood ash and leaves of lovage, crooked his elbow, lifted it to his nose, and sniffed the whole pinch up with no help from his thumb—and still without a word. And it was only when he felt in another pocket and brought out a checked blue cotton handkerchief that he muttered the saying, I believe it was, "Cast not thy pearls before swine." "There's bound to be a quarrel," I thought, seeing that Foma Grigorievich's fingers were moving as though to make a fig. Fortunately my old woman chose that moment to set butter and hot rolls on the table. We all set to work upon them. Foma Grigorievich's hand, instead of forming the rude gesture, stretched out for a hot roll, and as always happened, they all began praising the skill of my wife.

We have another storyteller, but he (night is not the time to think of him!) has such a store of frightening tales that it makes the hair stand up on one's head. I have purposely omitted them; good people might be so scared that they would be afraid of the beekeeper, as though he were the devil, God forgive me. If, please God, I live to the New Year and bring out another volume, then I might frighten my readers with the ghosts and wonders that were seen in old days in our Christian country. Among them, maybe, you will find some tales told by the beekeeper himself to his grandchildren. If only people will read and listen, I have enough of them stored away for ten volumes, if only I am not too damned lazy to rack my brains for them.

But there, I have forgotten what is most important: when you come to see me, gentlemen, take the main road straight to Dikanka. I have put the name on my title page on purpose so that our village may be more easily found. You have heard enough about Dikanka,

---

[5] As used by Gogol, synonymous with "nonbeliever," "pagan," "infidel," etc. (ed.)

I have no doubt, and indeed there is a dwelling there finer than the beekeeper's hut. And I need say nothing about the park: I don't suppose you would find anything like it in your Petersburg. When you reach Dikanka, you need only ask any little boy in a dirty shirt minding geese: "Where does the beekeeper Rudy Panko live?" "There," he will say, pointing with his finger, and if you like, he will lead you to the village. But one thing I must ask you: not to walk here lost in thought, nor to be too clever, in fact, for our village roads are not as smooth as those in front of your mansions. The year before last Foma Grigorievich, driving from Dikanka, fell into a ditch, with his new chaise and bay mare and all, though he himself was driving and had on a pair of spectacles too.

But when you do arrive, we will give you melons such as you have never tasted in your life, I think; and you will find no better honey in any village, I will take my oath on that. Just imagine: when you bring in the comb, the scent in the room is something beyond comprehension; it is as clear as a tear or a costly crystal such as you see in earrings. And what pies my old woman will feed you on! What pies, if only you knew: simply sugar, perfect sugar! And the butter fairly melts on your lips when you begin to eat them. Really, when one comes to think of it, what can't these women do! Have you, friends, ever tasted pear kvass flavored with sloes, or raisin and plum vodka? Or rice soup with milk? Good heavens, what dainties there are in the world! As soon as you begin eating them, it is a treat and no mistake about it: too good for words! Last year . . . But how I am running on! Only come, make haste and come; and we will give you such good things that you will talk about them to everyone you meet.

Rudy Panko
Beekeeper

THE FAIR
AT
SOROCHINTSY

I

I am weary of the hut,
Aie, take me from my home,
To where there's noise and bustle,
To where the girls are dancing gaily,
Where the boys are making merry!

From an old ballad

How intoxicating, how magnificent is a summer day in Little Russia! [1] How luxuriously warm the hours when midday glitters in stillness and sultry heat and the blue fathomless ocean covering the plain like a dome seems to be slumbering, bathed in languor, clasping the fair earth and holding it close in its ethereal embrace! Upon it, not a cloud; in the plain, not a sound. Everything might be dead; only above in the heavenly depths a lark is trilling, and from the airy heights the silvery notes drop down upon adoring earth, and from time to time the cry of a gull or the ringing note of a quail sounds in the steppe. The towering oaks stand, idle and apathetic, like aimless wayfarers, and the dazzling gleams of sunshine light up picturesque masses of leaves, casting onto others a shadow

---

[1] The name of the Ukraine before 1917. (ed.)

black as night, only flecked with gold when the wind blows. The insects of the air flit like sparks of emerald, topaz, and ruby about the gay vegetable gardens, topped by stately sunflowers. Gray haystacks and golden sheaves of wheat, like tents, stray over the plain. The broad branches of cherries, of plums, apples, and pears bent under their load of fruit, the sky with its pure mirror, the river in its green, proudly erect frame—how full of delight is the Little Russian summer!

Such was the splendor of a day in the hot August of eighteen hundred . . . eighteen hundred . . . yes, it will be about thirty years ago, when the road eight miles beyond the village of Sorochintsy bustled with people hurrying to the fair from all the farms, far and near. From early morning, wagons full of fish and salt had trailed in an endless chain along the road. Mountains of pots wrapped in hay moved along slowly, as though weary of being shut up in the dark; only here and there a brightly painted tureen or crock boastfully peeped out from behind the hurdle that held the high pile on the wagon, and attracted wishful glances from the devotees of such luxury. Many of the passers-by looked enviously at the tall potter, the owner of these treasures, who walked slowly behind his goods, carefully wrapping his proud crocks in the alien hay that would engulf them.

On one side of the road, apart from all the rest, a team of weary oxen dragged a wagon piled up with sacks, hemp, linen, and various household goods and followed by their owner, in a clean linen shirt and dirty linen trousers.[2] With a lazy hand he wiped from his swarthy face the streaming perspiration that even trickled from his long mustaches, powdered by the relentless barber who, uninvited, visits fair and foul alike and has for countless years forcibly sprinkled all mankind with dust. Beside him, tied to the wagon, walked a mare, whose meek air betrayed her advancing years.

Many of the passers-by, especially the young men, took off their caps as they met our peasant. But it was not his gray mustaches or his dignified step that led them to do so; one had but to raise one's eyes a little to discover the reason for this deference: on the wagon was sitting his pretty daughter, with a round face, black eyebrows[3] arching evenly above her clear brown eyes, carelessly

---

[2] *Sharovary*, very full trousers which are held below the knees by high boots. (ed.)

[3] A very common image in Gogol. Many Ukrainian women are blonde and

smiling rosy lips, and with red and blue ribbons twisted in the long braids which, with a bunch of wild flowers, crowned her charming head. Everything seemed to interest her; everything was new and wonderful . . . and her pretty eyes were racing all the time from one object to another. She might well be diverted! It was her first visit to a fair! A girl of eighteen for the first time at a fair! . . . But none of the passers-by knew what it had cost her to persuade her father to bring her, though he would have been ready enough but for her spiteful stepmother, who had learned to manage him as cleverly as he drove his old mare, now as a reward for long years of service being taken to be sold. The irrepressible woman . . . But we are forgetting that she, too, was sitting on the top of the load dressed in a smart green woolen pelisse, adorned with little tails to imitate ermine, though they were red in color, in a gorgeous *plakhta*⁴ checked like a chessboard, and a flowered chintz cap that gave a particularly majestic air to her fat red face, the expression of which betrayed something so unpleasant and savage that everyone hastened in alarm to turn from her to the bright face of her daughter.

The river Psiol gradually came into our travelers' view; already in the distance they felt its cool freshness, the more welcome after the exhausting, wearisome heat. Through the dark and light green foliage of the birches and poplars, carelessly scattered over the plain, there were glimpses of the cold glitter of the water, and the lovely river unveiled her shining silvery bosom, over which the green tresses of the trees drooped luxuriantly. Willful as a beauty in those enchanting hours when her faithful mirror so jealously frames her brow full of pride and dazzling splendor, her lily shoulders, and her marble neck, shrouded by the dark waves of her hair, when with disdain she flings aside one ornament to replace it by another and there is no end to her whims—the river almost every year changes her course, picks out a new channel, and surrounds herself with new and varied scenes. Rows of watermills tossed up great waves with their heavy wheels and flung them violently down again, churning them into foam, scattering froth and making

have light-colored eyebrows, i.e., are "eyebrowless," hence black or dark eyebrows bespeak something striking, beautiful. (ed.)
⁴ Ukrainian women wore a skirt made of two separate pieces of material, held together only by a girdle at the waist; the front breadth was the *zapaska,* and the back breadth the *plakhta.* (C.G.)

a great clatter. At that moment the wagon with the persons we have described reached the bridge, and the river lay before them in all her beauty and grandeur like a sheet of glass. Sky, green and dark blue forest, men, wagons of pots, watermills—all were standing or walking upside down, and not sinking into the lovely blue depths.

Our fair maiden mused, gazing at the glorious view, and even forgot to crack the sunflower seeds with which she had been busily engaged all the way, when all at once the words, "What a girl!" caught her ear. Looking around, she saw a group of young villagers standing on the bridge, of whom one, dressed rather more smartly than the others in a white jacket[5] and gray astrakhan cap, was jauntily looking at the passers-by with his arms akimbo. The girl could not but notice his sunburnt but pleasant face and fiery eyes, which seemed to look right through her, and she lowered her eyes at the thought that he might have uttered those words.

"A fine girl!" the young man in the white jacket went on, keeping his eyes fixed on her. "I'd give all I have to kiss her. And there's a devil sitting in front!"

There were peals of laughter all around; but the slow-moving peasant's gaily dressed wife was not pleased at such a greeting: her red cheeks blazed and a torrent of choice language fell like rain on the head of the unruly youth.

"I wish you'd choke, you worthless bum! May your father crack his head on a pot! May he slip down on the ice, the damned antichrist! May the devil singe his beard in the next world!"

"Isn't she swearing!" said the young man, staring at her as though puzzled at such a sharp volley of unexpected greetings. "And she can bring her tongue to utter words like that, the witch! She's a hundred if she's a day!"

"A hundred!" the elderly charmer interrupted. "You infidel! go and wash your face! You worthless rake! I've never seen your mother, but I know she's trash. And your father is trash, and your aunt is trash! A hundred, indeed! Why, the milk is scarcely dry on his . . ."

At that moment the wagon began to descend from the bridge and the last words could not be heard; but, without stopping to think, he picked up a handful of mud and threw it at her. The

---

[5] *Svitka*, a loose, long-sleeved jacket fastened by a girdle. (ed.)

throw achieved more than he could have hoped: the new chintz
cap was spattered all over, and the laughter of the rowdy pranksters
was louder than ever. The buxom charmer was boiling with rage;
but by this time the wagon was far away, and she wreaked her
vengeance on her innocent stepdaughter and her torpid husband,
who, long since accustomed to such onslaughts, preserved a determined silence and received the stormy language of his angry
spouse with indifference. In spite of all that, her tireless tongue
went on clacking until they reached the house of their old friend
and crony, the Cossack Tsibulya, on the outskirts of the village.
The meeting of the old friends, who had not seen each other for a
long time, put this unpleasant incident out of their minds for a
while, as our travelers talked of the fair and rested after their long
journey.

II

Good heavens! what isn't there at that fair! Wheels, windowpanes, tar, tobacco, straps, onions, all sorts of haberdashery . . . so
that even if you had thirty rubles in your purse you could not buy
everything at the fair.

From a Little Russian comedy[6]

You have no doubt heard a rushing waterfall when everything is
quivering and filled with uproar, and a chaos of strange vague
sounds floats like a whirlwind around you. Are you not instantly
overcome by the same feelings in the turmoil of the village fair,
when all the people become one huge monster that moves its mas-
sive body through the square and the narrow streets, with shouting,
laughing, and clatter? Noise, swearing, bellowing, bleating, roaring—all blend into one jarring uproar. Oxen, sacks, hay, gypsies,
pots, peasant women, cakes, caps—everything is bright, gaudy,
discordant, flitting in groups, shifting to and fro before your eyes.
The different voices drown one another, and not a single word
can be caught, can be saved from the deluge; not one cry is distinct.
Only the clapping of hands after each bargain is heard on all sides.
A wagon breaks down, there is the clank of iron, the thud of
boards thrown onto the ground, and one's head is so dizzy one does
not know which way to turn.

---

[6] This epigraph and those which appear in VI, VII, and X are from comedies.
by Gogol's father, an amateur playwright. (ed.)

The peasant whose acquaintance we have already made had been for some time elbowing his way through the crowd with his black-browed daughter; he went up to one wagonload, fingered another, inquired the prices; and meanwhile his thoughts kept revolving around his ten sacks of wheat and the old mare he had brought to sell. From his daughter's face it could be seen that she was not especially pleased to be wasting time by the wagons of flour and wheat. She longed to be where red ribbons, earrings, crosses made of copper and pewter, and coins were smartly displayed under linen awnings. But even where she was she found many objects worthy of notice: she was amused at the sight of a gypsy and a peasant, who clapped hands so that they both cried out with pain; of a drunken Jew kneeing a woman on the rump; of women hucksters quarreling with abusive words and gestures of contempt; of a Great Russian with one hand stroking his goat's beard, with another . . . But at that moment she felt someone pull her by the embroidered sleeve of her blouse. She looked around—and the bright-eyed young man in the white jacket stood before her. She started and her heart throbbed, as it had never done before at any joy or grief; it seemed strange and delightful, and she could not make out what had happened to her.

"Don't be frightened, dear heart, don't be frightened!" he said to her in a low voice, taking her hand. "I'll say nothing to hurt you!"

"Perhaps it is true that you will say nothing to hurt me," the girl thought to herself; "only it is strange . . . it might be the Evil One! One knows that it is not right . . . but I haven't the strength to take away my hand."

The peasant looked around and was about to say something to his daughter, but on the other side he heard the word "wheat." That magic word instantly made him join two dealers who were talking loudly, and riveted his attention upon them so that nothing could have distracted it. This is what the dealers were saying.

III

Do you see what a sort of a fellow he is?
Not many like him in the world.
Tosses off vodka like beer!

KOTLYAREVSKY,[7] *The Aeneid*

"So you think, neighbor, that our wheat won't sell well?" said a man, who looked like an artisan of some big village, in dirty tar-stained trousers of coarse homespun material, to another, with a big bump on his forehead, wearing a dark blue jacket patched in different parts.

"It's not a matter of thinking: I am ready to put a halter around my neck and hang from that tree like a sausage in the hut before Christmas, if we sell a single bushel."

"What nonsense are you talking, neighbor? No wheat has been brought except ours," answered the man in the homespun trousers.

"Yes, you may say what you like," thought the father of our beauty, who had not missed a single word of the dealer's conversation. "I have ten sacks here in reserve."

"Well, you see, it's like this: if there is any devilry mixed up in a thing, you will get no more profit from it than a hungry Muscovite,"[8] the man with the bump on his forehead said significantly.

"What do you mean by devilry?" retorted the man in the homespun trousers.

"Did you hear what people are saying?" went on he of the bumpy forehead, giving him a sidelong look out of his gloomy eyes.

"Well?"

"Ah, you may say, well! The assessor, may he never wipe his lips again after the gentry's plum brandy, has set aside an evil spot for the fair, where you may burst before you get rid of a single grain. Do you see that old dilapidated barn which stands there, see, under the hill?" (At this point the inquisitive peasant went closer and was all attention.) "All manner of devilish tricks go on in that barn, and not a single fair has taken place in this spot without trouble. The

---

[7] Ivan Kotlyarevsky (1769-1838), an important Ukrainian writer, considered by many the founder of modern Ukrainian literature. These lines are from his comic version of Vergil's epic poem. (ed.)

[8] Inhabitant of Great Russia. Traditionally, Cossacks hated Great Russians, but the hatred was not necessarily reciprocal. (ed.)

district clerk passed it late last night and all of a sudden a pig's snout looked out from the window of the loft, and grunted so that it sent a shiver down his back. You may be sure that the *red jacket* will be seen again!"

"What's that about a red jacket?"

Our attentive listener's hair stood up on his head at these words. He looked around in alarm and saw that his daughter and the young man were calmly standing in each other's arms, murmuring soft nothings to each other and oblivious of every colored jacket in the world. This dispelled his terror and restored his equanimity.

"Aha-ha-ha, neighbor! You know how to hug a girl, it seems! I had been married three days before I learned to hug my late Khveska, and I owed that to a friend who was my best man: he gave me a hint."

The youth saw at once that his fair one's father was not very bright, and began making a plan for disposing him in his favor.

"I believe you don't know me, good friend, but I recognized you at once."

"Maybe you did."

"If you like I'll tell you your name and your surname and everything about you: your name is Solopy Cherevik."

"Yes, Solopy Cherevik."

"Well, have a good look: don't you know me?"

"No, I don't know you. No offense meant: I've seen so many faces of all sorts in my day, how the hell can one remember them all?"

"I am sorry you don't remember Golopupenko's son!"

"Why, is Okhrim your father?"

"Who else? Maybe he's the devil if he's not!"

At this the friends took off their caps and proceeded to kiss each other; our Golopupenko's son made up his mind, however, to attack his new acquaintance without loss of time.

"Well, Solopy, you see, your daughter and I have so taken to each other that we are ready to spend our lives together."

"Well, Paraska," said Cherevik, laughing and turning to his daughter; "maybe you really might, as they say . . . you and he . . . graze on the same grass! Come, shall we shake hands on it? And now, my new son-in-law, buy me a glass!"

And all three found themselves in the famous refreshment bar of the fair—a Jewess's booth, decorated with a huge assortment of jars, bottles, and flasks of every kind and description.

"Well, you are a smart fellow! I like you for that," said Cherevik, a little exhilarated, seeing how his intended son-in-law filled a pint mug and, without winking an eyelash, tossed it off at a gulp, flinging down the mug afterward and smashing it to bits. "What do you say, Paraska? Haven't I found you a fine husband? Look, look how he downs his drink!"

And laughing and staggering he went with her toward his wagon; while our young man made his way to the booths where fancy goods were displayed, where there were even dealers from Gadyach and Mirgorod, the two famous towns of the province of Poltava, to pick out the best wooden pipe in a smart copper setting, a flowered red kerchief and cap, for wedding presents to his father-in-law and everyone else who must have one.

IV

If it's a man, it doesn't matter,
But if there's a woman, you see
There is need to please her.

KOTLYAREVSKY

"Well, wife, I have found a husband for my daughter!"

"This is a moment to look for husbands, I must say! You are a fool—a fool! It must have been ordained at your birth that you should remain one! Whoever has seen, whoever has heard of such a thing as a decent man running after husbands at a time like this? You had much better be thinking how to get your wheat off your hands. A nice young man he must be, too! I'm certain he is the shabbiest scarecrow in the place!"

"Oh, he's not anything like that! You should see what a young man he is! His jacket alone is worth more than your pelisse and red boots. And how he downs his vodka! The devil confound me and you too if ever I have seen a fellow before toss off a pint without winking!"

"To be sure, if he is a drunkard and a vagabond he is a man after your own heart. I wouldn't mind betting it's the very same rascal who pestered us on the bridge. I am sorry I haven't come across him yet: I'd let him know."

"Well, Khivrya, what if it were the same: why is he a rascal?"

"Eh! Why is he a rascal? Ah, you birdbrain! Do you hear? Why is he a rascal? Where were your stupid eyes when we were driving past the mills? They might insult his wife here, right before his snuff-clogged nose, and he would not care a damn!"

"I see no harm in him, anyway: he is a fine fellow! Except that he plastered your mug with dung for an instant."

"Aha! I see you won't let me say a word! What's the meaning of it? It's not like you! You must have managed to get a drop before you have sold anything."

Here Cherevik himself realized that he had said too much and instantly put his hands over his head, doubtless expecting that his wrathful wife would promptly seize his hair in her wifely claws.

"Go to the devil! So much for our wedding!" he thought to himself, retreating before his wife's attack. "I shall have to refuse a good fellow for no rhyme or reason. Merciful God! Why didst Thou send such a plague on us poor sinners? With so many trashy things in the world, Thou must needs go and create wives!"

V

Droop not, plane tree,
Still art thou green.
Fret not, little Cossack,
Still art thou young.

Little Russian song

The fellow in the white jacket sitting by his wagon gazed absent-mindedly at the crowd that moved noisily about him. The weary sun, after blazing through morning and noon, was tranquilly withdrawing from the earth, and the daylight was going out in a bright lovely glow. The tops of the white booths and tents stood out with dazzling brightness, suffused in a faint rosy tint of fiery light. The panes in the window frames piled up for sale glittered; the green goblets and bottles on the tables in the drinking booths flashed like fire; the heaps of melons and pumpkins looked as though they were cast in gold and dark copper. There was less talk, and the weary tongues of merchants, peasants, and gypsies moved more slowly and deliberately. Here and there lights began gleaming, and savory steam from cooking dumplings floated over the hushed streets.

"What are you grieving over, Grytsko?" a tall swarthy gypsy

cried, slapping our young friend on the shoulder. "Come, let me have your oxen for twenty rubles!"

"It's nothing but oxen and oxen with you. All that you gypsies care for is profit; cheating and deceiving honest folk!"

"Tfoo, the devil! You do seem to be in trouble! You are angered at having tied yourself up with a girl, maybe?"

"No, that's not my way: I keep my word; what I have once done stands forever. But it seems that old grumbler Cherevik has not a half pint of conscience: he gave his word, but he has taken it back. . . . Well, it is no good blaming him: he is a blockhead and that's the fact. It's all the doing of that old witch whom we jeered at on the bridge today! Ah, if I were the Czar or some great lord I would first hang all the fools who let themselves be saddled by women. . . ."

"Well, will you let the oxen go for twenty, if we make Cherevik give you Paraska?"

Grytsko stared at him in surprise. There was a look spiteful, malicious, ignoble, and at the same time haughty in the gypsy's swarthy face: any man looking at him would have recognized that there were great qualities in that strange soul, though their only reward on earth would be the gallows. The mouth, completely sunken between the nose and the pointed chin and forever curved in a mocking smile, the little eyes that gleamed like fire, and the lightning flashes of intrigue and enterprise forever flitting over his face—all this seemed in keeping with the strange costume he wore. The dark brown full coat which looked as though it would drop into dust at a touch; the long black hair that fell in tangled tresses on his shoulders; the shoes on his bare sunburnt feet, all seemed to be in character and part of him.

"I'll let you have them for fifteen, not twenty, if only you don't deceive me!" the young man answered, keeping his searching gaze fixed on the gypsy.

"Fifteen? Done! Mind you don't forget; fifteen! Here is a blue note[9] as a pledge!"

"But if you deceive me?"

"If I do, the pledge is yours!"

"Right! Well, let's shake hands on the bargain!"

"Let's!"

---

9 Colloquial for five rubles. (ed.)

VI

What a misfortune! Roman is coming; here he is, he'll give me a drubbing in a minute; and you, too, master Khomo, will not get off without trouble.

From a Little Russian comedy

"This way, Afanasy Ivanovich! The fence is lower here, put your foot up and don't be afraid: my idiot has gone off for the night with his crony to the wagons to see that the Muscovites don't steal anything but ill-luck."

So Cherevik's menacing spouse fondly encouraged the priest's son, who was faintheartedly clinging to the fence. He soon climbed onto the top and stood there for some time in hesitation, like a long terrible phantom, looking where he could best jump and at last coming down with a crash among the rank weeds.

"How dreadful! I hope you have not hurt yourself? Please God, you've not broken your neck!" Khivrya faltered anxiously.

"Sh! It's all right, it's all right, dear Khavronya Nikiforovna," the priest's son brought out in a painful whisper, getting onto his feet, "except for being afflicted by the nettles, that serpentlike weed, to use the words of our late head priest."

"Let us go into the house; there is nobody there. I was beginning to think you were ill or asleep, Afanasy Ivanovich: you did not come and did not come. How are you? I hear that your honored father has had a run of good luck!"

"Nothing to speak of, Khavronya Nikiforovna: during the whole fast Father has received nothing but fifteen sacks of spring wheat, four sacks of millet, a hundred buns; and as for fowls they don't amount to fifty, and the eggs were mostly rotten. But the truly sweet offerings, so to say, can only come from you, Khavronya Nikiforovna!" the priest's son continued, with a tender glance at her as he edged nearer.

"Here is an offering for you, Afanasy Ivanovich!" she said, setting some bowls on the table and coyly fastening the buttons of her jacket as though they had not been undone on purpose, "curd doughnuts, wheaten dumplings, buns, and cakes!"

"I bet they have been made by the cleverest hands of any daughter of Eve!" said the priest's son, setting to work upon the cakes and with the other hand drawing the curd doughnuts toward him.

"Though indeed, Khavronya Nikiforovna, my heart thirsts for a gift from you sweeter than any buns or dumplings!"

"Well, I don't know what dainty you will ask for next, Afanasy Ivanovich!" answered the buxom beauty, pretending not to understand.

"Your love, of course, incomparable Khavronya Nikiforovna!" the priest's son whispered, holding a doughnut in one hand and encircling her ample waist with his arm.

"Goodness knows what you are thinking about, Afanasy Ivanovich!" said Khivrya, bashfully casting down her eyes. "Why, I wouldn't be surprised if you tried to kiss me next!"

"As for that, I must tell you," the young man went on. "When I was still at the seminary, I remember as though it were today . . ."

At that moment there was a sound of barking and a knock at the gate. Khivrya ran out quickly and came back looking pale.

"Afanasy Ivanovich, we are caught: there are a lot of people knocking, and I think I heard Tsibulya's voice . . ."

A dumpling stuck in the young man's throat. . . . His eyes almost popped out of his head, as though someone had just come from the other world to visit him.

"Climb up here!" cried the panic-stricken Khivrya, pointing to some boards that lay across the rafters just below the ceiling, loaded with all sorts of domestic odds and ends.

Danger gave our hero courage. Recovering a little, he clambered on the stove and from there climbed cautiously onto the boards, while Khivrya ran headlong to the gate, as the knocking was getting louder and more insistent.

VII

But here are miracles, gentlemen!
From a Little Russian comedy

A strange incident had taken place at the fair: there were rumors all over the place that the *red jacket* had been seen somewhere among the wares. The old woman who sold pretzels thought she saw the devil in the shape of a pig, bending over the wagons as though looking for something. The news soon flew to every corner of the now resting camp, and everyone would have thought it a crime to disbelieve it, in spite of the fact that the pretzel seller, whose stall was next to the drinking booth, had been staggering about all day and could not walk straight. To this was added the story—by now greatly exaggerated—of the wonder seen by the district clerk in the dilapidated barn; so toward night people were all huddling together; their peace of mind was destroyed, and everyone was too terrified to close an eye; while those who were not cast in a heroic mold, and had secured a night's lodging in a hut, made their way homeward. Among the latter were Cherevik with his daughter and his friend Tsibulya, and they, together with the friends who had offered to keep them company, were responsible for the loud knocking that had so alarmed Khivrya. Tsibulya was already a little exhilarated. This could be seen from his twice driving around the yard with his wagon before he could find the hut. His guests, too, were all rather merry, and they unceremoniously pushed into the hut before their host. Our Cherevik's wife sat as though on thorns, when they began rummaging in every corner of the hut.

"Well, gossip," cried Tsibulya as he entered, "you are still shaking with fever?"

"Yes, I am not well," answered Khivrya, looking uneasily toward the boards on the rafters.

"Come, wife, get the bottle out of the wagon!" said Tsibulya to his wife, who had come in with him, "we will empty it with these good folk, for the damned women have given us such a scare that one is ashamed to admit it. Yes, friends, there was really no sense in our coming here!" he went on, taking a pull out of an earthenware jug. "I don't mind betting a new cap that the women thought they would have a laugh at us. Why, if it were Satan—who's Satan? Spit on him! If he stood here before me this very minute, I'll be a son of a bitch if I wouldn't make a fig at him!"

"Why did you turn so pale, then?" cried one of the visitors, who was a head taller than any of the rest and tried on every occasion to display his valor.

"I? . . . Bless you! Are you dreaming?"

The visitors laughed; the boastful hero smiled complacently.

"As though he could turn pale now!" put in another; "his cheeks are as red as a poppy; he is not a Tsibulya[10] now, but a beet—or, rather, the *red jacket* itself that frightened us all so."

The bottle went the round of the table, and made the visitors

---

[10] "Onion." (ed.)

more exhilarated than ever. At this point Cherevik, greatly disturbed about the *red jacket*, which would not let his inquisitive
mind rest, appealed to his friend:

"Come, friend, kindly tell me! I keep asking about this damned
jacket and can get no answer from anyone!"

"Eh, friend, it's not a thing to talk about at night; however, to
satisfy you and these good friends" (saying this he turned toward
his guests) "who want, I see, to know about these strange doings
as much as you do. Well, so be it. Listen!"

Here he scratched his shoulder, mopped his face with the skirt
of his coat, leaned both arms on the table, and began:

"Once upon a time a devil was kicked out of hell, what for I cannot say . . ."

"How so, friend?" Cherevik interrupted. "How could it be that
a devil was turned out of hell?"

"I can't help it, crony, if he was turned out, he was—as a peasant
turns a dog out of his hut. Perhaps a whim came over him to do a
good deed—and so they showed him the door. And the poor devil
was so homesick, so homesick for hell that he was ready to hang
himself. Well, what could he do about it? In his trouble he took to
drink. He settled in the broken-down barn which you have seen at
the bottom of the hill and which no good man will pass now without making the sign of the cross as a safeguard; and the devil became such a rake you would not find another like him among the
fellows: he sat day and night in the tavern!"

At this point Cherevik interrupted again:

"Goodness knows what you are saying, friend! How could anyone let a devil into a tavern? Why, thank God, he has claws on his
paws and horns on his head."

"Ah, that was just it—he had a cap and gloves on. Who could
recognize him? Well, he kept it up till he had drunk away all he had
with him. They gave him credit for a long time, but at last they
would give no more. The devil had to pawn his red jacket for less
than a third of its value to the Jew who sold vodka in those days at
Sorochintsy. He pawned it and said to him: 'Mind now, Jew, I shall
come to you for my jacket in a year's time; take care of it!' And he
disappeared and no more was seen of him. The Jew examined the
coat thoroughly: the cloth was better than anything you could get
in Mirgorod, and the red of it glowed like fire, so that one could not
take one's eyes off it! And it seemed to the Jew a long time to wait

till the end of the year. He scratched his earlocks and got nearly five gold pieces for it from a gentleman who was passing by. The Jew forgot all about the date set. But all of a sudden one evening a man turns up: 'Come, Jew, hand me over my jacket!' At first the Jew did not know him, but afterward when he had had a good look at him, he pretended he had never seen him before. 'What jacket? I have no jacket. I know nothing about your jacket!' The other walked away; only, when the Jew locked himself up in his room and, after counting over the money in his chests, flung a sheet around his shoulders and began saying his prayers in Jewish fashion, all at once he heard a rustle . . . and there were pigs' snouts looking in at every window."

At that moment an indistinct sound not unlike the grunt of a pig was audible; everyone turned pale. Drops of sweat stood out on Tsibulya's face.

"What was it?" cried the panic-stricken Cherevik.

"Nothing," answered Tsibulya, trembling all over.

"Eh?" responded one of the guests.

"Did you speak?"

"No!"

"Who was it grunted?"

"God knows why we are so flustered! It's nothing!"

They all turned about fearfully and began rummaging in the corners. Khivrya was more dead than alive.

"Oh, you are a bunch of women!" she shouted. "You are not fit to be Cossacks and men! You ought to sit spinning yarn! Maybe someone misbehaved, God forgive him, or someone's bench creaked, and you are all in a fluster as though you were out of your heads!"

This put our heroes to shame and made them pull themselves together. Tsibulya took a pull at the jug and went on with his story.

"The Jew fainted from terror; but the pigs with legs as long as stilts climbed in at the windows and so revived him in an instant with a three-thonged whip, making him skip higher than this ceiling. The Jew fell at their feet and confessed everything. . . . Only the jacket could not be restored in a hurry. The gentleman had been robbed of it on the road by a gypsy who sold it to a peddler woman, and she brought it back again to the fair at Sorochintsy; but no one would buy anything from her after that. The woman wondered and wondered and at last saw what it was: there was no doubt the red jacket was at the bottom of it; it was not for nothing that she had felt stifled when she put it on. Without stopping to think she flung it in the fire—the devilish thing would not burn! . . . 'Ah, that's a gift from the devil!' she thought. The woman managed to thrust it into the wagon of a peasant who had come to the fair to sell his butter. The silly fellow was delighted; but no one would ask for his butter. 'Ah, it's an evil hand foisted that red jacket on me!' He took his ax and chopped it into bits; he looked at it—and each bit joined up to the next till it was whole again! Crossing himself, he went at it with the ax again; he flung the bits all over the place and went away. But ever since then, just at the time of the fair, the devil walks all over the market place with the face of a pig, grunting and collecting the pieces of his jacket. Now they say there is only the left sleeve missing. People have been shy of the place ever since, and it is ten years since the fair has been held on it. But in an evil hour the assessor . . ."

The rest of the sentence died away on the speaker's lips: there was a loud rattle at the window, the panes fell tinkling on the floor, and a frightening pig's snout peered in through the window, rolling its eyes as though asking, "What are you doing here, folks?"

VIII

His tail between his legs like a dog,
Like Cain, trembling all over;
The snuff dropped from his nose.
KOTLYAREVSKY, *The Aeneid*

Everyone in the room was numb with horror. Tsibulya sat petri-fied with his mouth open; his eyes were bulging as if he wanted to shoot with them; his outspread fingers were frozen in the air. The tall hero, in overwhelming terror, leaped up and struck his head against the rafter; the boards shifted, and with a thud and a crash the priest's son fell to the floor.

"Aie, aie, aie!" one of the party screamed desperately, flopping on the locker in alarm, and waving his arms and legs.

"Save me!" wailed another, hiding his head under a sheepskin.

Tsibulya, roused from his numbness by this second horror, crept shuddering under his wife's skirts. The valiant hero crawled into the oven in spite of the narrowness of the opening, and closed the oven door on himself. And Cherevik, clapping a basin on his head instead of a cap, dashed to the door as though he had been scalded, and ran through the streets like a lunatic, not knowing where he was going; only weariness caused him to slacken his pace. His heart was thumping like an oil press; streams of perspiration rolled down him. He was on the point of sinking to the ground in exhaustion when all at once he heard someone running after him. . . . His breath failed him.

"The devil! The devil!" came a shout behind him, and all he felt was something falling with a thud on the top of him. Then his senses deserted him and, like the dread inmate of a narrow coffin, he remained lying dumb and motionless in the middle of the road.

IX

> In front, like anyone else;
> Behind, I swear, like a devil!
>
> *From a folk tale*

"Do you hear, Vlas?" one of the crowd asleep in the street said, sitting up; "someone spoke of the devil near us!"

"What is it to me?" the gypsy near him grumbled, stretching. "They may talk of all their kindred for all I care!"

"But he bawled, you know, as though he were being strangled!"

"A man will cry out anything in his sleep!"

"Say what you like, we must have a look. Strike a light!"

The other gypsy, grumbling to himself, rose to his feet, sent a shower of sparks flying like lightning flashes, blew the tinder with his lips, and with a *kaganets* in his hands—the usual Little Russian lamp consisting of a broken pot full of mutton fat—set off, lighting the way before him.

"Stop! There is something lying here! Show a light this way!"

Here they were joined by several others.

"What's lying there, Vlas?"

"Why, it looks like two men: one on top, the other under. Which of them is the devil I can't make out yet!"

"Why, who is on top?"

"A woman!"

"Oh, well, then that's the devil!"

A general shout of laughter roused almost the whole street.

"A woman straddling a man! I suppose she knows how to ride!" one of the bystanders exclaimed.

"Look, boys!" said another, picking up a broken piece of the basin of which only one half still remained on Cherevik's head, "what a cap this fine fellow put on!"

The growing noise and laughter brought our corpses to life, and Cherevik and his spouse, full of the panic they had known, gazed with bulging eyes in terror at the swarthy faces of the gypsies; in the dim and flickering light they looked like a wild horde of dark subterranean creatures, reeking of hell.

X

> Fie upon you, away with you, image of the Devil!
> *From a Little Russian comedy*

The freshness of morning breathed over the awakening folk of Sorochintsy. Clouds of smoke from all the chimneys floated to meet the rising sun. The fair began to hum with life. Sheep were bleating, horses neighing; the cackle of geese and peddler women sounded all over the encampment again—and terrible tales of the *red jacket*, which had roused such alarm in the mysterious hours of darkness, vanished with the return of morning.

Stretching and yawning, Cherevik lay drowsily under his friend Tsibulya's thatched barn among oxen and sacks of flour and wheat. And apparently he had no desire to part with his dreams, when all at once he heard a voice, familiar as his own stove, the blessed refuge of his lazy hours, or as the tavern kept by his cousin not ten paces from his own door.

"Get up, get up!" his tender wife squeaked in his ear, tugging at his arm with all her might.

Cherevik, instead of answering, blew out his cheeks and began waving his hands, as though beating a drum.

"Idiot!" she shouted, retreating out of reach of his arms, which almost struck her in the face.

Cherevik sat up, rubbed his eyes, and looked about him.

"The devil take me, my dear, if I didn't imagine that your face was a drum on which I was forced to beat an alarm, like a soldier, by those pig-faces that Tsibulya was telling us about. . . ."

"Stop talking nonsense! Go, make haste and take the mare to market! We are a laughingstock, upon my word: we've come to the fair and not sold a handful of hemp. . . ."

"Of course, wife," Cherevik agreed, "they will laugh at us now, to be sure."

"Go along, go along! They are laughing at you as it is!"

"You see, I haven't washed yet," Cherevik went on, yawning, scratching his back, and trying to gain time.

"What a moment to be fussy about cleanliness! When have you cared about that? Here's the towel, wipe your ugly face."

Here she snatched up something that lay crumpled up—and darted back in horror: it was the cuff of a red jacket!

"Go along and get to work," she repeated, recovering herself, on seeing that her husband was motionless with terror and his teeth were chattering.

"A fine sale there will be now!" he muttered to himself as he untied the mare and led her to the market place. "It was not for nothing that, while I was getting ready for this cursed fair, my heart was as heavy as though someone had put a dead cow on my back, and twice the oxen turned homeward of their own accord. And now that I come to think of it, I do believe it was Monday when we started. And so everything has gone wrong! [11] And the damned devil can never be satisfied: he might have worn his jacket without one sleeve—but no, he can't let honest folk rest in peace. Now if I were the devil—God forbid—do you suppose I'd go hanging around at night after a lot of damned rags?"

Here our Cherevik's meditations were interrupted by a thick harsh voice. Before him stood a tall gypsy.

"What have you for sale, good man?"

Cherevik was silent for a moment; he looked at the gypsy from head to foot and said with unruffled composure, neither stopping nor letting go the bridle:

"You can see for yourself what I am selling."

"Harness?" said the gypsy, looking at the bridle which the other had in his hand.

"Yes, harness, if a mare is the same thing as harness."

"But damn it, neighbor, one would think you had fed her on straw!"

"Straw?"

Here Cherevik would have pulled at the bridle to lead his mare

---

[11] Throughout Russia, Monday was traditionally considered a poor day on which to initiate anything—the result of an old superstition which died hard. (ed.)

forward and convict the shameless slanderer of his lie; but his hand slipped and struck his own chin. He looked—in it was a severed bridle, and tied to the bridle—oh horror! his hair stood up on his head—a piece of a red sleeve! . . . Spitting, crossing himself, and brandishing his arms, he ran away from the unexpected gift and, running faster than a boy, vanished in the crowd.

XI

For my own corn I have been beaten.

Proverb

"Catch him! catch him!" cried several young men at a narrow street corner, and Cherevik felt himself suddenly seized by strong hands.

"Tie him up! That's the fellow who stole an honest man's mare."

"Damn it! What are you tieing me up for?"

"Imagine his asking! Why did you want to steal a mare from a peasant at the fair, Cherevik?"

"You're out of your minds, fellows! Who has ever heard of a man stealing from himself?"

"That's an old trick! An old trick! Why were you running your hardest, as though the devil were on your heels?"

"Anyone would run when the devil's garment . . ."

"Aie, my good soul, try that on others! You'll catch it yet from the court assessor, to teach you to go scaring people with tales of the devil."

"Catch him! catch him!" came a shout from the other end of the street. "There he is, there is the runaway!"

And Cherevik beheld his friend Tsibulya in the most pitiful plight with his hands tied behind him, led along by several young men.

"Strange things are happening!" said one of them. "You should hear what this scoundrel says! You have only to look at his face to see he is a thief. When we began asking him why he was running like one possessed, he says he put his hand in his pocket and instead of his snuff pulled out a bit of the devil's jacket and it burst into a red flame—and he took to his heels!"

"Aha! why, these two are birds of a feather! We had better tie them together!"

XII

"In what am I to blame, good folks?
Why are you beating me?" said our poor wretch.
"Why are you falling upon me?
What for, what for?" he said, bursting into tears,
Streams of bitter tears, and clutching at his sides.
ARTEMOVSKY-GULAK,[12] *Master and Dog*

"Maybe you really have picked up something, friend?" Cherevik asked, as he lay bound beside Tsibulya in a thatched shanty.

"You too, friend! May my arms and legs wither if ever I stole anything in my life, except maybe buns and cream from my mother, and that only before I was ten years old."

"Why has this trouble come upon us? It's not so bad for you: you are charged, anyway, with stealing from somebody else; but what have I, unlucky wretch, done to deserve such a foul slander, as stealing my mare from myself? It seems it was written at our birth that we should have no luck!"

"Woe to us, forlorn and forsaken!"

At this point the two friends fell to weeping violently.

"What's the matter with you, Cherevik?" said Grytsko, entering at that moment. "Who tied you up like that?"

"Ah, Golopupenko, Golopupenko!" cried Cherevik, delighted. "Here, this is the fellow I was telling you about. Ah, he is a smart one! God strike me dead on the spot if he did not toss off a whole jug, almost as big as your head, and never turned a hair!"

"What made you ignore such a fine fellow, then, friend?"

"Here, you see," Cherevik went on, addressing Grytsko, "God has punished me, it seems, for having wronged you. Forgive me, good lad! I swear I'd be glad to do anything for you. . . . But what would you have me do? There's the devil in my old woman!"

"I am not one to hold a grudge, Cherevik! If you like, I'll set you free!"

Here he made a sign to the other fellows and the same ones who were guarding them ran to untie them.

"Then you must do your part, too: a wedding! And let us keep it up so that our legs ache with dancing for a year afterwards!"

"Good, good!" said Cherevik, striking his hands together. "I feel

---

[12] P. P. Artemovsky-Gulak (1790-1865), Ukrainian writer. *Master and Dog* is a short story in verse. (ed.)

as pleased as though the soldiers had carried off my old woman! Why give it another thought? Whether she likes it or not, the wedding shall be today—and that's all there is to it!"

"Mind now, Solopy: in an hour's time I will be with you; but now go home—there you will find purchasers for your mare and your wheat."

"What! has the mare been found?"

"Yes."

Cherevik was struck dumb with joy and stood still, gazing after Grytsko.

"Well, Grytsko, have we mishandled the job?" said the tall gypsy to the hurrying young man. "The oxen are mine now, aren't they?"

"Yours! yours!"

XIII

Fear not, fear not, little mother,
Put on your red boots
Trample your foes
Under foot
So that your ironshod
Heels may clang,
So that your foes
May be hushed and still.

A wedding song

Paraska mused, sitting alone in the hut with her pretty chin propped on her hand. Many dreams hovered about her little head. At times a faint smile stirred her crimson lips and some joyful feeling lifted her dark brows, while at times a cloud of pensiveness set them frowning above her clear brown eyes.

"But what if it does not come true as he said?" she whispered with an expression of doubt. "What if they don't let me marry him? If . . . No, no; that will not be! My stepmother does just as she likes; why mayn't I do as I like? I've plenty of obstinacy too. How handsome he is! How wonderfully his black eyes glow! How delightfully he says, 'Paraska darling!' How his white jacket suits him! But his belt ought to be a bit brighter! . . . I will weave him one when we settle in a new hut. I can't help being pleased when I think," she went on, taking from her bosom a little red-paper-framed mirror bought at the fair and gazing into it, "how I shall meet her one day somewhere and she may burst before I bow to her, nothing will induce me. No, stepmother, you've kicked me for the last time. The sand will rise up on the rocks and the oak bend down to the water like a willow before I bow down before you. But I was forgetting . . . let me try on a cap, even if it has to be my stepmother's, and see how it suits me to look like a wife?"

Then she got up, holding the mirror in her hand and bending her head down to it, walked in excitement about the room, as though in dread of falling, seeing below her, instead of the floor, the ceiling with the boards laid on the rafters from which the priest's son had so lately dropped, and the shelves set with pots.

"Why, I am like a child," she cried, "afraid to take a step!"

And she began tapping with her feet, growing bolder as she went on; at last she laid her left hand on her hip and went off into a dance, clinking with her metaled heels, holding the mirror before her, and singing her favorite song:

> Little green periwinkle,
>   Twine lower to me!
> And you, black-browed dear one,
>   Come nearer to me!
> Little green periwinkle,
>   Twine lower to me!
> And you, black-browed dear one,
>   Come nearer to me!

At that moment Cherevik peeped in at the door, and seeing his daughter dancing before the mirror, he stood still. For a long time he watched, laughing at the innocent prank of his daughter, who was apparently so absorbed that she noticed nothing; but when he heard the familiar notes of the song, his muscles began working: he stepped forward, his arms jauntily akimbo, and forgetting all he had to do, began dancing. A loud shout of laughter from his friend Tsibulya startled both of them.

"Here is a pretty thing! The dad and his daughter getting up a wedding on their own account! Make haste and come along: the bridegroom has arrived!"

At the last words Paraska flushed a deeper crimson than the ribbon which bound her head, and her lighthearted parent remembered his errand.

"Well, daughter, let us make haste! Khivrya is so pleased that I have sold the mare," he went on, looking timorously about him, "that she has run off to buy herself aprons and all sorts of rags, so we must get it all over before she is back."

Paraska had no sooner stepped over the threshold than she felt herself caught in the arms of the young man in the white jacket who with a crowd of people was waiting for her in the street.

"God bless you!" said Cherevik, joining their hands. "May their lives together cleave as the wreaths of flowers they weave." [13]

At this point a hubbub was heard in the crowd.

"I'd burst before I'd allow it!" screamed Cherevik's helpmate, who was being shoved back by the laughing crowd.

"Don't excite yourself, wife!" Cherevik said coolly, seeing that two sturdy gypsies held her hands, "what is done can't be undone: I don't like going back on a bargain!"

"No, no, that shall never be!" screamed Khivrya, but no one heeded her; several couples surrounded the happy pair and formed an impenetrable dancing wall around them.

A strange feeling, hard to put into words, would have overcome anyone watching how the whole crowd was transformed into a scene of unity and harmony, at one stroke of the bow of the fiddler, who had long twisted mustaches and wore a homespun jacket. Men whose sullen faces seemed to have known no gleam of a smile for years were tapping with their feet and wriggling their shoulders; everything was heaving, everything was dancing. But an even stranger and more disturbing feeling would have been stirred in the heart at the sight of old women, whose ancient faces breathed the indifference of the tomb, shoving their way between the young, laughing, living human beings. Caring for nothing, indifferent, long removed from the joy of childhood, wanting only drink, it was as if a puppeteer were tugging the strings that held his wooden puppets, making them do things that seemed human; yet they slowly wagged their drunken heads, dancing after the rejoicing crowd, not casting one glance at the young couple.

The sounds of laughter, song, and uproar grew fainter and fainter. The strains of the fiddle were lost in vague and feeble notes, and died away in the wind. In the distance there was still the sound of dancing feet, something like the faraway murmur of the sea, and soon all was stillness and emptiness again.

Is it not thus that joy, lovely and fleeting guest, flies from us? In

---

[13] The proverbial form of greeting to a newly wedded couple in Little Russia. (C.G.)

vain the last solitary note tries to express gaiety. In its own echo it hears melancholy and emptiness and listens to it, bewildered. Is it not thus that those who have been playful friends in free and stormy youth, one by one stray, lost, about the world and leave their old comrade lonely and forlorn at last? Sad is the lot of one left behind! Heavy and sorrowful is his heart and nothing can help him!

ST. JOHN'S EVE

A True Story Told by the Sexton

It was a special peculiarity of Foma Grigorievich's that he had a mortal aversion for repeating the same story. It sometimes happened that one persuaded him to tell a story over again, but then he would be bound to add something fresh, or would tell it so differently that you hardly knew it for the same. It happened that one of those people—it is hard for us, simple folk, to know what to call them, for scriveners they are not, but they are like the dealers at our fairs: they beg, they grab, they filch all sorts of things and bring out a little book, no thicker than a child's reader, every month or every week—well, one of these gentry got this story out of Foma Grigorievich, though he almost forgot all about it. And then that young gentleman in the pea-green coat of whom I have told you already and whose story, I believe, you have read arrives from Poltava, brings with him a little book, and opening it in the middle, shows it to us. Foma Grigorievich was just about to put

his spectacles astride his nose, but, recollecting that he had for-
gotten to mend them with thread and wax, he handed it to me.
As I know how to read after a fashion and do not wear spectacles,
I began reading it aloud. I had hardly read two pages when Foma
Grigorievich suddenly nudged my arm.

"Wait a minute: tell me first what it is you are reading."

I must admit I was a little taken aback by such a question.

"What I am reading, Foma Grigorievich? Your story, your own
words."

"Who told you it was my story?"

"What better proof do you want? It is printed here: 'Told by
the sexton of So-and-so.'"

"Hang the fellow who printed that! He's lying, the dog! Is that
how I told it? What is one to do when a man has a screw loose in
his head? Listen, I'll tell it to you now."

We moved up to the table and he began.

My grandfather (the kingdom of heaven be his! May he have
nothing but rolls made of fine wheat and poppy cakes with honey
to eat in the other world!) was a great hand at telling stories. Sometimes when he talked, one could sit listening all day without stirring. He was not like the gabblers nowadays who drive you to
pick up your cap and go out as soon as they begin spinning their
yarns in a voice which sounds as though they had had nothing
to eat for three days. I remember as though it were today—the
old lady, my mother, was living then—how, on a long winter
evening when frost crackled outside and sealed up the narrow
window of our hut, she would sit with her spindle pulling out
a long thread with one hand, rocking the cradle with her foot,
and singing a song which I can hear now. Sputtering and trembling as though it were afraid of something, the lamp lighted up
the hut. The spindle hummed while we children clustered together listening to Grandad, who was so old that he had hardly
climbed down from the stove for the last five years. But not even
his marvelous accounts of the old days, of the raids of the Cossacks,
and of the Poles, of the gallant deeds of Podkova, of Poltor-
Kozhukh and Sagaydachny,[1] interested us so much as stories of
strange things that had happened long ago; they always made our

---

[1] Famous Cossack headmen. (ed.)

hair stand on end and set us shuddering. Sometimes we were so terrified by them that in the evening you can't imagine how strange everything looked. Sometimes you would step out of the hut for something at night and think that some visitor from the other world had got into your bed. And, may I never live to tell this tale again, if I did not often mistake my coat rolled up as a pillow for the devil huddling there. But the main thing about Grandad's stories was that he never in his life told a lie and everything he told us had really happened.

One of his wonderful stories I am going to tell you now. I know there are lots of smart fellows who scribble in law courts and read even modern print, though if you put in their hands a simple prayer book they could not read a letter of it, and yet they are clever enough at grinning and mocking! Whatever you tell them they turn into ridicule. Such unbelief is spreading all over the world! Why—may God and the Holy Virgin look ill upon me!—you will hardly believe me: I dropped a word about witches one day, and there was a crazy fellow who didn't believe in witches! Here, thank God, I have lived all these long years and have met unbelievers who would tell a lie at confession as easily as I'd take a pinch of snuff, but even they made the sign of the cross in terror of witches. May they dream of—but I won't say what I would like them to dream of. . . . Better not speak of them.

How many years ago! over a hundred, my Grandad told us, no one would have known our village: it was a hamlet, the poorest of hamlets! A dozen huts or so, without plaster or proper roofs, stood up here and there in the middle of the fields. No fences, no real barns where cattle or carts could be housed. And it was only the rich who lived as well as that—you should have seen the likes of us poor ones: we used to dig a hole in the ground and that was our hut! You could only tell from the smoke that Christians were living there. You will ask, why did they live like that? It was not that they were poor, for in those days almost everyone was a Cossack and brought home plenty of good things from other lands, but more because it was no use to have a good hut. All sorts of folk were roaming about the country then: Crimeans, Poles, Lithuanians! And sometimes even fellow countrymen came in gangs and robbed us. All sorts of things used to happen.

In this village there often appeared a man, or rather the devil in human shape. Why he came and where he came from nobody knew.

He drank and made merry, and then vanished as though he had sunk into the water, and they heard no news of him. Then all at once he seemed to drop from the sky and was prowling about the streets of the village which was hardly more than a hundred paces from Dikanka, though there is no trace of it now. . . . He would join any stray Cossacks, and then there was laughter and singing, the money would fly, and vodka would flow like water. . . . Sometimes he'd set upon the girls, heap ribbons, earrings, necklaces on them, till they did not know what to do with them. To be sure, the girls did think twice before they took his presents: who knows, they might really come from the devil. My own grandfather's aunt, who used to keep a tavern on what is now the Oposhnyansky Road, where Basavriuk (that was the name of this devil of a fellow) often went for a drink, said she wouldn't take a present from him for all the riches in the world. And yet, how could they refuse? Everybody was terrified when he scowled with his shaggy eyebrows and looked from under them in a way that might make the stoutest take to his heels; and if a girl did accept, the very next night a friend of his from the marsh with horns on his head might pay her a visit and try to strangle her with the necklace around her neck, or bite her finger if she had a ring, or pull her hair if she had a ribbon in it. A plague take them, then, his fine presents! And the worst of it was, there was no getting rid of them: if you threw them into the water, the devilish necklace or ring would float on the top and come back straight into your hands.

In the village there was a church, and I think, if I remember right, it was St. Panteley's. The priest there in those days was Father Afanasy of blessed memory. Noticing that Basavriuk did not come to church even on Easter Sunday, he thought to reprimand him and threaten him with a church penance. But no such thing! It was he that caught it! "Look here, my good sir," Basavriuk bellowed in reply to him, "you mind your own business and don't meddle with other people's unless you want your billygoat's gullet choked with hot rice soup!" What was to be done with the cursed fellow? Father Afanasy merely declared that he should consider anyone who associated with Basavriuk a Catholic, an enemy of the Church of Christ and of the human race.

In the same village a Cossack called Korzh had a worker who was known as Petro the Kinless—perhaps because no one remem-

bered his parents. It is true that the churchwarden used to say that
they had died of the plague when he was a year old, but my grandfather's aunt would not hear of that and did her very utmost to pro-
vide him with relations, though poor Petro cared no more about
them than we do about last year's snow. She used to say that his
father was still in Zaporozhye, that he had been taken prisoner by
the Turks and suffered goodness knows what tortures, and that in
some miraculous way he had escaped, disguised as a eunuch. The
black-browed girls and young women cared nothing about his relations. All they said was that if he put on a new coat, a red belt, a
black astrakhan cap with a smart blue top to it, hung a Turkish
sword at his side, and carried a whip in one hand and a handsome
pipe in the other, he would outshine all the fellows of the place.
But the pity was that poor Petro had only one gray jacket with
more holes in it than gold pieces in a Jew's pocket. And that was
not what mattered; what did matter was that old Korzh had a
daughter, a beauty—such as I imagine you have never seen. My
grandfather's aunt used to say—and women, you know, would
rather kiss the devil, forgive the expression, than call any girl a
beauty—that the girl's round cheeks were as fresh and bright as a
poppy of the most delicate shade of pink when it glows, washed by
God's dew, unfolds its leaves, and preens itself in the rising sun;
that her brows, like black strings such as our girls buy nowadays to
hang crosses or coins on from traveling Russian peddlers, were
evenly arched and seemed to gaze into her clear eyes; that her little
mouth, at which the young men stared greedily, looked as though
it had been created to utter the notes of a nightingale; that her hair,
black as a raven's wings and soft as young flax, fell in rich curls on
her gold-embroidered jacket (in those days our girls did not tie
their hair in braids and twine them with bright-colored ribbons).
Ah, may God never grant me to sing "Alleluia" again in the choir,
if I could not kiss her on the spot now in spite of the gray which
is spreading all over the old stubble on my head, and of my old
woman, always at hand like a sty when she is not wanted. Well, if a
boy and a girl live near each other . . . you all know what is bound
to happen. Before the sun had fully risen, the footprints of the little
red boots could be seen on the spot where Pidorka had been talking
to her Petro. But Korzh would never have had an inkling that anything was amiss if—clearly it was the devil's prompting—one day

Petro had not been so unwary as to imprint, as they say, a heartfelt kiss on Pidorka's rosy lips in the outer room without taking a good look around; and the same devil—may he dream of the Holy Cross, the son of a bitch!—prompted the old bastard to open the door of the hut. Korzh stood petrified, clutching at the door, with his mouth wide open. The accursed kiss seemed to overwhelm him completely. It seemed louder to him than the racket a pestle makes when smashed against the wall, a technique practiced in our day by the peasants who wanted to frighten away the devil though they had no gun with which to make noise.

Recovering himself, he took his grandfather's whip from the wall and was about to flick it on Petro's back, when all of a sudden Pidorka's six-year-old brother Ivas ran in and threw his arms around the old man's legs in terror, shouting: "Father, Father, don't beat Petro!"

What was to be done? The father's heart was not made of stone. Hanging the whip on the wall, he quietly led Petro out of the hut. "If you ever show yourself again in my hut, or even under the windows, then listen: you will lose your black mustaches, and your forelock,[2] too—it is long enough to go twice around your ear—will take leave of your head, or my name is not Terenty Korzh!"

Saying this, he dealt him a light blow on the back of the neck, and Petro, caught unawares, flew headlong. So that was what his kisses brought him!

Our cooing doves were overwhelmed with sadness; and then there was a rumor in the village that a new visitor was continually seen at Korzh's—a Pole, all in gold braid, with mustaches, a saber, spurs, and pockets jingling like the bell on the bag that our sexton Taras carries about the church with him every day. Well, we all know why people visit a father when he has a black-browed daughter! So one day Pidorka, bathed in tears, took her little brother Ivas in her arms: "Ivas my dear, Ivas my darling, run fast as an arrow from the bow, my golden little one, to Petro. Tell him everything: I would love his brown eyes, I would kiss his fair face, but my fate says no. More than one towel I have soaked with my bitter tears. I am sick and sad at heart. My own father is my foe: he is forcing me

---

[2] Cossacks shaved their heads, but left a long forelock which they twirled around an ear. (ed.)

to marry the detested Pole. Tell him that they are making ready the wedding, only there will be no music at our wedding, the deacons will chant instead of the pipe and the lute. I will not walk out to dance with my bridegroom: they will carry me. Dark, dark will be my dwelling, of maple wood, and instead of a chimney a cross will stand over it!"

Standing motionless, as though turned to stone, Petro heard Pidorka's words lisped by the innocent child.

"And I, poor luckless fool, was thinking of going to the Crimea or Turkey to win gold in war, and, when I had money, to come to you, my sweet. But it is not to be! An evil eye has looked upon us! I, too, will have a wedding, my dear little fish; but there will be no clergy at that wedding—a black raven will croak over me instead of a priest; the open plain will be my dwelling, the gray storm clouds will be my roof; an eagle will peck out my brown eyes; the rains will wash my Cossack bones and the whirlwind will dry them. But what am I saying? To whom, of whom am I complaining? It is God's will, apparently. If I must perish, then perish!" and he walked straight to the tavern.

My grandfather's aunt was rather surprised when she saw Petro at the tavern and at an hour when a good Christian is at prayer, and she stared at him open-eyed as though half awake when he asked for a mug of vodka, almost half a pailful. But in vain the poor fellow sought to drown his sorrow. The vodka stung his tongue like a nettle and seemed to him bitterer than wormwood. He flung the mug upon the ground.

"Stop grieving, Cossack!" something boomed out in a bass voice above him.

He turned around: it was Basavriuk! Ugh, what he looked like! Hair like bristles, eyes like a bullock's.

"I know what it is you lack: it's this!" and then with a fiendish laugh he jingled the leather pouch he carried at his belt.

Petro started.

"Aha! Look how it glitters!" yelled the other, pouring the gold pieces into his hand. "Aha! how it rings! And you know, only one thing is asked for a whole pile of such baubles."

"The devil!" cried Petro. "Very well, I am ready for anything!" They shook hands on it.

"So, Petro, you are just in time: tomorrow is St. John the Baptist's Day. This is the only night in the year in which the fern blossoms.[3] Don't miss your chance! I will wait for you at midnight in the Bear's Ravine."

I don't think the hens are as eager for the minute when the goodwife brings their grain as Petro was for evening to come. He was continually looking whether the shadows from the trees were longer, whether the setting sun were not flushing red, and as the hours went on he grew more impatient. Ah, how slowly they went! It seemed as though God's day had lost its end somewhere. At last the sun was gone. There was only a streak of red on one side of the sky. And that, too, was fading. It turned colder. The light grew dimmer and dimmer till it was quite dark. At last! With his heart almost leaping out of his breast, he set off on his way and carefully went down through the thick forest to a deep hollow which was known as the Bear's Ravine. Basavriuk was there already. It was so dark that you could not see your hand before your face. Hand in hand, they made their way over a muddy bog, caught at by the thorns that grew over it and stumbling almost at every step. At last they reached a level place. Petro looked around—he had never chanced to come there before. Here Basavriuk stopped.

"You see there are three hillocks before you? There will be all sorts of flowers on them, but may the powers from above keep you from picking one of them. But as soon as the fern blossoms, pick it and do not look around, regardless of what you may think is behind you."

Petro wanted to question him further . . . but behold, he was gone. He went up to the three hillocks: where were the flowers? He saw nothing. Rank weeds overshadowed everything and smothered all else with their dense growth. But there came a flash of summer lightning in the sky, and he saw before him a whole bed of flowers, all marvelous, all new to him; and there, too, were the simple fronds of fern. Petro was puzzled and he stood in confusion with his arms akimbo.

"What is marvelous about this? One sees that green stuff a dozen times a day—what is there strange in it? Didn't the devil mean to make a fool of me?"

All at once a little flower began to turn red and to move as though

---

[3] Fern, of course, never blossoms. According to Ukrainian folklore, it blossoms once a year, on St. John the Baptist's Day. Legend has it that the sight of blossoming fern indicates a buried treasure beneath. (ed.)

it were alive. It really was a marvel! It moved and grew bigger and bigger and turned red like a burning coal. A little star suddenly flashed, something snapped—and the flower opened before his eyes, shedding light on the others about it like a flame.

"Now is the time!" thought Petro, and stretched out his hand. He saw that hundreds of shaggy hands were stretched from behind him toward it, and something seemed to be flitting to and fro behind his back. Shutting his eyes, he pulled at the stalk, and the flower was left in his hand. Everything was hushed. Basavriuk, looking blue as a corpse, appeared sitting on a stump. He did not stir a finger. His eyes were fastened on something which only he could see; his mouth was half open, and no answer came from it. Nothing stirred all around. Ugh, it was horrible! . . . But at last a whistle sounded, which turned Petro cold all over, and it seemed to him as though the grass were murmuring, and the flowers were talking among themselves with a voice as delicate and sweet as silver bells: the trees resounded with angry gusts. Basavriuk's face suddenly came to life, his eyes sparkled. "At last, you are back, old witch!" he growled through his teeth. "Look, Petro, a beauty will appear before you: do whatever she tells you, or you will be lost forever!"

Then with a gnarled stick he parted a thornbush and a little hut—on hen's legs,[4] as they say in fairy tales—stood before them. Basavriuk struck it with his fist and the wall tottered. A big black hound ran out to meet them, and changing into a cat, flew squealing at their eyes.

"Don't be angry, don't be angry, old devil!" said Basavriuk, spicing his words with an oath which would make a good man stop his ears. In an instant, where the cat had stood was an old hag wrinkled like a baked apple and bent double, her nose and chin meeting like the tongs of a nutcracker.

"A fine beauty!" thought Petro, and a shudder ran down his back.

The witch snatched the flower out of his hands, bent over it, and spent a long time muttering something and sprinkling it with water of some sort. Sparks flew out of her mouth, there were flecks of foam on her lips. "Throw it!" she said, giving him back the flower. Petro threw it and, marvelous to relate, the flower did not fall at

---

[4] Reference is to a becharmed dwelling in the woods inhabited by spirits and witches. Pushkin often refers to such places. (ed.)

once, but stayed for a long time like a ball of fire in the darkness, and floated in the air; at last it began slowly descending and fell so far away that it looked like a little star no bigger than a poppy seed. "Here!" the old woman wheezed in a hollow voice, and Basavriuk, giving him a spade, added: "Dig here, Petro; here you will see more gold than you or Korzh ever dreamed of."

Petro, spitting into his hands, took the spade, thrust at it with his foot, and threw out the earth, a second spadeful, a third, another . . . Something hard! . . . The spade clanked against something and would go no further. Then his eyes could distinguish clearly a small trunk. He tried to get hold of it, but the trunk seemed to sink deeper and deeper into the earth; and behind him he heard laughter that was like the hissing of snakes.

"No, you will never see the gold till you have shed human blood!" said the witch, and brought him a child about six years old covered with a white sheet, gesturing to him to cut off its head. Petro was struck dumb. A mere trifle! for no rhyme or reason to murder a human being, and an innocent child, too! Angrily he pulled the sheet off the child, and what did he see? Before him stood Ivas. The poor child crossed his arms and hung his head. . . . Like one possessed, Petro flew at the witch, knife in hand, and was just lifting his hand to strike . . .

"And what did you promise for the sake of the girl?" thundered Basavriuk, and his words smashed through Petro like a bullet. The witch stamped her foot; a blue flame shot out of the earth and shed light down into its center, so that it all looked as though made of crystal; and everything under the surface could be seen clearly. Gold pieces, precious stones in chests and in cauldrons were piled up in heaps under the very spot on which they were standing. His eyes glowed . . . his brain reeled . . . Frantic, he seized the knife and the blood of the innocent child spurted into his eyes. . . . Devilish laughter broke out all around him. Hideous monsters galloped in herds before him. Clutching the headless corpse in her hands, the witch drank the blood like a wolf. . . . His head was in a whirl! With a desperate effort he started running. Everything about him was lost in a red light. The trees all bathed in blood seemed to be burning and moaning. The blazing sky quivered. . . . Gleams of lightning like fire flashed before his eyes. At his last gasp he ran into his hut and fell on the ground like a sheaf of wheat. He sank into a deathlike sleep.

For two days and two nights he slept without waking. Waking on the third day, he stared for a long time into the corners of the hut. But he tried in vain to remember what had happened; his memory was like an old miser's pocket out of which you can't entice a copper. Stretching a little, he heard something clink at his feet. He looked: two sacks of gold. Only then he remembered, as though it were a dream, that he had been looking for a treasure, that he had been frightened and alone in the forest. . . . But at what price, how he had obtained it—that he could not recall.

Korzh saw the sacks and—was softened. Petro was this and Petro was that, and he could not say enough for him. "And wasn't I always fond of him, and wasn't he like my own son to me?" And the old fox carried on so sympathetically that Petro was moved to tears. Pidorka began telling him how Ivas had been stolen by some passing gypsies, but Petro could not even remember the child: that cursed devilry had so confounded him!

There was no reason for delay. They sent the Pole away after offering him a fig under his nose and began preparing the wedding. They baked wedding cakes, they hemmed towels and kerchiefs, rolled out a barrel of vodka, set the young people down at the table, cut the wedding loaf, played the lute, the pipe, the bandore, and the cymbals—and the merrymaking began. . . .

You can't compare weddings nowadays with what they used to be. My grandfather's aunt used to tell about them—it was a treat! How the girls in a smart headdress of yellow, blue, and pink ribbons, with gold braid tied over it, in fine smocks embroidered with red silk on every seam and adorned with little silver flowers, in morocco boots with high iron heels, danced around the room as gracefully as peacocks, swishing like a whirlwind. How the married women in a boat-shaped headdress, the whole top of which was made of gold brocade with a little slit at the back showing a peep of the gold cap below, with two little horns of the very finest black astrakhan, one in front and one behind, in blue coats of the very best silk with red borders, holding their arms with dignity akimbo, stepped out one by one and rhythmically danced the *gopak!* How the lads in high Cossack hats, in fine cloth jerkins with silver-embroidered belts, with a pipe in their teeth, danced attendance on them and cut all sorts of capers! Korzh himself, looking at the young couple, could not refrain from recalling his young days: with a bandore in his hand, smoking his pipe and singing, at the

same time balancing a goblet on his head, the old man began dancing in a half-squatting position. What won't people think of when
they are making merry? They would begin, for instance, putting
on masks—my goodness, they looked like monsters! Ah, it was a
very different thing from dressing up at weddings nowadays. What
do they do now? Only rig themselves out like gypsies or Muscovites. Why, in the old days one would dress himself as a Jew and
another as a devil; first they would kiss each other and then pull
each other's forelocks. . . . My God! one laughed till one held
one's sides. They would put on Turkish and Tartar garments, all
glittering like fire. . . . And as soon as they began fooling and
playing tricks . . . there were no limits to what they would do!
An amusing incident happened to my grandfather's aunt who was
at that wedding herself; she was wearing a full Tartar dress and,
goblet in her hand, she was entertaining the company. The devil
prompted someone to splash vodka over her from behind; another
one, it seems, was just as clever: at the same moment he struck
a light and set fire to her. . . . The flame flared up; the poor aunt,
terrified, began flinging off all her clothes before everybody. . . .
The din, the laughter, the hubbub that arose—it was like a fair. In
fact, the old people had never remembered such a merry wedding.

Pidorka and Petro began to live like lady and lord. They had
plenty of everything, it was all handsome . . . But good people
shook their heads a little as they watched the way they lived. "No
good comes from the devil," all said with one voice. "From whom
had his wealth come, if not from the tempter of good Christians?
Where could he have got such a pile of gold? Why had Basavriuk
vanished on the very day that Petro had grown rich?"

You may say that people imagine things! But really, before a
month was out, no one would have known Petro. What had happened to him, God only knows. He would sit still without stirring
and not say a word to anyone; he was always brooding as if he
wanted to remember something. When Pidorka did succeed in
making him talk, he would seem to forget his troubles and keep up
a conversation and even be merry, but if by chance his eye fell on
the bags, "Stop, stop, I have forgotten," he would say, and again he
would sink into thought and again try to remember something.
Sometimes after he had been sitting still for a long time it seemed
that in another moment he would recall it all . . . and then it
would pass away again. He fancied he had been sitting in a tavern;

they brought him vodka; the vodka stung him; the vodka was repulsive; someone came up, slapped him on the shoulder; he . . . but after that everything seemed shrouded in a fog. The sweat dropped down his face and he sat down again, feeling helpless.

What did not Pidorka do! She consulted sorcerers, poured wax into water, and burned a bit of hemp[5]—nothing was of any use. So the summer passed. Many of the Cossacks had finished their mowing and harvesting; many of the more reckless ones had gone off fighting. Flocks of ducks were still plentiful on our marshes, but there was not a nettle wren to be seen. The steppes turned red. Stacks of wheat, like Cossacks' caps, were dotted about the field here and there. Wagons laden with bundles of twigs and logs were on the roads. The ground was firmer and in places it was frozen. Snow began falling and the twigs on the trees were decked in hoarfrost like rabbit fur. Already one bright frosty day the red-breasted bullfinch was strutting about like a smart Polish gentleman, looking for seeds in the heaps of snow, and the children were whipping wooden tops on the ice with huge sticks while their fathers lay quietly on the stove, coming out from time to time with a lighted pipe between their teeth to swear roundly at the good Orthodox frost, or to get a breath of air and thrash the grain stored in the outer room.

At last the snow began to melt and "the perch smashed the ice with its tail," but Petro was still the same, and as time went on he was gloomier still. He would sit in the middle of the hut, as though riveted to the spot, with the bags of gold at his feet. He shunned company, let his hair grow, began to look dreadful, and thought only about one thing: he kept trying to remember something and was troubled and angry that he could not. Often he would wildly get up from his seat, wave his arms, fix his eyes on something as though he wanted to catch it; his lips would move as though trying to utter some long-forgotten word—and then would remain motionless. . . . He was overcome by fury; he would gnaw and bite his hands like a madman, and tear out his hair in handfuls until he

---

[5] When anyone has had a fright and wants to know what has caused it, melted tin or wax is thrown into water and it will take the shape of whatever has caused the patient's terror; and after that the terror passes off. Hemp is burned for sickness or stomach complaint. A piece of hemp is lighted, and thrown into a mug which is turned wrong side up over a bowl of water placed on the patient's stomach. Then, after a spell is repeated, a spoonful of the water is given to the patient to drink. (N. Gogol)

would grow quiet again and seem to sink into forgetfulness; and then he would begin to remember again, and again there would be fury and torment. . . . It was, indeed, a heaven-sent infliction.

Pidorka's life was not worth living. At first she was afraid to remain alone in her hut, but afterward she grew used to her trouble, poor thing. But no one would have known her for the Pidorka of earlier days. No color, no smile; she was pining and wasting away, she was crying her bright eyes out. Once someone must have taken pity on her and advised her to go to the witch in the Bear's Ravine, who was reputed able to cure all the diseases in the world. She made up her mind to try this last resource; little by little, she persuaded the old hag to go home with her. It was after sunset, on St. John's Eve. Petro was lying on the bench lost in forgetfulness and did not notice the visitor come in. But little by little he began to sit up and look at her. All at once he trembled, as though he were on the scaffold; his hair stood on end . . . and he broke into a laugh that cut Pidorka to the heart with terror. "I remember, I remember!" he cried with a fearful joy, and, snatching up an ax, flung it with all his might at the old hag. The ax made a cut two inches deep in the oak door. The hag vanished and a child of about seven in a white shirt, with its head covered, was standing in the middle of the hut. . . . The veil flew off. "Ivas!" cried Pidorka and rushed up to him, but the ghost was covered from head to foot with blood and shed a red light all over the hut. . . . She ran into the outer room in terror, but, recovering herself, wanted to help her brother; in vain! the door had slammed behind her so that she could not open it. Neighbors ran up; they began knocking, broke open the door: not a living soul within! The whole hut was full of smoke, and in the middle where Petro had stood was a heap of ashes from which smoke was still rising. They rushed to the bags: they were full of broken potsherds instead of gold pieces. The Cossacks stood as though rooted to the spot with their mouths open and their eyes starting out of their heads, not daring to move an eyelash, such terror did this miracle cause in them.

What happened afterward I don't remember. Pidorka took a vow to go on a pilgrimage. She gathered together all the goods left her by her father, and a few days later she vanished from the village. No one could say where she had gone. Some old women were so obliging as to declare that she had followed Petro where he had gone; but a Cossack who came from Kiev said he had seen a nun

in the convent there, wasted to a skeleton, who never ceased praying, and by every token the villagers recognized her as Pidorka; he
told them that no one had ever heard her say a word; that she had
come on foot and brought a frame for the icon of the Mother of
God with such bright jewels in it that it dazzled everyone who
looked at it.

But let me tell you, this was not the end of it all. The very day
that the devil carried off Petro, Basavriuk turned up again: but
everyone ran away from him. They knew now the kind of bird he
was: no one but Satan himself disguised in human form in order to
unearth buried treasure; and since unclean hands cannot touch the
treasure he entices young men to help him. The same year everyone deserted their old huts and moved into a new village, but even
there they had no peace from that cursed Basavriuk. My grandfather's aunt used to say that he was particularly angry with her for
having given up her old tavern on the Oposhnyansky Road and did
his utmost to get back at her. One day the elders of the village were
gathered at her tavern and were conversing according to their
rank, as the saying is, at the table, in the middle of which was stood
a whole roast ram, and it would be a lie to call it a small one. They
chatted of one thing and another; of wonders and strange happen-
ings. And all at once they imagined—and of course it would be
nothing if it were only one of them, but they all saw it at once—
that the ram raised its head, its sly black eyes gleamed and came to
life; it suddenly grew a black bristly mustache and meaningfully
twitched it at the company. They all recognized at once in the
ram's head the face of Basavriuk; my grandfather's aunt even
thought that in another minute he would ask for vodka. . . . The
worthy elders picked up their caps and hurried home. Another
day, the churchwarden himself, who liked at times a quiet half-
hour with the family goblet, had not drained it twice when he saw
the goblet bow down to him. "The devil take you!" and he began
crossing himself. . . . And at the same time a strange thing happened to his better half: she had only just mixed the dough in a
huge tub when suddenly the tub jumped away. "Stop, stop!" But it
wouldn't! Its arms akimbo, with dignity the tub danced all over the
hut. . . . You may laugh; but it was no laughing matter to our
forefathers. And in spite of Father Afanasy's going all over the village with holy water and driving the devil out of every street
with the sprinkler, my grandfather's aunt complained for a long

time that as soon as evening came on someone knocked on the roof
and scratched on the wall.

   But there! In this place where our village is located you would
think everything was quiet nowadays; but you know it is not so
long ago, within my father's memory—and indeed I remember it—
that no good man would pass the ruined tavern which the unbaptized tribe[6] repaired long afterward at their own expense. Smoke
poured out in clouds from the grimy chimney and, rising so high
that one's cap dropped off if one looked at it, scattered hot embers
all over the steppe, and the devil—no need to mention him, son of a
bitch—used to sob so plaintively in his hole that the frightened
birds rose up in flocks from the neighboring forest and scattered
with wild cries over the sky.

---

[6] I.e., Jews. (ed.)

A MAY NIGHT
OR
THE DROWNED
MAIDEN

The devil only knows what to make of it! If Christian folk begin
any task, they fret and fret themselves like dogs after a hare, and
all to no purpose; but as soon as the devil comes into it—in a jiffy—
lo and behold, the thing's done!

I

GANNA [1]

A resounding song flowed like a river down the streets of the village. It was the hour when, weary from the cares and labors of the
day, the boys and girls gather together in a ring in the glow of the
clear evening to pour out their gaiety in strains never far removed
from melancholy. And the brooding evening dreamily embraced
the dark blue sky, making everything seem vague and distant. It
was already dusk, yet still the singing did not cease. Levko, a young
Cossack, the son of the village mayor,[2] slipped away from the singers with a bandore in his hands. He was wearing an astrakhan cap.
The Cossack walked down the street strumming on the strings of

---

[1] Diminutive of Galina, as is Galya. (ed.)
[2] The village head, appointed by Cossack elders. (ed.)

his instrument and dancing to it. At last he stopped quietly before
the door of a hut surrounded by low-growing cherry trees. Whose
hut was it? Whose door was it? After a few moments of silence, he
began playing and singing:

> The sun is low, the evening's near
> Come out to me, my little dear

"No, it seems my bright-eyed beauty is sound asleep," said the
Cossack when he had finished the song, and he went nearer to the
window. "Galya! Galya, are you asleep, or don't you want to come
out to me? You are afraid, I suppose, that someone will see us, or
perhaps you don't want to put your fair little face out into the
cold? Don't be afraid: there is no one about, and the evening is
warm. And if anyone should appear, I will cover you with my
jacket, wrap my sash around you, or hide you in my arms—and no
one will see us. And if there is a breath of cold, I'll press you
warmer to my heart, I'll warm you with my kisses, I'll put my cap
over your little white feet. My heart, my little fish, my necklace!
Look out for a minute. At least put your little white hand out of
the window. . . . No, you are not asleep, proud maiden!" he said
more loudly, in the voice of one ashamed at having for a moment
demeaned himself; "you are pleased to mock at me; farewell!"

At this point he turned away, thrust his cap rakishly to one side,
and walked haughtily away from the window, softly strumming
the strings of the bandore. At that moment the wooden handle
turned: the door was flung open with a creak, and a girl in her
seventeenth spring looked about her timidly, shrouded in the dusk,
and, without leaving hold of the handle, stepped over the threshold.
Her bright eyes shone with welcome like stars in the semidark-
ness; her red coral necklace gleamed, and even the modest blush
that colored her cheeks could not escape the youth's eagle eye.

"How impatient you are!" she said to him in a low voice. "You
are angry already! Why did you choose this time? Crowds of
people are strolling up and down the street . . . I keep trembling . . ."

"Oh, do not tremble, my lovely willow! Cling closer to me!" said
the boy, putting his arms around her, and casting aside his bandore,
which hung on a long strap around his neck, he sat down with her
at the door of the hut. "You know it pains me to pass an hour
without seeing you."

"Do you know what I am thinking?" the girl broke in, pensively gazing at him. "Something seems to be whispering in my ear that from now on we shall not meet so often. People here are not good: the girls all look so envious, and the boys . . . I even notice that of late my mother has taken to watching me more strictly. I must admit, it was pleasanter for me with strangers."

A look of sadness passed over her face at these last words.

"Only two months at home and already you are weary of it! Perhaps you are tired of me, too?"

"Oh, I am not tired of you," she replied, laughing. "I love you, my black-browed Cossack! I love you because you have brown eyes, and when you look at me with them, it seems as if there is laughter in my heart; and it is gay and happy; because you twitch your black mustache so charmingly, because you walk along the streets singing and playing the bandore, and it's sweet to listen to you."

"Oh, my Galya!" he cried, kissing her and pressing her warmly to his heart.

"Stop! Enough, Levko! Tell me first, have you told your father?"

"Told him what?" he said, as though waking up from sleep. "That I want to marry and that you will be my wife? Yes, I have told him." But the words "I have told him" came despondently from his lips.

"Well?"

"What's one to do with him? He pretended to be deaf, the old rogue, as he always does; he wouldn't hear anything, and then began scolding me for strolling about all over the place, and playing pranks in the streets with the boys. But don't grieve, my Galya! I give you the word of a Cossack that I will get around him."

"Well, you have only to say the word, Levko, and you will have everything your own way. I know that from myself: sometimes I would like not to obey you, but you have only to say a word—and I can't help doing what you want. Look, look!" she went on, laying her head on his shoulder and turning her eyes upward to the warm Ukrainian sky that showed dark blue, unfathomable, through the leafy branches of the cherry trees that were before them. "Look, there; far away, the stars are twinkling, one, two, three, four, five . . . It's the angels of God, opening the windows of their bright dwellings in the sky and looking out at us, isn't it? Yes, Levko! They are looking at our earth, aren't they? If only people

had wings like birds, so they could fly there, high up, high up . . .
Oh, it's dreadful! Not one oak here reaches to the sky. But they
do say there is some tree in a distant land the top of which reaches
right to heaven and that God descends it on the night before Easter
when He comes down to the earth."

"No, Galya, God has a ladder reaching from heaven right down
to earth. The holy archangels put it up before Easter Sunday, and
as soon as God steps on the first rung of it, all the evil spirits fall
headlong and sink in heaps down to hell. And that is why at Easter
there isn't one evil spirit on earth."

"How softly the water murmurs, like a child lying in its cradle!"
Ganna went on, pointing to the pond in its gloomy setting of a
wood of maple trees and weeping willows, whose drooping boughs
dipped into it. Like a feeble old man, it held the dark distant sky
in its cold embrace, covering with its icy kisses the flashing stars,
which gleamed dimly in the warm ocean of the night air as though
they felt the approach of the brilliant sovereign of the night. An
old wooden house lay slumbering with closed shutters on the hill
by the grove of small trees; its roof was covered with moss and
weeds; leafy apple trees grew in all directions under the windows;
the wood, wrapping it in its shade, threw a peculiar gloom over
it; a thicket of nut trees lay at its foot and sloped down to the pond.

"I remember as though it were a dream," said Ganna, not taking
her eyes off him, "long, long ago when I was little and lived with
Mother, they used to tell some dreadful story about that house.
Levko, you must know it, tell it to me. . . ."

"Never mind about it, my darling! The women and silly folk tell
all sorts of stories. You will only upset yourself; you'll be frightened and won't sleep soundly."

"Tell me, tell me, dear black-browed lad!" she said, pressing her
face against his cheek and putting her arm around him. "No, I see
you don't love me; you have some other girl. I won't be frightened; I will sleep peacefully at night. Now I will not sleep if you
don't tell me. I'll be worried and thinking . . . Tell me,
Levko . . . !"

"It seems folk are right when they say that there is a devil of
curiosity in girls, egging them on. Well, listen, then. Long ago, my
little heart, there was a Cossack officer who used to live in that
house. He had a daughter, a fair maiden, white as snow, white as
your little face. His wife had long been dead; he took it into his

head to marry again. 'Will you care for me the same, Father, when you take another wife?' 'Yes, I shall, my daughter, I shall press you to my heart more warmly than ever! I shall, my daughter. I shall give you earrings and necklaces brighter than ever!'

"The father brought his young wife to her new home. The new wife was fair of face. All pink and white was the young wife; only she gave her stepdaughter such a terrible look that the girl uttered a shriek when she saw her, and the harsh stepmother did not say a word to her all day. Night came on. The father went with his young wife to his sleeping chamber, and the fair maiden shut herself up in her little room. She felt sad at heart and began to weep. She looked around, and a terrifying black cat was stealing up to her; there were sparks in its fur and its steely claws scratched on the floor. In terror she jumped on a bench; the cat followed her. She jumped on the oven step and the cat jumped after her, then suddenly leaped on her neck and was stifling her. Tearing herself away with a shriek, she flung it on the floor. Again the monstrous cat stole up. She was overcome with terror. Her father's sword was hanging on the wall. She snatched it up and brought it down with a crash on the floor; one paw with its steely claws flew off, and the squealing cat disappeared into a dark corner. All day the young wife did not come out of her room; on the third day she came out with her arm bandaged. The poor maiden guessed that her stepmother was a witch and that she had cut off her hand. On the fourth day the father bade his daughter fetch the water, sweep the house like a humble peasant girl, and not show herself in her father's rooms. It was a hard lot for the poor girl, but there was nothing she could do; she obeyed her father's will. On the fifth day the father turned his daughter, barefoot, out of the house and did not give her a bit of bread to take with her. Only then did the maiden begin sobbing, hiding her white face in her hands. 'You have sent your own daughter to perish, Father! The witch has ruined your sinful soul! God forgive you; and it seems it is not His will that I should live in this fair world. . . .' And over there, do you see . . . ?" At this point Levko turned to Ganna, pointing toward the house. "Look this way, there, on the very highest part of the bank! From that bank the maiden threw herself into the water. And from that hour she was seen no more. . . ."

"And the witch?" Ganna asked in a frightened voice, fastening her tearful eyes on him.

"The witch? The old women insist that ever since then all the maidens drowned in the pond have come out on moonlight nights into that garden to warm themselves, and the officer's daughter is leader among them. One night she saw her stepmother beside the pond; she pounced upon her and with a shriek dragged her into the water. But the witch saved herself even then: she changed under water into one of the drowned girls, and so escaped the scourge of green reeds with which the maidens meant to beat her. Trust a woman! They say, too, that the maiden assembles all the drowned girls every night and looks into the face of each, trying to discover the witch, but has not yet found her. And if she comes across any living man she makes him guess which it is: or else she threatens to drown him in the water. So, my Galya, that's how old people tell the story! . . . The present master wants to set up a distillery there and has sent a distiller here to see to it . . . But, I hear voices. It's our fellows coming back from singing. Good night, Galya! Sleep well and don't think about these old women's tales."

Saying this, he embraced her warmly, kissed her, and walked away.

"Good night, Levko," said Ganna, gazing dreamily at the dark wood.

At that moment a huge fiery moon began majestically rising from the earth. Half of it was still below the horizon, yet all the world was already flooded with its sublime light. The pond was covered with gleaming ripples. The shadow of the trees began to stand out clearly against the dark green grass.

"Good night, Ganna!" The words uttered behind her were accompanied by a kiss.

"You have come back," she said, looking around, but seeing a boy she did not know, she turned away.

"Good night, Ganna!" she heard again, and again she felt a kiss on her cheek.

"The Evil One has brought another!" she said angrily.

"Good night, dear Ganna!"

"That's the third one!"

"Good night, good night, good night, Ganna," and kisses were showered upon her from all sides.

"Why, there is a whole gang of them!" cried Ganna, tearing herself away from the crowd of boys, who fought with each other in trying to embrace her. "It is amazing that they are not sick of this eternal kissing! I swear that one won't be able to show oneself in the street soon!"

The door slammed upon these words and nothing more was heard but the iron bolt squeaking in its socket.

II

THE MAYOR

Do you know the Ukrainian night? Aie, you do not know the Ukrainian night! Look at it: the moon looks out from the center of the sky; the immense dome of heaven stretches further, more inconceivably immense than ever; it glows and breathes; the earth is all bathed in a silvery light; and the exquisite air is refreshing and warm and full of languor, and an ocean of fragrance is stirring. Heavenly night! Enchanting night! The woods stand motionless, mysterious, full of gloom, and cast huge shadows. Calm and still lie the ponds. The cold and darkness of their waters are walled in by the dark green gardens. The virginal thickets of wild cherry timidly stretch their roots into the cold of the water and from time to time murmur in their leaves, as though angry and indignant when the sweet rogue—the night wind—steals up suddenly and kisses them. All the countryside is sleeping. But overhead all is breathing; all is marvelous, triumphal. And the soul is full of the immensity and the marvel; and silvery visions rise up in harmonious multitudes from its depths. Divine night! Enchanting night! And suddenly it all springs into life: the woods, the ponds, and the stones. The glorious clamor of the Ukrainian nightingale bursts upon the night and one fancies the moon itself is listening in midheaven. . . . The hamlet on the upland sleeps as though spellbound. The groups of huts gleam whiter, fairer than ever in the moonlight; their low walls stand out more dazzlingly in the darkness. The singing has ceased. All is still. God-fearing people are asleep. Only here and there is a light in the narrow windows. Here and there before the doorway of a hut a family is still at supper.

"But that's not the way to dance the *gopak*. I feel that it won't be right somehow. What was that my crony was saying . . . ? Oh yes: hop, tra-la! hop, hop, hop!" So a middle-aged peasant, who had been drinking and was dancing down the street, talked to himself. "I swear, that's not the way to dance the *gopak*. Why should I tell a lie about it? I swear it's not right. Come: hop, tra-la! hop, tra-la! hop, hop, hop!"

"There's a man tipsy! And it's not as though it were a young man, but it's an old fool. It's enough to make the children laugh. Dancing in the street at night!" cried an elderly woman who passed by, carrying an armful of straw. "Go to your home! You ought to have been asleep long ago!"

"I am going," said the peasant, stopping. "I am going. I don't care about any mayor. He thinks (may the devil beat his father) that because he is the mayor, because he pours cold water over folks in the frost, he can turn up his nose at everyone! Mayor indeed! I am my own mayor. God strike me dead! Strike me dead, God! I am my own mayor. That's how it is and will remain," he went on, and going up to the first hut he reached and standing before the window, he passed his fingers over the windowpane and tried to find the door handle. "Wife, open! Look alive, I tell you, open! It's time the Cossack was asleep!"

"Where are you going, Kalenik? You are at somebody else's hut," some girls on their way home from the merry singing shouted from behind him, laughing. "Shall we show you where you live?"

"Show me the way, kind fair maidens!"

"Fair maidens! Do you hear," said one of them, "how polite Kalenik is? We must show him the way to his hut for that . . . but no, you dance on in front."

"Dance . . . ? Ah, you sneaky girls!" Kalenik drawled, laughing and shaking his finger at them, and he lurched forward because his legs were not steady enough to stand still. "Come, give me a kiss. I'll kiss you all, every one of you . . . !" And with staggering steps he fell to running after them. The girls shrieked and huddled together; then, growing bolder, ran over to the other side of the street, seeing that Kalenik was not very quick on his feet.

"There is your hut!" they shouted to him, pointing, as they walked away, to a hut, much larger than his own, which belonged to the mayor of the village. Kalenik obediently turned in that direction, beginning to curse the mayor again.

But who was this mayor who aroused such abuse and criticism? Oh, he was an important person in the village. While Kalenik is on his way we shall certainly have time to say something about this mayor. All the villagers took off their caps when they saw him, and the girls, even the youngest, wished him good day. Which of the young men would not have liked to be mayor? He was free to help himself to everyone's snuff, and the sturdy peasant would stand respectfully, cap in hand, all the time while the mayor fumbled with his fat, coarse fingers in the peasant's birchbark snuffbox. At the village council, although his power was limited to a few votes, he always took the upper hand and almost on his own authority sent whom he pleased to level and repair the roads or dig the ditches. He was austere, forbidding of aspect, and not fond of wasting words. Very long ago when the great Czarina Catherine, of blessed memory, was going to the Crimea, he had been chosen to act as a guide. For two whole days he had performed this duty, and had even been deemed worthy to sit on the box beside the Czarina's coachman. It was from that time that he had taken to bowing his head with a dignified and meditative air, to stroking his long, drooping mustaches, and to shooting hawklike glances from under his brows. And from that time, too, whatever subject was broached, the mayor always cleverly turned the conversation to the way in which he had guided the Czarina, and sat on the box of the Czarina's carriage. He liked at times to pretend to be deaf, especially when he heard something that he did not want to hear. He could not endure ostentation: he always wore a long coat of black homespun cloth, always with a colored woolen sash around his waist, and no one had ever seen him in any other costume, except on the occasion of the Czarina's visit to the Crimea, when he wore a dark blue Cossack coat. But hardly anyone in the village can remember that time; he still kept that one locked up in a chest. He was a widower, but he had living in the house with him his sister-in-law, who cooked the dinner and the supper, washed the benches, whitewashed the hut, wove him shirts, and looked after the house. They did say in the village that she was not his sister-in-law at all, but we have seen already that there were many who bore no good will to the mayor and were glad to circulate any scandal about him. Though, perhaps, what did lend credence to the story was the fact that the sister-in-law was displeased if he went out into a field that was full of girls reaping, or visited a Cossack who had a young daughter. The mayor had but one eye, but that eye was a shrewd villain and could see a pretty girl a long way off. He does not, however, fix it upon a bewitching face before he has taken a good look around to see whether his sister-in-law is watching him. But we have said almost all that we need about the mayor, while tipsy Kalenik was on his way there, still continuing to bestow on him the choicest epithets his slow and clumsy tongue could utter.

III

AN UNEXPECTED RIVAL

A Plot

"No, lads, no, I won't! What pranks you are up to! I wonder you are not sick of mischief. Goodness knows, people call us rogues frequently enough as is. You had better go to bed!" So said Levko to his rollicking companions who were persuading him to join in some new pranks. "Good night to you!" and with rapid steps Levko walked away from them down the street.

"Is my bright-eyed Ganna asleep?" he wondered, as he approached the hut with the cherry trees we've already described. Subdued voices could be heard in the stillness. Levko stood still. He could see the whiteness of a shirt through the trees. . . . "What does it mean?" he wondered, and stealing up a little nearer, hid behind a tree. The face of the girl who stood before him gleamed in the moonlight. . . . It was Ganna! But who was the tall man standing with his back toward him? In vain he gazed at him; the shadow covered him from head to foot. Only a little light fell upon him in front, but the slightest step forward would have exposed Levko to the unpleasant risk of being discovered. Quietly leaning against the tree, he resolved to remain where he was. The girl distinctly pronounced his name.

"Levko? Levko is still nursing," the tall man said huskily and in a low voice. "If I ever meet him here, I'll pull his forelock."

"I should like to know what scoundrel it is, boasting that he will pull me by my forelock!" murmured Levko softly, and he craned his neck, trying not to miss one word. But the intruder went on speaking so softly that he could not hear what was said.

"I am surprised that you are not ashamed!" said Ganna, when he had finished speaking. "You are lying, you are deceiving me; you don't love me; I shall never believe that you love me."

"I know," the tall man went on, "Levko has talked a lot of nonsense to you and has turned your head." (At this point the boy felt that the voice was not really unknown to him; it seemed as though he had heard it before.) "I'll show Levko what I am made of!" the voice went on in the same way. "He thinks I don't see all his malicious tricks. He shall find out, the young dog, what my fists are like!"

At those words, Levko could not restrain his rage. Taking three steps toward him, he swung his fist to give him a clout on the ear, which might have sent him flying for all his apparent strength; but at that instant the moonlight fell on his face, and Levko was stupefied to see standing before him—his father. An unconscious jerk of the head and a faint whistle were the only expression of his amazement. A rustle was heard. Ganna hurriedly flew into the hut, slamming the door after her.

"Good night, Ganna!" one of the boys cried at that moment, stealing up and putting his arm around the mayor, and skipped back with horror, meeting his stiff mustache.

"Good night, my beauty!" cried another; but this one was sent flying by a violent push from the mayor.

"Good night, good night, Ganna!" called several young men, hanging on his neck.

"Be off, you cursed hooligans!" cried the mayor, pushing them off and kicking them. "Ganna indeed! Go and be hanged like your fathers, you children from hell! They come around one like flies after honey! I'll teach you . . . !"

"The mayor, the mayor, it's the mayor!" shouted the young men and scattered in all directions.

"Aha, Father!" said Levko, recovering from his amazement and looking after the mayor as he walked away swearing. "So these are the tricks you are up to! A fine thing! And I have been brooding and wondering what was the meaning of his always pretending to be deaf when one begins speaking about it. Wait a moment, you old dog, I'll teach you to hang about under young girls' windows. I'll teach you to lure away other men's sweethearts! Hey, fellows! Come here, come here, this way!" he shouted, waving his hands to the boys who had gathered into a group again. "Come here! I advised you to go to bed, but now I have changed my mind and am ready to have fun with you."

"That's the way to talk!" said a stout, broad-shouldered fellow who was reckoned the merriest and most mischievous in the village. "It always makes me sick when we can't manage to have a decent

bit of fun and play some prank. I always feel as though I had missed
something, as though I had lost my cap or my pipe; not like a Cossack, in fact."

"What do you say to our giving the mayor a good going over?"

"The mayor?"

"Yes. What does he think he's doing? He rules us as though he
were a Hetman.[3] He is not satisfied with treating us as though we
were his serfs, but he has to go after our girls, too. I do believe
there is not a nice-looking girl in the whole village that he has not
tried to seduce."

"That's true, that's true!" they all shouted together.

"What's wrong with us, fellows? Aren't we the same sort as he
is? Thank God, we are free Cossacks! [4] Let us show him that we are
free Cossacks!"

"We'll show him," they shouted. "And if we give the devil to the
mayor, we won't spare his clerk either!"

"We won't spare the clerk! And I have just made up a splendid
song, it's the very thing for him. Come along, I will teach it to you,"
Levko went on, striking the strings of his bandore. "Dress up in
anything at hand!"

"Come on, brave Cossacks!" said the sturdy rogue, striking his
feet together and clapping his hands. "How glorious! What fun!
When you join in the fun you feel as though you were celebrating
bygone years. Your heart is light and free and your soul might be
in paradise. Hey, fellows! Hey, now for some fun . . . !"

And the crowd moved noisily down the street, and God-fearing
old women, awakened from their sleep by the shouts, pulled up
their windows and crossed themselves with drowsy hands, saying:
"Well, the boys are enjoying themselves now!"

IV

THE YOUNG MEN MAKE MERRY

Only one hut at the end of the village was still lighted up. It was
the mayor's. He had finished his supper long ago, and would no
doubt have been asleep by this time, but he had a visitor, the man

---

[3] Headman of the Cossacks appointed by the Poles. (ed.)
[4] In Czarist Russia the Cossacks were politically independent. They were not
subjected to serfdom. (ed.)

who had been sent to set up a distillery by the landowner who had a small piece of land among the free Cossacks. The visitor, a short, fat little man with little eyes that were always laughing and seeming to express the pleasure he took in smoking, sat in the place of honor under the icons, continually spitting and catching with his fingers the tobacco ash that kept dropping out of his short pipe. Clouds of smoke were spreading rapidly over him and enveloping him in a gray-blue fog. It seemed as though a big chimney of some distillery, weary of sitting on its roof, had thought it would like a change, and was sitting decorously in the mayor's hut. Short thick mustaches stuck out below his nose; but they so indistinctly appeared and disappeared in the smoky atmosphere that they seemed like a mouse that the distiller, infringing the monopoly of the granary cat, had caught and held in his mouth. The mayor, being in his own house, was sitting in his shirt and linen trousers. His eagle eye was beginning little by little to close and grow dim like the setting sun. One of the village constables who made up the mayor's staff was smoking a pipe at the end of the table, and out of respect to his host still kept on his coat.

"Are you thinking of setting up your distillery soon?" the mayor asked, addressing the distiller and making the sign of the cross over his mouth as he yawned.

"With God's help, I bet you that by fall Mr. Mayor will be walking zigzag down the road, dragging his feet."

As he uttered these words, the distiller's eyes disappeared; where they had been were wrinkles stretched to his ears; his whole frame began to quiver with laughter, and for an instant his mirthful lips abandoned the pipe that belched forth clouds of smoke.

"Please God I may," said his host, twisting his face into something that looked like a smile. "Now, thank God, distilleries are doing better. But years ago, when I was guiding the Czarina by the Pereyaslav Road, Bezborodko, now deceased . . ."

"Well, old friend, that was a time! In those days there were only two distilleries all the way from Kremenchug to Romny. But now . . . have you heard what the damned Germans are going to do? They say that instead of burning wood in distilleries like all decent Christians, they are soon going to use some kind of devilish steam. . . ." As he said this the distiller looked thoughtfully at the table and at his hands lying on it. "How it is done with steam—I swear, I don't know!"

"What fools they are, those Germans, God forgive me!" said the mayor. "I'd give them hell, the bunch of bastards! Did anyone ever hear the like of boiling anything by steam? According to that, you couldn't take a spoonful of soup without boiling your lips like a young sucking pig."

"And you, friend," the sister-in-law, who was sitting on the bed with her feet tucked under her, interrupted, "are you going to stay with us all that time without your wife?"

"Why, what do I want with her? It would be different if she were something worth having."

"Isn't she good-looking?" asked the mayor, fixing his eye upon him.

"Good-looking, indeed! Old as the devil. Her face all wrinkles like an empty purse." And the stubby frame of the distiller shook with laughter again.

At that moment something began fumbling at the door; the door opened—and a peasant crossed the threshold without taking off his cap, and stood in the middle of the hut as though in hesitation, gaping and staring at the ceiling. This was our friend Kalenik.

"Here I am home at last," he said, sitting down on the bench near the door, and taking no notice of the company present. "God, how that damned devil lengthened the road! You go on and on, and no end to it! I feel as though someone had broken my legs. Woman, get the sheepskin to put down for me. I am not coming up beside you on the stove, that I am not, my legs ache! Get it, it's lying there under the icons; only mind you don't upset the pot with the snuff. Or no, don't touch it, don't touch it! Maybe you are drunk today . . . Let me get it myself."

Kalenik tried to get up, but an overpowering force riveted him to his seat.

"I like that," said the mayor. "Walks into another man's home and gives orders as though he were at his own place. Throw him out on his rear end!"

"Let him stay and rest, friend!" said the distiller, holding him back by the arm. "He is a useful man; if there were more folk like him, our distillery would do well. . . ."

It was not kindness, however, that dictated this remark. The distiller believed in omens of all sorts, and to turn a man out who had already sat down on the bench would have meant provoking misfortune.

"It seems as though age is creeping up on me . . ." muttered Kalenik, lying down on the bench. "It would be all right if I were drunk, but I am not drunk. No, indeed, I am not drunk. Why tell a lie about it? I am ready to tell the mayor himself so. What do I care for the mayor. May he choke, the son of a bitch! I spit on him. I wish a wagon would run over him, the one-eyed devil! Why does he drench people in the frost?"

"Aha, the pig has made its way into the hut, and is putting its feet on the table," said the mayor, wrathfully rising from his seat; but at that moment a heavy stone, smashing the window to fragments, fell at their feet. He stopped short. "If I knew," he said, picking up the stone, "if I knew what jailbird flung that stone, I'd teach him to throw stones! What devilry!" he went on, looking with angry eyes at the stone in his hand. "May he choke with this stone . . . !"

"Stop, stop, God preserve you, friend!" cried the distiller, turning pale. "God preserve you in this world and the next from blessing anyone with such abuse!"

"Here's a protector! Damn him!"

"Think nothing of it, friend! I suppose you don't know what happened to my late mother-in-law?"

"Your mother-in-law?"

"Yes, my mother-in-law. One evening, a little earlier than it is now, they sat down to supper: my mother-in-law and father-in-law and their hired man and their hired girl and their five children. My mother-in-law shook some dumplings out of a big cauldron into a bowl to cool them. They were all hungry after their work and did not want to wait for the dumplings to get cool. Picking them up on long wooden skewers, they began eating them. All at once a man appeared: where he came from no one can say; who he was, God only knows. He asks them to let him sit down to the table. Well, there is no refusing a hungry man food. They gave him a skewer, too. Only the visitor stowed away the dumplings like a cow eating hay. While the others had eaten one each, and were prodding after more with their skewers, the bowl was as clean as a gentleman's floor. My mother-in-law put out some more; she thought the visitor had had enough and would take less. Nothing of the sort: he began gulping them down faster than ever and emptied the second bowl. "And may you choke with the dumplings!" thought my hungry mother-in-law, when all of a sudden the man choked and fell on the floor. They rushed up to him, but the spirit had departed. He had choked."

"And serve him right, the damned glutton!" said the mayor.

"Quite so, but it didn't end with that: from that time on my mother-in-law had no peace. As soon as night came the dead man rose from the dead. He sat straddling the chimney, the cursed fellow, holding a dumpling in his teeth. In the daytime all was quiet and they didn't hear a sound from him, but as soon as it began to get dusk, look at the roof and there you would see him, straddling the chimney, the son of a bitch."

"And a dumpling in his teeth?"

"And a dumpling in his teeth."

"How marvelous, friend! I had heard something of the sort about your mother-in-law—"

The speaker stopped short. Under the window they heard an uproar and the sound of dancing feet. First there was the soft strumming of the bandore strings, then a voice joined in. The strings twanged more loudly, several voices joined in, and the singing rose up like a whirlwind.

> Boys, have you heard the news now!
> Mayors it seems are none too sound!
> Our one-eyed mayor's a barrelhead
> Whose staves have come unbound!
> Come, cooper, knock upon it hard,
> And bind with hoops of steel!
> Come hammer, cooper, on the head
> And hit with right good will!
> Our mayor is gray and has one eye;
> Old as sin, and what a blockhead!
> Full of whims and lewd fancies;
> Flatters the girls . . . the blockhead!
> You must try to ape the young ones!
> When you should be in your coffin,
> Flung in by the scruff and whiskers!
> By the forelock you're so proud of!

"A fine song, friend!" said the distiller, inclining his head a little to one side and turning toward his host, who was struck dumb with amazement at such insolence. "Fine! it's only a pity that they refer to the mayor in rather disrespectful terms. . . ."

And again he put his hands on the table with a sort of gleeful delight in his eyes, preparing himself to hear more, for from below came peals of laughter and shouts of "Again! again!" However, a penetrating eye could have seen at once that it was not astonishment that kept the mayor from moving. An old experienced cat will sometimes in the same way let an inexperienced mouse run around his tail while he is rapidly making a plan to cut off its way back to its hole. The mayor's solitary eye was still fixed on the window, and already his hand, after gesturing to the constable, was on the wooden door-handle, when all at once a shout rose from the street. . . . The distiller, curiosity being one of his characteristics, hurriedly filled his pipe and ran out into the street; but the rogues had already scattered in all directions.

"No, you won't get away from me!" cried the mayor, dragging a man in a black sheepskin, put on inside out, by the arm. The distiller, seizing the opportunity, ran to have a look at this disturber of the peace, but he staggered back in alarm at seeing a long beard and a horribly colored face. "No, you won't escape me!" shouted the mayor, still dragging his captive into the outer room. The prisoner offered no resistance but followed quietly, as though he were going to his own hut. "Karpo, open the storeroom!" said the mayor to the constable; "we'll put him in the dark storeroom. And then we will wake the clerk, get the constables together, catch all these hooligans, and today we will pass judgment on them all."

The constable clanked a small padlock in the outer room and opened the storeroom. At that instant his captive, taking advantage of the dark storeroom, wrenched himself out of his hands with a violent effort.

"Where are you off to?" cried the mayor, clutching him more tightly than ever by the collar.

"Let's go, it's me!" cried a thin shrill voice.

"That won't help you, that won't help you, my boy. You may squeal like a devil, as well as a woman, you won't fool me," and he shoved him into the dark storeroom, so that the poor prisoner uttered a moan as he fell on the floor, while, accompanied by the constable and followed by the distiller, puffing like a steamer, the mayor went off to the clerk's hut.

They walked along all three with their eyes on the ground, lost in meditation, when, turning into a dark lane, all of them at once uttered a shriek, from a violent bang on their foreheads, and a similar cry of pain echoed in response. The mayor, screwing up his eye, saw with surprise the clerk and two constables.

"I was coming to see you, worthy clerk!"

"And I was coming to your worship, honored mayor."

"Strange things have been happening, worthy clerk."

"Very strange things, honored mayor!"

"Why, what?"

"The boys have gone crazy! They are behaving disgracefully in the street, whole gangs of them. They describe your honor in language . . . I should be ashamed to repeat it. A drunken soldier couldn't bring his dirty tongue to utter such words." (All this the lanky clerk, in striped linen breeches and a vest the color of wine dregs, accompanied by craning his neck forward and dragging it back again to its former position.) "I had just dropped into a doze, when the cursed rogues roused me from my bed with their indecent songs and racket! I meant to take stern measures with them, but while I was putting on my breeches and vest they all ran away in different directions. The ringleader did not get away, though. He is singing now in the hut where we keep criminals. I was eager to find out what bird it was we'd caught, but his face is all sooty like the devils who forge nails for sinners."

"And how is he dressed, worthy clerk?"

"In a black sheepskin put on inside out, the bastard, honored mayor."

"Aren't you lying, clerk? What if that rascal is sitting now in my storeroom?"

"No, honored mayor! You yourself, not in anger be it said, are a little in error!"

"Give me a light! We will have a look at him!"

The light was brought, the door unlocked, and the mayor uttered a groan of amazement when he saw his sister-in-law facing him!

"Tell me, please," with these words she pounced upon him, "have you lost what little wits you ever had? Was there a grain of sense in your thick head, you one-eyed fool, when you pushed me into the dark storeroom? It was lucky I did not hit my head against the iron hook. Didn't I scream out to you that it was me? This damned bear seizes me in his iron paws and shoves me in! May the devils treat you the same in the other world . . . !"

The last words were uttered in the street, where she had gone for some purpose of her own.

"Yes, I see that it's you," said the mayor, recovering his wits.

"What do you say, worthy clerk? Isn't this a cunning rogue?"

"He is a cunning rogue, honored mayor."

"Isn't it high time that we gave all these rascals a good lesson and set them to work?"

"It's high time, high time, honored mayor!"

"They have taken it into their heads, the fools . . . What the devil? I thought I heard my sister-in-law scream in the street. . . . They have taken it into their heads, the fools, that they are as good as I am. They think I am one of them, a simple Cossack! . . ." The little cough that followed this, and the way he looked around from under his brows indicated that the mayor was about to speak of something important. "In the year eighteen . . . I never can remember these damned dates—Ledachy, who was then commissar, was given orders to pick out from the Cossacks the most intelligent of them all. Aie!" (that "Aie!" he pronounced with his finger in the air) "the most intelligent! to act as guide to the Czarina. At that time I . . ."

"Why tell us? We all know that, honored mayor! We all know how you won the royal favor. Admit now that I was right. You took a sin upon your soul when you said that you had caught that rogue in the black sheepskin."

"Well, as for that devil in the black sheepskin, we'll put him in chains and punish him severely as an example to others! Let him know what authority means! By whom is the mayor appointed if not by the Czar? Then we'll get hold of the other fellows: I have not forgotten how the confounded hooligans drove a herd of pigs into my vegetable garden that ate up all my cabbages and cucumbers; I have not forgotten how the sons of bitches refused to thrash my grain; I have not forgotten . . . But plague take them, I must find out who that rascal is wearing a sheepskin inside out."

"He's a wily bird, it seems!" said the distiller, whose cheeks during the whole of this conversation were continually being charged with smoke, like a siege cannon, and whose lips, abandoning the short pipe, were ejecting a perfect fountain of smoke. "It wouldn't be amiss, anyway, to keep the fellow for working in the distillery; or better still, hang him from the top of an oak tree like a church candlestick."

Such a witticism did not seem quite foolish to the distiller, and he at once decided, without waiting for the approval of the others, to reward himself with a husky laugh.

At that moment they drew near a small hut that had almost sunk into the earth. Our friends' curiosity grew keener: they all crowded around the door. The clerk took out a key and jingled it about the lock; but it was the key to his chest. Their impatience became acute. Thrusting his hand into his pocket he began fumbling for it, and swearing because he could not find it.

"Here!" he said at last, bending down and taking it from the depths of the roomy pocket with which his full striped trousers were provided.

At that word the hearts of all our heroes merged into one, and that one giant heart beat so violently that the sound of its uneven throb was not lost despite the creaking of the lock. The door was opened, and . . . the mayor turned white as a sheet, the distiller was aware of a cold chill, and the hair of his head seemed rising up toward heaven; horror was depicted on the face of the clerk; the constables were rooted to the spot, and were incapable of closing their mouths, which had fallen open simultaneously: before them stood the sister-in-law.

No less amazed than they, she, however, pulled herself together, and made a movement as though to approach them.

"Stop!" cried the mayor in a wild voice, and slammed the door in her face. "Gentlemen, it is Satan!" he went on. "A light! quick, a light! I won't spare the hut, though it is Crown property. Set fire to it, set fire to it, so that the devil's bones may not be left on earth!"

The sister-in-law screamed in terror, hearing this sinister decision through the door.

"What are you doing, friends!" said the distiller. "Your hair, thank God, is almost white, but you have not gained sense yet: a witch won't burn with ordinary fire! Only a light from a pipe can burn one of these creatures! Wait, I will manage it in a minute!"

Saying this, he scattered some burning ash out of his pipe on a wisp of straw, and began blowing on it. The poor sister-in-law was meanwhile overwhelmed with despair; she began loudly imploring and beseeching them.

"Stop, friends! Why take a sin upon us in vain? Perhaps it is not Satan!" said the clerk. "If it, whatever it may be that is sitting there, consents to make the sign of the cross, that's a sure token that it is not a devil."

The proposition was approved.

"Get thee behind me, Satan!" said the clerk, putting his lips to the keyhole. "If you don't stir from your place we will open the door."

The door was opened.

"Cross yourself!" said the mayor, looking behind him as though scouting for a safe place in case of retreat.

The sister-in-law crossed herself.

"The devil! it really is my sister-in-law! What evil spirit dragged you to this hole?"

And the sister-in-law, sobbing, told them that the boys had seized her in the street and, in spite of her resistance, had forced her in at the wide window of the hut and had nailed up the shutter. The clerk looked: the staples of the broad shutter had been pulled out, and it was only attached by a board at the top.

"All right, you one-eyed bastard!" she screamed, stepping up to the mayor, who staggered back and still scanned her with his solitary eye. "I know your plan. You would have been glad to do me in, to be free to run after the girls, to have no one see the gray-headed old grandad playing the fool. You think I don't know what you were saying this evening to Ganna? Oh, I know all about it. It's hard to deceive me, let alone for a blockhead like you. I am long-suffering, but when I do lose patience, you'll have something to put up with."

Saying this, she shook her fist at him and walked away quickly, leaving him completely stupefied.

"Well, Satan has certainly had a hand in it this time," he thought, scratching his head vigorously.

"We've caught him," cried the constables, coming in at that instant.

"Caught whom?" asked the mayor.

"The devil with his sheepskin inside out."

"Bring him here!" shouted the mayor, seizing the prisoner by the arm. "You are mad! this is the drunkard, Kalenik."

"What a strange thing! We had him in our hands, honored mayor!" answered the constables. "The confounded boys came around us in the lane, began dancing and capering, tugging at us, putting out their tongues and snatching him out of our hands . . . Damnation take it! . . . And how we hit on this crow instead of him, the devil only knows!"

"By my authority and that of all the members of the parish council, the command is given," said the mayor, "to catch that rascal this minute, and in the same way all whom you find in the street, and to bring them to me to be questioned!"

"Upon my word, honored mayor . . . !" cried some of them, bowing down to his feet. "You should have seen those ugly faces; we have been born and been christened but strike us dead if we have ever seen such horrid faces. Trouble may come of it, honored mayor. They may give a simple man such a fright that there isn't a woman in the place who would undertake to cure him of his panic."

"Panic, indeed! Why? Are you refusing to obey? I expect you are hand in glove with them! You are mutinying! What's this . . . ! What's the meaning of it . . . ? You are getting up a rebellion . . . ! You . . . you . . . I'll report it to the commissar. This minute, do you hear, this minute! Run, fly like a bird! I'll show you . . . you'll show me . . ."

They all ran off in different directions.

V

THE DROWNED MAIDEN

The instigator of all this turmoil, undisturbed by anything and untroubled by the search parties that were being sent in all directions, walked slowly toward the old house and the pond. I think that I need hardly say that it was Levko. His black sheepskin was unbuttoned; he held his cap in his hand; the sweat ran down his face in streams. The maple wood stood majestic and gloomily black, only sprinkled with delicate silver on the side facing the moon. A refreshing coolness from the motionless pond breathed on the tired wanderer and lured him to rest for a while on the bank. All was still. The only sound was the trilling of the nightingale in the deepest recesses of the wood. An overpowering drowsiness soon made his eyes close; his tired limbs were about to sink into sleep and forgetfulness; his head drooped. . . . "No, if I go on like this I'll fall asleep here!" he said, getting to his feet and rubbing his eyes.

He looked around and the night seemed even more brilliant. A strange enchanting radiance was mingled with the light of the moon. He had never seen anything like it before. A silvery mist had fallen over everything around him. The fragrance of the apple blossom and the night-scented flowers flooded the whole earth. He gazed in awe at the motionless water of the pond: the old manor house, reflected in the water, was distinct and looked serenely dignified. Instead of gloomy shutters there were bright glass windows and doors. There was a glitter of gilt through the clean panes. And then it seemed as though a window opened. Holding his breath, not stirring, nor taking his eyes from the pond, he seemed to pass into its depths and saw—first, a white elbow appeared in the window; then a charming little head, with sparkling eyes softly shining through her dark brown locks, peeped out and rested on the elbow, and he saw her slightly nod her head. She beckoned, she smiled . . . His heart suddenly began throbbing . . . The water quivered and the window was closed again. He moved slowly away from the pond and looked at the house; the gloomy shutters were open; the windowpanes gleamed in the moonlight. "See how little one can trust what people say," he thought to himself. "It's a new house; the paint is as fresh as though it had been painted today. Someone is living there." And in silence he went up closer to it, but all was quiet in the house. The glorious singing of the nightingales rang out loud and melodious, and when it seemed to die away, there was heard the rustle and churr of the grasshoppers, or the deep note of some marsh bird, striking his slippery beak on the broad mirror of the water. There was a sense of sweet stillness and space and freedom in Levko's heart. Tuning his bandore, he began playing it and singing:

> Oh, thou moon, my darling moon!
> And thou, glowing clear sunrise!
> Oh, shine brightly o'er the hut
> Where my lovely maiden lies!

The window slowly opened and the head whose reflection he had seen in the pond looked out, listening intently to the song. Her long eyelashes half hid her eyes. She was white all over, like a sheet, like the moonlight. How exquisite, how lovely! She laughed . . . ! Levko started.

"Sing me a song, young Cossack!" she said softly, bending her head on one side and veiling her eyes completely with her thick eyelashes.

"What song shall I sing you, my fair lady?"

Tears rolled slowly down her pale face. "Youth," she said, and there was something inexpressibly touching in her speech. "Youth,

find me my stepmother! I will grudge you nothing. I will reward
you. I will reward you richly, sumptuously. I have sleeves embroidered with silk, corals, necklaces. I will give you a girdle
adorned with pearls. I have gold. Youth, find me my stepmother!
She is a terrible witch. I had no peace in life because of her. She
tormented me, she made me work like a simple peasant girl. Look
at my face. With her foul spells she drew the roses from my cheeks.
Look at my white neck: they will not wash off, they will not wash
off, they never will be washed away, those dark blue marks left by
her claws of steel! Look at my white feet: far have they trodden,
not on carpets only, but on the hot sand, on the damp earth, on
sharp thorns have they trodden! And at my eyes, look at my eyes:
they have grown dim with weeping! Find her, youth, find me my
stepmother . . . !"

Her voice, which had risen, sank into silence. Tears streamed
down her pale face. The young man's heart was oppressed by a
painful feeling of pity and sadness.

"I am ready to do anything for you, my fair lady!" he said with
heartfelt emotion, "but how can I, where can I find her?"

"Look, look!" she said quickly, "she is here, she is on the bank,
playing games among my maidens, bathing herself in the moonlight. She is sly and cunning, she has taken the form of a drowned
maiden; but I know, I feel that she is here. I am oppressed, I am
stifled by her. I cannot swim lightly and easily like a fish, because
of her. I drown and sink to the bottom like a stone. Find her,
youth!"

Levko looked toward the bank: in the delicate silvery mist there
were maidens flitting, light as shadows, in smocks white as a
meadow dotted with lilies-of-the-valley; gold necklaces, strings of
beads, coins glittered on their necks; but they were pale; their
bodies looked as though molded out of transparent clouds, and it
seemed as though the moonlight shone through them. The maidens,
singing and playing, drew nearer to him. He heard their voices.

"Let us play hawk and chickens," they murmured like river
reeds kissed by the ethereal lips of the wind at the quiet hour of
twilight.

"Who will be the hawk?"

They cast lots, and one of the girls stepped out of the group.
Levko looked at her carefully. Her face, her dress, all was exactly
like the rest. The only thing he noticed was that she did not enjoy

playing her part. The group drew out in a chain; it raced rapidly away from the pursuit of the bird of prey.

"No, I don't want to be the hawk," said the maiden, weary and exhausted. "I am sorry to snatch the chickens from their poor mother."

"You are not the witch!" thought Levko.

"Who will be hawk?" The maidens made ready to cast lots again.

"I will be hawk!" One in the center of the group volunteered.

Levko began looking intently at her face. Boldly and swiftly she pursued the chain, and darted from side to side to capture her victim. At that point Levko noticed that her body was not so translucent as the others; something black could be seen in the inside. Suddenly there was shrieking; the hawk had pounced on one of the chain, seized her, and Levko thought that she put out her claws, and that there was a spiteful gleam of joy in her face.

"The witch!" he said suddenly, pointing his finger at her and turning toward the house.

The maiden at the window laughed, and the girls, shouting, led away the one who had played hawk.

"How am I to reward you, youth? I know you have no need of gold: you love Ganna, but your unreasonable father will not let you marry her. Now he will not hinder it: take this note and give it to him. . . ."

Her white hand was outstretched, her face seemed in a marvelous way full of light and radiance. . . . With his heart beating painfully, overwhelmed with excitement, he clutched the note, and . . . woke up.

VI

THE AWAKENING

"Can I have been asleep?" Levko wondered, getting up from the little hillock. "It was as vivid as though it were real . . . ! Strange, strange!" he said, looking about him. The moon standing right over his head showed that it was midnight; everywhere all was still, and a chill air rose from the pond; above him stood the old house with its shutters closed. The moss and high grass showed that it had been abandoned long ago. Then he opened his hand, which had been tightly closed all the time he had been asleep, and cried out with astonishment, feeling a note in it. "Oh, if I could only read!" he thought, turning it over and looking at it on all sides. At that moment he heard a noise behind him.

"Don't be afraid, seize him straight away! Why are you so scared? there are a dozen of us. I bet you anything it is a man and not a devil . . . !" That's what the mayor shouted to his companions, and Levko felt himself seized by several hands, some of which were trembling with fear.

"Throw off your dreadful mask, friend! Stop making fools of folk," said the mayor, seizing him by the collar; but he was astounded when he turned his eye upon him. "Levko! Son!" he cried, stepping back in amazement and dropping his hands. "It's you, you bastard! Aie, you child of hell! I was wondering who the rascal could be, what devil turned inside out was playing these tricks. And it seems it is all your doing—you half-cooked pudding sticking in your father's throat! You like to start fights in the street, compose songs . . . ! Ah, ah, Levko! What's the meaning of it? It seems your back is itching for the rod! Seize him!"

"Stop, Father! I was told to give you this letter," said Levko.

"This is not the time for letters, my boy! Tie him up."

"Stop, honored mayor," said the clerk, opening the note, "it is the commissar's handwriting."

"The commissar's," the constable repeated mechanically.

"The commissar's? Strange! It is more incomprehensible than ever!" Levko thought to himself.

"Read it, read it!" said the mayor. "What does the commissar write?"

"We shall hear what the commissar writes," said the distiller, holding his pipe in his teeth and striking a light.

The clerk cleared his throat and began reading:

"Instruction to the mayor, Yevtukh Makogonenko. The news has reached us that you, old fool, instead of collecting past arrears and setting the village in order, have become an ass and been behaving disgracefully . . ."

"I swear," the mayor interrupted, "I don't hear a word!"

The clerk began over again: "Instruction to the major, Yevtukh Makogonenko. The news has reached us that you, old foo . . ."

"Stop, stop! you needn't go on," cried the mayor. "Though I

can't hear it, I know that what matters isn't that. Read what comes later!"

"And therefore I command you to marry your son Levko Makogonenko to Ganna Petrychenkova, a Cossack maiden of your village, and also to mend the bridges on the high road, and do not without my authorization give the villagers' horses to the clerks, even if they have come straight from the government office. If on my coming I find my commands not carried out, I shall hold you alone responsible. Commissar, retired Lieutenant, Kozma Derkach-Drishpanovsky."

"Well!" said the mayor, gaping with wonder. "Do you hear that, do you hear? The mayor is responsible for it all, and so you must obey me unconditionally, or you will catch hell! . . . As for you," he went on, turning to Levko, "since it's the commissar's orders, though I can't understand how it came to his ears, I'll marry you: only first you shall have a taste of my whip! You know the one that hangs on the wall near the icons. I'll repair it tomorrow. . . . Where did you get that note . . . ?"

In spite of Levko's astonishment at this unexpected turn of events, he had the wit to prepare an answer and to conceal the true explanation of the way he had received the letter.

"I was in the town yesterday evening," he said, "and met the commissar getting out of his chaise. Learning that I came from this village, he gave me the letter and told me to give you the message, Father, and that on his way back he will come and dine with us."

"He told you that?"

"Yes."

"Do you hear," said the mayor with an air of dignity, turning to his companions, "the commissar is coming in person to the likes of us, that is to me, to dinner. Oh . . ." Here he held up his finger and lifted up his head as though he were listening to something. "The commissar, do you hear, the commissar is coming to dine with me! What do you think, worthy clerk, and you, friend? That's honor not to be sneezed at! Isn't it?"

"To the best of my recollection," chimed in the clerk, "no village mayor has ever yet entertained the commissar at dinner."

"There are mayors and mayors," said the mayor with a self-satisfied air. His mouth twisted and something in the nature of a husky laugh more like the rumbling of distant thunder came from his lips. "What do you think, worthy clerk? Shouldn't we for this distinguished visitor give orders that every hut should send at least a chicken and, well, some linen and anything else . . . eh?"

"We should, we should, honored mayor."

"And when is the wedding to be, Father?" asked Levko.

"Wedding? I'll teach you to talk about weddings . . . ! Oh well, for the sake of our distinguished visitor . . . tomorrow the priest shall marry you. Damn you! Let the commissar see what punctual discharge of duty means! Well, boys, now it is bedtime! Go home . . . ! What has happened today reminds me of the time when I . . ." At these words the mayor glanced from under his brows with his habitual air of importance and dignity.

"Now the mayor's going to tell us how he guided the Czarina," said Levko, and with rapid steps he made his way joyfully toward the familiar hut, surrounded by low-growing cherry trees. "God give you the kingdom of heaven, kind and lovely lady!" he thought to himself. "May you in the other world be smiling forever among the holy angels. I shall tell no one of the wonder that has happened this night; to you only, Galya, I will tell it. Only you will believe me and together we will pray for the peace of the soul of the luckless drowned maiden!"

Here he drew near the hut: the window was open, the moonlight shone through it upon Ganna as she lay asleep with her head upon her arm, a soft glow on her cheeks; her lips moved, faintly murmuring his name. "Sleep, my beauty, dream of all that is fairest in the world, though that will not be better than our awakening."

Making the sign of the cross over her he closed the window and gently moved away.

And in a few minutes all the village was asleep; only the moon floated, radiant and marvelous in the infinite spaces of the glorious Ukrainian sky. There was the same triumphal splendor on high, and the night, the divine night, glowed majestically. The earth was as lovely in the wonderful silvery light, but no one was enchanted by it; all were sunk in sleep. But from time to time the silence was broken for a moment by the bark of a dog, and for a long while drunken Kalenik was still staggering along the slumbering street looking for his hut.

THE LOST LETTER

A Tale Told by the Sexton
of N——— Church

So you want me to tell you another story about Grandad? Certainly, why not amuse you with some more . . . ? Ah, the old days, the old days! What joy, what gladness it brings to the heart when one hears of what was done in the world so long, long ago, that the year and the month are forgotten! And when some kinsman of one's own is mixed up in it, a grandfather or great-grandfather—then I'm done for: may I choke while praying to St. Varvara if I don't think that I'm doing it all myself, as though I had crept into my great-grandfather's soul, or my great-grandfather's soul were playing tricks in me. . . . But then, our girls and young women are to blame for plaguing me; if I only let them catch a glimpse of me, it's "Foma Grigorievich! Foma Grigorievich! Come now, some terrible tale! Come now, come now . . . !" Tara-ta-ta, ta-ta-ta and they keep on and on. . . . I don't grudge telling them a story, of course, but you should see what happens to them when they are in bed. Why, I know every one of them is trembling under the quilt as though she were in a fever and would be glad to creep under her sheepskin, head and all. If a rat scratches against a pot, or she herself touches the poker with her foot—it's "Lord preserve us!" and her heart's in her heels. But

it's all over the next day; she'll pester me again to tell her a frightening story, and that's how it goes. Well, what am I to tell you? Nothing comes into my mind at the minute . . . oh yes, I'll tell you
how the witches played "Fools" [1] with my grandfather. But I must
beg you first, good friends, not to interrupt me or I will make a
hash of it not fit to put to one's lips. My Grandad, I must tell you,
was a leading Cossack in his day. He knew his ABC's and even how
to abbreviate. On a saint's day, he would boom out the Acts of the
Apostles in a voice that would make a priest's son of today feel
small. Well, you know without my telling you that in those days if
you collected all who could read and write from the whole of Baturin you wouldn't need your cap to contain them: there wouldn't
be a handful altogether. So it's no wonder that everyone who met
my Grandad offered him a bow, and a low one too.

One day our noble Hetman took it into his head to send a letter to
the Czarina about something. The secretary of the regiment in
those days—damn, I can't remember his name, the devil take him
. . . Viskryak, no, that's not it, Motuzochka, that's not it, Goloputsek—no, not Goloputsek . . . all I know is that it was a peculiar
name that began in an odd way—he sent for my Grandad and told
him that the Hetman himself had named him as messenger to the
Czarina. My Grandad never liked to waste time getting ready: he
sewed the letter in his cap, led out his horse, kissed his wife and his
two sucking pigs, as he used to call his sons, of whom one was my
own father, and he made the dust fly behind him that day as though
fifteen fellows had been playing a rough game in the middle of the
street. The cock had not crowed for the fourth time next morning before Grandad had already reached Konotop. There used to
be a fair there in those days: there were such crowds moving up
and down the streets that it made one giddy to watch them. But as
it was early the people were all stretched out on the ground asleep.
Beside a cow would be lying a rakish boy with a nose as red as a
bullfinch; a little further a peddler woman with flints, packets of
bluing, buckshot, and pretzels was snoring where she sat; a gypsy
lay under a cart, a dealer on a wagon of fish; while a Muscovite with
a big beard, carrying belts and sleeves for sale, sprawled with his
legs stuck out in the middle of the road. . . . In fact, there was
rabble of all sorts, as there always is at fairs. My Grandad stopped

---

[1] *Durak*, a very popular card game. (ed.).

to have a good look around. Meanwhile, little by little, there began
to be a stir in the booths: the Jewesses made a clatter with the bottles; smoke rolled up in rings here and there, and the smell of hot
doughnuts floated all over the encampment. It came into my
Grandad's mind that he had no steel and tinder nor tobacco with
him, so he began sauntering about the fair. He had not gone twenty
paces when he met a Dnieper Cossack.[2] Trousers red as fire, a full-
skirted blue coat and bright-flowered girdle, a saber at his side, and
a pipe with a fine brass chain right down to his heels—a regular
Dnieper Cossack, that's all you can say! Ah, they were something!
One would stand up, stretch himself, stroke his gallant mustaches,
clink with his iron heels—and off he would go! And how he would
go! And how he would go! His legs would whirl around like a
spindle in a woman's hands: his fingers would pluck at all the strings
of the bandore like a whirlwind, and then pressing it to his side he
would begin dancing, burst into song—his whole soul rejoicing
. . . ! Yes, the good old days are over; you don't see such Cossacks
nowadays! No. So they met. One word leads to another, it doesn't
take long to make friends. They fell to chatting and chatting, so
that Grandad quite forgot about his journey. They had a drinking
bout, as at a wedding before Lent. Only at last I suppose they got
tired of smashing the pots and flinging money to the crowd, and indeed, one can't stay forever at a fair! So the new friends agreed not
to part, but to travel on together. It was getting on toward evening
when they rode out into the open country. The sun had set; here
and there streaks of red glowed in the sky where the sun had been;
the country was gay with different-colored fields like the checked
petticoats our black-browed peasant wives wear on holidays.

Our Dnieper Cossack talked away like mad. Grandad and
another jaunty fellow who had joined them began to think that
there was a devil in him. Where did it all come from? Tales and
stories of such marvels that sometimes Grandad held his sides and
almost split his stomach with laughing. But the farther they went
the darker it grew, and with it the gay talk grew more disconnected. At last our storyteller was completely silent and started at
the slightest rustle.

"Aha, neighbor!" they said to him, "you have started nodding in

---

[2] *Zaporozhets*, a Cossack belonging to the military community settled at
Zaporozhye (i.e., Beyond the Falls) on the Dnieper River. The community
is fully described in *Taras Bulba*. (ed.)

earnest: you are wishing now that you were at home and on the stove!"

"It's no use keeping secrets from you," he said, suddenly turning around and fixing his eyes upon them. "Do you know that I sold my soul to the devil long ago?"

"As though that were something unheard of! Who hasn't had dealings with the devil in his day? That's why you must drain the cup of pleasure to the dregs, as the saying is."

"Ah, friends! I would, but this night the fatal hour has come! Brothers!" he said, clasping their hands, "do not give me up! Watch over me one night! Never will I forget your friendship!"

Why not help a man in such trouble? Grandad vowed straight off he'd sooner have the forelock cut off his own head than let the devil sniff his snout at a Christian soul.

Our Cossacks would perhaps have ridden on further, if the whole sky had not clouded over as though covered by a black blanket and if it had not turned as dark as under a sheepskin. But there was a light twinkling in the distance and the horses, feeling that a stall was near, quickened their pace, pricking up their ears and staring into the darkness. It seemed as though the light flew to meet them, and the Cossacks saw before them a tavern, leaning on one side like a peasant woman on her way home from a merry christening party. In those days taverns were not what they are now. There was nowhere for a good man to turn around or dance a *gopak*—indeed, he had nowhere to lie down, even if the drink had gone to his head and his wobbly legs began making circles all over the floor. The yard was all blocked up with dealers' wagons; under the sheds, in the mangers, in the barns, men were snoring like tomcats, one curled up and another sprawling. But one was busy. The tavern keeper, in front of his little pot-lamp, was making notches in a stick to mark the number of quarts and pints the dealers had drained.

Grandad, after ordering a third of a pailful for the three of them, went off to the barn. They lay down side by side. But before he had time to turn around he saw that his friends were already sleeping like the dead. Waking the third Cossack, the one who had joined them, Grandad reminded him of the promise given to their comrade. The man sat up, rubbed his eyes, and fell asleep again. There was nothing he could do; he had to watch alone. To drive away sleep in some way, he examined all the wagons, looked at the horses, lighted his pipe, came back, and sat down again beside his comrades. All was still; it seemed as though not a fly were moving. Then he imagined that something gray poked out its horns from a wagon close by. . . . Then his eyes began to close, so that he was obliged to rub them every minute with his fist and to keep them open with the rest of the vodka. But soon, when they were a little clearer, everything had vanished. At last a little later something strange showed itself again under the wagon. . . . Grandad opened his eyes as wide as he could, but the cursed sleepiness made everything misty before them; his hands felt numb, his head rolled back, and he fell into such a sound sleep that he lay as though dead. Grandad slept for hours, and he only sprang to his feet when the sun was baking his shaven head. After stretching twice and scratching his back, he noticed that there were no longer so many wagons standing there as in the evening. The dealers, it seemed, had trailed off before dawn. He looked for his companions—the Cossack was still asleep, but the Dnieper Cossack was gone. No one could tell him anything when he asked; only his coat was still lying in the same place. Grandad was frightened and didn't know what to think. He went to look for the horses—no sign of his or the Dnieper Cossack's! What could that mean? Supposing the Evil One had taken the Dnieper Cossack, who had taken the horses? Thinking it over, Grandad concluded that probably the devil had come on foot, and as it's a long journey to hell he had carried off his horse. He was terribly upset at not having kept his Cossack word.

"Well," he thought, "there is nothing to be done; I will go on foot. Maybe I shall come across some horse dealer on his way from the fair. I shall manage somehow to buy a horse." But when he reached for his cap, his cap was not there either. Grandad wrung his hands when he remembered that the day before he had changed caps for a time with the Dnieper Cossack. Who else could have carried it off if not the devil himself! Some Hetman's messenger! A nice job he'd made of taking the letter to the Czarina! At this point my Grandad fell to bestowing such names on the devil as I imagine must have set him sneezing more than once in hell. But cursing is not much use, and however often my Grandad scratched his head, he could not think of any plan. What was he to do? He turned to ask advice of others: he got together all the good folk who were in the tavern at the time, dealers and simple wayfarers, told them how it all happened and what a misfortune had befallen him. The dealers pondered for a long time. Leaning their chins on their whips, they shook their heads and said that they had never heard of such a marvel in Christendom as a devil carrying off a Hetman's letter. Others added that when the devil or a Muscovite stole anything, you whistle in the dark for it. Only the tavern keeper sat silent in the corner. Grandad went up to him, too. When a man says nothing, you may be sure he thinks a great deal. But the tavern keeper was sparing of his words, and if Grandad had not felt in his pocket for five silver coins, he might have gone on standing before him to no purpose.

"I will tell you how to find the letter," said the tavern keeper, leading him aside. His words lifted a weight from Grandad's heart. "I see from your eyes that you are a Cossack and not a woman. Listen now! Near the tavern you will find a turn on the right into the forest. As soon as it begins to grow dark you must be ready to start. There are gypsies living in the forest and they come out of their dens to forge iron on nights on which none but witches go abroad on their pokers. What their real trade is you had best not inquire. There will be much knocking in the forest, only don't you go where you hear the knocking; there'll be a little path facing you near a burnt tree: go by that little path, go on and on. . . . The thorns may scratch you, thick bushes may block the path, but you continue on and do not stop until you come to a little stream. There you will see whom you need. But don't forget to take in your pockets that for which pockets are made. . . . You understand, both devils and men prize that." Saying this, the tavern keeper went off to his corner and would not say another word.

My late Grandad was by no means a coward; if he met a wolf, he would grab him straightway by the tail; if he used his fist among the Cossacks, they would fall to the ground like pears. But a shudder ran down him when he stepped into the forest on such a dark night. Not one little star in the sky. Dark and dim as a wine cellar; there was no sound, except far, far overhead a cold wind playing in the treetops, and the trees swayed like the heads of drunken Cossacks while their leaves whispered a tipsy song. And there was such a cold blast that Grandad thought of his sheepskin, and all at once it was as though a hundred hammers began tapping in the forest with a noise that set his ears ringing. And the whole forest was lit up for a moment as though by summer lightning. At once Grandad caught sight of a little path winding between the bushes. And here was the burnt tree and here were the thorn bushes! So everything was as he had been told; no, the tavern keeper had not deceived him. It was not altogether pleasant tearing his way through the prickly bushes; he had never in his life known the damned thorns and twigs to scratch so badly. He almost cried out at every step. Little by little he came into an open place, and as far as he could see the trees seemed wider apart, and as he went on he came upon bigger trees than he had ever seen even on the other side of Poland. And behold, among the trees gleamed a little stream, dark as tempered steel. For a long time Grandad stopped on the bank, looking in all directions. On the other bank a light was twinkling; it seemed every minute on the point of going out, and then it was reflected again in the stream, trembling like a Pole in the hands of Cossacks. And here was the little bridge!

"Perhaps only the devil's chariot uses this bridge," he said. Grandad stepped out boldly, however, and before another man would have had time to get out his horn and take a pinch of snuff he was on the other side. Only now he saw that there were people sitting around a fire, and they had such charming pig-faces that at any other time God knows he would have given anything to escape making their acquaintance. But now he couldn't avoid it: he had to make friends with them. So Grandad tossed off a low bow, saying: "God help you, good people!"

No one nodded his head; they all sat in silence and kept dropping something into the fire. Seeing one place empty, Grandad, without making a fuss, sat down. The charming pig-faces said nothing, Grandad said nothing either. For a long time they sat in silence. Grandad was already beginning to be bored; he fumbled in his pocket, pulled out his pipe, looked around—not one of them glanced at him.

"Well, your honors, will you be so kind; as a matter of fact, in a manner of speaking . . ." (Grandad had knocked about the world a good bit and knew how to turn a phrase, and maybe even if he had been before the Czar he would not have been at a loss.)

"In a manner of speaking, not to forget myself nor to slight you —a pipe I have, but that with which to light it I lack." To this speech, too, there was not a word. But one of the pig-faces thrust a hot brand straight into Grandad's face, so that if he had not turned aside a little he might have parted with one eye forever. At last, seeing that time was being wasted, he made up his mind to tell his story whether the pig-faces would listen or not.

They pricked up their ears and stretched out their paws. Grandad guessed what that meant; he pulled out all the money he had with him and flung it to them as though to dogs. As soon as he had flung the money, everything was in a turmoil before him, the earth shook, and all at once—he never knew how to explain this part— he found himself almost in hell itself.

"Merciful heavens!" groaned Grandad when he had taken a good look around. What wonders were here! One ugly face after another, as the saying is. The witches were as many as the snow-flakes that fall on occasion at Christmas. They were all dressed up and painted like fine ladies at a fair. And the whole bunch of them were dancing some sort of devil's jig as though they were drunk. What a dust they raised, God help us! Any Christian would have shuddered to see how high the devils skipped. In spite of his terror, my Grandad started laughing when he saw the devils, with their dogs' faces on their little German legs, wag their tails, twist, and turn about the witches, like our boys about the pretty girls, while the musicians beat on their cheeks with their fists as though they were tambourines and whistled with their noses as though they were horns. As soon as they saw Grandad, they pressed around him in a crowd. Pig-faces, dog-faces, goat-faces, bird-faces, and horse-faces—all craned forward, and here they were actually trying to kiss him. Grandad could not help spitting, he was so disgusted! At last they caught hold of him and made him sit down at a table, as long, maybe, as the road from Konotop to Baturin.[3]

"Well, this is not altogether so bad!" thought Grandad, seeing on the table pork, sausages, onion minced with cabbage, and many other dainties. "The damned scum doesn't keep the fasts, it seems."

My Grandad, I may as well tell you, was by no means averse to good fare on occasion. He ate with good appetite, the dear man, and so without wasting words he pulled toward him a bowl of sliced bacon fat and a smoked ham, took up a fork not much smaller than those with which a peasant pitches hay, picked out the most solid piece, laid it on a piece of bread, and—lo and behold!—put it in another mouth just close beside his very ear, and, indeed, there was the sound of another fellow's jaws chewing it and clack-ing with his teeth, so that all the table could hear. Grandad didn't mind; he picked up another piece, and this time it seemed as though

---

[3] I.e., eighteen miles. (ed.)

he had caught it with his lips, but again it did not go down his gullet. A third time he tried—again he missed it. Grandad flew into a rage; he forgot his fright and in whose claws he was, and ran up to the witches: "Do you mean to mock me, you pagan bitches? If you don't this very minute give me back my Cossack cap—may I be a Catholic if I don't twist your pig-snouts to the back of your heads!"

He had finished the last word when the monsters grinned and set up such a roar of laughter that it sent a chill to my Grandad's heart.

"Good!" shrieked one of the witches, whom Grandad took to be the leader among them because she was almost the greatest beauty of the lot; "we will give you back your cap, but not until you win it back from us in three games of 'Fools'!"

What was he to do? For a Cossack to sit down and play "Fools" with a lot of women! Grandad kept refusing and refusing, but in the end sat down. They brought the cards, a greasy pack such as we only see used by priests' wives to tell the girls their fortunes and what their husbands will be like.

"Listen!" barked the witch again: "if you win one game, the cap is yours; if you are left 'Fool' in every one of the three games, it's no use your fuming: you'll never see your cap nor maybe the world again!"

"Deal, deal, you old witch! What will be, will be."

Well, the cards were dealt. Grandad picked up his—he couldn't bear to look at them, they were such trash; they could have at least given him one trump just for the fun of it. Of the other suits the highest was a ten and he hadn't even a pair; while the witch kept giving him five at once. It was his fate to be left "Fool"! As soon as Grandad was left "Fool," the monsters began neighing, barking, and grunting on all sides: "Fool, fool, fool!"

"Shout till you burst, you bitches," cried Grandad putting his fingers in his ears.

"Well," he thought, "the witch didn't play fair; now I am going to deal myself." He dealt; he turned up the trump and looked at his cards; they were first-rate, he had trumps. And at first things could not have gone better; till the witch put down five cards with kings among them.

Grandad had nothing in his hand but trumps! In a flash he beat all the kings with trumps!

"Ha-ha! but that's not like a Cossack! What are you covering them with, neighbor?"

"What with? With trumps!"

"Maybe to your thinking they are trumps, but to our thinking they are not!"

Lo and behold! the cards were really of another suit! What devilry was this? A second time he was "Fool" and the devils started shrieking again: "Fool! fool!" so that the table rocked and the cards danced upon it.

Grandad flew into a passion; he dealt for the last time. Again he had a good hand. The witch put down five again; Grandad covered them and took from the pack a handful of trumps.

"Trump!" he shouted, flinging a card on the table so that it spun around like a basket; without saying a word she covered it with the eight of another suit.

"What are you beating my trump with, old devil?"

The witch lifted her card and under it was the six of another suit not trumps.

"What damned trickery!" said Grandad, and in his great anger he struck the table with his fist as hard as he could. Luckily the witch had a poor hand; this time, as luck would have it, Grandad had pairs. He began drawing cards out of the pack, but it was of no use; such trash came that Grandad let his hands fall. There was not one good card in the pack. So he just played anything—a six. The witch had to take it, and she could not cover it. "So there! What do you say to that? Aie, Aie! There is something wrong, I'll be damned!" Then on the sly under the table Grandad made the sign of the cross over the cards, and behold—he had in his hand the ace, king, and jack of trumps, and the card he had just played was not a six but the queen!

"Well, I've been the fool! King of trumps! Well, have you taken it? Aie, you bitches! Would you like the ace too? The ace! the jack . . . !"

Thunder boomed in hell; the witch went into convulsions, and all of a sudden the cap flew smack into Grandad's face.

"No, no, that's not enough!" shouted Grandad, plucking up his courage and putting on his cap. "If my gallant horse is not standing before me at once, may a thunderbolt strike me dead in this foul place if I do not make the sign of the holy cross over all of you!"

And he was just raising his hand to do it when the horse's bones rattled before him.

"Here is your horse!"

The poor man burst out crying like an infant as he looked at the bones. He grieved for his old comrade!

"Give me some sort of a horse," he said, "to get out of your den!" A devil cracked a whip—a highly spirited horse rose up under him and Grandad soared upward like a bird.

Terror came over him, however, when the horse, heeding neither shout nor rein, galloped over ditches and bogs. The places he went through were such that it made him shudder at the mere telling of it. He looked down and was more terrified than ever: an abyss, a fearful precipice! But that was nothing to the satanic beast; he leaped straight over it. Grandad tried to hold on; he could not. Over tree stumps, over hillocks he flew headlong into a ditch, and fell so hard on the ground at the bottom that it seemed he had breathed his last. Anyway, he could remember nothing of what happened to him then; and when he came to himself a little and looked about him, it was broad daylight; he caught glimpses of familiar places and found himself lying on the roof of his own hut.

Grandad crossed himself as he climbed down. What devils' tricks! Damn it all! What strange things befall a man! He looked at his hands: they were bathed in blood; he looked into a pail of water— and saw that his face was also bathed in blood. Washing himself thoroughly so that he would not scare the children, he went quietly into the hut—and what did he see! The children staggered back toward him and pointed in alarm, saying: "Look! Look! Mother's jumping like mad!" And indeed, his wife was sitting asleep before her loom, holding her spindle in her hands, and in her sleep was bouncing up and down on the bench. Grandad, taking her gently by the hand, woke her. "Good morning, wife! Are you quite well?" For a long while she gazed at him with bulging eyes, but at last recognized Grandad and told him that she had dreamed that the stove was riding around the hut shoveling out the pots and tubs with a spade . . . and devil knows what else.

"Well," said Grandad, "you have had it asleep, I have had it awake. I see I must have our hut blessed; but I cannot linger now."

Saying this Grandad rested a little, then got out his horse and did not stop by day or by night till he arrived and gave the letter to the Czarina herself. There Grandad beheld such wonderful things that for long after he used to tell the tale: how they brought him to the palace, and it was so high that if you were to set ten huts one on top of another they probably would still not be high enough; how he glanced into one room—nothing, into another—nothing, into a third—still nothing, into a fourth even—nothing, but in the fifth there she was sitting in her golden crown, in a new gray gown and red boots, eating golden dumplings; how she had bade them fill a whole cap with five-ruble notes for him; how . . . I can't remember it all! As for his rumpus with the devils, Grandad forgot even to think about it; and if it happened that someone reminded him of it, Grandad would say nothing, as though the matter did not concern him, and we had the greatest trouble persuading him to tell us how it had all happened. And apparently to punish him for not rushing out at once after that to have the hut blessed, every year just at that same time a strange thing happened to his wife— she would dance and nothing could stop her. No matter what anyone did, her legs would go their own way, and something forced her to dance.

EVENINGS ON
A FARM
NEAR DIKANKA, II

Preface

Here is a second part for you, and I had better say the last one! I did
not want, I did not at all want to bring it out. One should not outstay
one's welcome. I must tell you they are already beginning to laugh
at me in the village. "The old fellow has become stupid," they say,
"he is amusing himself with children's toys in his old age!" And, indeed, it is high time to rest. I expect you imagine, dear readers, that
I am only pretending to be old. Pretend, indeed, when I have no
teeth left in my mouth! Now, if anything soft comes my way I
manage to chew it, but I can't tackle anything hard. So here is another book for you! Only don't scold me! It is not nice to scold at
parting, especially when God only knows whether one will soon
meet again. In this book you will find stories told by people you do
not know at all, except, perhaps, Foma Grigorievich. That gentleman in the pea-green coat who talked in such refined language that
many of the wits, even Muscovites, could not understand him, has
not been here for a long time. He hasn't visited us since he quarreled
with us all. I did not tell you about it, did I? It was a regular comedy.
Last year, some time in the summer, I believe it was on my Saint's

Day, I had visitors to see me. . . . (I must tell you, dear readers, that my neighbors, God give them good health, do not forget the old man.) It is fifty years since I began keeping my name day; but just how old I am neither I nor my old woman could say. It must be somewhere about seventy. The priest at Dikanka, Father Kharlampy, knew when I was born, but I am sorry to say he has been dead these fifty years. So I had visitors to see me: Zakhar Kirilovich Chukhopupenko, Stepan Ivanovich Kurochka, Taras Ivanovich Smachnenky, the assessor Kharlampy Kirilovich Khlost; there was another one . . . I forget his name . . . Osip . . . Osip . . . I swear, everyone in Mirgorod knows him! Whenever he begins speaking he snaps his fingers and puts his arms akimbo. . . . Well, God help him! I shall think of it presently. The gentleman from Poltava whom you already know came too. Foma Grigorievich I do not count: he is one of us. Everybody talked (I must tell you that our conversation is never about trifles; I always like pleasant conversation, so as to combine pleasure and profit, as the saying is) —we discussed how to pickle apples. My old woman began saying that first you had to wash the apples thoroughly, then soak them in kvass, and then . . . "All that is no use whatever!" the gentleman from Poltava interrupted, thrusting his hand into his pea-green coat and pacing about the room majestically, "not the slightest use! First you must sprinkle them with tansy and then . . ." Well, I ask you, dear readers, did you ever hear of apples being sprinkled with tansy? It is true, people do use black-currant leaves, swineherb, trefoil; but to put in tansy . . . I have never heard of such a thing! And I imagine no one knows more about these things than my old woman. But there you are! I quietly drew him aside, as a good neighbor: "Come now, Makar Nazarovich, don't make people laugh! You are a man of some consequence; you have dined at the same table with the governor, as you told us yourself. Well, if you were to say anything like this there, you would set them all laughing at you!" And what do you imagine he said to that? Nothing! He spat on the floor, picked up his cap, and went out. He might have said goodbye to somebody, he might have given us a nod; all we heard was his chaise with a bell on it drive up to the gate; he got into it and drove off. And a good thing too! We don't want guests like that. I tell you what, dear readers, there is nothing in the world worse than these high-class people. Because his uncle was a commissar once, he turns up his nose at everyone. As though there were no rank in the world higher than a commissar! Thank God, there are people greater than commissars. No, I don't like these high-class people. Now Foma Grigorievich, for instance—he is not a high-class man, but just look at him: there is a serene dignity in his face. Even when he takes a pinch of ordinary snuff you can't help feeling respect for him. When he sings in the choir in the church there is no describing how touching it is. You feel as though you were melting . . . ! While that other . . . But there, God help the man. He thinks we cannot do without his tales. But here, you see, is a book of them without him.

I promised you, I remember, that in this book there should be my story too. And I did mean to put it in. But I found that for my story I should need three books of this size, at least. I did think of printing it separately, but I thought better of it. I know you: you would be laughing at the old man. No, I shall not! Goodbye. It will be a long time before we meet again, if we ever do. But then, it would not matter to you if I had never existed at all. One year will pass and then another—and none of you will remember or miss the old bee-keeper.

RUDY PANKO

CHRISTMAS EVE

The last day before Christmas had passed. A clear winter night had come; the stars peeped out; the moon rose majestically in the sky to light good people and all the world so that all might enjoy singing *kolyadki*[1] and praising the Lord. It was freezing harder than in the morning; but it was so still that the crunch of the snow under the boot could be heard half a mile away. Not one group of boys had appeared under the hut windows yet; only the moon peeped in at them stealthily as though calling to the girls who were dressing up in their best to make haste and run out on the crunching snow. At that moment the smoke rose in puffs from a hut chimney and passed like a cloud over the sky, and a witch on a broomstick rose up in the air with the smoke.

If the assessor of Sorochintsy, in his cap edged with lambskin and cut like a Turk's, in his dark blue overcoat lined with black

---

[1] Among us it is the custom to sing under the window on Christmas Eve carols that are called *kolyadki*. The mistress or master or whoever is left in the house always drops into the singer's bag some sausage or bread or a copper or whatever he has plenty of. It is said that once upon a time there was a blockhead called Kolyada who was taken to be a god and that these *kolyadki* came from that. Who knows? It is not for plain folk like us to give our opinion about it. Last year Father Osip was for forbidding them to sing *kolyadki* about the farms, saying that folk were honoring Satan by doing so, though to tell the truth there is not a word about Kolyada in the *kolyadki*. They often sing about the birth of Christ, and at the end wish good health to the master, the mistress, the children, and the entire household. (*The beekeeper's note*)

astrakhan, had driven by at that moment with his three hired horses and the fiendishly braided whip with which it is his habit to urge on his coachman, he would certainly have noticed her, for there is not a witch in the world who could elude the eyes of the Sorochintsy assessor. He can count on his fingers how many suckling pigs every peasant woman's sow has farrowed and how much linen is lying in her chest and just which of her clothes and household belongings her good man pawns on Sunday at the tavern. But the Sorochintsy assessor did not drive by, and, indeed, what business is it of his? He has his own district. Meanwhile, the witch rose so high in the air that she was only a little black patch gleaming aloft. But wherever that little patch appeared, there the stars one after another vanished. Soon the witch had gathered a whole sleeveful of them. Three or four were still shining. All at once from the opposite side another little patch appeared, grew larger, began to lengthen out, and was no longer a little patch. A shortsighted man would never have made out what it was, even if he had put the wheels of the commissar's chaise on his nose as spectacles. At first it looked like a regular German:[2] the narrow little face, continually twisting and turning and sniffing at everything, ended in a little round heel, like our pigs' snouts; the legs were so thin that if the mayor of Yareski had had legs like that, he would certainly have broken them in the first Cossack dance. But from behind he was for all the world a district attorney in uniform, for he had a tail as long and pointed as the uniform coattails are nowadays. It was only from the goat-beard under his chin, from the little horns sticking from his forehead, and from his being no whiter than a chimney sweep, that one could tell that he was not a German or a district attorney, but simply the devil, who had one last night left him to wander about the wide world and teach good folk to sin. On the morrow when the first bells rang for prayer, he would run with his tail between his legs straight off to his lair.

Meanwhile the devil stole silently up to the moon and stretched his hand out to seize it, but drew it back quickly as though he were scorched, sucked his fingers and danced about, then ran up from the other side and again skipped away and drew back his hand. But

---

[2] Among us everyone is called a German who comes from a foreign country; even if he is a Frenchman, a Hungarian, or a Swede—he is still a German. (N. Gogol)

in spite of all his failures the sly devil did not give up his tricks. Running up, he suddenly seized the moon with both hands; grimacing and blowing, he kept flinging it from one hand to the other, like a peasant who has picked up an ember for his pipe with bare fingers; at last, he hurriedly put it in his pocket and ran on as though nothing had happened.

No one in Dikanka noticed that the devil had stolen the moon. It is true the district clerk, crawling out of the tavern on all fours, saw the moon for no reason whatever dancing in the sky, and he swore that he had to the whole village; but people shook their heads and even made fun of him. But what motive led the devil to this illegal act? Why, this was how it was: he knew that the rich Cossack, Chub,[3] had been invited by the sexton to a supper of rice soup at which a kinsman of the sexton's, who had come from the bishop's choir, wore a dark blue coat and could take the very lowest bass note, the mayor, the Cossack Sverbiguz, and some others were to be present, and at which besides the Christmas soup there were to be spiced vodka, saffron vodka, and good things of all sorts. And meanwhile his daughter, the greatest beauty in the village, was left at home, and there was no doubt that the blacksmith, a very strong and fine young fellow, would pay her a visit, and him the devil hated more than Father Kondrat's sermons. In his spare time the blacksmith had taken up painting and was reckoned the finest artist in the whole countryside. Even the Cossack officer L——ko, who was still strong and hearty in those days, sent for him to Poltava expressly to paint a picket fence around his house. All the bowls from which the Cossacks of Dikanka gulped their borsht had been painted by the blacksmith. He was a God-fearing man and often painted icons of the saints: even now you may find his Luke the Evangelist in the church of T——. But the triumph of his art was a picture painted on the church wall in the chapel on the right. In it he depicted St. Peter on the Day of Judgment with the keys in his hand driving the Evil Spirit out of hell; the frightened devil was running in all directions, foreseeing his doom, while the sinners, who had been imprisoned before, were chasing him and striking him with whips, blocks of wood, and anything they could get hold of. While the artist was working at this picture and painting it on a

---

[3] "Forelock." (ed.)

big wooden board, the devil did all he could to hinder him; he gave him a nudge on the arm, unseen, blew some ashes from the forge in the smithy, and scattered them on the picture; but, in spite of it all, the work was finished, the picture was brought into the church and put on the wall of the side chapel, and from that day the devil had sworn to revenge himself on the blacksmith.

He had only one night left to wander upon earth; but he was looking for some means of venting his anger on the blacksmith that night. And that was why he made up his mind to steal the moon, reckoning that old Chub was lazy and slow to move, and the sexton's hut a good distance away: the road passed by cross paths beside the mills and the graveyard and went around a ravine. On a moonlight night spiced vodka and saffron vodka might have tempted Chub; but in such darkness it was doubtful whether anyone could drag him from the stove and bring him out of the cottage. And the blacksmith, who had for a long time been on bad terms with him, would on no account have ventured, strong as he was, to visit the daughter when the father was at home.

And so, as soon as the devil had hidden the moon in his pocket, it became so dark all over the world that not everyone could have found the way to the tavern, let alone to the sexton's. The witch shrieked when she suddenly found herself in darkness. Then the devil running up, all bows and smiles, put his arm around her, and began whispering in her ear the sort of thing that is usually whispered to all females. Things are oddly arranged in our world! All who live in it are always trying to outdo and imitate one another. In the old days the judge and the police captain were the only ones in Mirgorod who used to wear cloth overcoats lined with sheepskin in the winter, while all the minor officials wore plain sheepskin; but nowadays the assessor and the chamberlain have managed to get themselves new cloth overcoats lined with astrakhan. The year before last the treasury clerk and the district clerk bought dark blue duck at sixty kopeks a yard. The sexton has got himself cotton trousers for the summer and a striped vest of camel's hair. In fact everyone tries to be somebody! When will folks give up being vain! I am ready to bet that many would be surprised to see the devil carrying on in that way. What is most annoying is that, no doubt, he fancies himself a handsome fellow, though his figure is a shameful sight. With a face, as Foma Grigorievich used to say, the abomination of abominations, yet even he plays the dashing hero! But in the sky and under the sky it was growing so dark that there was no seeing what followed between them.

"So you have not been to see the sexton in his new hut, friend?" said the Cossack Chub, coming out at his door, to a tall lean peasant in a short sheepskin, whose stubby beard showed that for at least two weeks it had not been touched by the broken piece of scythe with which, for lack of a razor, peasants usually shave their beards. "There will be a fine drinking party there tonight!" Chub went on, grinning as he spoke. "If only we are not late!"

Hereupon Chub set straight the belt that closely girt his sheepskin, pulled his cap more firmly on his head, and gripped his whip, the terror and the enemy of tiresome dogs; but glancing upward, he stopped. "What the hell! Look! look, Panas . . . !"

"What?" articulated his friend, and he too turned his face upward.

"What, indeed! There is no moon!"

"What a nuisance! There really is no moon."

"That's just it, there isn't!" Chub said, with some annoyance at his friend's imperturbable indifference. "You don't care, I'll bet."

"Well, what can I do about it?"

"Some devil," Chub went on, wiping his mustaches with his sleeve, "has to go and meddle—may he never have a glass of vodka to drink in the mornings, the dog! I swear it's as though to mock us. . . . As I sat indoors I looked out of the window and the night was lovely! It was light, the snow was sparkling in the moonlight; you could see everything as though it were day. And here, before I'm out of the door, you can't see your hand before your face! May he break his teeth on a crust of buckwheat bread!"

Chub went on grumbling and swearing for a long while, and at the same time he was hesitant about what to decide. He had a desperate longing to gossip about all sorts of nonsense at the sexton's where no doubt the mayor was already sitting, as well as the bass choir singer, and Mikita, the tar dealer, who used to come once every two weeks on his way to Poltava, and who cracked such jokes that all the village worthies held their sides from laughing. Already in his mind's eye Chub saw the spiced vodka on the table. All this was enticing, it is true, but the darkness of the night recalled the charms of laziness so dear to every Cossack. How nice it would be now to lie on the stove with his legs tucked under him, quietly smoking his pipe and listening through a delicious drowsiness to the songs and carols of the lighthearted boys and girls who gathered in groups under the windows! He would undoubtedly have decided on the latter course had he been alone; but for the two together, it was not so dreary and terrible to go through the dark night; besides he did not care to seem sluggish and cowardly to others. When he had finished swearing he turned again to his friend.

"So there is no moon, friend?"

"No!"

"It's strange, really! Let me have a pinch of snuff! You have splendid snuff, friend! Where do you get it?"

"Splendid! What the hell do you mean by splendid?" answered the friend, shutting the birchbark snuffbox with patterns pricked out upon it. "It wouldn't make an old hen sneeze!"

"I remember," Chub still went on, "the innkeeper, Zuzulya, once brought me some snuff from Nyezhin. Ah, that was snuff! it was good snuff! So what is it to be? It's dark, you know!"

"So maybe we'll stay at home," his friend said, taking hold of the door handle.

If his friend had not said that, Chub would certainly have made up his mind to stay at home; but now something seemed egging him on to oppose it. "No, friend, let us go! It won't do; we must go!"

Even as he was saying it, he was angry with himself for having said it. He very much disliked going out on such a night, but it was a comfort to him that he was acting on his own decision and not following advice.

His friend looked around and scratched his shoulders with the handle of his whip, without the slightest sign of anger on his face, like a man to whom it is a matter of complete indifference whether he sits at home or goes out—and the two friends set off on their road.

Now let us see what Chub's daughter, the beauty, was doing all by herself. Before Oksana was seventeen, people were talking about nothing but her in almost the whole world, both on this side of Dikanka and on the other side of Dikanka. The young men were unanimous in declaring that there never had been and never would be a finer girl in the village. Oksana heard and knew all that was said about her and, like a beauty, was full of caprices. If, instead of a checked skirt and an apron, she had been dressed as a lady, she could never have kept a servant. The young men ran after her in crowds, but, losing patience, by degrees gave up on the obstinate beauty, and turned to others who were not so spoiled. Only the blacksmith was persistent and would not abandon his courtship, although he was treated not a bit better than the rest. When her father went out, Oksana spent a long while dressing herself in her best and preening before a little mirror in a pewter frame; she could not tear herself away from admiring herself.

"What put it into folks' heads to spread it abroad that I am pretty?" she said, as it were without thinking, simply to talk to herself about something. "Folks lie, I am not pretty at all!"

But the fresh animated face reflected in the mirror, its youthfulness, its sparkling black eyes and inexpressibly charming smile that stirred the soul, at once proved the contrary.

"Can my black eyebrows and my eyes," the beauty went on, still holding the mirror, "be so beautiful that there are none like them in the world? What is there pretty in that turned-up nose, and in those cheeks and those lips? Is my black hair pretty? Ough, my curls might frighten one in the evening, they twist and twine around my head like long snakes! I see now that I am not pretty at all!" And, moving the mirror a little further away, she cried out: "No, I am pretty! Ah, how pretty! Wonderful! What a joy I shall be to the man whose wife I become! How my husband will admire me! He'll be wild with joy. He will kiss me to death!"

"Wonderful girl!" whispered the blacksmith, coming in softly. "And hasn't she a little conceit! She's been standing looking in the mirror for an hour and can't tear herself away, and praising herself aloud, too!"

"Yes, boys, I am a match for you! Just look at me!" the pretty coquette went on: "how gracefully I step; my chemise is embroidered with red silk. And the ribbons on my head! You will never see richer braid! My father bought me all this so that the finest young man in the world may marry me." And, laughing, she turned around and saw the blacksmith. . . .

She uttered a shriek and stood still, coldly facing him.

The blacksmith's hands dropped helplessly to his sides.

It is hard to describe what the dark face of the lovely girl expressed. There was sternness in it, and through the sternness a sort of defiance of the embarrassed blacksmith, and at the same time a hardly perceptible flush of anger delicately suffused her face; and all this was so mingled and so indescribably pretty that to give her a million kisses was the best thing that could have been done at the moment.

"Why have you come here?" was how Oksana began. "Do you want me to shove you out of the door with a spade? You are all very clever at coming to see us. You sniff out in a minute when there are no fathers in the house. Oh, I know you! Well, is my chest ready?"

"It will be ready, my little heart, it will be ready after Christmas. If only you knew how I have worked at it; for two nights I didn't leave the smithy. But then, no priest's wife will have a chest like it. The iron I bound it with is better than what I put on the officer's chariot, when I worked at Poltava. And how it will be painted! You won't find one like it if you wander over the whole neighborhood with your little white feet! Red and blue flowers will be scattered over the whole ground. It will glow like fire. Don't be angry with me! Allow me at least to speak to you, to look at you!"

"Who's forbidding you? Speak and look!"

Then she sat down on the bench, glanced again in the mirror, and began arranging her hair. She looked at her neck, at her chemise embroidered in red silk, and a subtle feeling of complacency could be read on her lips and fresh cheeks, and was reflected in her eyes.

"Allow me to sit beside you," said the blacksmith.

"Sit down," said Oksana, with the same emotion still perceptible on her lips and in her gratified eyes.

"Wonderful, lovely Oksana, allow me to kiss you!" ventured the blacksmith, growing bolder, and he drew her toward him with the intention of snatching a kiss. But Oksana turned away her cheek, which had been very close to the blacksmith's lips, and pushed him away.

"What more do you want? When there's honey he must have a spoonful! Go away, your hands are harder than iron. And you smell of smoke. I believe you have smeared me all over with your soot."

Then she picked up the mirror and began preening again.

"She does not love me!" the blacksmith thought to himself, hanging his head. "It's all a game to her while I stand before her like a fool and cannot take my eyes off her. And I should like to stand before her always and never to take my eyes off her! Wonderful girl! What would I not give to know what is in her heart, and whom she loves. But no, she cares for nobody. She is admiring herself; she is tormenting poor me, while I am so sad that everything is darkness to me. I love her as no man in the world ever has loved or ever will."

"Is it true that your mother's a witch?" Oksana said, and she laughed. And the blacksmith felt that everything within him was laughing. That laugh echoed as if it were at once in his heart and in his softly tingling veins, and for all that, his soul was angry that he had not the right to kiss that sweetly laughing face.

"What care I for Mother? You are father and mother to me and all that is precious in the world. If the Czar summoned me and said: 'Smith Vakula, ask me for all that is best in my kingdom; I will give you anything. I will bid them make you a golden forge and you shall work with silver hammers.' 'I don't care,' I should say to the Czar, 'for precious stones or a golden forge nor for all your kingdom: give me rather my Oksana.' "

"You see, what a fellow you are! Only my father's no fool either. You'll see that, when he doesn't marry your mother!" Oksana said, smiling slyly. "But the girls are not here. . . . What's the meaning of it? We ought to have been singing long ago. I am getting tired of waiting."

"Let them stay away, my beauty!"

"I should hope not! I expect the boys will come with them. And then there will be dances. I can imagine what funny stories they will tell!"

"So you'll be merry with them?"

"Yes, merrier than with you. Ah! someone knocked; I expect it is the girls and the boys."

"What's the use of my staying longer?" the blacksmith said to himself. "She is jeering at me. I am no more to her than an old rusty horseshoe. But if that's so, anyway I won't let another man laugh at me. If only I see for certain that she likes someone better than me, I'll teach him to keep away . . ."

A knock at the door and a cry of "Open!" ringing out sharply in the frost interrupted his reflections.

"Stop, I'll open the door," said the blacksmith, and he went out, intending in his anger to break the ribs of anyone who might be there.

The frost grew sharper, and up above it turned so cold that the devil kept hopping from one hoof to the other and blowing into his fists, trying to warm his frozen hands. And indeed it is small wonder that he should be cold, being used day after day to knocking about in hell, where, as we all know, it is not so cold as it is with us in winter, and where, putting on his cap and standing before the hearth, like a real cook, he fries sinners with as much satisfaction as a peasant woman fries a sausage at Christmas.

The witch herself felt that it was cold, although she was warmly clad; and so, throwing her arms upward, she stood with one foot out, and putting herself into the attitude of a man flying along on skates, without moving a single muscle, she dropped through the air, as though on an icy slope, and straight into her chimney.

The devil started after her in the same way. But as the creature is nimbler than any dandy in stockings, there is no wonder that he reached the top of the chimney almost on the neck of his mistress, and both found themselves in a roomy oven among the pots.

The witch stealthily moved back the oven door to see whether her son, Vakula, had invited visitors to the hut; but seeing that there was no one, except the sacks that lay in the middle of the floor, she crept out of the oven, flung off her warm pelisse, rearranged her clothing, and no one could have told that she had been riding on a broom the minute before.

Vakula's mother was not more than forty years old. She was neither pretty nor ugly. Indeed, it is hard to be pretty at such an age. However, she was so clever at attracting even the resolute Cossacks (who, it may not be amiss to observe, do not care much about beauty) that the mayor and the sexton, Osip Nikiforovich (if his wife were not at home, of course), and the Cossack Korny Chub, and the Cossack Kasian Sverbiguz, were all lavishing attentions on her. And it must be said to her credit that she was very skillful in managing them: not one of them dreamed that he had a rival. If a God-fearing peasant or a gentleman (as the Cossacks call themselves) wearing a cape with a hood went to church on Sunday or, if the weather was bad, to the tavern, how could he fail to look in on Solokha, eat curd dumplings with sour cream, and gossip in the warm hut with its chatty and agreeable mistress? And the Cossack would purposely go a long way around before reaching the tavern, and would call that "looking in on his way." And when Solokha went to church on a holiday, dressed in a bright-checked *plakhta* with a cotton *zapaska*,[4] and above it a dark blue overskirt on the back of which gold flourishes were embroidered, and took up her stand close to the right side of the choir, the sexton would be sure to begin coughing and unconsciously screw up his eyes in her direction; the mayor would smooth his mustaches, begin twisting the curl behind his ear, and say to the man standing next to him: "Ah, a nice woman, a hell of a woman!" Solokha would bow to each one of them, and each one would think that she was bowing to him alone.

But anyone fond of meddling in other people's business would notice at once that Solokha was most gracious to the Cossack Chub. Chub was a widower. Eight stacks of wheat always stood before his hut. Two pairs of stalwart oxen poked their heads out of the barn with the thatched roof by the roadside and mooed every time they saw their crony, the cow, or their uncle, the fat bull, pass. A bearded billygoat used to clamber onto the roof, from which he would bleat in a harsh voice like the police captain's, taunting the turkeys when they came out into the yard, and turning his back when he saw his enemies, the boys, who used to jeer at his beard. In Chub's trunks there was plenty of linen and many caftans and old-fashioned overcoats with gold braid on them; his wife had been fond of fine clothes. In his vegetable patch, besides poppies, cabbages, and sunflowers, two beds were sown every year with tobacco. All this Solokha thought would not be improper to join to her own farm, and, already reckoning in what good condition it would be when it passed into her hands, she felt doubly well-disposed to old Chub. And to prevent her son Vakula from courting Chub's daughter[5] and succeeding in getting possession of it all himself (then he would very likely not let her interfere in anything), she had recourse to the common maneuver of all women of forty—that is, setting Chub against the blacksmith as often as she could. Possibly these sly tricks and subtleties were the reason that the old women were beginning here and there, particularly when they had drunk a drop too much at some merry gathering, to say that Solokha was certainly a witch, that the boy Kizyakolupenko had seen a tail on her back no bigger than a peasant woman's spindle;

---

[4] See p. 10, n. 4. (ed.)

[5] Had her son married Chub's daughter, she could not by the rules of the Russian Church have married Chub. (C.G.)

that, no longer ago than the Thursday before last, she had run across the road in the form of a black cat; that on one occasion a sow had run up to the priest's wife, had crowed like a cock, put Father Kondrat's cap on her head, and run away again. . . .

It happened that just when the old women were talking about this, a cowherd, Tymish Korostyavy, came up. He did not fail to tell them how in the summer, just before St. Peter's Fast, when he had lain down to sleep in the stable, putting some straw under his head, he saw with his own eyes a witch, with her hair down, in nothing but her chemise, begin milking the cows, and he could not stir he was so spellbound, and she had smeared his lips with something so nasty that he was spitting the whole day afterwards. But all that was somewhat doubtful, for the only one who can see a witch is the assessor of Sorochintsy. And so all the notable Cossacks waved their hands impatiently when they heard such tales. "They are lying, the bitches!" was their usual answer.

After she had crept out of the stove and rearranged herself, Solokha, like a good housewife, began tidying up and putting everything in its place; but she did not touch the sacks. "Vakula brought those in, let him take them out himself!" she thought. Meanwhile the devil, who had chanced to turn around just as he was flying into the chimney, had caught sight of Chub arm-in-arm with his neighbor already a long way from home. Instantly he flew out of the chimney, cut across their road, and began flinging up heaps of frozen snow in all directions. A blizzard sprang up. All was whiteness in the air. The snow zigzagged behind and in front and threatened to plaster up the eyes, the mouth, and the ears of the friends. And the devil flew back to the chimney again, certain that Chub would go back home with his neighbor, would find the blacksmith there and probably give him such a scolding that it would be a long time before he would be able to handle a brush and paint offensive caricatures.

As a matter of fact, as soon as the blizzard began and the wind blew straight in their faces, Chub expressed his regret, and pulling his hood further down on his head showered abuse on himself, the devil, and his friend. His annoyance was feigned, however. Chub was really glad of the snowstorm. They had still eight times as far to go as they had gone already before they would reach the sexton's. They turned around. The wind blew on the back of their heads, but they could see nothing through the whirling snow.

"Stop, friend! I think we are going wrong," said Chub, after walking on a little. "I do not see a single hut. Oh, what a snow-storm! You go a little that way and see whether you find the road, and meanwhile I'll look this way. It was the foul fiend put it into my head to go trudging out in such a storm! Don't forget to shout when you find the road. Oh, what a heap of snow Satan has driven into my eyes!"

The road was not to be seen, however. Chub's friend, turning off, wandered up and down in his high boots, and at last came straight upon the tavern. This lucky find so cheered him that he forgot everything and, shaking the snow off, walked straight in, not worrying himself in the least about the friend he had left on the road. Meanwhile Chub thought that he had found the road. Standing still, he started shouting at the top of his voice, but, seeing that his friend did not appear, he made up his mind to go on alone. After walking on a little he saw his own hut. Snowdrifts lay all about it and on the roof. Clapping his frozen hands together, he began knocking on the door and shouting peremptorily to his daughter to open it.

"What do you want here?" the blacksmith called grimly, as he came out.

Chub, recognizing the blacksmith's voice, stepped back a little. "Ah, no, it's not my hut," he said to himself. "The blacksmith doesn't come into my hut. Though, as I look it over, it is not the blacksmith's either. Whose place can it be? I know! I didn't recognize it! It's where lame Levchenko lives, who has lately married a young wife. His is the only hut that is like mine. I did think it was a little strange that I had reached home so soon. But Levchenko is at the sexton's now, I know that. Why is the blacksmith here . . . ? Ah, a-ha! he comes to see his young wife. So that's it! Good . . . ! Now I understand it all."

"Who are you and what are you hanging about at people's doors for?" said the blacksmith more grimly than before, coming closer to him.

"No, I am not going to tell him who I am," thought Chub. "I wouldn't be surprised if he gave me a good beating, the damned brute." And, disguising his voice, he answered: "It's me, good man! I have come for your pleasure, to sing carols under your windows."

"Go to hell with your carols!" Vakula shouted angrily. "Why are you standing there? Do you hear! Get out of here!"

Chub already had that prudent intention; but it annoyed him to be forced to obey the blacksmith's orders. It seemed as though some evil spirit nudged his arm and compelled him to say something contradictory. "Why are you screaming like that?" he said in the same voice. "I want to sing carols and that's all there is to it!"

"Aha! I see words aren't enough for you!" And with that Chub felt a very painful blow on his shoulder.

"So I see you are beginning to fight now!" he said, stepping back a little.

"Get away, get away!" shouted the blacksmith, giving Chub another shove.

"Well, you are the limit!" said Chub in a voice that betrayed pain, annoyance, and timidity. "You are fighting in earnest, I see, and hitting pretty hard, too."

"Get away, get away!" shouted the blacksmith, and slammed the door.

"Look, how he swaggered!" said Chub when he was left alone in the road. "Just try going near him! What a fellow! He's a somebody! Do you suppose I won't have the law on you? No, my dear boy, I am going straight to the commissar. I'll teach you! I don't care if you are a blacksmith and a painter. But I must look at my back and shoulders; I believe they are black and blue. The bastard must have hit hard. It's a pity that it is cold, and I don't want to take off my pelisse. You wait, you fiend of a blacksmith; may the devil give you a beating and your smithy, too; I'll make you dance! Ah, the damned rascal! But he is not at home, now. I expect Solokha is all alone. H'm . . . it's not far off, I might go! It's such weather now that no one will interrupt us. There's no saying what may happen. . . . Aie, how hard that damned blacksmith did hit!"

Here Chub, rubbing his back, started off in a different direction. The agreeable possibilities awaiting him in a tryst with Solokha eased the pain a little and made him insensible even to the frost, the crackling of which could be heard on all the roads in spite of the howling of the storm. At moments a look of mawkish sweetness came into his face, though the blizzard soaped his beard and mustaches with snow more briskly than any barber who tyrannically holds his victim by the nose. But if everything had not been hidden by the flying snow, Chub might have been seen long afterward stopping and rubbing his back as he said: "The damned blacksmith did hit hard!" and then going on his way again.

While the nimble dandy with the tail and goat-beard was flying out of the chimney and back again into the chimney, the pouch which hung on a shoulder-belt at his side, and in which he had put the stolen moon, chanced to catch in something in the stove and came open—and the moon took advantage of this accident to fly up through the chimney of Solokha's hut and to float smoothly through the sky. Everything was flooded with light. It was as though there had been no snowstorm. The snow sparkled, a broad silvery plain, studded with crystal stars. The frost seemed less cold. Groups of boys and girls appeared with sacks. Songs rang out, and under almost every hut window were crowds of carol singers.

How wonderful is the light of the moon! It is hard to put into words how pleasant it is on such a night to mingle in a group of singing, laughing girls and among boys ready for every jest and sport which the gaily smiling night can suggest. It is warm under the thick pelisse; the cheeks glow brighter than ever from the frost, and the devil himself prompts to mischief.

Groups of girls with sacks burst into Chub's hut and gathered around Oksana. The blacksmith was deafened by the shouts, the laughter, the stories. They fought with one another in telling the beauty some bit of news, in emptying their sacks and boasting of the little loaves, sausages, and curd dumplings of which they had already gathered a fair harvest from their singing. Oksana seemed to be highly pleased and delighted; she chatted first with one and then with another and laughed without ceasing.

With what envy and anger the blacksmith looked at this gaiety, and this time he cursed the carol singing, though he was passionately fond of it himself.

"Ah, Odarka!" said the lighthearted beauty, turning to one of the girls, "you have some new slippers. Ah, how pretty! And with gold on them! It's nice for you, Odarka, you have a man who will buy you anything, but I have no one to get me such splendid slippers."

"Don't grieve, my precious Oksana!" said the blacksmith. "I will get you slippers such as not many a lady wears."

"You!" said Oksana, with a quick and proud glance at him. "I should like to know where you'll get hold of slippers such as I could put on my feet. Perhaps you will bring me the very ones the Czarina[6] wears?"

"You see the sort she wants!" cried the crowd of girls, laughing.

"Yes!" the beauty went on proudly, "all of you be my witnesses: if the blacksmith Vakula brings me the very slippers the Czarina wears, here's my word on it: I'll marry him that very day."

The girls carried off the capricious beauty with them.

"Laugh away! Laugh away!" thought the blacksmith as he followed them out. "I laugh at myself! I wonder and can't think what I have done with my senses! She does not love me—well, let her go! As though there were no one in the world but Oksana. Thank God, there are lots of fine girls besides her in the village. And what is Oksana? She'll never make a good housewife; the only thing she is good at is dressing up. No, it's enough! It's time I gave up playing the fool!"

But at the very time when the blacksmith was making up his mind to be resolute, some evil spirit set floating before him the laughing image of Oksana saying mockingly, "Get me the Czarina's slippers, blacksmith, and I will marry you!" Everything within him was stirred and he could think of nothing but Oksana.

The crowds of carol singers, the boys in one party and the girls in another, hurried from one street to the next. But the blacksmith went on and saw nothing, and took no part in the merrymaking which he had once loved more than anything.

Meanwhile the devil was making love in earnest at Solokha's: he kissed her hand with the same airs and graces as the assessor does the priest's daughter's, put his hand on his heart, sighed, and said bluntly that, if she would not consent to gratify his passion and reward his devotion in the usual way, he was ready for anything: would fling himself in the water and let his soul go straight to hell. Solokha was not so cruel; besides, the devil, as we know, was alone with her. She was fond of seeing a crowd hanging about her and was rarely without company. That evening, however, she was expecting to spend alone, because all the noteworthy inhabitants of the village had been invited to keep Christmas Eve at the sexton's. But it turned out otherwise: the devil had only just urged his suit,

---

[6] Catherine II (1729-96); became empress in 1762, after her husband, Peter III, was dethroned by a conspiracy. (ed.)

when suddenly they heard a knock and the voice of the resolute mayor. Solokha ran to open the door, while the nimble devil crept into a sack that was lying on the floor.

The mayor, after shaking the snow off his cap and drinking a glass of vodka from Solokha's hand, told her that he had not gone to the sexton's because it had begun to snow, and seeing a light in her hut, had dropped in, meaning to spend the evening with her.

The mayor had hardly had time to say this when they heard a knock at the door and the voice of the sexton: "Hide me somewhere," whispered the mayor. "I don't want to meet him now."

Solokha thought for some time where to hide so bulky a visitor; at last she selected the biggest coalsack. She shot the coal out into a barrel, and the brave mayor, mustaches, head, pelisse, and all, crept into the sack.

The sexton walked in, clearing his throat and rubbing his hands, and told her that no one had come to his party and that he was heartily glad of this opportunity to enjoy a visit to her and was not afraid of the snowstorm. Then he went closer to her and, with a cough and a smirk, touched her plump bare arm with his long fingers and said with an air expressive both of slyness and satisfaction: "And what have you here, magnificent Solokha?" and saying this he stepped back a little.

"What do you mean? My arm, Osip Nikiforovich!" answered Solokha.

"H'm! your arm! He-he-he!" cried the sexton, highly delighted with his opening. And he paced up and down the room.

"And what have you here, incomparable Solokha . . . ?" he said with the same air, going up to her again, lightly touching her neck and skipping back again in the same way.

"As though you don't see, Osip Nikiforovich!" answered Solokha; "my neck and my necklace on my neck."

"H'm! A necklace on your neck! He-he-he!" and the sexton walked again up and down the room, rubbing his hands.

"And what have you here, incomparable Solokha . . . ?" There's no telling what the sexton (a carnal-minded man) might have touched next with his long fingers, when suddenly they heard a knock at the door and the voice of the Cossack Chub.

"Oh dear, someone who's not wanted!" cried the sexton in alarm. "What now if I am caught here, a person of my position . . . ! It will come to Father Kondrat's ears. . . ."

But the sexton's apprehensions were really of a different nature; he was more afraid that his doings might come to the knowledge of his better half, whose terrible hand had already turned his thick mane into a very scanty one. "For God's sake, virtuous Solokha!" he said, trembling all over, "your loving-kindness, as it says in the Gospel of St. Luke, chapter thirt . . . thirt . . . What a knocking, aie, what a knocking! Ough, hide me somewhere!"

Solokha turned the coal out of another sack, and the sexton, whose proportions were not too ample, crept into it and settled at the very bottom, so that another half-sack of coal might have been put in on top of him.

"Good evening, Solokha!" said Chub, as he came into the hut. "Maybe you didn't expect me, eh? You didn't, did you? Perhaps I am in the way . . . ?" Chub went on with a good-humored and significant expression on his face, which betrayed that his slow-moving mind was at work and preparing to utter some sarcastic and amusing jest.

"Maybe you had some entertaining companion here . . . ! Maybe you have someone in hiding already? Eh?" And enchanted by this observation of his, Chub laughed, inwardly triumphant at being the only man who enjoyed Solokha's favor. "Come, Solokha, let me have a drink of vodka now. I believe my throat's frozen stiff with this damned frost. God has sent us weather for Christmas Eve! How it has come on, do you hear, Solokha, how it has come on . . . ? Ah, my hands are stiff, I can't unbutton my sheepskin! How the storm has come on . . ."

"Open the door!" a voice rang out in the street, accompanied by a thump on the door.

"Someone is knocking," said Chub, standing still.

"Open!" the shout rang out louder still.

"It's the blacksmith!" cried Chub, grabbing his pelisse. "Solokha, put me where you like; for nothing in the world will I show myself to that damned brute. May he have a pimple as big as a pile of hay under each of his eyes, the bastard!"

Solokha, herself alarmed, flew about like one distraught and, forgetting what she was doing, gestured to Chub to creep into the very sack in which the sexton was already sitting. The poor sexton dared not betray his pain by a cough or a groan when the heavy Cossack sat down almost on his head and put a frozen boot on each side of his face.

The blacksmith walked in, not saying a word nor removing his cap, and almost fell down on the bench. It could be seen that he was in a very bad humor.

At the very moment when Solokha was shutting the door after him, someone knocked at the door again. This was the Cossack Sverbiguz. He could not be hidden in the sack, because no sack big enough could be found anywhere. He was fatter than the mayor and taller than Chub's neighbor Panas. And so Solokha led him into the garden to hear from him there all that he had to tell her.

The blacksmith looked absent-mindedly at the corners of his hut, listening from time to time to the voices of the carol singers floating far away through the village. At last his eyes rested on the sacks. "Why are those sacks lying there? They ought to have been cleared away long ago. This foolish love has made me stupid. Tomorrow's Christmas and trash of all sorts is still lying about the hut. I'll carry them to the smithy!"

The blacksmith stooped down to the huge sacks, tied them up more tightly, and prepared to hoist them on his shoulders. But it was evident that his thoughts were straying, God knows where, or he would have heard how Chub gasped when the hair of his head was twisted in the string that tied the sack and the brave mayor began hiccuping quite distinctly.

"Can nothing drive that wretched Oksana out of my head?" the blacksmith was saying. "I don't want to think about her; but I keep thinking and thinking and, as luck will have it, of her and nothing else. How is it that thoughts creep into the mind against the will? The devil! The sacks seem to have grown heavier than they were! Something besides coal must have been put into them. I am a fool! I forget that now everything seems heavier to me. In the old days I could bend and unbend a copper coin or a horseshoe with one hand, and now I can't lift sacks of coal. I shall be blown over by the wind next . . . No!" he cried, pulling himself together after a pause, "I am not a weak woman! I won't let anyone make an ass of me! If there were ten such sacks, I would lift them all." And he briskly hoisted on his shoulders the sacks which two strong men could not have carried. "I'll take this one too," he went on, picking up the little one at the bottom of which the devil lay curled up. "I believe I put my tools in this one." Saying this he went out of the hut whistling the song: "I Can't Be Bothered with a Wife."

The singing, laughter, and shouts sounded louder and louder in the streets. The crowds of jostling people were reinforced by newcomers from neighboring villages. The boys were full of mischief and wild pranks. Often among the carols some gay song was heard which one of the young Cossacks had made up on the spot. All at once one of the crowd would sing out a New Year's song instead of a carol and bawl at the top of his voice:

> Kind one, good one
> Give us a dumpling,
> A heap of *kasha*[7]
> And a ring of sausage!

A roar of laughter rewarded the wag. Little windows were thrown up and the withered hand of an old woman (the old women, together with the sedate fathers, were the only people left indoors) was thrust out with a sausage or a piece of pie.

The boys and the girls fought with one another in holding out their sacks and catching their booty. In one place the boys, coming together from all sides, surrounded a group of girls. There was loud noise and clamor; one flung a snowball, another pulled away a sack full of all sorts of good things. In another place, the girls caught a boy, gave him a kick, and sent him flying headlong with his sack into the snow. It seemed as though they were ready to make merry the whole night through. And, as though by design, the night was so splendidly warm. And the light of the moon seemed brighter still from the glitter of the snow.

The blacksmith stood still with his sacks. He thought he heard among the crowd of girls the voice and shrill laugh of Oksana. Every vein in his body throbbed; flinging the sacks on the ground so that the sexton at the bottom groaned over the bruise he received, and the mayor gave a loud hiccup, he strolled with the little sack on his shoulders together with a group of boys after a crowd of girls, among whom he heard the voice of Oksana.

"Yes, it is she! She stands like a queen, her black eyes sparkling. A handsome boy is telling her something. It must be amusing, for she is laughing. But she is always laughing." As it were unconsciously, he could not say how, the blacksmith squeezed his way through the crowd and stood beside her.

---

[7] Groats. (ed.)

"Oh, Vakula, you here! Good evening!" said the beauty, with a smile which almost drove Vakula mad. "Well, have you sung many carols? Oh, but what a little sack! And have you got the slippers that the Czarina wears? Get me the slippers and I will marry you . . . !" And laughing, she ran off with the other girls.

The blacksmith stood as though rooted to the spot. "No, I cannot bear it; it's too much for me . . ." he said at last. "But, my God, why is she so fiendishly beautiful? Her eyes, her words and everything, well, they scorch me, they fairly scorch me. . . . No, I cannot control myself. It's time to put an end to it all. Damn my soul, I'll go and drown myself in the hole in the ice and it will all be over!"

Then with a resolute step he walked on, caught up with the group of girls, overtook Oksana, and said in a firm voice: "Farewell, Oksana! Find any lover you like, make a fool of whom you like; but me you will not see again in this world."

The beauty seemed amazed and would have said something, but with a wave of his hand the blacksmith ran away.

"Where are you off to, Vakula?" said the boys, seeing the blacksmith running.

"Goodbye, friends!" the blacksmith shouted in answer. "Please God we shall meet again in the other world, but we shall not walk together again in this. Farewell! Do not remember evil of me! Tell Father Kondrat to sing a requiem mass for my sinful soul. Sinner that I am, for the sake of worldly things I did not finish painting the candles for the icons of the Martyr and the Virgin Mary. All the goods which will be found in my chest are for the Church. Farewell!"

Saying this, the blacksmith started running again with the sack upon his back.

"He has gone crazy!" said the boys.

"A lost soul!" an old woman, who was passing, muttered devoutly. "I must go and tell them that the blacksmith has hanged himself!"

Meanwhile, after running through several streets, Vakula stopped to catch his breath. "Where am I running?" he thought, "as though everything were over already. I'll try one way more: I'll go to the

Dnieper Cossack Puzaty[8] Patsyuk; they say he knows all the devils and can do anything he likes. I'll go to him, for my soul is lost anyway!"

At that the devil, who had lain for a long while without moving, skipped for joy in the sack; but the blacksmith, thinking that he had somehow twitched the sack with his hand and caused the movement himself, gave the sack a punch with his big fist and, shaking it on his shoulders, set off to Puzaty Patsyuk.

This Puzaty Patsyuk certainly at one time had been a Dnieper Cossack; but no one knew whether he had been turned out of the camp or whether he had run away from Zaporozhye of his own accord.

For a long time, ten years or perhaps fifteen, he had been living in Dikanka. At first he had lived like a true Dnieper Cossack: he had done no work, slept three-quarters of the day, eaten as much as six hay cutters, and drunk almost a whole pailful at a time. He had somewhere to put it all, however, for though Patsyuk was not very tall he was fairly bulky horizontally. Moreover, the trousers he used to wear were so full that, however long a step he took, no trace of his leg was visible, and it seemed as though a wine distiller's machine were moving down the street. Perhaps it was this that gave rise to his nickname, Puzaty. Before many weeks had passed after his coming to the village, everyone had found out that he was a wizard. If anyone were ill, he called in Patsyuk at once: Patsyuk had only to whisper a few words and it was as though the ailment had been lifted off by his hand. If it happened that a hungry gentleman was choked by a fishbone, Patsyuk could punch him so skillfully on the back that the bone went the proper way without causing any harm to the gentleman's throat. Of late years he was rarely seen anywhere. The reason for that was perhaps laziness, though possibly also the fact that it was every year becoming increasingly difficult for him to pass through a doorway. People had of late been obliged to go to him if they had need of him.

Not without some timidity, the blacksmith opened the door and saw Patsyuk sitting Turkish-fashion on the floor before a little tub on which stood a bowl of dumplings. This bowl stood as though purposely planned on a level with his mouth. Without moving a sin-

[8] "Paunchy." (ed.)

gle finger, he bent his head a little toward the bowl and sipped the soup, from time to time catching the dumplings with his teeth.

"Well," thought Vakula to himself, "this fellow's even lazier than Chub: he does eat with a spoon, at least, while this fellow won't even lift his hand!"

Patsyuk must have been entirely engrossed in the dumplings, for he seemed to be quite unaware of the entrance of the blacksmith, who offered him a very low bow as soon as he stepped on the threshold.

"I have come to ask you a favor, Patsyuk!" said Vakula, bowing again.

Puzaty Patsyuk lifted his head and again began swallowing dumplings.

"They say that you—no offense meant . . ." the blacksmith said, taking heart, "I speak of this not by way of any insult to you— that you are a little akin to the devil."

When he had uttered these words, Vakula was alarmed, thinking that he had expressed himself too bluntly and had not sufficiently softened his language; and, expecting that Patsyuk would pick up the tub together with the bowl and fling them straight at his head, he turned aside a little and covered his face with his sleeve so that the hot dumpling soup might not spatter it. But Patsyuk looked up and again began swallowing the dumplings.

The blacksmith, reassured, made up his mind to go on. "I have come to you, Patsyuk. God give you everything, goods of all sorts in abundance and bread in proportion!" (The blacksmith would sometimes throw in a fashionable word: he had got into the way of it during his stay in Poltava when he was painting the fence for the officer.) "There is nothing but ruin before me, a sinner! Nothing in the world will help! What will be, will be. I have to ask help from the devil himself. Well, Patsyuk," the blacksmith said, trying to break Patsyuk's silence, "what am I to do?"

"If you need the devil, then go to the devil," answered Patsyuk, not lifting his eyes to him, but still chewing away at the dumplings.

"It is for that that I have come to you," answered the blacksmith, offering him another bow. "I suppose that nobody in the world but you knows the way to him!"

Patsyuk answered not a word, but ate up the remaining dumplings. "Do me a kindness, good man, do not refuse me!" persisted the blacksmith. "Whether it is pork or sausage or buckwheat flour or linen, say—millet or anything else in case of need . . . as is usual between good people . . . we will not grudge it. Tell me at least how, for instance, to get on the road to him."

"He need not go far who has the devil on his shoulders!" Patsyuk pronounced carelessly, without changing his position.

Vakula fastened his eyes upon him as though the interpretation of those words were written on his brow. "What does he mean?" his face asked dumbly, while his mouth stood half-open ready to swallow the first word like a dumpling.

But Patsyuk was still silent.

Then Vakula noticed that there were neither dumplings nor a tub before him; but two wooden bowls were standing on the floor instead—one was filled with turnovers, the other with some cream. His thoughts and his eyes unconsciously fastened on these dainties. "Let us see," he said to himself, "how Patsyuk will eat the turnovers. He certainly won't want to bend down to lap them up like the dumplings; besides he couldn't—he must first dip the turnovers in the cream."

He had hardly time to think this when Patsyuk opened his mouth, looked at the turnovers, and opened his mouth wider still. At that moment a turnover popped out of the bowl, splashed into the cream, turned over on the other side, leaped upward, and flew straight into his mouth. Patsyuk ate it and opened his mouth again, and another turnover went through the same performance. The only trouble he took was to munch it up and swallow it.

"What a miracle!" thought the blacksmith, his mouth dropping open with surprise, and at the same moment he was aware that a turnover was creeping toward him and was already smearing his mouth with cream. Pushing away the turnover and wiping his lips, the blacksmith began to reflect what marvels there are in the world and to what subtle devices the evil spirit may lead a man, saying to himself at the same time that no one but Patsyuk could help him.

"I'll bow to him once more; maybe he will explain properly. . . . He's a devil, though! Why, today is a fast day and he is eating turnovers with meat in them! What a fool I am, really. I am standing here and preparing to sin! Back . . . !" And the pious blacksmith ran headlong out of the hut.

But the devil, sitting in the sack and already gloating over his prey, could not endure letting such a glorious capture slip through his fingers. As soon as the blacksmith put down the sack the devil skipped out of it and straddled his neck.

A cold shudder ran over the blacksmith's skin; pale and scared, he did not know what to do; he was on the point of crossing himself. . . . But the devil, putting his snout down to Vakula's right ear, said: "It's me, your friend; I'll do anything for a friend and comrade! I'll give you as much money as you like," he squeaked into his left ear. "Oksana shall be yours this very day," he whispered, turning his snout again to the right ear. The blacksmith stood still, hesitating.

"Very well," he said at last; "for such a price I am ready to be yours!"

The devil clasped his hands in delight and began galloping up and down on the blacksmith's neck. "Now the blacksmith is done for!" he thought to himself: "now I'll pay you back, my sweet fellow, for all your paintings and false tales thrown up at the devils! What will my comrades say now when they learn that the most pious man of the whole village is in my hands!"

Here the devil laughed with joy, thinking how he would taunt all the long-tailed crew in hell, how furious the lame devil, who was considered the most resourceful among them, would be.

"Well, Vakula!" piped the devil, not dismounting from his neck, as though afraid he might escape, "you know nothing is done without a contract."

"I am ready!" said the blacksmith. "I have heard that among you contracts are signed with blood. Wait. I'll get a nail out of my pocket!"

And he put his hand behind him and caught the devil by the tail.

"What a man you are for a joke!" cried the devil, laughing. "Come, let go, that's enough mischief!"

"Wait a minute, friend!" cried the blacksmith, "and what do you think of this?" As he said that he made the sign of the cross and the devil became as meek as a lamb. "Wait a minute," said the blacksmith, pulling him by the tail to the ground: "I'll teach you to entice good men and honest Christians into sin."

Here the blacksmith leaped on the devil and lifted his hand to make the sign of the cross.

"Have mercy, Vakula!" the devil moaned piteously; "I will do anything you want, anything; only let me off with my life: do not lay the terrible cross upon me!"

"Ah, so that's your tone now, you damned German! Now I know what to do. Carry me at once on your back! Do you hear? And fly like a bird!"

"Where?" asked the miserable devil.

"To Petersburg, straight to the Czarina!" And the blacksmith almost fainted with terror as he felt himself soaring into the air.

Oksana stood for a long time pondering on the strange words of the blacksmith. Already an inner voice was telling her that she had treated him too cruelly. "What if he really does make up his mind to do something dreadful! I wouldn't be surprised! Perhaps his sorrow will make him fall in love with another girl, and in his anger he will begin calling her the greatest beauty in the village. But no, he loves me. I am so beautiful! He will not give me up for anything; he is playing, he is pretending. In ten minutes he will come back to look at me, for certain. I really was angry. I must, as though it were against my will, let him kiss me. Won't he be delighted!" And the frivolous beauty went back to jesting with her companions.

"Stop," said one of them, "the blacksmith has forgotten his sacks: look what fat sacks! He has made more by his carol singing than we have. I bet they must have put here at least a quarter of a sheep, and I am sure that there are no end of sausages and loaves in them. Wonderful! we shall have enough to feast on all Christmas week!"

"Are they the blacksmith's sacks?" asked Oksana. "We had better drag them to my hut and have a good look at what he has put in them."

All the girls laughingly approved of this proposal.

"But we can't lift them!" the whole group cried, trying to move the sacks.

"Wait a minute," said Oksana; "let us run for a sled and take them away on it!"

And the crowd of girls ran out to get a sled.

The captives were terribly bored with staying in the sacks, although the sexton had poked a fair-sized hole to peep through. If there had been no one about, he might have found a way to creep out; but to creep out of a sack in front of everybody, to be a laughingstock . . . that thought restrained him, and he made up his mind to wait, only uttering a slight groan under Chub's ill-mannered boots.

Chub himself was no less eager for freedom, feeling that there

was something under him that was terribly uncomfortable to sit
upon. But as soon as he heard his daughter's plan, he felt relieved
and did not want to creep out, reflecting that it must be at least a
hundred paces and perhaps two hundred to his hut; if he crept out,
he would have to rearrange himself, button up his sheepskin, fasten
his belt—such a lot of trouble! Besides, his winter cap had been left
at Solokha's. Let the girls drag him in the sled.

But things turned out not at all as Chub was expecting. Just
when the girls were running to fetch the sled, his lean neighbor,
Panas, came out of the tavern, upset and ill-humored. The woman
who kept the tavern could not be persuaded to serve him on credit.
He thought to sit on in the tavern in the hope that some godly gentleman would come along and treat him; but as ill-luck would have
it, all the gentlefolk were staying at home and like good Christians
were eating rice and honey in the bosom of their families. Meditat-
ing on the degeneration of manners and the hard heart of the Jewess who kept the tavern, Panas made his way up to the sacks and
stopped in amazement. "My word, what sacks somebody has flung
down in the road!" he said, looking about him in all directions. "I'll
bet there is pork in them. Some carol singer is in luck to get so
many gifts of all sorts! What fat sacks! Suppose they are only
stuffed full of buckwheat cake and biscuits, that's worth having; if
there should be nothing but biscuits in them, that would be welcome, too; the Jewess would give me a dram of vodka for each
cake. Let's make haste and get them away before anyone sees."

Here he flung on his shoulder the sack with Chub and the sexton
in it, but felt it was too heavy. "No, it'll be too heavy for one to
carry," he said; "and here by good luck comes the weaver Shap-
uvalenko. Good evening, Ostap!"

"Good evening!" said the weaver, stopping.

"Where are you going?"

"Oh, nowhere in particular."

"Help me carry these sacks, good man! Someone has been singing carols, and has dropped them in the middle of the road. We'll
share the things."

"Sacks? sacks of what? White loaves or biscuits?"

"Oh, all sorts of things, I expect."

They hurriedly pulled some sticks out of the fence, laid the sack
on them, and carried it on their shoulders.

"Where shall we take it? To the tavern?" the weaver asked on the way.

"That's just what I was thinking; but, you know, the damned Jewess won't trust us, she'll think we have stolen it somewhere; besides, I have only just come from the tavern. We'll take it to my hut. No one will hinder us there; the wife's not at home."

"Are you sure she is not at home?" the cautious weaver inquired.

"Thank God that I am not quite a fool yet," said Panas; "the devil would hardly take me where she is. I'm sure she will be trailing around with the other women till daybreak."

"Who is there?" shouted Panas' wife, opening the door of the hut as she heard the noise in the porch made by the two friends with the sack. Panas was dumbfounded.

"Well, that's it!" said the weaver, letting his hands fall.

Panas' wife was a treasure of a kind that is not uncommon in this world. Like her husband, she hardly ever stayed at home, but almost every day visited various cronies and well-to-do old women, flattered them, and ate with good appetite at their expense; she only quarreled with her husband in the mornings, as it was only then that she sometimes saw him. Their hut was twice as old as the district clerk's trousers; there was no straw in places on their thatched roof. Only the remnants of a fence could be seen, for everyone, as he went out of his house, thought it unnecessary to take a stick for the dogs, relying on passing by Panas' vegetable garden and pulling one out of his fence. The stove was not heated for three days at a time. Whatever the tender wife managed to beg from good Christians she hid as far as possible out of her husband's reach, and often robbed him of his gains if he had not had time to spend them on drink. In spite of his habitual imperturbability Panas did not like to give way to her, and consequently left his house every day with both eyes blackened, while his better half, sighing and groaning, waddled off to tell her old friends of her husband's unmannerliness and the blows she had to put up with from him.

Now you can imagine how disconcerted were the weaver and Panas by this unexpected apparition. Dropping the sack, they stood before it, and concealed it with the skirts of their coats, but it was already too late: Panas' wife, though she did not see well with her old eyes, had observed the sack.

"Well, that's good!" she said, with a face which betrayed the

joy of a vulture. "That's good, that you have gained so much singing carols! That's how it always is with good Christians; but no,
I'm sure you have stolen it somewhere. Show me your sack at once,
do you hear, show me this very minute!"

"The bald devil may show you, but we won't," said Panas, assuming a dignified air.

"What's it to do with you?" said the weaver. "We've sung the
carols, not you."

"Yes, you will show me, you wretched drunkard!" screamed the
wife, striking her tall husband on the chin with her fist and forcing
her way toward the sack. But the weaver and Panas manfully defended the sack and compelled her to beat a retreat. Before they recovered themselves the wife ran out again with a poker in her
hands. She nimbly hit her husband a blow on the arms and the
weaver one on his back and reached for the sack.

"Why did we let her pass?" said the weaver, regaining his senses.

"Yes, we let her pass! Why did you let her pass?" said Panas
coolly.

"Your poker is made of iron, it seems!" said the weaver after a
brief silence, rubbing his back. "My wife bought one last year at
the fair, gave twenty-five kopeks; that one's all right . . . it doesn't
hurt . . ."

Meanwhile the triumphant wife, setting a lamp on the floor, untied the sack and peeped into it.

But her old eyes, which had so well described the sack, this time
certainly deceived her.

"Oh, but there is a whole pig lying here!" she shrieked, clapping
her hands in glee.

"A pig! Do you hear, a whole pig!" The weaver nudged Panas.
"And it's all your fault."

"It can't be helped!" replied Panas, shrugging his shoulders.

"Can't be helped! Why are we standing still? Let us take away the
sack! Here, come on! Go away, go away, it's our pig!" shouted the
weaver, stepping forward.

"Move away, move away, you devilish woman! It's not your
property!" said Panas, approaching.

His wife picked up the poker again, but at that moment Chub
crawled out of the sack and stood in the middle of the room,
stretching like a man who has just waked up from a long sleep.

Panas' wife shrieked, slapping her skirts, and they all stood with open mouths.

"Why did she say it was a pig, the ass! It's not a pig!" said Panas, staring open-eyed.

"God! What a man has been dropped into a sack!" said the weaver, staggering back in alarm. "You may say what you please, you can burst if you like, but the foul fiend has had a hand in it. Why, he would not go through a window!"

"It's Chub!" cried Panas, looking more closely.

"Why, who did you think it was?" said Chub, laughing. "Well, haven't I played you a fine trick? I'll bet you meant to eat me as pork! Wait a minute, I'll console you: there is something in the sack; if not a whole pig, it's certainly a little porker or some live beast. Something kept moving under me."

The weaver and Panas flew to the sack, the lady of the house clutched at the other side of it, and the battle would have been renewed had not the sexton, seeing that now he had no chance of concealment, scrambled out of the sack of his own accord.

The woman, astounded, let go of the leg by which she was beginning to drag the sexton out of the sack.

"Here's another of them!" cried the weaver in horror, "the devil knows what has happened to the world. . . . My head's going around. . . . Men are put into sacks instead of cakes or sausages!"

"It's the sexton!" said Chub, more surprised than any of them. "Well, then! You're a nice one, Solokha! To put one in a sack . . . I thought at the time her hut was very full of sacks. . . . Now I understand it all: she had a couple of men hidden in each sack. While I thought it was only me she . . . So now you know her!"

The girls were a little surprised on finding that one sack was missing.

"Well, there is nothing we can do, we must be content with this one," murmured Oksana.

The mayor made up his mind to keep quiet, reasoning that if he called out to them to untie the sack and let him out, the foolish girls would run away in all directions; they would think that the devil was in the sack—and he would be left in the street till next day. Meanwhile the girls, linking arms together, flew like a whirlwind with the sled over the crunching snow. Many of them sat on the sled for fun; others even clambered on top of the mayor. The mayor made up his mind to endure everything.

At last they arrived, threw open the door into the outer room of the hut, and dragged in the sack amid laughter.

"Let us see what is in it," they all cried, hastening to untie it.

At this point the hiccup which had tormented the mayor became so much worse that he began hiccuping and coughing loudly.

"Ah, there is someone in it!" they all shrieked, and rushed out of doors in horror.

"What the devil is it? Where are you tearing off to as though you were all possessed?" said Chub, walking in at the door.

"Oh, Daddy!" cried Oksana, "there is someone in the sack!"

"In the sack? Where did you get this sack?"

"The blacksmith threw it in the middle of the road," they all said at once.

"So that's it; didn't I say so?" Chub thought to himself. "What are you frightened at? Let us look. Come now, my man—I beg you won't be offended at our not addressing you by your proper name —crawl out of the sack!"

The mayor did crawl out.

"Oh!" shrieked the girls.

"So the mayor got into one, too," Chub thought to himself in bewilderment, scanning him from head to foot. "Well, I'll be damned!" He could say nothing more.

The mayor himself was no less confused and did not know how to begin. "I think it is a cold night," he said, addressing Chub.

"There is a bit of a frost," answered Chub. "Allow me to ask you what you rub your boots with, goose fat or tar?" He had not meant to say that; he had meant to ask: "How did you get into that sack, mayor?" and he did not himself understand how he came to say something utterly different.

"Tar is better," said the mayor. "Well, good night, Chub!" And pulling his winter cap down over his head, he walked out of the hut.

"Why was I such a fool as to ask him what he rubbed his boots with?" said Chub, looking toward the door by which the mayor had gone out.

"Well, Solokha is a fine one! To put a man like that in a sack . . . ! My word, she is a devil of a woman! While I, poor fool . . . But where is that damned sack?"

"I flung it in the corner, there is nothing more in it," said Oksana.

"I know all about that; nothing in it, indeed! Give it here; there is another one in it! Shake it well . . . What, nothing? My word, the cursed woman! And to look at her she is like a saint, as though she had never tasted anything but lenten fare . . . !"

But we will leave Chub to pour out his anger at leisure and will go back to the blacksmith, for it must be past eight o'clock.

At first it seemed dreadful to Vakula, particularly when he rose up from the earth to such a height that he could see nothing below, and flew like a fly so close under the moon that if he had not bent down he would have caught his cap in it. But in a little while he gained confidence and even began mocking the devil. (He was extremely amused by the way the devil sneezed and coughed when he took the little cyprus-wood cross off his neck and held it down to him. He purposely raised his hand to scratch his head, and the devil, thinking he was going to make the sign of the cross over him, flew along more swiftly than ever.) It was quite light at that height. The air was transparent, bathed in a light silvery mist. Everything was visible, and he could even see a sorcerer whisk by them like a hurricane, sitting in a pot, and the stars gathering together to play hide-and-seek, a whole swarm of spirits whirling away in a cloud, a devil dancing in the light of the moon and taking off his cap at the sight of the blacksmith galloping by, a broom flying back home, from which evidently a witch had just alighted at her destination. . . . And they met many other nasty things. They all stopped at the sight of the blacksmith to stare at him for a moment, and then whirled off and went on their way again. The blacksmith flew on till all at once Petersburg flashed before him, glittering with lights. (For a certain reason the city was illuminated that day.) The devil, flying over the city gate, turned into a horse and the blacksmith found himself mounted on a fiery steed in the middle of the street.

My goodness! the clatter, the uproar, the brilliant light; the walls rose up, four stories on each side; the thud of the horses' hoofs and the rumble of the wheels echoed and resounded from every quarter; houses seemed to pop up out of the ground at every step; the bridges trembled; carriages raced along; sled drivers and postilions shouted; the snow crunched under the thousand sleds flying from all parts; people passing along on foot huddled together, crowded under the houses which were studded with little lamps, and their immense shadows flitted over the walls with their heads reaching the roofs and the chimneys.

The blacksmith looked about him in amazement. It seemed to him as though all the houses had fixed their innumerable fiery eyes upon him, watching. Good Lord! he saw so many gentlemen in cloth fur-lined overcoats that he did not know whom to take off his cap to. "Good God, how many gentlemen are here!" thought the blacksmith. "I think everyone who comes along the street in a fur coat is the assessor and again the assessor! And those who are driving about in such wonderful chaises with glass windows, if they are not police captains they certainly must be commissars or perhaps something even more important." His words were cut short by a question from the devil:

"Am I to go straight to the Czarina?"

"No, I'm frightened," thought the blacksmith. "The Dnieper Cossacks, who marched in the autumn through Dikanka, are stationed here, where I don't know. They came from the camp with papers for the Czarina; anyway, I might ask their advice. Hey, Satan! creep into my pocket and take me to the Dnieper Cossacks."

And in one minute the devil became so thin and small that he had no difficulty creeping into the blacksmith's pocket. And before Vakula had time to look around he found himself in front of a big house, went up a staircase, hardly knowing what he was doing, opened a door, and drew back a little from the brilliant light on seeing the smartly furnished room; but he regained confidence a little when he recognized the Cossacks who had ridden through Dikanka and now, sitting on silk-covered sofas, their tar-smeared boots tucked under them, were smoking the strongest tobacco, usually called "root."

"Good day to you, gentlemen! God be with you, this is where we meet again," said the blacksmith, going up to them and tossing off a low bow.

"What man is that?" the one who was sitting just in front of the blacksmith asked another who was further away.

"You don't know me?" said the blacksmith. "It's me, Vakula the blacksmith! When you rode through Dikanka in the autumn you stayed nearly two days with me. God give you all health and long years! And I put a new iron hoop on the front wheel of your chaise!"

"Oh!" said the same Cossack, "it's that blacksmith who paints so well. Good day to you, neighbor! How has God brought you here?"

"Oh, I just wanted to have a look around. I was told . . ."

"Well, neighbor," said the Cossack, drawing himself up with dignity and wishing to show he could speak Russian too, "well, it's a big city."

The blacksmith, too, wanted to preserve his reputation and not to seem like a novice. Moreover, as we have had occasion to see before, he too could speak as if from a book.

"A considerable town!" he answered casually. "There is no denying the houses are very large, the pictures that are hanging up are uncommonly good. Many of the houses are painted exuberantly with letters in gold leaf. The configuration is superb, there is no other word for it!"

The Dnieper Cossacks, hearing the blacksmith express himself in such a manner, drew the most flattering conclusions in regard to him.

"We will have a little more talk with you, neighbor; now we are going at once to the Czarina."

"To the Czarina? Oh, be so kind, gentlemen, as to take me with you!"

"You?" a Cossack pronounced in the tone in which an old man speaks to his four-year-old charge when the latter asks to be seated on a real, big horse. "What would you do there? No, we can't do that. We are going to talk about our own affairs to the Czarina." And his face assumed an expression of great significance.

"Please take me!" the blacksmith persisted.

"Ask them to!" he whispered softly to the devil, banging on the pocket with his fist.

He had hardly said this, when another Cossack said: "Let's take him, friends!"

"Yes, let's take him!" others joined in.

"Put on the same clothing as we are wearing, then."

The blacksmith was hastily putting on a green coat when all at once the door opened and a man covered with gold braid said it was time to go.

Again the blacksmith was moved to wonder, as he was whisked along in an immense coach swaying on springs, as four-storied houses raced by him on both sides and the rumbling pavement seemed to be moving under the horses' hoofs.

"My goodness, how light it is!" thought the blacksmith to himself. "At home it is not so light as this in the daytime."

The coaches stopped in front of the palace. The Cossacks got out, went into a magnificent vestibule, and began ascending a brilliantly lighted staircase.

"What a staircase!" the blacksmith murmured to himself, "it's a pity to trample it with one's feet. What decorations! They say the stories are untrue! The devil they are! My goodness! what banisters, what workmanship! At least fifty rubles must have been spent on the iron alone!"

When they had mounted the stairs, the Cossacks walked through the first drawing room. The blacksmith followed them timidly, afraid of slipping on the parquet at every footstep. They walked through three drawing rooms, the blacksmith still overwhelmed with admiration. On entering the fourth, he could not help going up to a picture hanging on the wall. It was the Holy Virgin with the Child in her arms.

"What a picture! What a wonderful painting!" he thought. "It seems to be speaking! It seems to be alive! And the Holy Child! It's pressing its little hands together and laughing, poor thing! And the colors! My goodness, what colors! I think there is not a kopek-worth of ochre on it; it's all emerald green and crimson lake. And the blue simply glows! A fine piece of work! I'm sure the background was put in with the most expensive white lead. Wonderful as that painting is, though, this copper handle," he went on, going up to the door and fingering the lock, "is even more wonderful. Ah, what a fine finish! That's all done, I imagine, by German blacksmiths, and it must be terribly expensive."

Perhaps the blacksmith would have gone on reflecting for a long time, if a flunkey in livery had not nudged his arm and reminded him not to lag behind the others. The Cossacks passed through two more rooms and then stopped. They were told to wait in the third, in which there was a group of several generals in gold-braided uniforms. The Cossacks bowed in all directions and stood together.

A minute later, a rather thickset man of majestic stature, wearing the uniform of a Hetman and yellow boots, walked in, accompanied by a retinue. His hair was in disorder, he squinted a little, his face wore an expression of haughty dignity, and the habit of command could be seen in every movement. All the generals, who had been walking up and down rather superciliously in their gold uniforms, bustled about and seemed with low bows to be hanging on every word he uttered and even on his slightest gesture, so as to fly at once to carry out his wishes. But the Hetman did not even notice all that: he barely nodded to them and went up to the Cossacks.

The Cossacks all bowed low, to the ground.

"Are you all here?" he asked deliberately, speaking a little through his nose.

"All, little father!" answered the Cossacks, bowing again.

"Don't forget to speak as I have told you!"

"No, little father, we will not forget."

"Is that the Czar?" asked the blacksmith of one of the Cossacks.

"Czar, indeed! It's Potiomkin[9] himself," answered the other.

Voices were heard in the other room, and the blacksmith did not know which way to look for the number of ladies who walked in, wearing satin gowns with long trains, and courtiers in gold-laced coats with their hair tied in a tail at the back. He could see a blur of brilliance and nothing more.

The Cossacks all bowed down at once to the floor and cried out with one voice: "Have mercy, little mother, mercy!"

The blacksmith, too, though seeing nothing, stretched himself very zealously on the floor.

"Get up!" An imperious and at the same time pleasant voice sounded above them. Some of the courtiers bustled about and nudged the Cossacks.

"We will not get up, little mother! We will not get up! We will die, but we will not get up!" they shouted.

Potiomkin bit his lips. At last he went up himself and whispered sternly to one of the Cossacks. They rose to their feet.

Then the blacksmith, too, ventured to raise his head, and saw standing before him a short and, indeed, rather stout woman with blue eyes, and at the same time with that majestically smiling air which was so well able to subdue everything and could only belong to a queen.

---

[9] Grigory Aleksandrovich Potiomkin (1739-91), of a noble but impoverished Polish family, attracted the notice of Catherine II while serving in the Russian army, and in 1774 became her recognized favorite, and, in fact, directed Russian policy. (ed.)

"His Excellency has promised to make me acquainted today with my people whom I have not seen before," said the lady with the blue eyes, scrutinizing the men with curiosity.

"Are you well cared for here?" she went on, going nearer to them.

"Thank you, little mother! The provisions they give us are excellent, though the mutton here is not at all like what we have in Zaporozhye . . . What does our daily fare matter . . . ?"

Potiomkin frowned, seeing that the Cossacks were saying something quite different from what he had taught them. . . .

One of them, drawing himself up with dignity, stepped forward:

"Be gracious, little mother! How have your faithful people angered you? Have we taken the hand of the vile Tartar? Have we come to agreement with the Turk? Have we been false to you in deed or in thought? How have we lost your favor? First we heard that you were commanding fortresses to be built everywhere against us; then we heard you mean to turn us into carbineers; now we hear of new oppressions. How are your Zaporozhye troops in fault? In having brought your army across the Perekop and helped your generals to slaughter the Tartars in the Crimea . . . ?"

Potiomkin casually rubbed with a little brush the diamonds with which his hands were studded and said nothing.

"What is it you want?" Catherine asked anxiously.

The Cossacks looked meaningly at one another.

"Now is the time! The Czarina asks what we want!" the blacksmith said to himself, and he suddenly flopped down on the floor.

"Your Imperial Majesty, do not command me to be punished! Show me mercy! Of what, be it said without offense to your Imperial Graciousness, are the little slippers made that are on your feet? I think there is no Swede nor a shoemaker in any kingdom in the world who can make them like that. Merciful heavens, if only my wife could wear such slippers!"

The Empress laughed. The courtiers laughed too. Potiomkin frowned and smiled at the same time. The Cossacks began nudging the blacksmith under the arm, wondering whether he had not gone out of his mind.

"Stand up!" the Empress said graciously. "If you wish to have slippers like these, it is very easy to arrange it. Bring him at once the very best slippers with gold on them! Indeed, this simpleheartedness greatly pleases me! Here you have a subject worthy of your witty pen!" the Empress went on, turning to a gentleman with a full but rather pale face, who stood a little apart from the others and whose modest coat with big mother-of-pearl buttons on it showed that he was not one of the courtiers.

"You are too gracious, your Imperial Majesty. It needs a La Fontaine[10] at least to do justice to it!" answered the man with the mother-of-pearl buttons, bowing.

"I tell you sincerely, I have not yet got over my delight at your *Brigadier*.[11] You read so wonderfully well! I have heard, though," the Empress went on, turning again to the Cossacks, "that none of you are married in your camp." [12]

"What next, little mother! Why, you know yourself, a man cannot live without a wife," answered the same Cossack who had talked to the blacksmith, and the blacksmith wondered, hearing him address the Czarina, as though purposely, in coarse language, speaking like a peasant, as it is commonly called, though he could speak as if from a book.

"They are sly fellows!" he thought to himself. "I'll bet he does not do that for nothing."

"We are not monks," the Cossack went on, "but sinful folk. Ready like all honest Christians to fall into sin. There are among us many who have wives, but do not live with them in the camp. There are some who have wives in Poland; there are some who have wives in the Ukraine; there are some who have wives even in Turkey."

At that moment they brought the blacksmith the slippers.

"God, what fine embroidery!" he cried joyfully, taking the slippers. "Your Imperial Majesty! If the slippers on your feet are like this—and in them Your Honor, I expect, goes skating on the ice—what must the feet themselves be like! They must be made of pure sugar at least, I should think!"

The Empress, who had in fact very well-shaped and charming. feet, could not help smiling at hearing such a compliment from the

---

[10] French poet (1621-95); author of popular fables. (ed.)

[11] She is speaking to Denis Fonvizin (1744-92). *Brigadier* is his famous comedy. (ed.)

[12] *Sech*, Cossack military camp established in a clearing near the Dnieper River. A full description of a *sech* is given in *Taras Bu̇ba.* (ed.)

lips of a simplehearted blacksmith, who in his Dnieper Cossack uniform might be considered a handsome fellow in spite of his swarthy face.

Delighted with such gracious attention, the blacksmith would have liked to question the pretty Czarina thoroughly about everything: whether it was true that Czars eat nothing but honey, fat bacon, and such; but, feeling that the Cossacks were digging him in the ribs, he made up his mind to keep quiet. And when the Empress, turning to the older men, began questioning them about their manner of life and customs in the camp, he, stepping back, stooped down to his pocket, and said softly: "Get me away from here, quickly!" And at once he found himself outside the city gates.

"He is drowned! I swear he is drowned! May I never leave this spot if he is not drowned!" lisped the weaver's fat wife, standing with a group of Dikanka women in the middle of the street.

"Why, am I a liar, then? Have I stolen anyone's cow? Have I put the evil eye on someone, that I am not to be believed?" shouted a purple-nosed woman in a Cossack coat, waving her arms. "May I never want to drink water again if old Dame Pereperchikha didn't see with her own eyes the blacksmith hanging himself!"

"Has the blacksmith hanged himself? Well, I never!" said the mayor, coming out of Chub's hut, and he stopped and pressed closer to the group.

"You had better say, may you never want to drink vodka, you old drunkard!" answered the weaver's wife. "He must be as crazy as you to hang himself! He drowned himself! He drowned himself in the hole in the ice! I know that as well as I know that you were in the tavern just now."

"You disgrace! See what she throws up at me!" the woman with the purple nose retorted wrathfully. "You had better hold your tongue, you wretch! Do you think I don't know that the sexton comes to see you every evening?"

The weaver's wife flared up.

"What about the sexton? Whom does he go to? What lies are you telling?"

"The sexton?" piped the sexton's wife, squeezing her way up to the combatants, in an old blue cotton coat lined with hareskin. "I'll let the sexton know! Who was it said the sexton?"

"Well, this is the lady the sexton visits!" said the woman with the purple nose, pointing to the weaver's wife.

"So it's you, you bitch!" said the sexton's wife, stepping up to the weaver's wife. "So it's you, is it, witch, who cast a spell over him and gave him foul poison to make him come to you!"

"Get behind me, Satan!" said the weaver's wife, staggering back.

"Oh, you cursed witch, may you never live to see your children! Wretched creature! Tfoo!"

Here the sexton's wife spat straight into the other woman's face.

The weaver's wife tried to do the same, but spat instead on the unshaven chin of the mayor, who had come close to the combatants so that he might hear the quarrel better.

"Ah, nasty woman!" cried the mayor, wiping his face with the skirt of his coat and lifting his whip.

This gesture sent them all flying in different directions, cursing loudly.

"How disgusting!" repeated the mayor, still wiping his face. "So the blacksmith is drowned! My goodness! What a fine painter he was! What good knives and reaping hooks and plows he could forge! What a strong man he was! Yes," he went on musing; "there are not many fellows like that in our village. To be sure, I did notice while I was in that damned sack that the poor fellow was very much depressed. So that is the end of the blacksmith! He was and is not! And I was meaning to have my dapple mare shod . . . !" And filled with such Christian reflections, the mayor quietly made his way to his own hut.

Oksana was much troubled when the news reached her. She put little faith in the woman Pereperchikha's having seen it and in the women's talk; she knew that the blacksmith was too pious a man to bring himself to send his soul to perdition. But what if he really had gone away, intending never to return to the village? And, indeed, in any place it would be hard to find as fine a fellow as the blacksmith. And how he had loved her! He had endured her whims longer than any one of them. . . . All night long the beauty turned over from her right side to her left and her left to her right, and could not fall asleep. Naked, she tossed sensuously in the darkness of her room. She reviled herself almost aloud; grew peaceful; made up her mind to think of nothing—and kept thinking all the time. She was in a perfect fever, and by the morning head over ears in love with the blacksmith.

Chub expressed neither pleasure nor sorrow at Vakula's fate. His thoughts were absorbed by one subject: he could not forget the treachery of Solokha and never stopped abusing her even in his sleep.

Morning came. Even before daybreak the church was full of people. Elderly women in white linen wimples, in white cloth tunics, crossed themselves piously at the church porch. Ladies in green and yellow blouses, some even in dark blue overdresses with gold streamers behind, stood in front of them. Girls who had a whole shopful of ribbons twined on their heads, and necklaces, crosses, and coins around their necks, tried to make their way closer to the icon-stand. But in front of all stood the gentlemen and humble peasants with mustaches, with forelocks, with thick necks and newly shaven chins, for the most part wearing hooded cloaks, below which peeped a white or sometimes a dark blue jacket. Wherever one looked every face had a festive air. The mayor was licking his lips in anticipation of the sausage with which he would break his fast; the girls were thinking how they would skate with the boys on the ice; the old women murmured prayers more zealously than ever. All over the church one could hear the Cossack Sverbiguz bowing to the ground. Only Oksana stood feeling unlike herself: she prayed without praying. So many different feelings, each more amazing, each more distressing than the other, crowded upon her heart that her face expressed nothing but overwhelming confusion; tears quivered in her eyes. The girls could not think why it was and did not suspect that the blacksmith was responsible. However, not only Oksana was concerned about the blacksmith. All the villagers observed that the holiday did not seem like a holiday, that something was lacking. To make things worse, the sexton was hoarse after his travels in the sack and he wheezed scarcely audibly; it is true that the chorister who was on a visit to the village sang the bass splendidly, but how much better it would have been if they had had the blacksmith too, who used always when they were singing *Our Father* or the *Holy Cherubim* to step up into the choir and from there sing it with the same chant with which it is sung in Poltava. Moreover, he alone performed the duty of a churchwarden. Matins were already over; after matins mass was over. . . . Where indeed could the blacksmith have vanished to?

It was still night as the devil flew even more swiftly back with the blacksmith, and in a flash Vakula found himself inside his own hut. At that moment the cock crowed.

"Where are you off to?" cried the blacksmith, catching the devil by his tail as he was about to run away. "Wait a moment, friend, that's not all: I haven't thanked you yet." Then, seizing a switch, he gave him three lashes, and the poor devil started running like a peasant who has just had a beating from the tax assessor. And so, instead of tricking, tempting, and fooling others, the enemy of mankind was fooled himself. After that Vakula went into the outer room, made himself a hole in the hay, and slept till dinner-time. When he woke up he was frightened at seeing that the sun was already high. "I've overslept myself and missed matins and mass!"

Then the worthy blacksmith was overwhelmed with distress, thinking that no doubt God, as a punishment for his sinful intention of damning his soul, had sent this heavy sleep, which had prevented him from even being in church on this solemn holiday. However, comforting himself with the thought that next week he would confess all this to the priest and that from that day he would begin making fifty genuflections a day for a whole year, he glanced into the hut; but there was no one there. Apparently Solokha had not yet returned.

Carefully he drew out from the breast of his coat the slippers and again marveled at the costly workmanship and at the wonderful adventure of the previous night. He washed and dressed himself in his best, put on the very clothes which he had got from the Dnieper Cossacks, took out of a chest a new cap of good astrakhan with a dark blue top not once worn since he had bought it while staying in Poltava; he also took out a new girdle of rainbow colors; he put all this together with a whip in a kerchief and set off straight to see Chub.

Chub opened his eyes wide when the blacksmith walked into his hut, and did not know what to wonder at most: the blacksmith's having risen from the dead, the blacksmith's having dared to come to see him, or the blacksmith's being dressed up as such a dandy, like a Dnieper Cossack. But he was even more astonished when Vakula untied the kerchief and laid before him a new cap and a girdle such as had never been seen in the village, and then fell down on his knees before him, and said in a tone of entreaty: "Have mercy, father! Be not angry! Here is a whip; beat me as much as your heart may desire. I give myself up, I repent of everything! Beat, but only be not angry. You were once a comrade of my father's, you ate bread and salt together and drank the cup of good-will."

It was not without secret satisfaction that Chub saw the black-smith, who had never bowed to anyone in the village and who could twist five-kopek pieces and horseshoes in his hands like pan-cakes, lying now at his feet. In order to maintain his dignity still further, Chub took the whip and gave him three strokes on the back. "Well, that's enough; get up! Always obey the old! Let us forget everything that has passed between us. Come, tell me now what is it that you want?"

"Give me Oksana for my wife, father!"

Chub thought a little, looked at the cap and the girdle. The cap was delightful and the girdle, too, was not inferior to it; he thought of the treacherous Solokha and said resolutely: "Good! send the matchmakers!"

"Aie!" shrieked Oksana, as she crossed the threshold and saw the blacksmith, and she gazed at him with astonishment and delight.

"Look, what slippers I have brought you!" said Vakula, "they are the same as the Czarina wears!"

"No, no! I don't want slippers!" she said, waving her arms and keeping her eyes fixed upon him. "I am ready without slip-pers . . ." She blushed and could say no more.

The blacksmith went up to her and took her by the hand; the beauty looked down. Never before had she looked so exquisitely lovely. The enchanted blacksmith gently kissed her; her face flushed crimson and she was even lovelier.

The bishop of blessed memory was driving through Dikanka. He admired the site on which the village stands, and as he drove down the street stopped before a new hut.

"And whose is this hut so gaily painted?" asked his Reverence of a beautiful woman, who was standing near the door with a baby in her arms.

"The blacksmith Vakula's!" Oksana, for it was she, told him, bowing.

"Splendid! splendid work!" said his Reverence, examining the doors and windows. The windows were all outlined with a ring of red paint; everywhere on the doors there were Cossacks on horse-back with pipes in their teeth.

But his Reverence was even warmer in his praise of Vakula when he learned that by way of church penance he had painted free of charge the whole of the left choir in green with red flowers.

But that was not all. On the wall, to one side as you go in at the church, Vakula had painted the devil in hell—such a loathsome figure that everyone spat as he passed. And the women would take a child up to the picture, if it would go on crying in their arms, and would say: "There, look! What a *kaka!*" [13] And the child, restrain-ing its tears, would steal a glance at the picture and nestle closer to its mother.

❖《◆《

A TERRIBLE
VENGEANCE

I

There was a bustle and an uproar in a quarter of Kiev: Gorobets, Captain of the Cossacks, was celebrating his son's wedding. A great many people had come as guests to the wedding. In the old days they liked good food, better still liked drinking, and best of

---

[13] Literally, "defecator," but this hardly does justice to the original which, being Gogol at his outrageous best, has a marvelously funny ring to it: *"Yaka kaka!"* (What a *kaka!*) (ed.)

all they liked merrymaking. Among others the Dnieper Cossack
Mikitka came on his sorrel horse straight from a riotous orgy at the
Pereshlay Plain, where for seven days and seven nights he had been
entertaining the Polish king's soldiers with red wine. The Captain's
adopted brother, Danilo Burulbash, came too, with his young wife
Katerina and his year-old son, from beyond the Dnieper where his
farmstead lay between two mountains. The guests marveled at the
fair face of the young wife Katerina, her eyebrows as black as German velvet, her beautiful cloth dress and underskirt of blue silk,
and her boots with silver heels; but they marveled still more that
her old father had not come with her. He had been living in that region for scarcely a year, and for twenty-one years before nothing
had been heard of him and he had only come back to his daughter
when she was married and had borne a son. No doubt he would
have many strange stories to tell. How could he fail to have them,
after being so long in foreign parts! Everything there is different:
the people are not the same and there are no Christian churches.
. . . But he had not come.

They brought the guests spiced vodka with raisins and plums in
it and wedding bread on a big dish. The musicians began on the
bottom crust, in which coins had been baked, and put their fiddles,
cymbals, and tambourines down for a brief rest. Meanwhile the
girls and young women, after wiping their mouths with embroidered handkerchiefs, stepped out again to the center of the
room, and the young men, putting their arms akimbo and looking
haughtily about them, were on the point of going to meet them,
when the old Captain brought out two icons to bless the young
couple. These icons had come to him from the venerable hermit,
Father Varfolomey. They had no rich setting, there was no gleam
of gold or silver on them, but no evil power dare approach the man
in whose house they stand. Raising the icons on high the Captain
was about to deliver a brief prayer . . . when all at once the children playing on the ground cried out in terror, and the people drew
back, and everyone pointed with their fingers in alarm at a Cossack who was standing in their midst. Who he was nobody knew.
But he had already danced splendidly and had diverted the people
standing around him. But when the Captain lifted up the icons, at
once the Cossack's face completely changed: his nose grew longer
and twisted to one side, his rolling eyes turned from brown to
green, his lips turned blue, his chin quivered and grew pointed like

a spear, a tusk peeped out of his mouth, a hump appeared behind his head, and the Cossack turned into an old man.

"It is he! It is he!" shouted the crowd, huddling close together.

"The sorcerer has appeared again!" cried the mothers, snatching up their children.

Majestically and with dignity the Captain stepped forward and, turning the icons toward him, said in a loud voice: "Away, image of Satan! This is no place for you!" And, hissing and clacking his teeth like a wolf, the strange old man vanished.

Talk and conjecture arose among the people and the hubbub was like the roar of the sea in bad weather.

"What is this sorcerer?" asked the young people, who knew nothing about him.

"There will be trouble!" muttered their elders, shaking their heads. And everywhere about the spacious courtyard folks gathered in groups listening to the story of the dreadful sorcerer. But almost everyone told it differently and no one could tell anything certain about him.

A barrel of mead was rolled out and many gallons of Greek wine were brought into the yard. The guests regained their lightheartedness. The orchestra struck up—the girls, the young women, the gallant Cossacks in their gay-colored coats flew around in the dance. After a glass, old folks of ninety, of a hundred, began dancing too, remembering the years that had passed. They feasted till late into the night and feasted as none feast nowadays. The guests began to disperse, but only a few made their way home; many of them stayed to spend the night in the Captain's wide courtyard; and even more Cossacks dropped to sleep uninvited under the benches, on the floor, by their horses, by the stables; wherever the tipplers stumbled, there they lay, snoring for the whole town to hear.

II

There was a soft light all over the earth: the moon had come up from behind the mountain. It covered the steep bank of the Dnieper as with a costly damask muslin, white as snow, and the shadows drew back further into the pine forest.

A boat, hollowed out of an oak tree, was floating in the Dnieper. Two young Cossacks were sitting in the bow; their black Cossack caps were cocked on one side; and the drops flew in all directions from their oars as sparks fly from a flint.

Why were the Cossacks not singing? Why were they not telling of the Polish priests who go about the Ukraine forcing the Cossack people to turn Catholic, or of the two days' fight with the Tartars at the Salt Lake? How could they sing, how could they tell of gallant deeds? Their lord, Danilo, was deep in thought, and the sleeve of his crimson coat hung out of the boat and was dipped in the water; their mistress, Katerina, was softly rocking her child and keeping her eyes fixed upon it, while her beautiful gown was made wet by the spray which fell like fine gray dust.

Sweet it is to look from mid-Dnieper at the lofty mountains, at the broad meadows, at the green forests! Those mountains are not mountains; they end in peaks below, as above, and both under and above them lie the high heavens. Those forests on the hills are not forests: they are the hair that covers the shaggy head of the wood demon. Down below he washes his beard in the water, and under his beard and over his head lie the high heavens. Those meadows are not meadows: they are a green girdle encircling the round sky; and above and below the moon hovers over them.

Lord Danilo looks not about him; he looks at his young wife. "Why are you so deep in sadness, my young wife, my golden Katerina?"

"I am not deep in sadness, Danilo! I am full of dread at the strange tales of the sorcerer. They say when he was born he was terrible to look at . . . and not one of the children would play with him. Listen, Danilo, what dreadful things they say: he thought all were mocking him. If he met a man in the dark he thought that he opened his mouth and grinned at him; and next day they found that man dead. I marveled and was frightened hearing those tales," said Katerina, taking out a kerchief and wiping the face of the sleeping child. The kerchief had been embroidered by her with leaves and fruits in red silk.

Lord Danilo said not a word, but looked into the darkness where far away beyond the forest there was the dark ridge of an earthen wall and beyond the wall rose an old castle. Three lines furrowed his brow; his left hand stroked his gallant mustaches.

"It is not that he is a sorcerer that is cause for fear," he said, "but that he is here for some evil. What whim has brought him here? I have heard it said that the Poles mean to build a fort to cut off our

way to the Dnieper Cossacks. That may be true. . . . I will scatter
that devil's nest if any rumor reaches me that he harbors our foes
there. I will burn the old sorcerer so that even the crows will find
nothing to peck at. And I think he lacks not store of gold and
wealth of all kinds. It's there the devil lives! If he has gold . . . We
shall soon row by the crosses—that's the graveyard! There lie his
evil forefathers. I am told they were all ready to sell themselves to
Satan for a brass coin—soul and threadbare coat and all. If truly he
has gold, there is no time to lose: there is not always booty to be
won in war. . . ."

"I know what you are planning: my heart tells me no good will
come from your meeting him. But you are breathing so hard, you
are looking so fierce, your brows are knitted so angrily above
your eyes . . ."

"Hold your tongue, woman!" said Danilo wrathfully. "If one has
dealings with you, one will turn into a woman, oneself. You, give
me a light for my pipe!" Here he turned to one of the rowers who,
knocking some hot ash from his pipe, began putting it into his
master's. "She would scare me with the sorcerer!" Danilo went on.
"A Cossack, thank God, fears neither devil nor Catholic priest.
What should we come to if we listened to women? No good,
should we, boys? The best wife for us is a pipe and a sharp sword!"

Katerina sat silent, looking down into the slumbering river; and
the wind ruffled the water into eddies and all the Dnieper shim-
mered with silver like a wolf's skin in the night.

The boat turned and hugged the wooded bank. A graveyard
came into sight; tumbledown crosses stood huddled together. No
guelder rose grows among them, no grass is green there; only the
moon warms them from the heavenly heights.

"Do you hear the shouts? Someone is calling for our help!" said
Danilo, turning to his oarsmen.

"We hear shouts, and they are coming from that bank," the two
young men cried together, pointing to the graveyard.

But all was still again. The boat turned, following the curve of
the projecting bank. All at once the rowers dropped their oars and
stared before them without moving. Danilo stopped too: a chill of
horror surged through the Cossack's veins.

A cross on one of the graves tottered and a withered corpse rose
slowly up out of the earth. Its beard reached to its waist; the nails
on its fingers were longer than the fingers themselves. It slowly

raised its hands upward. Its face was all twisted and distorted. One could see it was suffering terrible torments. "I am stifling, stifling!" it moaned in a strange, inhuman voice. Its voice seemed to scrape on the heart like a knife, and suddenly it disappeared under the earth. Another cross tottered and again a dead body came forth, more frightening and taller than the one before; it was all hairy, with a beard to its knees and even longer claws. Still more terribly it shouted: "I am stifling!" and vanished into the earth. A third cross tottered, a third corpse appeared. It seemed like a skeleton rising from the earth; its beard reached to its heels; the nails on its fingers pierced the ground. Terribly it raised its hands toward the sky as though it would seize the moon, and shrieked as though someone were sawing its yellow bones. . . .

The child asleep on Katerina's lap screamed and woke up; the lady screamed too; the oarsmen let their caps fall in the river; even their master shuddered.

Suddenly it all vanished as though it had never been; but it was a long time before the rowers took up their oars again. Burulbash looked anxiously at his young wife who, panic-stricken, was rocking the screaming child in her arms; he pressed her to his heart and kissed her on the forehead.

"Fear not, Katerina! Look, there is nothing!" he said, pointing around. "It is the sorcerer who frightens people so that they will not break into his foul lair. He only scares women! Let me hold my son!"

With those words Danilo lifted up his son and kissed him. "Why, Ivan, you are not afraid of sorcerers, are you? Say: 'No, Daddy, I'm a Cossack!' Stop crying! soon we shall be home! Then Mother will give you your porridge, put you to bed in your cradle, and sing:

> Lullaby, my little son,
> Lullaby to sleep!
> Play about and grow a man!
> To the glory of the Cossacks
> And destruction of our foes.

Listen, Katerina! It seems that your father will not live at peace with us. He was sullen, gloomy, as though angry, when he came. . . . If he doesn't like it, why come? He would not drink to Cossack freedom! He has never fondled the child! At first I would have trusted him with all that lay in my heart, but I could not do it; the words stuck in my throat. No, he has not a Cossack heart! When

Cossack hearts meet, they almost leap out of the breast to greet each other! Well, my friends, is the bank near? I will give you new caps. You, Stetsko, I will give one made of velvet and gold. I took it from a Tartar with his head; I got all his gear, too; I let nothing go but his soul. Well, here is land! Here, we are home, Ivan, but still you cry! Take him, Katerina . . . !"

They all got out. A thatched roof came into sight behind the mountain: it was Danilo's ancestral home. Beyond it was another mountain, and then the open plain, and there you might travel a hundred miles and not see a single Cossack.

III

Danilo's farm lay between two mountains in a narrow valley that ran down to the Dnieper. It was a low-pitched house like the hut of an ordinary Cossack, and there was only one large room in it; but he and his wife and their old maidservant and ten picked young Cossacks all had their places in it. There were oak shelves running around the walls at the top. Bowls and cooking pots were piled upon them. Among them were silver goblets and drinking cups mounted in gold, gifts or booty brought from the war. Lower down hung costly swords, guns, spears; willingly or unwillingly, they had come from the Tartars, the Turks, and the Poles, and many a dent there was in them. Looking at them, Danilo was reminded of his encounters. At the bottom of the wall were smooth-planed oak benches; beside them, in front of the stove, the cradle hung on cords from a ring fixed in the ceiling. The whole floor of the room was leveled and plastered with clay. On the benches slept Danilo and his wife; on the stove the old maidservant; the child played and was lulled to sleep in the cradle; and on the floor the young Cossacks slept in a row. But a Cossack likes best to sleep on the flat earth in the open air; he needs no feather bed or pillow; he piles fresh hay under his head and stretches at his ease upon the grass. It rejoices his heart to wake up in the night and look up at the lofty sky spangled with stars and to shiver at the chill of night which refreshes his Cossack bones; stretching and muttering through his sleep, he lights his pipe and wraps himself more closely in his sheepskin.

Burulbash did not wake early after the merrymaking of the day before; when he woke he sat on a bench in a corner and began sharpening a new Turkish saber, for which he had just bartered something; and Katerina set to work embroidering a silken towel with gold thread.

All at once Katerina's father came in, angry and frowning, with an outlandish pipe in his teeth; he went up to his daughter and began questioning her sternly, asking what was the reason she had come home so late the night before.

"It is not her but me you should question about that, father-in-law! Not the wife but the husband is responsible. That's our way here, don't be disturbed about it," said Danilo, going on with his work. "Perhaps in infidel lands it is not so—I don't know."

The color came into the father-in-law's face; there was an ominous gleam in his eye. "Who, if not a father, should watch over his daughter!" he muttered to himself. "Well, I ask you: where were you roving so late at night?"

"Ah, that's it at last, dear father-in-law! To that I will answer that I have left swaddling clothes behind me long ago. I can ride a horse, I can wield a sharp sword, and there are other things I can do . . . I can refuse to answer to anyone for what I do."

"I know, I see, Danilo, you seek a quarrel! A man who is not frank has some evil in his mind."

"You may think as you please," said Danilo, "and I will think as I please. Thank God, I've had no part in any dishonorable deed so far; I have always stood for the Orthodox faith and my fatherland, not like some vagabonds who go tramping God knows where while good Christians are fighting to the death, and afterward come back to reap the harvest they have not sown. They are worse than the Uniats: they never go into the Church of God. It is such men that should be strictly questioned as to where they have been."

"Ah, Cossack! Do you know . . . I am no great shot; my bullet only pierces the heart at seven hundred feet; I am nothing to boast of at swordplay either: I leave bits of my opponent behind, though in truth, the pieces are smaller than the grains you use for porridge."

"I am ready," said Danilo jauntily, making the sign of the cross in the air with the saber, as though he knew what he had sharpened it for.

"Danilo!" Katerina cried aloud, seizing him by the arm and hanging on it, "think what you are doing, madman, see against whom you are lifting your hand! Father, your hair is white as snow, but you have flown into a rage like a senseless boy!"

"Wife!" Danilo cried menacingly, "you know I will have no interference! You mind your woman's business!"

There was a terrible clatter of swords; steel hacked steel and the Cossacks sent sparks flying like dust. Katerina went out weeping into another room, flung herself on the bed, and covered her ears that she might not hear the clash of the swords. But the Cossacks did not fight so faintheartedly that she could smother the sound of their blows. Her heart was ready to break; she seemed to hear all over her the clank of the swords. "No, I cannot bear it, I cannot bear it. . . . Perhaps the red blood is already flowing out of his white body; maybe by now my dear one is helpless, and I am lying here!" And pale all over, scarcely breathing, she went back.

A terrible and even fight it was; neither of the Cossacks was winning the day. At one moment Katerina's father attacked and Danilo seemed to give way; then Danilo attacked and the sullen father seemed to yield; and again they were equal. They boiled with rage, they swung their swords . . . Ough! The swords clashed . . . and with a clatter the blades flew out of the handles.

"Thank God!" said Katerina, but she screamed again when she saw that the Cossacks had picked up their muskets. They put in the flints and drew the triggers.

Danilo fired and missed. Her father took aim . . . He was old, he did not see so well as the younger man, but his hand did not tremble. A shot rang out . . . Danilo staggered; the red blood stained the left sleeve of his Cossack coat.

"No!" he cried, "I will not yield so easily. Not the left but the right hand is master. I have a Turkish pistol hanging on the wall: never yet has it failed me. Come down from the wall, old comrade! Do your friend a service!" Danilo stretched out his hand.

"Danilo!" cried Katerina in despair, clutching his hands and falling at his feet. "Not for myself I beseech you. There is but one end for me: unworthy is the wife who will outlive her husband; Dnieper, the cold Dnieper, will be my grave. . . . But look at your son, Danilo, look at your son! Who will cherish the poor child? Who will be kind to him? Who will teach him to race on the black stallion, to fight for faith and freedom, to drink and carouse like a Cossack? You must perish, my son, you must perish! Your father will not think of you! See how he turns away his head. Oh, I know you now! You are a wild beast and not a man! You have the heart of a wolf and the mind of a crafty reptile! I thought there was a drop of pity in you, that there was human feeling in your breast of stone. I have been terribly deceived! This will be a delight to you. Your bones will dance in the grave with joy when they hear the foul brutes of Poles throwing your son into the flames, when your son shrieks under the knife or the scalding water. Oh, I know you! You would be glad to rise up from the grave and fan the flames under him with your cap!"

"Stop, Katerina! Come, my precious Ivan, let me kiss you! No, my child, no one shall touch a hair of your head. You shall grow up to the glory of your fatherland; like a whirlwind you shall fly at the head of the Cossacks with a velvet cap on your head and a sharp sword in your hand. Give me your hand, Father! Let us forget what has been between us! For what wrong I have done you I ask pardon. Why do you not give me your hand?" said Danilo to Katerina's father, who stood without moving, with no sign of anger nor of reconciliation on his face.

"Father!" cried Katerina, embracing and kissing him, "don't be merciless, forgive Danilo: he will never offend you again!"

"For your sake only, my daughter, I forgive him!" he answered, kissing her with a strange glitter in his eyes.

Katerina shuddered faintly: the kiss and the strange glitter seemed uncanny to her. She leaned her elbows on the table, at which Danilo was bandaging his wounded hand, while he wondered if he had acted like a Cossack in asking pardon when he had done no wrong.

IV

The day broke, but without sunshine: the sky was overcast and a fine rain was falling on the plains, on the forest, and on the broad Dnieper. Katerina woke up, but not joyfully: her eyes were tear-stained, and she was restless and uneasy.

"My dear husband, my precious husband! I have had a strange dream!"

"What dream, my sweet wife Katerina?"

"I had a strange dream, and as vivid as though it were real, that my father was that very monster whom we saw at the Captain's.

But I beg you, do not put faith in the dream: one dreams all manner of foolishness. I dreamed that I was standing before him, was trembling and frightened, my whole body racked with pain at every word he said. If only you had heard what he said . . ."

"What did he say, my darling Katerina?"

"He said: 'Look at me, Katerina, how handsome I am! People are wrong in saying I am ugly. I should make you a fine husband. See what a look there is in my eyes!' Then he turned his fiery eyes upon me. I cried out and woke up . . ."

"Yes, dreams tell many a true thing. But do you know that all is not quiet beyond the mountain? I believe the Poles may have begun to show themselves again. Gorobets sent me a message to keep alert, but he need not have troubled—I am not asleep as it is. My Cossacks have piled up a dozen barricades during the night. We will treat Poland to leaden plums and the Poles will dance to our sticks."

"And Father, does he know of this?"

"Your father is a burden on my back! I'll be damned if I can understand him. Perhaps he has committed many sins in foreign lands. What other reason can there be? Here he has lived with us more than a month and not once has he made merry like a true Cossack! He would not drink mead! Do you hear, Katerina, he would not drink the mead which I wrung out of the Jews at Brest. Boy!" cried Danilo, "run to the cellar, boy, and bring me the Jews' mead! He won't even drink vodka! What do you make of that? I believe, my lády Katerina, that he does not believe in Christ. Eh, what do you think?"

"God forgive you for what you are saying, my lord Danilo!"

"Strange, wife!" Danilo went on, taking the earthenware mug from the Cossack, "even the damned Catholics have a weakness for vodka; it is only the Turks who do not drink. Well, Stetsko, have you had a good sip of mead in the cellar?"

"I just tried it, sir."

"You are lying, you son of a bitch! See how the flies have settled on your mustache! I can see from your eyes that you have gulped down half a pailful. Oh, you Cossacks! What reckless fellows! Ready to give all else to a comrade, but he keeps his drink to himself. It is a long time, my lady Katerina, since I have been drunk. Eh?"

"A long time indeed! Why, last . . ."

"Don't be afraid; don't be afraid, I won't drink more than a mugful! And here is the Turkish abbot at the door!" he muttered through his teeth, seeing his father-in-law stooping to come in.

"What's this, my daughter!" said the father, taking his cap off his head and adjusting his girdle where hung a saber set with precious stones; "the sun is already high and your dinner is not ready."

"Dinner is ready, my lord and father, we will serve it at once! Bring out the pot of dumplings!" said the young mistress to the old maidservant who was wiping the wooden bowls. "Stop, I had better get it out myself, while you call the men."

They all sat down on the floor in a ring; facing the icons sat the father, on his left Danilo, on his right Katerina, and ten of Danilo's most trusted Cossacks in blue and yellow coats.

"I don't like these dumplings!" said the father, laying down his spoon after eating a little. "There is no flavor in them!"

"I know you like Jewish noodles better," thought Danilo. "Why do you say there is no flavor in the dumplings, father-in-law? Are they badly made or what? My Katerina makes dumplings such as the Hetman does not often taste. And there is no need to despise them: it is a Christian dish! All holy people and godly saints have eaten dumplings!"

Not a word from the father. Danilo, too, said no more.

They served roast boar with cabbage and plums.

"I don't like pork," said Katerina's father, picking out a spoonful of cabbage.

"Why don't you like pork?" said Danilo. "It is only Turks and Jews who won't eat pork."

The father frowned more angrily than ever.

He ate nothing but some baked flour pudding with milk over it, and instead of vodka drank some black liquid from a bottle he took out of his bosom.

After dinner Danilo slept like a hero and only woke toward evening. He sat down to write to the Cossack troops, while his young wife sat on the stove, rocking the cradle with her foot. The lord Danilo sat there, his left eye on his writing while his right eye looked out of the window. From the window far away he could see the shining mountains and the Dnieper; beyond the Dnieper lay the dark blue forest; overhead glimmered the clear night sky. But the lord Danilo was not gazing at the faraway sky and the blue forest; he was watching the projecting tongue of land on which stood the old castle. He thought that a light gleamed at a narrow little window in the castle. But everything was still; it must have been his imagination. All he could hear was the hollow murmur of the Dnieper down below and, from three sides, the resounding splash of the waves suddenly awakening. It was not in turmoil. Like an old man, it merely muttered and grumbled, finding nothing that pleased it. Everything about it had changed; it was feuding with the mountains, the woods, and the meadows on its banks, carrying its complaints to the Black Sea.

And now on the wide expanse of the Dnieper the black speck of a boat appeared and again there was a gleam of light in the castle. Danilo gave a low whistle and the faithful servant ran in at the sound.

"Make haste, Stetsko, bring with you a sharp sword and a musket, and follow me!"

"Are you going out?" asked Katerina.

"I am, wife. I must inspect everything and see that all is in order."

"But I am afraid to be left alone. I am weary with sleep: what if I should have the same dream again? And, indeed, I am not sure it was a dream—it was all so vivid."

"The old woman will stay with you, and there are Cossacks sleeping in the porch and in the courtyard."

"The old woman is asleep already, and somehow I put no trust in the Cossacks. Listen, Danilo: lock me in the room and take the key with you. Then I shall not be so afraid; and let the Cossacks lie before the door."

"So be it!" said Danilo, wiping the dust off his musket and loading it with powder.

The faithful Stetsko stood ready with all the Cossack's equipment. Danilo put on his astrakhan cap, closed the window, bolted and locked the door, and stepping between his sleeping Cossacks, went out of the courtyard toward the mountains.

The sky was almost completely clear again. A fresh breeze blew lightly from the Dnieper. But for the wail of a gull in the distance all was silent. But a faint rustle stirred . . . Burulbash and his faithful servant stealthily hid behind the brambles that screened a barricade of felled trunks. Someone in a scarlet coat, with two pistols and a sword at his side, came down the mountainside. "It's my father-in-law," said Danilo, watching him from behind the bushes.

"Where is he going at this hour, and what is he up to? Be alert, Stetsko: keep a sharp watch which road your mistress's father takes."

The man in the scarlet coat went down to the riverbank and turned toward the jutting tongue of land.

"Ah, so that is where he is going," said Danilo. "Tell me, Stetsko, hasn't he gone to the sorcerer's den?"

"Nowhere else, for certain, my lord Danilo! Or we should have seen him on the other side; but he disappeared near the castle."

"Wait a minute: let us get out and follow his track. There is some secret in this. Yes, Katerina, I told you your father was an evil man; he does nothing like a good Christian."

Danilo and his faithful servant leaped out on the tongue of land. Soon they were out of sight; the slumbering forest around the castle hid them. A gleam of light came into an upper window; the Cossacks stood below wondering how to climb to it; no gate nor door was to be seen; doubtless there was a door in the courtyard, but how could they climb in? They could hear in the distance the clanking of chains and the stirring of dogs.

"Why am I wasting time?" said Danilo, seeing a big oak tree by the window. "Stay here, friend! I will climb up the oak; from it I can look straight into the window."

With this he took off his girdle, put down his sword so that it might not jingle, and gripping the branches, lifted himself up. There was still a light at the window. Sitting on a branch close to the window, he held on to the tree and looked in: it was light in the room but there was no candle. On the wall were mysterious symbols; weapons were hanging there, but all were strange—not such as are worn by Turks or Tartars or Poles or Christians or the gallant Swedish people. Bats flitted to and fro under the ceiling and their shadows flitted to and fro over the floor, the doors, and the walls. Then the door noiselessly opened. Someone in a scarlet coat walked in and went straight up to the table, which was covered with a white cloth. "It is he; it is my father-in-law!" Danilo crept a little lower down and huddled closer to the tree.

But his father-in-law had no time to look whether anyone were peeping in at the window. He came in, morose and ill-humored; he drew the cloth off the table, and at once the room was filled with transparent blue light, but the waves of pale golden light with which the room had been filled, eddied and dived, as in a blue sea, without mingling with it, and ran through it in streaks like the lines in marble. Then he set a pot upon the table and began scattering some herbs in it.

Danilo looked more attentively and saw that he was no longer wearing the scarlet coat; and that now he had on wide trousers, such as Turks wear, with pistols in his girdle, and on his head a strange cap embroidered all over with letters that were neither Russian nor Polish. As he looked at his face the face began to change: his nose grew longer and hung right down over his lips; in one instant his mouth stretched to his ears; a crooked tooth peeped out beyond his lips; and Danilo saw before him the same sorcerer who had appeared at the Captain's wedding feast. "Your dream was true, Katerina!" thought Burulbash.

The sorcerer began pacing around the table; the symbols on the wall began changing more rapidly, the bats flitted more swiftly up and down and to and fro. The blue light grew dimmer and dimmer and at last seemed to fade away. And now there was only a dim pinkish light in the room. It spread through the room and a faint ringing sound was heard. The light seemed to flood every corner, and suddenly it vanished and all was darkness. Nothing was heard but a murmur like the wind in the quiet evening hour when hovering over the mirrorlike water it bends the silvery willows lower into its depths. And it seemed to Danilo as though the moon were shining in the room, the stars were moving, there were vague glimpses of the bright blue sky within it, and he even felt the chill of night coming from it. And Danilo imagined (he began fingering his mustaches to make sure he was not dreaming) that it was no longer the sky but his own hut he was seeing through the window; his Tartar and Turkish swords were hanging on the walls; around the walls were the shelves with pots and pans; on the table stood bread and salt; the cradle hung from the ceiling . . . but hideous faces appeared where the icons should have been; on the stove . . . but a thick mist hid all and it was dark again. And accompanied by a faint ringing sound the rosy light flooded the room again, and again the sorcerer stood motionless in his strange turban. The sounds grew louder and deeper, the delicate rosy light shone more brilliant, and something white like a cloud hovered in the middle of the room; and it seemed to Danilo that the cloud was not a cloud, but that a woman was standing there; but what was she made of? Surely not of air? Why did she stand without touching the floor, without leaning on anything, why did the rosy light and the magic symbols on the wall show through her? And now she moved her transparent head; a soft light shone in her pale blue eyes; her hair curled and fell over her shoulders like a pale gray mist; a faint flush colored her lips like the scarcely perceptible crimson glimmer of dawn glowing through the white transparent sky of morning; the brows darkened a little . . . Ah, it was Katerina! Danilo felt his limbs turned to stone; he tried to speak, but his lips moved without uttering a sound.

The sorcerer stood without moving. "Where have you been?" he asked, and the figure standing before him trembled.

"Oh, why did you call me up?" she moaned softly. "I was so happy. I was in the place where I was born and lived for fifteen years. Ah, how good it was there! How green and fragrant was the meadow where I used to play in childhood! The darling wild flowers were the same as ever, and our hut and the garden! Oh, how my dear mother embraced me! How much love there was in her eyes! She caressed me, she kissed my lips and my cheeks, combed out my fair hair with a fine comb . . . Father!" Then she bent her pale eyes on the sorcerer. "Why did you murder my mother?"

The sorcerer shook his finger at her menacingly. "Did I ask you to speak of that?" And the ethereal beauty trembled. "Where is your mistress now?"

"My mistress Katerina has fallen asleep and I was glad of it: I flew up and darted off. For long years I have longed to see my mother. I was suddenly fifteen again, I felt light as a bird. Why have you sent for me?"

"You remember all I said to you yesterday?" the sorcerer said, so softly that it was hard to catch the words.

"I remember, I remember! But what would I not give to forget them. Poor Katerina, there is much she doesn't know that her soul knows!"

"It is Katerina's soul," thought Danilo, but still he dared not stir.

"Repent, Father! Is it not dreadful that after every murder you commit the dead rise up from their graves?"

"You are at your old tune again!" said the sorcerer menacingly. "I will have my way, I will make you do as I will. Katerina shall love me . . ."

"Oh, you are a monster and not my father!" she moaned. "No,

your will shall not be done! It is true that by your foul spells you have power to call up and torture her soul; but only God can make her do what He wills. No, never shall Katerina, so long as I am living in her body, bring herself to so ungodly a deed. Father, a terrible judgment is at hand! Even if you were not my father, you would never make me false to my faithful and beloved husband. Even if my husband were not true and dear to me, I would not betray him, for God detests souls that are faithless and false to their vows."

Then she fixed her pale eyes on the window under which Danilo was sitting, and was silent and still as death.

"What are you looking at? Whom do you see there . . . ?" cried the sorcerer.

The wraith of Katerina trembled. But already Danilo was on the ground and with his faithful Stetsko making his way to his mountain home. "Terrible, terrible!" he murmured to himself, feeling a thrill of fear in his Cossack heart, and he rapidly crossed his courtyard, in which the Cossacks slept as soundly as ever, all but one who sat on guard smoking a pipe.

The sky was all studded with stars.

V

"How glad I am you have awakened me!" said Katerina, wiping her eyes with the embroidered sleeve of her nightgown and looking intently at her husband as he stood facing her. "What a terrible dream I have had! I could hardly breathe! Ough . . . ! I thought I was dying. . . ."

"What was your dream? Was it like this?" And Burulbash told his wife all that he had seen.

"How did you know it, husband?" asked Katerina in amazement. "But no, many things you tell me I did not know. No, I did not dream that my father murdered my mother; I did not dream of the dead. No, Danilo, you have not told the dream right. Oh, what a terrible man my father is!"

"And it is no wonder that you have not dreamed of that. You do not know a tenth part of what your soul knows. Do you know your father is the Antichrist? Only last year when I was getting ready to go with the Poles against the Crimean Tartars (I was still allied with that faithless people then), the Father Superior of the

Bratsky Monastery (he is a holy man, wife) told me that the Antichrist has the power to call up every man's soul; for the soul wanders freely when the body is asleep and flies with the archangels about the dwelling of God. I disliked your father's face from the first. I would not have married you had I known you had such a father; I would have given you up and not have taken upon myself the sin of being allied to the brood of Antichrist."

"Danilo!" cried Katerina, hiding her face in her hands and bursting into tears. "In what have I been to blame? Have I been false to you, my beloved husband? How have I roused your wrath? Have I not served you truly? Do I say a word to cross you when you come back merry from a drinking bout? Have I not borne you a black-browed son?"

"Do not weep, Katerina; now I know you and nothing would make me abandon you. The sin all lies at your father's door."

"No, do not call him my father! He is not my father. God is my witness I disown him, I disown my father! He is Antichrist, a rebel against God! If he were perishing, if he were drowning, I would not hold out a hand to save him; if his throat were parched by some magic herb I would not give him a drop of water. You are my father!"

VI

In a deep underground cellar at Danilo's the sorcerer lay bound in iron chains behind a door with three locks, while his devilish castle above the Dnieper was on fire and the waves, glowing red as blood, splashed and surged around the ancient walls. It was not for sorcery, it was not for ungodly deeds that the sorcerer lay in the underground cellar—for his wickedness God was his judge; it was for secret treachery that he was imprisoned, for plotting with the foes of Orthodox Russia to sell to the Catholics the Ukrainian people and burn Christian churches. The sorcerer was gloomy; thoughts black as night strayed through his mind; he had but one day left to live and on the morrow he would take leave of the world; his punishment was awaiting him on the morrow. It was no light one: it would be an act of mercy if he were boiled alive in a cauldron or his sinful skin were flayed from him. The sorcerer was sad, his head was bowed. Perhaps he was already repenting on the eve of death; but his sins were not such as God would forgive. Above him was a little window covered with an iron grating. Clanking his chains, he stood to look out of the window and see whether his daughter were passing. She was gentle and forgiving as a dove; would she not have mercy on her father . . . ? But there was no one. The road ran below the window; no one passed along it. Beneath it rippled the Dnieper; it cared for no one; it murmured, and it splashed monotonously, drearily.

Then someone appeared upon the road—it was a Cossack! And the prisoner heaved a deep sigh. Again the road was empty. In the distance someone was coming down the hill . . . a green overskirt flapped in the wind . . . a golden headdress glittered on her head . . . It was she! He pressed still closer to the window. Now she was coming nearer . . .

"Katerina, daughter! Have pity on me, be merciful!"

She was silent, she would not listen, she did not turn her eyes toward the prison, and had already passed, already vanished. The whole world was empty; dismally the Dnieper murmured; it made hearts sad; but did the sorcerer know anything of such sadness?

The day was drawing to a close. Now the sun was setting; now it had vanished. Now it was evening, it was cool; an ox was lowing somewhere; sounds of voices floated from afar: people doubtless going home from their work and making merry; a boat flashed into sight on the Dnieper . . . no one thought of the prisoner. A silver crescent gleamed in the sky; now someone came along the road in the opposite direction; it was hard to tell the figure in the darkness; it was Katerina coming back.

"Daughter, for Christ's sake! even the savage wolf cubs will not tear their mother in pieces—daughter, give one look at least to your guilty father!"

She heeded not but walked on.

"Daughter, for the sake of your unhappy mother . . ."

She stopped.

"Come close and hear my last words!"

"Why do you call me, enemy of God? Do not call me daughter! There is no kinship between us. What do you want of me for the sake of my unhappy mother?"

"Katerina, my end is near; I know that your husband means to tie me to the tail of a wild mare and send it racing in the open country, and maybe he will invent an end more dreadful yet . . ."

"But is there in the world a punishment bad enough for your sins? You may be sure no one will plead for you."

"Katerina! It is not punishment in this world that I fear but in the next. . . . You are innocent, Katerina; your soul will fly about God in paradise; but your ungodly father's soul will burn in a fire everlasting and never will that fire be quenched; it will burn more and more hotly; no drop of dew will fall upon it, nor will the wind breathe on it . . ."

"I can do nothing to ease that punishment," said Katerina, turning away.

"Katerina, stay for one word! You can save my soul! You know not yet how good and merciful is God. Have you heard of the Apostle Paul, what a sinful man he was—but afterward he repented and became a saint?"

"What can I do to save your soul?" said Katerina. "It is not for a weak woman like me to think of that."

"If I could but get out, I would abandon everything. I will repent, I will go into a cave, I will wear a hair shirt next to my skin and spend day and night in prayer. I will give up not only meat, but even fish I will not taste! I will lay nothing under me when I lie down to sleep! And I will pray without ceasing, pray without ceasing! And if God's mercy does not release me from at least a hundredth part of my sins, I will bury myself up to the neck in the earth or entomb myself in a wall of stone; I will take neither food nor drink and perish; and I will give all my goods to the monks that they may sing a requiem for me for forty days and forty nights."

Katerina pondered. "If I were to unlock you I could not undo your fetters."

"I do not fear chains," he said. "You say that they have fettered my hands and feet? No, I threw a mist over their eyes and held out a dry tree instead of hands. Here, see: I have not a chain upon me now!" he said, walking into the middle of the cellar. "I should not have been contained by these walls either; but your husband does not know what walls these are: they were built by a holy hermit, and no evil power can deliver a prisoner from them without the very key with which the hermit used to lock his cell. Just such a cell will I build for myself, incredible sinner that I have been, when I am free again."

"Listen, I will let you out; but what if you deceive me," said Katerina, standing still at the door, "and instead of repenting, again become the devil's comrade?"

"No, Katerina, I have not long left to live; my end is near even if I am not put to death. Can you believe that I will give myself up to eternal punishment?"

The key grated in the lock.

"Farewell! God in His mercy keep you, my child!" said the sorcerer, kissing her.

"Do not touch me, you fearful sinner; make haste and go . . ." said Katerina.

But he was gone.

"I let him out!" she said to herself, terror-stricken, looking wildly at the walls. "What answer shall I give my husband now? I am undone. There is nothing left but to bury myself alive!" and sobbing she almost fell upon the block on which the prisoner had been sitting. "But I have saved a soul," she said softly. "I have done a godly deed; but my husband . . . I have deceived him for the first time. Oh, how terrible, how hard it will be for me to lie to him! Someone is coming! It is he! my husband!" She uttered a desperate shriek and fell senseless on the ground.

VII

"It is I, my daughter! It is, I, my darling!" Katerina heard, as she revived and saw the old maidservant before her. The woman bent down and seemed to whisper to her, and stretching out her withered old hand, sprinkled her with water.

"Where am I?" said Katerina, sitting up and looking around her. "The Dnieper is splashing before me, behind me are the mountains . . . Where have you taken me, granny?"

"I have taken you out; I have carried you in my arms from the stifling cellar; I locked up the cellar again that you might not be in trouble with my lord Danilo."

"Where is the key?" asked Katerina, looking at her girdle. "I don't see it."

"Your husband has taken it, to have a look at the sorcerer, my child."

"To look! Granny, I am lost!" cried Katerina.

"God mercifully preserve us from that, my child! Only hold your peace, my little lady, no one will know anything."

"He has escaped, the cursed Antichrist! Do you hear, Katerina, he has escaped!" said Danilo, coming up to his wife. His eyes flashed fire; his sword hung clanking at his side. His wife was like one dead.

"Has someone let him out, dear husband?" she brought out trembling.

"Yes, someone has—you are right: the devil. Look, where he was is a log chained to the wall. It is God's pleasure, it seems, that the devil should not fear a Cossack's hands! If any one of my Cossacks had dreamed of such a thing and I knew of it . . . I could find no punishment bad enough for him!"

"And if I had done it?" Katerina could not resist saying, and she stopped, panic-stricken.

"If you had done it you would be no wife to me. I would sew you up in a sack and drown you in mid-Dnieper . . . !"

Katerina could hardly breathe and she felt the hair stand up on her head.

VIII

On the frontier road the Poles had gathered at a tavern and feasted there for two days. There were not a few of the rabble. They had doubtless met for some raid: some had muskets; there was jingling of spurs and clanking of swords. The nobles made merry and boasted; they talked of their marvelous deeds; they mocked at the Orthodox Christians, calling the Ukrainian people their serfs, and insolently twirled their mustaches and sprawled on the benches. There was a Catholic priest among them, too; but he was like them and had not even the semblance of a Christian priest; he drank and caroused with them and uttered shameful words with his foul tongue. The servants were no better than their masters: tucking up the sleeves of their tattered coats, they walked about with a swagger as though they were of consequence. They played cards, struck each other on the nose with cards; they had brought with them other men's wives; there was shouting, quarreling . . . ! Their masters were at the height of their revelry, playing all sorts of tricks; pulling the Jewish tavern keeper by the beard, painting a cross on his impious brow, shooting blanks at the women, and dancing the *Cracovienne* with their impious priest. Such sinfulness had never been seen on Russian soil even among the Tartars; it was God's chastisement, seemingly, for the sins of Russia that she should be put to so great a shame! In the midst of the bedlam, talk could be heard of lord Danilo's farmstead above the Dnieper, of his lovely wife . . . The gang of thieves was plotting foul deeds!

IX

The lord Danilo sat at the table in his house, leaning on his elbow, thinking. The lady Katerina sat on the stove, singing.

"I am sad, my wife!" said lord Danilo. "My head aches and my heart aches. I feel weighed down. It seems my death is hovering not far away."

"Oh, my precious husband! lean your head upon me! Why do you cherish such black thoughts?" thought Katerina, but dared not utter the words. It was bitter to her, feeling her guilt, to receive her husband's caresses.

"Listen, wife!" said Danilo, "do not desert our son when I am no more. God will give you no happiness either in this world or the next if you forsake him. Sad it will be for my bones to rot in the damp earth; sadder still it will be for my soul!"

"What are you saying, my husband? Was it not you who mocked at us weak women? And now you are talking like a weak woman yourself. You must live many years yet."

"No, Katerina, my heart feels death near at hand. The world has become a sad place; cruel days are coming. Ah, I remember, I remember the good years—they will not return! He was living then, the honor and glory of our army, old Konashevich! The Cossack regiments pass before my eyes as though it were today. Those were golden days, Katerina! The old Hetman sat on a black stallion; his mace shone in his hand; the soldiers stood around him, and on each side moved the red sea of the Dnieper Cossacks. The Hetman began to speak—and all stood as though turned to stone. The old man wept when he told us of old days and battles long ago. Ah, Katerina, if only you knew how we fought in those days with the Turks! The scar on my head shows even now. Four bullets pierced me in four places and not one of the wounds has quite healed. How much gold we took in those days! The Cossacks filled their caps with precious stones. What horses, Katerina! If you only knew, what horses, Katerina, we drove away with us! Ah, I shall never fight like that! One would think I am not old and I am strong in body, yet the sword drops out of my hand, I live doing nothing

and know not what I live for. There is no order in the Ukraine:
the colonels and the captains quarrel like dogs: there is no chief
over them all. Our gentry imitate Polish fashions and have copied
their sly ways . . . they have sold their souls, accepting the Uniat
faith. The Jews are oppressing the poor. Oh, those days, those days!
Those days that are past! Whither have you fled, my years? Go to
the cellar, boy, and bring me a jug of mead! I will drink to the life
of the past and to the years that have gone!"

"How shall we receive our guests, lord Danilo? The Poles are
coming from the direction of the meadow," said Stetsko, coming
into the hut.

"I know what they are coming for," said Danilo. "Saddle the
horses, my faithful men! Put on your harness! Bare your swords!
Don't forget to take your rations of lead: we must do honor to our
guests!"

But before the Cossacks had time to saddle their horses and load
their guns, the Poles covered the mountainside as leaves cover the
ground in autumn.

"Ah, here we have foes to try our strength with!" said Danilo,
looking at the stout Poles swaying majestically on their gold-
harnessed steeds in the front ranks. "It seems it is my lot to have
one more glorious jaunt! Take your pleasure, Cossack soul, for the
last time! Go ahead, Cossacks, the festival for which we waited has
come!"

And the festival was kept on the mountains and great was the
merrymaking: swords were playing, bullets flying, horses neighing
and prancing. The shouting dazed the brain; the smoke blinded the
eye. All was confusion, but the Cossack knew where was friend,
where was foe; whenever a bullet whistled a gallant rider dropped
from the saddle, whenever a sword flashed—a head fell to the
ground, babbling meaningless words.

But the red crest of Danilo's Cossack cap could always be seen in
the crowd; the gold girdle of his dark blue coat gleamed bright, the
mane on his black horse fluttered in the breeze. Like a bird he flew
here and there, shouting and waving his Damascus sword and hack-
ing to right and to left. Hack away, Cossack, make merry! Cheer
your gallant heart; but look not at the gold trappings and tunics:
trample under foot the gold and jewels! Stab, Cossack! Wreak your
will, Cossack! But look back: already the godless Poles are setting

fire to the huts and driving away the frightened cattle. And like a whirlwind Danilo turned around, and the cap with the red crest gleamed now by the huts while the crowd about him scattered.

Hour after hour the Poles fought with the Cossacks; there were not many left of either; but lord Danilo did not slacken; with his long spear he thrust Poles from the saddle and his spirited steed trampled them under foot. Already his courtyard was almost cleared, already the Poles were flying in all directions; already the Cossacks were stripping the golden coats and rich trappings from the slain; already Danilo was setting off in pursuit, when he looked around to call his men together . . . and was overwhelmed with fury: he saw Katerina's father. There he stood on the hillside aiming his musket at him. Danilo urged his horse straight upon him . . . Cossack, you go to your doom! Then came the crack of a shot —and the sorcerer vanished behind the hill. Only the faithful Stetsko caught a glimpse of the scarlet coat and the strange hat. The Cossack staggered and fell to the ground. The faithful Stetsko flew to his master's aid: his lord lay stretched on the ground with his bright eyes closed while the red blood spurted from his breast. But he became aware of his faithful servant's presence; slowly he raised his eyelids and his eyes gleamed: "Farewell, Stetsko! Tell Katerina not to forsake her son! And do not you, my faithful servant, forsake him either!" and he ceased. His gallant soul flew from his noble body; his lips turned blue; the Cossack slept, never to wake again.

His faithful servant sobbed and beckoned to Katerina: "Come, lady, come! deeply has your lord been carousing; in drunken sleep he lies on the damp earth; and long will it be before he awakens!"

Katerina wrung her hands and fell like a sheaf of wheat on the dead body: "Husband, is it you lying here with closed eyes? Rise up, stretch out your hand! Stand up! Look, if only once, at your Katerina, move your lips, utter one word . . . ! But you are mute, you are mute, my noble lord! You have turned blue as the Black Sea. Your heart is not beating! Why are you so cold, my lord? It seems my tears are not scalding, they have no power to warm you! It seems my weeping is not loud, it will not waken you! Who will lead your regiments now? Who will gallop on your black horse, loudly calling, and lead the Cossacks, waving your sword? Cossacks, Cossacks, where is your honor and glory? Your honor and glory is lying with closed eyes on the damp earth. Bury me, bury me with him! Throw earth upon my eyes! Press the maple boards upon my white breasts! My beauty is useless to me now!"

Katerina grieved and wept; while the distant horizon was covered with dust: the old Captain Gorobets was galloping to the rescue.

X

Lovely is the Dnieper in tranquil weather when, freely and smoothly, its waters glide through forests and mountains. Not a sound, not a ripple is stirring. You look and cannot tell whether its majestic expanse moves or does not move; and it might be of molten crystal and like a blue road made of mirror, immeasurably broad, endlessly long, twining and twisting about the green world. Sweet it is then for the burning sun to peep at itself from the heights and to plunge its beams in the cool of its glassy waves, and for the forests on the banks to watch their bright reflections in the water. Wreathed in green, they press with the wild flowers close to the river's edge, and bending over look in and are never tired of gazing and admiring their bright reflection, and smile and greet it with nodding branches. In mid-Dnieper they dare not look: none but the sun and the blue sky gaze into it; rarely a bird flies to the middle of the river. Glorious it is! No river like it in the world! Lovely too is the Dnieper on a warm summer night when all are sleeping— man, beast, and bird—while God alone majestically surveys earth and heaven and majestically shakes His robe, showering stars that glow and shine above the world and are all reflected together in the Dnieper. All of them the Dnieper holds in its dark bosom; not one escapes it till quenched in the sky. The black forests dotted with sleeping crows and the mountains cleft asunder in ages past strive, hanging over, to conceal the river in their long shadows, but in vain! There is nothing in the world that could hide the Dnieper. Deep, deep blue it flows, spreading its waters far and wide at midnight as at midday; it is seen far, far away, as far as the eye of man can see. Shrinking from the cold of night and huddling closer to the bank, it leaves behind a silver trail gleaming like the blade of a Damascus sword, while the deep blue water slumbers again. Lovely then, too, is the Dnieper, and no river is like it in the world! When dark blue storm clouds pile in masses over the sky, the dark forest totters to its roots, the oaks creak, and the lightning slashing through the storm clouds suddenly lights up the whole world—terrible then is the Dnieper! Then its mountainous billows roar, flinging themselves against the hillside, and flashing and moaning rush back and wail and lament in the distance. So the old mother laments as she lets her Cossack son go to the war. Bold and reckless, he rides his black stallion, arms akimbo and jaunty cap on one side, while she, sobbing, runs after him, seizes him by the stirrup, catches the bridle, and wrings her hands over him, bathed in bitter tears.

Strange and black are the burnt tree stumps and stones on the jutting bank between the warring waves. And the landing boat is beaten against the bank, thrown upward, and flung back again. What Cossack dared row out in a boat when the old Dnieper was raging? Surely he knew not that the river swallows men like flies.

The boat reached the bank; out of it stepped the sorcerer. He was in no happy mood: bitter to him was the funeral feast which the Cossacks had kept over their slain master. Heavily had the Poles paid for it: forty-four of them in all their harness and thirty-three servants were hacked to pieces, while the others were captured with their horses to be sold to the Tartars.

He went down stone steps between the burnt stumps to a place where he had a cave dug deep in the earth. He went in softly, not letting the door creak, put a pot on the table that was covered with a cloth, and began with his long hands strewing into it some strange herbs; he took a ladle made of some rare wood, scooped up some water with it, and poured it out, moving his lips and repeating an incantation. The cave was flooded with rosy light and his face was terrible to look upon: it seemed covered with blood, only the deep wrinkles showed up black upon it, and his eyes blazed as though they were on fire. Foul sinner! His beard was gray, his face was lined with wrinkles, he was shriveled with age, and still he persisted in his godless design. A white cloud began to hover in the cave and something like joy gleamed in his face; but why did he suddenly stand motionless with his mouth open, not daring to stir; why did his hair rise up on his head? The features of a strange face appeared to him from the cloud. Unbidden, uninvited it had come to visit him; it grew more distinct and fastened its eyes immovably upon him. The features, eyebrows, eyes, lips—all were unfamiliar; never in his life had he seen them. And there was nothing terrible, seemingly, about it, but he was overwhelmed with horror. The strange, marvelous face still looked fixedly at him from the cloud. Then the cloud vanished, but the unfamiliar face was more distinct than ever and the piercing eyes were still riveted on him. The sorcerer turned white as a sheet; he shrieked in a wild, unnatural voice and overturned the pot . . . The face disappeared.

XI

"Take comfort, my dear sister!" said old Captain Gorobets. "Rarely do dreams come true!"

"Lie down, sister," said his young daughter-in-law. "I will fetch a wise woman; no evil power can stand against her; she will help you."

"Fear nothing!" said his son, touching his sword. "No one shall harm you!"

Gloomily and with dull eyes Katerina looked at them all and found no word to say.

"I myself brought about my ruin: I let him out!" she said at last. "He gives me no peace! Here I have been ten days with you in Kiev and my sorrow is no less. I thought that at least I could bring up my son to avenge . . . I dreamed of him, looking terrible! God forbid that you should ever see him like that! My heart is still throbbing. 'I will kill your child, Katerina,' he shouted, 'if you do not marry me . . . ' " And she flung herself sobbing on the cradle; and the frightened child stretched out its little hands and cried.

The Captain's son was boiling with anger as he heard such words.

The Captain himself was roused. "Let him try coming here, the accursed Antichrist; he will learn whether there is still strength in the old Cossack's arm. God sees," he said, turning his keen eyes to heaven, "whether I did not hasten to give a hand to brother Danilo. It was His holy will! I found him lying on the cold bed upon which so many, many Cossacks have been laid. But what a funeral feast we had for him! We did not leave a single Pole alive! Be comforted, my child. No one shall dare to harm you, so long as I or my son live."

As he finished speaking the old Cossack captain approached the cradle, and the child saw hanging from a strap his red pipe set in silver and the pouch with the shiny flints, and stretched out its arms toward him and laughed. "He takes after his father," said the old captain, unfastening the pipe and giving it to the child. "He is not out of the cradle, but he is thinking of a pipe already!"

Katerina heaved a sigh and fell to rocking the cradle. They agreed to spend the night together and soon afterward they were all asleep; Katerina, too, fell asleep.

All was quiet in the courtyard; everyone slept but the Cossacks who were keeping watch. Suddenly Katerina woke with a scream, and the others woke too. "He is slain, he is murdered!" she cried, and flew to the cradle. All surrounded the cradle and were numb with horror when they saw that the child in it was dead. None uttered a sound, not knowing what to think of so horrible a crime.

XII

Far from the Ukraine, beyond Poland and the populous town of Lemberg, run ranges of high mountains. Mountain after mountain, like chains of stone flung to the right and to the left over the land, they fetter it with layers of rock to keep out the resounding turbulent sea. These stony chains stretch into Wallachia and the Sedmigrad region and stand like a huge horseshoe between the Galician and Hungarian peoples. There are no such mountains in our country. The eye shrinks from viewing them and no human foot has climbed to their tops. They are a wonderful sight. Were they perhaps caused by some angry sea that broke away from its wide shores in a storm and threw its monstrous waves aloft only to have them turn to stone, and remain motionless in the air? Or did heavy storm clouds fall from heaven and cumber up the earth? For they have the same gray color and their white crests flash and sparkle in the sun.

Until you get to the Carpathian Mountains you may hear Russian speech, and just beyond the mountain there are still here and there echoes of our native tongue; but further beyond, faith and speech are different. The numerous Hungarian people live there; they ride, fight, and drink like any Cossack, and do not grudge gold pieces from their pockets for their horses' trappings and costly coats. There are great wide lakes among the mountains. They are still as glass and reflect bare mountaintops and the green slopes below like mirrors.

But who rides through the night on a huge black horse whether stars shine or not? What hero of superhuman stature gallops under the mountains, above the lakes, is mirrored with his gigantic horse in the still waters and throws his vast reflection on the mountains?

His plated armor glitters; his saber rattles against the saddle; his helmet is tilted forward; his mustaches are black; his eyes are closed, his eyelashes are drooping—he is asleep and drowsily holds the reins; and on the same horse sits with him a young child, and he too is asleep and drowsily holds on to the hero. Who is he, where goes he, and why? Who knows? Not one day nor two has he been traveling over the mountains. Day breaks, the sun shines, and he is seen no more; only from time to time the mountain people behold a long shadow flitting over the mountains, though the sky is bright and there is no cloud upon it. But as soon as night brings back the darkness, he appears again and is reflected in the lakes and his quivering shadow follows him. He has crossed many mountains and at last he reaches Krivan. There is no mountain in the Carpathians higher than this one; it towers like a monarch above the others. There the horse and his rider halted and sank into even deeper slumber and the clouds descended and covered them and hid them from view.

XIII

"Hush . . . don't knock like that, nurse: my child is asleep. My baby cried a long time, now he is asleep. I am going to the forest, nurse! But why do you look at me like this? You are hideous: there are iron pincers coming out of your eyes . . . ugh, how long they are, and they blaze like fire! You must be a witch! Oh, if you are a witch, go away! You will steal my son. How absurd the Captain is; he thinks it is enjoyable for me to live in Kiev. No, my husband and my son are here. Who will look after the house? I went out so quietly that even the dog and the cat did not hear me. Do you want to grow young again, nurse? That's not hard at all; you need only dance. Look, how I dance."

And uttering these incoherent sentences Katerina began dancing, looking wildly about her and putting her arms akimbo. With a shriek she tapped with her feet; her silver heels clanked regardless of time or tune. Her black tresses floated loose about her white neck. Like a bird she flew around without resting, waving her hands and nodding her head, and it seemed as though she must either fall helpless to the ground or soar away from earth altogether.

The old nurse stood mournfully, her wrinkled face wet with tears; the trusty Cossacks had heavy hearts as they looked at their mistress. At last she was exhausted and languidly tapped with her feet on the same spot, imagining that she was dancing. "I have a necklace, lads," she said, stopping at last, "and you have not . . . ! Where is my husband?" she cried suddenly, drawing a Turkish dagger out of her girdle. "Oh, this is not the knife I need." With that, tears of grief came into her eyes. "My father's heart is far away; it will not reach it. His heart is wrought of iron; it was forged by a witch in the furnace of hell. Why does not my father come? Does not he know that it is time to stab him? He wants me to come myself, it seems . . ." and breaking off she laughed strangely. "A funny story came into my mind: I remembered how my husband was buried. He was buried alive, you know . . . It did make me laugh . . . ! Listen, listen!" and instead of speaking she began to sing:

> A bloodstained cart races on,
> A Cossack lies upon it
> Shot through the breast, stabbed to the heart.
> In his right hand he holds a spear
> And blood is trickling from it,
> A stream of blood is flowing.
> A plane tree stands over the river,
> Above the tree a raven croaks.
> A mother is weeping for the Cossack.
> Weep not, mother, do not grieve!
> For your son is married.
> He chose a pretty lady for his bride,
> A mound of earth in the bare fields
> Without a door or window.
> And this is how my story ends.
> A fish was dancing with a crab,
> And may a fever take his mother
> If he will not love me!

This was how she muddled lines from different songs. She had been living two days in her own house and would not hear of Kiev. She would not say her prayers, refused to see anyone, and wandered from morning till night in the dark oak thickets. Sharp twigs scratched her white face and shoulders; the wind fluttered her loose hair; the autumn leaves rustled under her feet—she looked at nothing. At the hour when the glow of sunset dies away and before the stars come out or the moon shines, it is frightening to walk in the forest: unbaptized infants claw at the trees and clutch at the branches; sobbing and laughing, they hover over the road and the expanses of nettles; maidens who have lost their souls rise up one after the other from the depths of the Dnieper, their green tresses stream over their shoulders, the water drips splashing to the ground from their long hair; and a maiden shines through the water as through a veil of crystal; her lips smile mysteriously, her cheeks glow, her eyes bewitch the soul . . . as though she might burn with love, as though she might kiss one to death. Flee, Christian! Her lips are ice, her bed—the cold water; she will drag you under water. Katerina looked at no one; in her frenzy she had no fear of the water sprites; she wandered at night with her knife, seeking her father.

In the early morning a visitor arrived, a man of handsome appearance in a scarlet coat, and inquired for the lord Danilo; he heard all the story, wiped his tear-stained eyes with his sleeves, and shrugged his shoulders. He said that he had fought side by side with Burulbash; side by side they had done battle with the Turks and the Crimeans; never had he thought that the lord Danilo would meet with such an end. The visitor told them many other things and wanted to see the lady Katerina.

At first Katerina heard nothing of what the guest said; but afterward she began to listen to his words as though understanding. He told her how Danilo and he had lived together like brothers; how once they had hidden under a dam from the Crimeans . . . Katerina listened and kept her eyes fixed upon him.

"She will recover," the Cossacks thought, looking at her, "this guest will heal her! She is listening like one who understands!"

The visitor began meanwhile describing how Danilo had once, in a confidential conversation, said to him: "Listen, brother Kopryan, when it is God's will that I am gone, you take Katerina, take her for your wife . . ."

Katerina looked piercingly at him. "Aie!" she shrieked, "it is he, it is my father!" and she flew at him with her knife.

For a long time he struggled, trying to snatch the knife from her; at last he snatched it away, raised it to strike—and a terrible deed was done: the father killed his crazed daughter.

The astounded Cossacks rushed at him, but the sorcerer had already leaped upon his horse and was gone.

XIV

An extraordinary marvel appeared outside Kiev. All the nobles and the hetmans assembled to see the miracle: in all directions even the ends of the earth had become visible. Far off was the dark blue of the mouth of the Dnieper and beyond that the Black Sea. Men who had traveled recognized the Crimea jutting like a mountain out of the sea and the marshy Sivash. On the right could be seen the Galician land.

"And what is that?" people asked the old men, pointing to white and gray crests looming far away in the sky, looking more like clouds than anything else.

"Those are the Carpathian Mountains!" said the old men. "Among them are some that are forever covered with snow, and the clouds cling to them and hover there at night."

Then a new miracle happened: the clouds vanished from the highest peak and on the top of it appeared a horseman, in full knightly armor, with his eyes closed, and he could be distinctly seen as though he were standing close to them.

Then among the marveling and fearful people, one leaped on a horse, and looking wildly about him as though to see whether he were pursued, hurriedly set his horse galloping at its utmost speed. It was the sorcerer. Why was he so panic-stricken? Looking in terror at the marvelous knight, he had recognized the face which had appeared to him when he was working his spells. He could not have said why his whole soul was thrown into confusion at this sight, and looking fearfully about him, he raced till he was overtaken by night and the stars began to come out. Then he turned homeward, perhaps to ask the Evil One what was meant by this marvel. He was just about to leap with his horse over a stream which lay across his path when his horse suddenly stopped in full gallop, looked around at him—and, marvelous to relate, laughed aloud! Two rows of white teeth gleamed horribly in the darkness. The sorcerer's hair stood up on his head. He uttered a wild scream, wept like one frantic, and turned his horse straight for Kiev. He felt as though he were being pursued on all sides: the trees that surrounded him in the dark forest strove to strangle him, nodding their black beards and stretching out their long branches; the stars seemed to be racing ahead of him and pointing to the sinner; the very road seemed to be flying after him.

The desperate sorcerer fled to the holy places in Kiev.

XV

A holy hermit sat alone in his cave before a little lamp and did not take his eyes off the holy book. It was many years since he had first shut himself up in his cave; he had already made himself a coffin in which he would lie down to sleep. The holy man closed his book and fell to praying. . . . Suddenly a man of a strange and terrible aspect ran into the cave. At first the holy hermit was astounded and stepped back upon seeing such a man. He was trembling all over like an aspen leaf; his eyes rolled in their sockets, a light of terror gleamed in them; his hideous face made one shudder.

"Father, pray! pray!" he shouted desperately, "pray for a lost soul!" and he sank to the ground.

The holy hermit crossed himself, took up his book, opened it, and stepped back in horror, dropping the book: "No, incredible sinner! There is no mercy for you! Away! I cannot pray for you!"

"No?" the sorcerer cried frantically.

"Look! the letters in the holy book are dripping with blood. . . . There has never been such a sinner in the world!"

"Father! you are mocking me!"

"Away, accursed sinner! I am not mocking you. I am overcome with fear. It is not good for a man to be with you!"

"No, no! You are mocking, say not so . . . I see that your lips are smiling and the rows of your old teeth are gleaming white!"

And like one possessed he flew at the holy hermit and killed him.

A terrible moan was heard and echoed through the forest and the fields. Dry withered arms with long claws rose up from beyond the forest; they trembled and disappeared.

And now he felt no fear. All was confusion: there was a noise in his ears, a noise in his head as though he were drunk, and everything before his eyes was veiled as though by spiders' webs. Leaping on his horse he rode straight to Kanev, thinking from there to go through Cherkassy direct to the Crimean Tartars, though he knew not why. He rode one day and a second and still Kanev was not in sight. The road was the same; he should have reached it long before, but there was no sign of Kanev. Far away there gleamed the cupolas of churches; but that was not Kanev but Shumsk. The sorcerer was amazed to find that he had traveled the wrong way. He turned back toward Kiev, and a day later a town appeared—not Kiev but Galich, a town further from Kiev than Shumsk and not far from Hungary. At a loss what to do he turned back, but felt again that he was going backward as he went on. No one in the world could tell what was in the sorcerer's mind; and had anyone seen and known, he would never have slept peacefully at night or laughed again in his life. It was not malice, not terror, and not fierce anger. There is no word in the world to say what it was. He was burning, scalding; he would have liked to trample the whole country from Kiev to Galich with all the people and everything in it and drown it in the Black Sea. But it was not from malice he would do it: no, he knew not why he wanted it. He shuddered when he saw the Carpathian Mountains and lofty Krivan, its crest capped with a gray cloud; the horse still galloped on and now was racing among the mountains. The clouds suddenly lifted, and facing him appeared the horseman in his terrible majesty. . . . The sorcerer tried to stop, he tugged at the rein; the horse neighed wildly, tossed its mane, and dashed toward the horseman. Then the sorcerer felt everything die within him, while the motionless horseman stirred and suddenly opened his eyes, saw the sorcerer flying toward him, and roared with laughter. The wild laugh echoed through the mountains like a clap of thunder and resounded in the sorcerer's heart, setting his whole body throbbing. He felt that some mighty being had taken possession of him and was moving within him, hammering on his heart and his veins . . . so fearfully did that laugh resound within him!

The horseman stretched out his mighty hand, seized the sorcerer, and lifted him into the air. The sorcerer died instantly and he opened his eyes after his death: but he was dead and looked out of dead eyes. Neither the living nor the risen from the dead have such a terrible look in their eyes. He rolled his dead eyes from side to side and saw dead men rising up from Kiev, from Galicia and the Carpathian Mountains, exactly like him.

Pale, very pale, one taller than another, one bonier than another, they thronged around the horseman who held this awful prey in his hand. The horseman laughed once more and dropped the sorcerer down a precipice. And all the corpses leaped into the precipice and fastened their teeth in the dead man's flesh. Another, taller and more terrible than all the rest, tried to rise from the ground but could not—he had not the power, he had grown so immense in the earth; and if he had risen he would have overturned the Carpathians and the whole of the Sedmigrad and the Turkish lands. He only stirred slightly, but that set the whole earth quaking, and overturned many huts and crushed many people.

And often in the Carpathians a sound is heard as though a thousand mills were churning up the water with their wheels: it is the sound of the dead men gnawing a corpse in the endless abyss which no living man has seen for none dares to approach it. It sometimes happens that the earth trembles from one end to another: that is said by the learned men to be due to a mountain near the sea from which flames issue and hot streams flow. But the old men who live in Hungary and Galicia know better, and say that it is the dead man who has grown so immense in the earth trying to rise that makes the earth quake.

XVI

A crowd had gathered around an old bandore player in the town of Glukhov and had been listening for an hour to the blind man's playing. No bandore player sang so well and such marvelous songs. First he sang of the leaders of the Dnieper Cossacks in the old days, of Sagaydachny and Khmelnitzky. Times were different then: the Cossacks were at the height of their glory, they trampled their foes underfoot and no one dared to mock them. The old man sang merry songs too, and looked about at the crowd as though his eyes could see, and his fingers with little sheaths of bone fixed to them danced like flies over the strings, and it seemed that the strings themselves were playing; and the crowd, the old people looking down and the young staring at the singer, dared not even whisper.

"Now," said the old man, "I will sing to you of what happened long ago." The people pressed closer and the blind man sang:

"In the days of Stepan, prince of Sedmigrad (the prince of Sedmigrad was also king of the Poles), there lived two Cossacks: Ivan and Petro. They lived together like brothers: 'See here, Ivan,' said Petro, 'whatever you gain, let us go halves; when one is merry, the other is merry too; when one is sad, the other is sad too; when one wins booty, we share it; when one gets taken prisoner, the other sells everything to ransom him or else goes himself into captivity.'

And, indeed, whatever the Cossacks gained they shared equally: if they drove away herds of cattle or horses—they shared them.

"King Stepan waged war on the Turks. He had been fighting with the Turks three weeks and could not drive them out. And the Turks had a Pasha who with a few janissaries could slaughter a whole regiment. So King Stepan proclaimed that if a brave warrior could be found to bring him the Pasha dead or alive he would give him a reward equal to the pay of the whole army.

" 'Let us go and catch the Pasha, brother,' said Ivan to Petro. And the two Cossacks set off, one one way, one the other.

"Whether Petro would have been successful or not there is no telling; but Ivan brought the Pasha with a lasso around his neck to the King. 'Brave fellow!' said King Stepan, and he commanded that he should be given a sum equal to the pay of the whole army, and that he should be given land wherever he chose and as many cattle as he pleased. As soon as Ivan received the reward from the King, he shared the money that very day with Petro. Petro took half of the King's money, but could not bear the thought that Ivan had been so honored by the King, and he hid deep in his heart desire for vengeance.

"The two Cossacks were journeying to the land beyond the Carpathians that the King had granted to Ivan. Ivan had set his son on the horse behind him, tying the child to himself. The boy had fallen asleep; Ivan, too, began to doze. A Cossack should not sleep, the mountains paths are perilous . . . ! But the Cossack had a horse who knew the way; it would not stumble or leave the path. There is a precipice between the mountains; no one has ever seen the bottom of it; it is deep as the sky is high. The road passed just above the precipice; two men could ride abreast on it, but for three it was too narrow. The horse began stepping cautiously with the slumbering Cossack on its back. Petro rode beside him; he trembled all over and was breathless with joy. He looked around and thrust his sworn brother into the precipice; and the horse, the Cossack, and the baby fell into the abyss.

"But Ivan grasped a branch and only the horse dropped to the bottom. He began scrambling up with his son upon his back. He looked up when he was nearly at the top and saw that Petro was holding a lance ready to push him back. 'Merciful God! better I had never raised my eyes again than I should see my own brother holding a lance ready to push me back . . . ! Dear brother, stab me if that is my fate, but take my son: what has the innocent child done that he should be doomed to so cruel a death?' Petro laughed and thrust at him with the lance; the Cossack fell with his child to the bottom. Petro took all his goods and began to live like a Pasha. No one had such droves of horses as Petro; no one had such flocks of sheep. And Petro died.

"After he was dead, God summoned the two brothers, Ivan and Petro, to the judgment seat. 'This man is a great sinner,' said God. 'Ivan, it will take me long to find a punishment for him; you select a punishment for him!' For a long time Ivan pondered what punishment to fix and at last he said:

" 'That man did me a great injury: he betrayed his brother like a Judas and robbed me of my honorable name and offspring. And a man without honorable name and offspring is like a seed of wheat dropped into the earth only to die there. If it does not sprout, no one knows that the seed has been dropped into the earth.

" 'Let it be, O Lord, that none of his descendants may be happy upon earth; that the last of his race may be the worst criminal that has ever been seen, and that at every crime he commits, his ancestors, unable to rest in their graves and suffering torments unknown to the world of the living, should rise from the tomb! And that the Judas, Petro, should be unable to rise and that hence he should suffer pain all the more intense; that he should bite the earth like one possessed and writhe in the ground in anguish!

" 'And when the time comes that that man's wickedness has reached its full measure, let me, O Lord God, rise on my horse from the precipice to the highest peak of the mountains, and let him come to me and I will throw him from that mountain into the deepest abyss. And let all his dead ancestors, wherever they lived in their lifetime, come from various parts of the earth to gnaw him for the sufferings he inflicted upon them, and let them gnaw him forever, and I shall rejoice looking at his sufferings. And let the Judas, Petro, be unable to rise out of the earth. Let him lust to gnaw but be forced to gnaw himself, and let his bones grow bigger and bigger as time goes on, so that his pain may be the greater. That torture will be worse for him than any other, for there is no greater

torture for a man than to long for vengeance and be unable to accomplish it.'

" 'A terrible punishment thou has devised, O man . . . !' God
said. 'All shall be as thou hast said; but thou shalt sit forever on thy
horse there and shalt not enter the kingdom of heaven!' And so it
all was fulfilled; the strange horseman still sits on his steed in the
Carpathians and sees the dead men gnawing the corpse in the bottomless abyss and feels how the dead Petro grows larger under the
earth, gnaws his bones in dreadful agony, and sets the earth quaking fearfully."

The blind man had finished his song; he began thrumming the
strings again and singing amusing ballads about Khoma and Yeri-
oma and Stkyar Stokoza. . . . But his listeners, old and young,
could not rouse themselves from reverie; they still stood with
bowed heads, thinking of the terrible story of long ago.

IVAN FIODOROVICH SHPONKA AND HIS AUNT

There is a story about this story: we were told it by Stepan Ivanovich Kurochka, who came over from Gadyach. You must know
that my memory is incredibly poor: you may tell me a thing or not

tell it, it is all the same. It is just pouring water into a sieve. Being aware of this weakness, I purposely begged him to write the story down in a notebook. Well, God give him good health, he was always a kind man to me, he began to work and wrote it down. I put it in the little table; I believe you know it: it stands in the corner as you come in by the door. . . . But there, I forgot that you had never been in my house. My old woman, with whom I have lived thirty years, has never learned to read—no use hiding one's shortcomings. Well, I noticed that she baked the pies on paper of some sort. She bakes pies beautifully, dear readers; you will never taste better pies anywhere. I happened to look on the underside of a pie —what did I see? Written words! My heart seemed to tell me at once: I went to the table; only half the book was there! All the other pages she had carried off for the pies. What could I do? There is no fighting at our age!

Last year I happened to be passing through Gadyach. Before I reached the town I purposely tied a knot in my handkerchief so that I might not forget to ask Stepan Ivanovich about it. That was not all: I vowed to myself that as soon as ever I sneezed in the town I would be sure to think of it. It was all no use. I drove through the town and sneezed and blew my nose too, but still I forgot it; and I only thought of it nearly six miles after I had passed through the town gate. Well, it couldn't be helped, I had to publish it without the end. However, if anyone particularly wants to know what happened later on in the story, he need only go on purpose to Gadyach and ask Stepan Ivanovich. He will be glad to tell the story all over again from the beginning. He lives not far from the brick church. There is a little lane close by, and as soon as you turn into the lane it is the second or third gate. Or better still, when you see a big post with a quail on it in the yard and coming to meet you a fat peasant woman in a green skirt (you should know, he is a bachelor), that is his yard. Though you may also meet him in the market, where he is to be seen every morning before nine o'clock, choosing fish and vegetables for his table and talking to Father Antip or the Jewish contractor. You will know him at once, for there is no one else who has trousers of printed linen and a yellow cotton coat. And another thing to help you recognize him—he always swings his arms as he walks. Denis Petrovich, the assessor, now deceased, always used to say when he saw him in the distance: "Look, look, here comes our windmill!"

I

IVAN FIODOROVICH SHPONKA

It is four years since Ivan Fiodorovich retired from the army
and came to live on his farm Vytrebenki. When he was still Vanyusha,[1] he was at the Gadyach district school, and I must say he was a
very well-behaved and industrious boy. Nikifor Timofeevich Dee-
prichastie[2] the teacher of Russian grammar, used to say that if all
the boys had been as anxious to do their best as Shponka, he would
not have brought into the classroom the maplewood ruler with
which, as he confessed, he was tired of hitting the lazy and mischievous boys' hands. Vanyusha's exercise book was always neat,
with a ruled margin, and not the tiniest blot anywhere. He always
sat quietly with his arms folded and his eyes fixed on the teacher,
and he never used to stick scraps of paper on the back of the boy sitting in front of him, never cut the bench, and never played at
shoving the other boys off the bench before the teacher came in. If
anyone wanted a penknife to sharpen his quill, he immediately
asked Ivan Fiodorovich, knowing that he always had a penknife,
and Ivan Fiodorovich, then called simply Vanyusha, would take it
out of a little leather case attached to a buttonhole of his gray coat,
and would only request that the sharp edge should not be used for
scraping the quill, pointing out that there was a blunt side for the
purpose. Such good conduct soon attracted the attention of the
Latin teacher, whose cough in the passage was enough to reduce
the class to terror, even before his frieze coat and pockmarked face
had appeared in the doorway. This terrifying teacher, who always
had two birches lying on his desk and half of whose pupils were always on their knees, made Ivan Fiodorovich monitor, although
there were many boys in the class of much greater ability. Here I
cannot omit an incident which had an influence on the whole of his
future life. One of the boys entrusted to his charge tried to induce
his monitor to write *scit*[3] on his report, though he had not learned
his lesson, by bringing into class a pancake soaked in butter and
wrapped in paper. Though Ivan Fiodorovich was usually conscientious, on this occasion he was hungry and could not resist the

[1] Diminutive of Ivan, i.e., a child. (ed.)
[2] "Participle," i.e., Nikifor Timofeevich Participle. (ed.)
[3] Latin for "knows," i.e., a good grade. (ed.)

temptation; he took the pancake, held a book up before him, and began eating it, and he was so absorbed in this occupation that he did not observe that a deathly silence had fallen upon the class. He woke up with horror only when a terrible hand protruding from a frieze overcoat seized him by the ear and dragged him into the middle of the room. "Hand over that pancake! Hand it over, I tell you, you rascal!" said the terrifying teacher; he seized the buttery pancake in his fingers and flung it out of the window, sternly forbidding the boys running about in the yard to pick it up. Then he proceeded on the spot to whack Ivan Fiodorovich very painfully on the hands; and quite rightly—the hands were responsible for taking it and no other part of the body. Anyway, the timidity which had always been characteristic of him was more marked from that time forward. Possibly the same incident was the explanation of his feeling no desire to enter the civil service, having learned by experience that one is not always successful in hiding one's misdeeds.

He was very nearly fifteen when he advanced to the second class,[4] where instead of the four rules of arithmetic and the abridged catechism, he went on to the unabridged one, the book describing the duties of man, and fractions. But seeing that the further you went into the forest the thicker the wood became, and receiving the news that his father had departed this life, he stayed only two years longer at school, and with his mother's consent went into the P—— infantry regiment.

The P—— infantry regiment was not at all of the class to which many infantry regiments belong, and, although it was for the most part stationed in villages, it was in no way inferior to many cavalry regiments. The majority of the officers drank hard and were really as good at dragging Jews around by their earlocks as any Hussars; some of them even danced the mazurka, and the colonel of the regiment never missed an opportunity of mentioning the fact when he was talking to anyone in company. "Among my officers," he used to say, patting himself on the belly after every word, "a number dance the mazurka, quite a number of them, really a great number of them indeed." To show our readers the degree of culture of the P—— infantry regiment, we must add that two of the officers were passionately fond of the game of bank[5] and used to

4 Ivan was not too bright. He should have advanced to the second class—roughly equivalent to the sixth grade—at eleven. (ed.)
5 *Shtoss*, a variation of faro. (ed.)

gamble away their uniforms, caps, overcoats, sword knots, and even their underclothes, which is more than you could say about every cavalry regiment.

Contact with such comrades did not, however, diminish Ivan Fiodorovich's timidity; and as he did not drink hard liquor, preferring instead a wineglassful of ordinary vodka before dinner and supper, did not dance the mazurka or play bank, naturally he was bound to be always left alone. And so it came to pass that while the others were driving about with hired horses, visiting the less important landowners, he, sitting at home, spent his time in pursuits peculiar to a mild and gentle soul: he either polished his buttons, or read a fortunetelling book[6] or set mousetraps in the corners of his room, or failing everything he would take off his uniform and lie on his bed.

On the other hand, no one in the regiment was more punctual in his duties than Ivan Fiodorovich, and he drilled his platoon in such a way that the commander of the company always held him up as a model to the others. Consequently in a short time, only eleven years after becoming an ensign, he was promoted to be a second lieutenant.

During that time he had received the news that his mother was dead, and his aunt, his mother's sister, whom he only knew from her bringing him in his childhood—and even sending him when he was at Gadyach—dried pears and extremely nice honeycakes which she made herself (she was on bad terms with his mother and so Ivan Fiodorovich had not seen her in later years), this aunt, in the goodness of her heart, undertook to look after his little estate and in due time informed him of the fact by letter.

Ivan Fiodorovich, having the fullest confidence in his aunt's good sense, continued to perform his duties as before. Some men in his position would have grown conceited at such promotion, but pride was a feeling of which he knew nothing, and as lieutenant he was the same Ivan Fiodorovich as he had been when an ensign. He spent another four years in the regiment after his promotion, an event of great importance to him, and was about to leave the Mogiliov district for Great Russia with his regiment when he received a letter as follows:

---

[6] Fortunetelling and dream-interpreting books were enormously popular throughout Russia. (ed.)

My Dear Nephew, Ivan Fiodorovich,

I am sending you some linen: five pairs of socks and four shirts of fine linen; and what is more I want to talk to you of something serious; since you have already a rank of some importance, as I suppose you are aware, and have reached a time of life when it is fitting to take up the management of your land, there is no reason for you to remain longer in military service. I am getting old and can no longer see to everything on your farm; and in fact there is a great deal that I want to talk to you about in person.

Come, Vanyusha! Looking forward to the real pleasure of seeing you, I remain your very affectionate aunt

VASILISA TSUPCHEVSKA

P.S.—There is a wonderful turnip in our vegetable garden, more like a potato than a turnip.

A week after receiving this letter Ivan Fiodorovich wrote an answer as follows:

Honored Madam, Auntie, Vasilisa Kashporovna,

Thank you very much for sending the linen. My socks especially are very old; my orderly has darned them four times and that has made them very tight. As to your views in regard to my service in the army, I completely agree with you, and the day before yesterday I sent in my papers. As soon as I get my discharge I will engage a chaise. As to your commission in regard to the wheat seed and Siberian grain, I cannot carry it out; there is none in all the Mogiliov province. Pigs here are mostly fed on brewers' grains together with a little beer when it has grown flat. With the greatest respect, honored madam and auntie, I remain your nephew

IVAN SHPONKA

At last Ivan Fiodorovich received his discharge with the grade of lieutenant, hired for forty rubles a Jew to drive from Mogiliov to Gadyach, and set off in the chaise just at the time when the trees are clothed with young and still scanty leaves, the whole earth is bright with fresh green, and there is the fragrance of spring over all the fields.

II

THE JOURNEY

Nothing of great interest occurred on the journey. They traveled more than two weeks. Ivan Fiodorovich might have arrived a little sooner than that, but the devout Jew kept the Sabbath on the Saturdays and, putting his horse blanket[7] over his head, prayed the whole day. Ivan Fiodorovich, however, as I have had occasion to mention already, was a man who did not give way to being bored. During these intervals he undid his trunk, took out his underclothes, inspected them thoroughly to see whether they were properly washed and folded; carefully removed the fluff from his new uniform, which had been made without epaulets, and repacked it all in the best possible way. He was not fond of reading in general; and if he did sometimes look into a fortunetelling book, it was because he liked to find again what he had already read several times. In the same way one who lives in the town goes every day to the club, not for the sake of hearing anything new there, but in order to meet there friends with whom it has been his habit to chat at the club from time immemorial. In the same way a government clerk will read a directory of addresses with immense satisfaction several times a day with no ulterior object; he is simply entertained by the printed list of names. "Ah! Ivan Gavrilovich So-and-so . . ." he murmurs mutely to himself. "And here again am I! h'm . . . !" and next time he reads it over again with exactly the same exclamations.

After a two-week journey Ivan Fiodorovich reached a little village some eighty miles from Gadyach. This was on Friday. The sun had long set when with the chaise and the Jew he reached an inn.

This inn differed in no respects from other little village inns. As a rule the traveler is zealously regaled in them with hay and oats, as though he were a posthorse. But should he want to lunch as decent people lunch, he keeps his appetite intact for some future opportunity. Ivan Fiodorovich, knowing all this, had provided himself beforehand with two bundles of pretzels and a sausage, and asking for a glass of vodka, of which there is never a shortage in any inn, he began his supper, sitting down on a bench before an oak table which was fixed immovably in the clay floor.

Meanwhile he heard the rattle of a chaise. The gates creaked but it was a long while before the chaise drove into the yard. A loud voice was engaged in scolding the old woman who kept the inn. "I will drive in," Ivan Fiodorovich heard, "but if I am bitten by a

---

7 I.e., prayer shawl. (ed.)

single bug in your inn, I will beat you, I swear I will, you old witch! and I won't give you anything for your hay either!"

A minute later the door opened and there walked—or rather squeezed himself—in a fat man in a green coat. His head rested immovably on his short neck, which seemed even thicker because of a double chin. To judge from his appearance, he belonged to that class of men who do not trouble their heads about trifles and whose whole life has passed easily.

"I wish you good day, honored sir!" he pronounced on seeing Ivan Fiodorovich.

Ivan Fiodorovich bowed in silence.

"Allow me to ask, to whom have I the honor of speaking?" the fat newcomer continued.

At such a question Ivan Fiodorovich involuntarily got up and stood at attention as he usually did when the colonel asked him a question. "Retired Lieutenant Ivan Fiodorovich Shponka," he answered.

"And may I ask what place you are bound for?"

"My own farm Vytrebenki."

"Vytrebenki!" cried the stern questioner. "Allow me, honored sir, allow me!" he said, going toward him, and waving his arms as though someone were hindering him or as though he were making his way through a crowd, he folded Ivan Fiodorovich in an embrace and kissed him first on the right cheek and then on the left and then on the right again. Ivan Fiodorovich was much gratified by this kiss, for his lips were pressed against the stranger's fat cheeks as though against soft cushions.

"Allow me to make your acquaintance, my dear sir!" the fat man continued: "I am a landowner of the same district of Gadyach and your neighbor; I live not more than four miles from your Vytrebenki in the village of Khortyshche; and my name is Grigory Grigorievich Storchenko. You really must, sir, you really must pay me a visit at Khortyshche. I won't speak to you if you don't. I am in haste now on business . . . Why, what's this?" he said in a mild voice to his lackey, a boy in a Cossack coat with patched elbows and a bewildered expression, who came in and put bundles and boxes on the table. "What's this, what's the meaning of it?" and by degrees Grigory Grigorievich's voice grew more and more threatening. "Did I tell you to put them here, my good lad? Did I tell you to put them here, you rascal? Didn't I tell you to heat the chicken up first, you dirty scoundrel? Get out!" he shouted stamping. "Wait, you ugly rogue! Where's the basket with the bottles? Ivan Fiodorovich!" he said, pouring out a glass of liqueur, "I beg you to take some cordial!"

"Oh, really, I cannot . . . I have already had occasion . . ." Ivan Fiodorovich began hesitatingly.

"I won't hear a word, sir!" the gentleman raised his voice, "I won't hear a word! I won't budge till you drink it. . . ."

Ivan Fiodorovich, seeing that it was impossible to refuse, not without gratification emptied the glass.

"This is a chicken, sir," said the fat Grigory Grigorievich, carving it in its wooden box. "I must tell you that my cook Yavdokha is fond of a drop at times and so she makes things too dry. Hey, boy!" here he turned to the boy in the Cossack coat who was bringing in a feather bed and pillows, "make my bed on the floor in the middle of the room! Make sure you put plenty of hay under the pillow! And pull a bit of hemp from the woman's spindle to stop up my ears for the night! I must tell you, sir, that I have the habit of stopping up my ears at night ever since the damned occasion when a cockroach crawled into my left ear in a Great Russian inn. Those damned Russians, as I found out afterward, eat their soup with cockroaches in it. Impossible to describe what happened to me; there was such a tickling, such a tickling in my ear . . . I was almost mad! I was cured by a simple old woman in our district, and by what, do you suppose? Simply by charming it. What do you think, my dear sir, about doctors? What I think is that they simply hoax us and make fools of us: some old women know a dozen times as much as all these doctors."

"Indeed, what you say is perfectly true, sir. There certainly are cases . . ." Here Ivan Fiodorovich paused as though he could not find the right word. It may not be improper to mention here that he was at no time lavish of words. This may have been due to timidity, or it may have been due to a desire to express himself elegantly.

"Shake up the hay properly, shake it up properly!" said Grigory Grigorievich to his servant. "The hay is so bad around here that you may come upon a twig in it any minute. Allow me, sir, to wish you a good night! We shall not see each other tomorrow. I am setting off before dawn. Your Jew will keep the Sabbath because tomorrow is Saturday, so it is no good for you to get up early. Don't forget my invitation; I won't speak to you if you don't come to see me at Khortyshche."

At this point Grigory Grigorievich's servant pulled off his coat and high boots and gave him his dressing gown instead, and Grigory Grigorievich stretched on his bed, and it looked as though one huge feather bed were lying on another.

"Hey, boy! where are you, rascal? Come here and arrange my quilt. Hey, boy, prop up my head with hay! Have you watered the horses yet? Some more hay! here, under this side! And arrange the bedspread properly, you rascal! That's right, more! Ough . . . !"

Then Grigory Grigorievich heaved two sighs and filled the whole room with a terrible whistling through his nose, snoring so loudly at times that the old woman who was snoozing on the stove, suddenly waking up, looked about her in all directions, but seeing nothing, subsided and went to sleep again.

When Ivan Fiodorovich woke up next morning, the fat gentleman was no longer there. This was the only noteworthy incident that occurred on the journey. Two days later he drew near his little farm.

He felt his heart begin to throb when the windmill waving its sails peeped out and, as the Jew drove his nag up the hill, the row of willows came into sight below. The pond gleamed bright and shining through them and a breath of freshness rose from it. Here he used to bathe in the old days; in that pond he used to wade with the peasant lads up to his neck after crayfish. The covered cart mounted the dam and Ivan Fiodorovich saw the little old house thatched with reeds, and the apple trees and cherry trees which he used to climb on the sly as a boy. He had no sooner driven into the yard than dogs of all kinds, brown, black, gray, spotted, ran up from every side. Some flew under the horse's hoofs, barking; others ran behind the cart, noticing that the axle was smeared with bacon fat; one, standing near the kitchen and keeping his paw on a bone, uttered a volley of shrill barks; and another barked from the distance, running to and fro wagging his tail and seeming to say: "Look, good Christians! What a fine young fellow I am!" Boys in dirty shirts ran out to stare. A sow who was promenading in the yard with sixteen little pigs lifted her snout with an inquisitive air and grunted louder than usual. In the yard a number of hempen sheets were lying on the ground covered with wheat, millet, and barley drying

in the sun. A good many different kinds of herbs, such as wild
chicory and hawkweed, were drying on the roof.

Ivan Fiodorovich was so occupied looking at all this that he was
only roused when a spotted dog bit the Jew on the calf of his leg as
he was getting down from the box. The servants who ran out, that
is, the cook and another woman and two girls in woolen petticoats,
after the first exclamations: "It's our young master!" informed him
that his aunt was sowing sweet corn together with the girl Palashka
and Omelko the coachman, who often performed the duties of a
gardener and watchman also. But his aunt, who had seen the covered cart in the distance, was already on the spot. And Ivan Fiodorovich was astonished when she almost lifted him from the
ground in her arms, hardly able to believe that this could be the
aunt who had written to him of her old age and infirmities.

III

THE AUNT

Aunt Vasilisa Kashporovna was at this time about fifty. She had
never married, and commonly declared that she valued her maiden
state above everything. Though, indeed, to the best of my memory,
no one ever courted her. This was due to the fact that all men were
rather timid in her presence, and never had the courage to make
her an offer. "A girl of great character, Vasilisa Kashporovna!" all
the young men used to say, and they were quite right, too, for there
was no one Vasilisa Kashporovna could not get the better of. With
her own manly hand, tugging every day at his forelock, she could,
unaided, turn the drunken miller, a worthless fellow, into a perfect
treasure. She was of almost gigantic stature and her breadth and
strength were fully in proportion. It seemed as though nature had
made an unpardonable mistake in condemning her to wear a dark
brown gown with little flounces on weekdays and a red cashmere
shawl on Sunday and on her name day, though a dragoon's mustaches and high topboots would have suited her better than anything. On the other hand, her pursuits completely corresponded
with her appearance: she rowed the boat herself and was more
skillful with the oars than any fisherman; shot game; stood over
the mowers all the while they were at work; knew the exact number of the melons, of all kinds, in the vegetable garden; took a toll

of five kopeks from every wagon that crossed her dam; climbed the trees and shook down the pears; beat lazy vassals with her terrible hand and with the same menacing hand bestowed a glass of vodka on the deserving. Almost at the same moment she was scolding, dyeing yarn, racing to the kitchen, brewing kvass, making jam with honey; she was busy all day long and everywhere in the nick of time. The result of all this was that Ivan Fiodorovich's little property, which had consisted of eighteen serfs at the last census, was flourishing in the fullest sense of the word. Moreover, she had a very warm affection for her nephew and carefully saved kopeks for him.

From the time of his arrival at his home Ivan Fiodorovich's life was completely changed and took an entirely different turn. It seemed as though nature had designed him expressly for looking after an estate of eighteen serfs. His aunt observed that he would make an excellent farmer, though she did not yet permit him to meddle in every branch of the management. "He's still a child," she used to say, though Ivan Fiodorovich was in fact not far from forty. "How should he know it all?"

However, he was always in the fields with the reapers and mowers, and this was a source of unutterable pleasure to his gentle heart. The sweep of a dozen or more gleaming scythes in unison; the sound of the grass falling in even swathes; the caroling songs of the reapers at intervals, at one time joyous as the welcoming of a guest, at another mournful as a parting; the calm pure evening—and what an evening! How free and fresh the air! How everything revived; the steppe flushed red, then turned dark blue and gleamed with flowers; quails, bustards, gulls, grasshoppers, thousands of insects, and all of them whistling, buzzing, chirping, calling, and suddenly blending into a harmonious chorus; nothing was silent for an instant, while the sun set and was hidden. Oh, how fresh and delightful it was! Here and there about the fields campfires were built and cauldrons set over them, and around the fires the mowers sat down; the steam from the dumplings floated upward; the twilight turned grayer. . . . It is hard to say what passed in Ivan Fiodorovich at such times. When he joined the mowers, he forgot to try their dumplings, though he liked them very much, and stood motionless, watching a gull disappear in the sky or counting the sheaves of wheat dotted over the field.

In a short time Ivan Fiodorovich was spoken of as a great farmer.

His aunt never tired of rejoicing over her nephew and never lost an opportunity of boasting of him. One day—it was just after the end of the harvest, that is, at the end of July—Vasilisa Kashporovna took Ivan Fiodorovich by the arm with a mysterious air, and said she wanted now to speak to him of a matter which had long been on her mind.

"You are aware, dear Ivan Fiodorovich," she began "that there are eighteen serfs on your farm, though, indeed, that is by the census register, and in reality they may amount to more, they may be twenty-four. But that is not the point. You know the copse that lies behind our vegetable ground, and no doubt you know the broad meadow behind it; there are very nearly sixty acres in it; and the grass is so good that it is worth a hundred rubles every year, especially if, as they say, a cavalry regiment is to be stationed at Gadyach."

"To be sure, Auntie, I know: the grass is very good."

"You needn't tell me the grass is very good, I know it; but do you know that all that land is by rights yours? Why do you look so surprised? Listen, Ivan Fiodorovich! You remember Stepan Kuzmich? What am I saying: 'you remember'! You were so little that you could not even pronounce his name. Yes, indeed! How could you remember! When I came on the very eve of Christmas and took you in my arms, you almost ruined my dress; luckily I was just in time to hand you to your nurse, Matryona; you were such a horrid little thing then . . . ! But that is not the point. All the land beyond our farm, and the village of Khortyshche itself belonged to Stepan Kuzmich. I must tell you that before you were in this world he used to visit your mama—though, indeed, only when your father was not at home. Not that I say it to blame her—God rest her soul!—though your poor mother was always unfair to me! But that is not the point. Be that as it may, Stepan Kuzmich made a gift to you of that same estate of which I have been speaking. But your poor mama, in confidence, was a very strange character. The devil himself (God forgive me for the nasty word!) would have been puzzled trying to understand her. What she did with that deed —God only knows. It's my opinion that it is in the hands of that old bachelor, Grigory Grigorievich Storchenko. That potbellied scoundrel has got hold of the whole estate. I'd bet anything you like that he has hidden that deed."

"Allow me to ask, Auntie: isn't he the Storchenko whose acquaintance I made at the inn?" Here Ivan Fiodorovich described his meeting with Storchenko.

"Who knows," said his aunt after a moment's thought, "perhaps he is not a rascal. It's true that it's only six months since he came to live among us; there's no finding out what a man is in that time. The old lady, his mother, is a very sensible woman, so I hear, and they say she is a great hand at pickling cucumbers; her own serf girls can make wonderful rugs. But as you say he gave you such a friendly welcome, go and see him; perhaps the old sinner will listen to his conscience and will give up what is not his. If you like you can go in the chaise, only those confounded brats have pulled out all the nails at the back; we must tell the coachman, Omelko, to nail the leather on better everywhere."

"What for, Auntie? I will take the trap that you sometimes go out shooting in."

With that the conversation ended.

IV

THE DINNER

It was about dinnertime when Ivan Fiodorovich drove into the hamlet of Khortyshche, and he felt a little timid as he approached the country house. It was a long house, not thatched with reeds like the houses of many of the neighboring landowners, but with a wooden roof. Two barns in the yard also had wooden roofs: the gate was of oak. Ivan Fiodorovich felt like a dandy who, on arriving at a ball, sees everyone more smartly dressed than himself. He stopped his horse by the barn as a sign of respect and went on foot toward the front door.

"Ah, Ivan Fiodorovich!" cried the fat man Grigory Grigorievich, who was crossing the yard in his coat but without necktie, vest, and suspenders. But apparently this attire weighed oppressively on his bulky person, for the perspiration was streaming down him.

"Why, you said you would come as soon as you had seen your aunt, and all this time you have not been here?" After these words Ivan Fiodorovich's lips found themselves again in contact with the same cushions.

"I've been busy looking after the land . . . I have come just for a minute to see you on business. . . ."

"For a minute? Well, that won't do. Hey, boy!" shouted the fat gentleman, and the same boy in the Cossack coat ran out of the kitchen. "Tell Kasian to shut the gate tight, do you hear! make it fast! And unharness this gentleman's horse this minute. Please come indoors; it is so hot out here that my shirt's soaked."

On going indoors Ivan Fiodorovich made up his mind to lose no time and in spite of his shyness to act with decision.

"My aunt had the honor . . . she told me that a deed of the late Stepan Kuzmich's . . ."

It is difficult to describe the unpleasant grimace made by the broad face of Grigory Grigorievich at these words.

"Oh dear, I hear nothing!" he responded. "I must tell you that a cockroach got into my left ear (those damned Russians breed cockroaches in all their huts); no pen can describe what agony it was, it kept tickling and tickling. An old woman cured me by the simplest means . . ."

"I meant to say . . ." Ivan Fiodorovich ventured to interrupt, seeing that Grigory Grigorievich was intentionally changing the subject; "that in the late Stepan Kuzmich's will mention is made, so to speak, of a deed . . . According to it I ought . . ."

"I know; so your aunt has told you that story already. It's a lie, I swear it is! My uncle made no deed. Though, indeed, some such thing is referred to in the will. But where is it? No one has produced it. I tell you this because I sincerely wish you well. I assure you it is a lie!"

Ivan Fiodorovich said nothing, reflecting that possibly his aunt really might be mistaken.

"Ah, here comes Mother with my sisters!" said Grigory Grigorievich, "so dinner is ready. Let us go!"

And he drew Ivan Fiodorovich by the hand into a room in which vodka and snacks were on a table.

At the same time a short little old lady, a coffeepot in a cap, with two young ladies, one fair and one dark, came in. Ivan Fiodorovich, like a well-bred gentleman, went up to kiss the old lady's hand and then to kiss the hands of the two young ladies.

"This is our neighbor, Ivan Fiodorovich Shponka, Mother," said Grigory Grigorievich.

The old lady looked intently at Ivan Fiodorovich, or perhaps it only seemed that she looked intently at him. She was good-natured simplicity itself, though; she looked as though she would like to ask Ivan Fiodorovich: "How many cucumbers has your aunt pickled for the winter?"

"Have you had some vodka?" the old lady asked.

"You can't be yourself, Mother," said Grigory Grigorievich. "Who asks a visitor whether he has had anything? You offer it to him, that's all. Whether he wants to drink or not is his business. Ivan Fiodorovich! the centaury-flavored vodka or the Trofimov brand? Which do you prefer? And you, Ivan Ivanovich, why are you standing there?" Grigory Grigorievich said, turning around, and Ivan Fiodorovich saw the gentleman so addressed approaching the vodka, in a frock coat and an immense stand-up collar, which covered the whole back of his head, so that his head sat in it, as though it were a chaise.

Ivan Ivanovich went up to the vodka and rubbed his hands, carefully examined the wineglass, filled it, held it up to the light, and poured all the vodka at once into his mouth. He did not, however, swallow it at once, but rinsed his mouth thoroughly with it first before finally swallowing it, and then after eating some bread and salted mushrooms, he turned to Ivan Fiodorovich.

"Is it not Ivan Fiodorovich, Mr. Shponka, I have the honor of addressing?"

"Yes, certainly," answered Ivan Fiodorovich.

"You have changed a great deal, sir, since I saw you last. Why!" he continued, "I remember you when you were that high!" As he spoke he held his hand a yard from the floor. "Your poor father, God grant him the kingdom of heaven, was a rare man. He used to have melons such as you never see anywhere now. Here, for instance," he went on, drawing him aside, "they'll set melons before you on the table—such melons! You won't care to look at them! Would you believe it, sir, he used to have watermelons," he pronounced with a mysterious air, flinging out his arms as if he were about to embrace a stout tree trunk, "God bless me, they were as big as this!"

"Come to dinner!" said Grigory Grigorievich, taking Ivan Fiodorovich by the arm.

Grigory Grigorievich sat down in his usual place at the end of the table, draped with an enormous tablecloth which made him resemble the Greek heroes depicted by barbers on their signs. Ivan Fiodorovich, blushing, sat down in the place assigned to him, facing the two young ladies; and Ivan Ivanovich did not let slip the chance of sitting down beside him, inwardly rejoicing that he had someone to whom he could impart his various bits of information.

"You shouldn't take the end, Ivan Fiodorovich! It's a turkey!" said the old lady, addressing Ivan Fiodorovich, to whom the village waiter in a gray frock coat patched with black was offering a dish. "Take the back!"

"Mother! no one asked you to interfere!" commented Grigory Grigorievich. "You may be sure our visitor knows what to take himself! Ivan Fiodorovich! take a wing, the other one there with the gizzard! But why have you taken so little? Take a leg! Why do you gape at him?" he asked the waiter holding the dish. "Ask him! Go down on your knees, rascal! Say, at once, 'Ivan Fiodorovich, take a leg!'"

"Ivan Fiodorovich, take a leg!" the waiter bawled, kneeling down.

"H'm! do you call this a turkey?" Ivan Ivanovich muttered in a low voice, turning to his neighbor with an air of disdain. "Is that what a turkey ought to look like? If you could see my turkeys! I assure you there is more fat on one of them than on a dozen of these. Would you believe me, sir, they are really a repulsive sight when they walk about my yard, they are so fat . . . !"

"Ivan Ivanovich, you are telling lies!" said Grigory Grigorievich, overhearing these remarks.

"I tell you," Ivan Ivanovich went on talking to his neighbor, affecting not to hear what Grigory Grigorievich had said, "last year when I sent them to Gadyach, they offered me fifty kopeks apiece for them, and I wouldn't take even that."

"Ivan Ivanovich! I tell you, you are lying!" observed Grigory Grigorievich, dwelling on each syllable for greater distinctness and speaking more loudly than before.

But Ivan Ivanovich behaved as though the words could not possibly refer to him; he went on as before, but in a much lower voice: "Yes, sir, I would not take it. There is not a gentleman in Gadyach . . ."

"Ivan Ivanovich! You are a fool, and that's the truth," Grigory Grigorievich said in a loud voice. "Ivan Fiodorovich knows all about it better than you do, and doesn't believe you."

At this Ivan Ivanovich was really offended: he said no more, but began downing the turkey, even though it was not so fat as those that were a repulsive sight.

The clatter of knives, spoons, and plates took the place of conversation for a time, but loudest of all was the sound made by Grigory Grigorievich, smacking his lips over the marrow of the mutton bones.

"Have you," inquired Ivan Ivanovich after an interval of silence, poking his head out of the chaise, "read *The Travels of Korobeynikov to Holy Places*? [8] It's a real delight to heart and soul! Such books aren't published nowadays. I very much regret that I did not notice in what year it was written."

Ivan Fiodorovich, hearing mention of a book, applied himself diligently to taking sauce.

"It is truly marvelous, sir, when you think that a humble artisan visited all those places: over two thousand miles, sir! over two thousand miles! Truly, it was divine grace that enabled him to reach Palestine and Jerusalem."

"So you say," said Ivan Fiodorovich, who had heard a great deal about Jerusalem from his orderly, "that he visited Jerusalem."

"What are you saying, Ivan Fiodorovich?" Grigory Grigorievich inquired from the end of the table.

"I had occasion to observe what distant lands there are in the world!" said Ivan Fiodorovich, genuinely gratified that he had succeeded in uttering so long and difficult a sentence.

"Don't you believe him, Ivan Fiodorovich!" said Grigory Grigorievich, who had not quite caught what he said. "He always tells fibs!"

Meanwhile dinner was over. Grigory Grigorievich went to his own room, as his habit was, for a little nap; and the visitors followed their aged hostess and the young ladies into the drawing room, where the same table on which they had left vodka when they went out to dinner was now as though by some magical transformation covered with little saucers of jam of various sorts and dishes of cherries and different kinds of melons.

The absence of Grigory Grigorievich could be seen in everything: the old lady became more disposed to talk and, of her own

---

[8] I.e., *The Travels of a Moscow Merchant, Trifon Korobeynikov, and His Comrades to Jerusalem, Egypt, and Mount Sinai in 1583,* which first saw print in 1783, was frequently reprinted. (ed.)

accord, without being asked, revealed several secrets in regard to the making of apple cheese and the drying of pears. Even the young ladies began talking; though the fair one, who looked some six years younger than her sister and who was apparently about twenty-five, was rather silent.

But Ivan Ivanovich was more talkative and livelier than anyone. Feeling secure that no one would snub or contradict him, he talked of cucumbers and of planting potatoes and of how much more sensible people were in the old days—no comparison with what people are now!—and of how as time goes on everything improves and the most intricate inventions are discovered. He was, indeed, one of those persons who take great pleasure in relieving their souls by conversation and will talk of anything that possibly can be talked about. If the conversation touched upon grave and solemn subjects, Ivan Ivanovich sighed after each word and nodded his head slightly: if the subject were of a more domestic character, he would pop his head out of his chaise and make faces from which one could almost, it seemed, read how to make pear kvass, how large were the melons of which he was speaking, and how fat were the geese that were running about in his yard.

At last, with great difficulty and not before evening, Ivan Fiodorovich succeeded in taking his leave, and although he was usually ready to give way and they almost kept him for the night by force, he persisted in his intention of going—and went.

V

HIS AUNT'S NEW PLANS

"Well, did you get the deed out of the old reprobate?" Such was the question with which Ivan Fiodorovich was greeted by his aunt, who had been expecting him for some hours in the porch and had at last been unable to resist going out to the gate.

"No, Auntie," said Ivan Fiodorovich, getting out of the trap: "Grigory Grigorievich has no deed!"

"And you believed him? He was lying, the damned scoundrel! Some day I'll come across him and I will give him a drubbing with my own hands. Oh, I'd get rid of some of his fat for him! Though perhaps we ought first to consult our court assessor and see if we couldn't get the law on him. . . . But that's not the point now. Well, was the dinner good?"

"Very . . . yes, excellent, Auntie!"

"Well, what did you have? Tell me. The old lady, I know, is a great hand at looking after the cooking."

"Curd fritters with sour cream, Auntie; a stew of stuffed pigeons . . ."

"And a turkey with pickled plums?" asked his aunt, for she was herself very skillful in the preparation of that dish.

"Yes, there was a turkey, too . . . ! Very handsome young ladies, Grigory Grigorievich's sisters, especially the fair one!"

"Ah!" said Auntie, and she looked intently at Ivan Fiodorovich, who dropped his eyes, blushing. A new idea flashed into her mind. "Come, tell me," she said eagerly and with curiosity, "what are her eyebrows like?" We should note that the aunt considered fine eyebrows as the most important item in a woman's looks.

"Her eyebrows, Auntie, are exactly like what you described yours as being when you were young. And there are little freckles all over her face."

"Ah," commented his aunt, well pleased with Ivan Fiodorovich's observation, though he had had no idea of paying her a compliment. "What sort of dress was she wearing? Though, indeed, it's hard to get good material nowadays, such as I have here, for instance, in this dress. But that's not the point. Well, did you talk to her about anything?"

"Talk . . . how do you mean, Auntie? Perhaps you are imagining . . ."

"Well, what of it, there would be nothing strange in that! Such is God's will! It may have been ordained at your birth that you should make a match of it."

"I don't know how you can say such a thing, Auntie. That shows that you don't know me at all. . . ."

"Well, well, now he is offended," said his aunt. "He's still only a child!" she thought to herself: "he knows nothing! We must bring them together—let them get to know each other!"

The aunt went to have a look at the kitchen and left Ivan Fiodorovich alone. But from that time on she thought of nothing but seeing her nephew married as soon as possible and fondling his little ones. Her brain was absorbed in making preparations for the wedding, and it was noticeable that she bustled about more busily than ever, though the work was the worse rather than the better for it. Often when she was making the pies, a job which she never left to the cook, she would forget everything, and imagining that a tiny great-nephew was standing by her asking for some pie, would absently hold out her hands with the nicest bit for him, and the watchdog, taking advantage of this, would snatch the dainty morsel and by its loud munching rouse her from her reverie, for which it was always beaten with the poker. She even abandoned her favorite pursuits and did not go out shooting, especially after she shot a crow by mistake for a partridge, a thing which had never happened to her before.

At last, four days later, everyone saw the chaise brought out of the carriage house into the yard. The coachman Omelko (he was also the gardener and the watchman) had been hammering from early morning, nailing on the leather and continually chasing away the dogs who licked the wheels. I think it my duty to inform my readers that this was the very chaise in which Adam used to drive; and therefore, if anyone tries to convince you that some other chaise was Adam's, it is an absolute lie, and his chaise is certainly not the genuine article. It is impossible to say how it survived the Flood. It must be supposed that there was a special carriage house for it in Noah's Ark. I am very sorry that I cannot give a vivid picture of it for my readers. It is enough to say that Vasilisa Kashporovna was very well satisfied with its structure and always expressed regret that the old style of carriages had gone out of fashion. The chaise had been constructed a little on one side, that is, the right half was much higher than the left, and this pleased her particularly, because, as she said, a fat person could sit on one side and a tall person on the other. Inside the chaise, however, there was room for five small persons or three as big as the aunt.

About midday Omelko, having finished with the chaise, brought out of the stable three horses that were only a little younger than the chaise, and began harnessing them to the magnificent vehicle with a rope. Ivan Fiodorovich and his aunt, one on the left side and the other on the right, stepped in and the chaise drove off. The peasants they met on the road, seeing this sumptuous chaise (Vasilisa Kashporovna rarely drove out in it), stopped respectfully, taking off their caps and bowing low.

Two hours later the chaise stopped at the front door—I think I need not say—of Storchenko's house. Grigory Grigorievich was not at home. His old mother and the two young ladies came into the dining room to receive the guests. The aunt walked in with a majestic step, with a great air stopped short with one foot forward, and said in a loud voice:

"I am delighted, dear madam, to have the honor to offer you my respects in person; and at the same time to thank you for your hospitality to my nephew, who has been warm in his praises of it. Your buckwheat is very good, madam—I saw it as we drove into the village. May I ask how many sheaves you get to the acre?"

After that followed kisses all around. As soon as they were seated in the drawing room, the old lady began:

"About the buckwheat I cannot tell you: that's Grigory Grigorievich's department: it's long since I have had anything to do with the farming; indeed I am not equal to it, I am old now! In the old days I remember the buckwheat stood up to my waist; now goodness knows what it is like, though they do say everything is better now." At that point the old lady heaved a sigh, and some observers would have heard in that sigh the sigh of a past age, of the eighteenth century.

"I have heard, madam, that your own serf girls can make excellent carpets," said Vasilisa Kashporovna, and with that touched on the old lady's most sensitive nerve; at those words she seemed to brighten up, and she talked readily of the way to dye the yarn and prepare the thread.

From carpets the conversation passed easily to the pickling of cucumbers and drying of pears. In short, before the end of an hour the two ladies were talking together as though they had been friends all their lives. Vasilisa Kashporovna had already said a great deal to her in such a low voice that Ivan Fiodorovich could not hear what she was saying.

"Yes, would you like to have a look at them?" said the old lady, getting up.

The young ladies and Vasilisa Kashporovna also got up and all moved toward the serf girls' room. The aunt signaled, however, to Ivan Fiodorovich to remain, and whispered something to the old lady.

"Mashenka," said the latter, addressing the fair-haired young lady, "stay with our visitor and talk with him, so that he doesn't become bored!"

The fair-haired young lady remained and sat down on the sofa. Ivan Fiodorovich sat on his chair as though on thorns, blushed and cast down his eyes; but the young lady appeared not to notice this and sat unconcernedly on the sofa, carefully scrutinizing the windows and the walls, or watching the cat timorously running around under the chairs.

Ivan Fiodorovich grew a little bolder and would have begun a conversation; but it seemed as though he had lost all his words on the way. Not a single idea came into his mind.

The silence lasted for nearly a quarter of an hour. The young lady went on sitting as before.

At last Ivan Fiodorovich plucked up his courage.

"There are a great many flies in summer, madam!" he said in a half-trembling voice.

"A very great many!" answered the young lady. "My brother has made a swatter out of an old slipper of Mama's but there are still lots of them."

Here the conversation stalled again, and Ivan Fiodorovich was utterly unable to find anything to say.

At last the old lady and his aunt and the dark-haired young lady came back again. After a little more conversation, Vasilisa Kashporovna took leave of the old lady and her daughters in spite of their entreaties that they stay the night. The three ladies came out on the steps to see their visitors off, and continued for some time nodding to the aunt and nephew, as they looked out of the chaise.

"Well, Ivan Fiodorovich, what did you talk about when you were alone with the young lady?" his aunt asked him on the way home.

"Maria Grigorievna is a modest and well-behaved young lady!" said Ivan Fiodorovich.

"Listen, Ivan Fiodorovich, I want to talk seriously to you. Here you are thirty-eight, thank God; you have obtained a good rank in the service—it's time to think about children! You must have a wife . . ."

"What, Auntie!" cried Ivan Fiodorovich, panic-stricken, "a wife! No, Auntie, for goodness' sake . . . You make me quite ashamed . . . I've never had a wife . . . I wouldn't know what to do with her!"

"You'll find out, Ivan Fiodorovich, you'll find out," said his aunt, smiling, and she thought to herself: "What next, he is a perfect baby, he knows nothing!" "Yes, Ivan Fiodorovich!" she went on aloud, "we could not find a better wife for you than Maria Grigorievna. Besides, you are very much attracted by her. I have had a good talk with the old lady about it: she'll be delighted to see you her son-in-law. It's true that we don't know what that old scoundrel Grigorievich will say to it; but we won't consider him, and if he takes it into his head not to give her a dowry, we'll have the law on him. . . ."

At that moment the chaise drove into the yard and the ancient nags grew more lively, feeling that their stable was not far off.

"Listen, Omelko! Let the horses have a good rest first, and don't take them down to drink the minute they are unharnessed; they are overheated."

"Well, Ivan Fiodorovich," his aunt went on as she got out of the chaise, "I advise you to think it over carefully. I must run to the kitchen: I forgot to tell Solokha what to get for supper, and I expect the wretched girl won't have thought of it herself."

But Ivan Fiodorovich stood as though thunderstruck. It was true that Maria Grigorievna was a very nice-looking young lady; but to get married . . . ! It seemed to him so strange, so peculiar, he couldn't think of it without horror. Living with a wife . . . ! Unthinkable! He would not be alone in his own room, but they would always have to be together . . . ! Perspiration came out on his face as he sank more deeply into meditation.

He went to bed earlier than usual but in spite of all his efforts he could not go to sleep. But at last sleep, that universal comforter, came to him; but such sleep! He had never had such incoherent dreams. First, he dreamed that everything was whirling noisily around him, and he was running and running, as fast as his legs could carry him . . . Now he was at his last gasp . . . All at once someone caught him by the ear. "Aie! who is it?" "It is I, your wife!" a voice resounded loudly in his ear—and he woke up. Then he imagined that he was married, that everything in their little house was so peculiar, so strange: a double bed stood in his room instead of a single one; his wife was sitting on a chair. He felt strange; he did not know how to approach her, what to say to her, and then he noticed that she had the face of a goose. He turned aside and saw another wife, also with the face of a goose. Turning in another direction, he saw still a third wife; and behind him was still another. Then he was seized by panic: he dashed away into the garden; but there it was hot. He took off his hat, and—saw a wife sitting in it. Drops of sweat came out on his face. He put his hand in his pocket for his handkerchief and in his pocket too there was a

wife; he took some cotton out of his ear—and there too sat a wife.
. . . Then he suddenly began hopping on one leg, and his aunt,
looking at him, said with a dignified air: "Yes, you must hop on
one leg now, for you are a married man." He went toward her, but
his aunt was no longer an aunt but a belfry, and he felt that someone was dragging him by a rope up the belfry. "Who is it pulling
me?" Ivan Fiodorovich asked plaintively. "It is I, your wife. I am
pulling you because you are a bell." "No, I am not a bell, I am Ivan
Fiodorovich," he cried. "Yes, you are a bell," said the colonel of the
P—— infantry regiment, who happened to be passing. Then he
suddenly dreamed that his wife was not a human being at all but a
sort of woolen material, and that he went into a shop in Mogiliov.
"What sort of material would you like?" asked the shopkeeper.
"You had better take a wife, that is the most fashionable material! It
wears well! Everyone is having coats made of it now." The shopkeeper measured and cut off his wife. Ivan Fiodorovich put her under his arm and went off to a Jewish tailor. "No," said the Jew, "that
is poor material! No one has coats made of that now. . . ."

Ivan Fiodorovich woke up in terror, not knowing where he was;
he was dripping with cold perspiration.

As soon as he got up in the morning, he went at once to his fortunetelling book, at the end of which a virtuous bookseller had in
the goodness of his heart and unselfishness inserted an abridged
dream interpreter. But there was absolutely nothing in it that re-
motely resembled this incoherent dream.

Meanwhile a new scheme, of which you shall hear more in the
following chapter, matured in his aunt's brain.

A BEWITCHED PLACE

A True Story Told by the Sexton

I swear, I am sick of telling stories! Why, what would you expect? It really is tiresome; one goes on telling stories and there is
no getting out of it! Oh, very well, I will tell you a story, then;
only remember, it is for the last time. Well, we were talking
about a man's being able to get the better, as the saying is, of the
devil. To be sure, if it comes to that, all sorts of things do happen
in this world. . . . Better not say so, though: if the devil wants
to bamboozle you he will, I swear he will. . . . Now, you see,
my father had the four of us; I was only a moron then, I wasn't
more than eleven, no, not yet eleven. I remember as though it
were today when I was running on all fours and began barking
like a dog, my dad shouted at me, shaking his head: "Aie, Foma,
Foma, you are almost old enough to be married and you are as
foolish as a young mule."

My grandfather was still living then and fairly—may his hiccup ease up in the other world—strong on his legs. At times he
would imagine things . . . But how am I to tell a story like this?
Here one of you has been raking an ember for his pipe out of
the stove for the last hour and the other has run behind the cup-
board for something. It's too much . . . ! It wouldn't bother me
if you didn't want to hear what I had to say, but you kept annoying me for a story . . . If you want to listen, then listen!

Just at the beginning of spring Father went with the wagons to the Crimea to sell tobacco; but I don't remember whether he loaded two or three wagons; tobacco brought a good price in those days. He took my three-year-old brother with him to train him early as a dealer. Grandad, Mother, and I and a brother and another brother were left at home. Grandad had sown melons on a bit of ground by the roadway and went to stay at the shanty there; he took us with him, too, to scare the sparrows and the magpies away from the garden. I can't say we didn't enjoy it: sometimes we'd eat so many cucumbers, melons, turnips, onions, and peas that I swear, you would have thought there were cocks crowing in our stomachs. Well, to be sure, it was profitable too: travelers jog along the road, everyone wants to treat himself to a melon, and, besides that, from the neighboring farms they would often bring us fowls, turkeys, eggs, to exchange for our vegetables. We did very well.

But what pleased Grandad more than anything was that some fifty dealers would pass with their wagonloads every day. They are people, you know, who have seen life: if one of them wants to tell you anything, you would do well to perk up your ears, and to Grandad it was like dumplings to a hungry man. Sometimes there would be a meeting with old acquaintances—everyone knew Grandad—and you know yourself how it is when old folks get together: it is this and that, and so then and so then, and so this happened and that happened . . . Well, they just go on. They remember things that happened, God knows when.

One evening—why, it seems as though it might have happened today—the sun had begun to set. Grandad was walking about the garden removing the leaves with which he covered the watermelons in the day to save them from being scorched by the sun.

"Look, Ostap," I said to my brother, "here come some wagoners!"

"Where are the wagoners?" said Grandad, as he put a mark on the big melon so that the boys wouldn't eat it by accident.

There were, as a fact, six wagons trailing along the road; a wagoner, whose mustache had gone gray, was walking ahead of them. He was still—what shall I say?—ten paces off, when he stopped.

"Good day, Maxim, so it has pleased God we should meet here."

Grandad screwed up his eyes. "Ah, good day, good day! Where do you come from? And Bolyachka here, too! Good day, good day, brother! What the devil! why, they are all here: Krutotry-shchenko too! and Pecherytsya! and Koveliok and Stetsko! Good day! Ha, ha, ho, ho . . . !" And they began kissing each other.

They took the oxen out of the shafts and let them graze on the grass; they left the wagons on the road and they all sat down in a circle in front of the shanty and lit their pipes. Though they had no thought for their pipes; well, between telling stories and chattering, I don't believe they smoked a pipe apiece.

After supper Grandad began regaling his visitors with melons. So, taking a melon each, they trimmed it neatly with a knife (they were all old hands, had been about a good deal, and knew how to eat in company—I daresay they would have been ready to sit down even at a gentleman's table); after cleaning the melon well, everyone made a hole with his finger in it, drank the juice, and began cutting it up into pieces and putting them into his mouth.

"Why are you standing there gaping, boys?" said my grand-father. "Dance, you sons of bitches! Where's your pipe, Ostap? Now then, the Cossack dance! Foma, arms akimbo! Come, that's it, hey, hop!"

I was an energetic boy in those days. Cursed old age! Now I can't move like that; instead of cutting capers, my legs can only trip and stumble. For a long time Grandad watched us as he sat with the dealers. I noticed that his legs wouldn't keep still; it was as though something was tugging at them.

"Look, Foma," said Ostap, "if the old fellow isn't going to dance."

What do you think, he had hardly uttered the words when the old man could resist it no longer! He wanted, you know, to show off in front of the dealers.

"Now, you little bastards, is that the way to dance? This is the way to dance!" he said, getting up on his feet, stretching out his arms, and tapping with his heels.

Well, there is no denying that he did dance; he couldn't have danced better if it had been with the Hetman's wife. We stood aside and the old man went whirling all over the flat area beside the cucumber beds. But as soon as he had got halfway through the dance and wanted to do his best and cut some more capers, his feet wouldn't lift from the ground, no matter what he did! "What a plague!" He moved backwards and forwards again, got to the middle of the dance again, but he couldn't go on with it! Whatever he did—he couldn't do it, and he didn't do it! His legs were stiff as though made of wood. "Look, the place is bewitched, look, it is a spell of Satan! The enemy of mankind has a hand in it!" Well, he couldn't disgrace himself before the dealers like that, could he? He made a fresh start and began cutting tiny trifling capers, a joy to see; up to the middle—then no! it wouldn't be danced, and that is all!

"Ah, you damned Satan! I hope you choke on a rotten melon, that you perish before you grow up, you son of a bitch. See what shame he has brought me to in my old age . . . !" And indeed someone did laugh behind his back.

He looked around: no melon garden, no dealers, nothing; behind, in front, on both sides was a flat field. "Ay! Sss! . . . Well, I never!" he began screwing up his eyes—the place doesn't seem quite unfamiliar: on one side a copse, behind the copse some sort of post sticking up which can be seen far away against the sky. Damn it all! but that's the dovehouse in the priest's garden! On the other side, too, there is something grayish; he looked closer: it was the district clerk's threshing barn. So this was where the devil had dragged him! Going around in a circle, he found a little path. There was no moon; instead of it a white blur glimmered through a dark cloud.

"There will be a high wind tomorrow," thought Grandad. All at once there was the gleam of a light on a little grave to one side of the path. "Well, I never!" Grandad stood still, put his arms akimbo, and stared at it. The light went out; far away and a little further yet, another twinkled. "A treasure!" cried Grandad. "I'll bet anything it's a treasure!" And he was just about to spit on his hands to begin digging when he remembered that he had no spade or shovel with him. "Oh, what a pity! Well—who knows?—maybe I've only to lift the turf and there it lies, the precious dear! Well, there's nothing I can do; I'll mark the place anyway so as not to forget it afterwards."

So pulling along a large branch that must have been broken off by a high wind, he laid it on the little grave where the light gleamed and then he continued along the path. The young oak copse grew thinner; he caught a glimpse of a fence. "There, didn't I say that it was the priest's garden?" thought Grandad. "Here's his fence; now it is not three-quarters of a mile to the melon patch."

It was pretty late, though, when he came home, and he wouldn't have any dumplings. Waking my brother Ostap, he only asked him whether it was long since the dealers had gone, and then rolled himself up in his sheepskin. And when Ostap started to ask him: "And what did the devils do with you today, Grandad?" "Don't ask," he said, wrapping himself up tighter than ever, "don't ask, Ostap, or your hair will turn gray!"

And he began snoring so that the startled sparrows which had been flocking together to the melon patch rose up in the air and flew away. But how was it that he could sleep? There's no denying, he was a sly beast. God give him the kingdom of heaven, he could always get out of any scrape; sometimes he would pitch such a yarn that you would have to bite your lips.

Next day as soon as it began to get light Grandad put on his coat, fastened his belt, took a spade and shovel under his arm, put on his cap, drank a mug of kvass, wiped his lips with the skirt of his coat, and went straight to the priest's vegetable garden. He passed both the hedges and the low oak copse, and there was a path winding out between the trees and coming out into the open country; it seemed the same. He came out of the copse and the place seemed exactly the same as yesterday. He saw the dovehouse sticking out, but he could not see the threshing barn. "No, this isn't the place, it must be a little farther; it seems I must turn a little toward the threshing barn!" He turned back a little and began going along another path—then he could see the barn but not the dovehouse. Again he turned, and a little nearer to the dovehouse the barn was hidden. As though to spite him it began to drizzle. He ran again toward the barn—the dovehouse vanished; toward the dovehouse—the barn vanished.

"You damned Satan, may you never live to see your children!" he cried. And the rain came down in buckets.

Taking off his new boots and wrapping them in a handkerchief, so that they might not be warped by the rain, he ran off at a trot like some gentleman's saddle horse. He crept into the shanty, drenched through, covered himself with his sheepskin, and began grumbling between his teeth and cursing the devil with words such as I had never heard in my life. I must admit I would really have blushed if it had happened in broad daylight.

Next day I woke up and looked; Grandad was walking about the melon patch as though nothing had happened, covering the melons with burdock leaves. At dinner the old man began talking again and scaring my young brother, saying he would trade him for a fowl instead of a melon; and after dinner he made a pipe out of a bit of wood and began playing on it; and to amuse us gave us a melon which was twisted in three coils like a snake; he called it a Turkish one. I don't see such melons anywhere nowadays; it is true he got the seed from somewhere far away. In the evening, after supper, Grandad went with the spade to dig a new bed for late pumpkins. He began passing that bewitched place and he couldn't resist saying, "Cursed place!" He went into the middle of it, to the spot where he could not finish the dance the day before, and in his anger struck it with his spade. In a flash—that same field was all around him again: on one side he saw the dovehouse and on the other the threshing barn. "Well, it's a good thing I brought my spade. And there's the path, and there is the little grave! And there's the branch lying on it, and there, see there, is the light! If only I have made no mistake!"

He ran up stealthily, holding the spade in the air as though he were going to hit a hog that had poked its nose into a melon patch, and stopped before the grave. The light went out. On the grave lay a stone overgrown with weeds. "I must lift up that stone," thought Grandad, and tried to dig around it on all sides. The damned stone was huge! But planting his feet on the ground he shoved it off the grave. "Goo!" it rolled down the slope. "That's the right road for you to take! Now we'll get things done quickly!"

At this point Grandad stopped, took out his horn, sprinkled a little snuff in his hand, and was about to raise it to his nose when all at once—"Tchee-hee!" something sneezed above his head so that the trees shook and Grandad's face was spattered all over. "You might at least turn aside when you want to sneeze," said Grandad, wiping his eyes. He looked around—there was no one there. "No, it seems the devil doesn't like the snuff," he went on, putting back the horn in his bosom and picking up his spade. "He's a fool! Neither his grandfather nor his father ever had a pinch of snuff like that!" He began digging; the ground was soft, the spade had no trouble biting into it. Then something clanked. Pushing aside the earth he saw a cauldron.

"Ah, you darling, here you are!" cried Grandad, thrusting the spade under it.

"Ah, you darling, here you are!" piped a bird's beak, pecking the cauldron.

Grandad looked around and dropped the spade.

"Ah, you darling, here you are!" bleated a sheep's head from the top of the trees.

"Ah, you darling, here you are!" roared a bear, poking its snout out from behind a tree. A shudder ran down Grandad's back.

"Why, one is afraid to say a word here!" he muttered to himself.

"One is afraid to say a word here!" piped the bird's beak.

"Afraid to say a word here!" bleated the sheep's head.

"To say a word here!" roared the bear.

"Hm!" said Grandad, and he felt terrified.

"Hm!" piped the beak.

"Hm!" bleated the sheep.

"Hm!" roared the bear.

Grandad turned around in astonishment. Heaven help us, what a night! No stars nor moon; pits all around him, a bottomless precipice at his feet and a crag hanging over his head and looking every minute as though it would break off and come down on him. And Grandad imagined that a horrible face peeped out from behind it. "Oo! Oo!" a nose like a blacksmith's bellows. You could pour a bucket of water into each nostril! Lips like two logs! Red eyes seemed to be popping out, and a tongue was thrust out too, and jeering. "The devil take you!" said Grandad, flinging down the cauldron. "Damn you and your treasure! What an ugly snout!" And he was just going to cut and run, but he looked around and stopped, seeing that everything was as before. "It's only the damned devil trying to frighten me!"

He set to work at the cauldron again. No, it was too heavy! What was he to do? He couldn't leave it now! So exerting himself to his utmost, he clutched at it. "Come, heave ho! again, again!" and he dragged it out. "Ough, now for a pinch of snuff!"

He took out his horn. Before shaking any out, though, he took a good look around to be sure there was no one there. He thought there was no one; but then it seemed to him that the trunk of the tree was gasping and blowing, ears made their appearance, there were red eyes, puffing nostrils, a wrinkled nose and it seemed on the point of sneezing. "No, I won't have a pinch of snuff!" thought Grandad, putting away the horn. "Satan will be spitting in my eyes again!" He made haste to snatch up the cauldron and began running as fast as his legs could carry him; only he felt something behind him scratching on his legs with twigs. . . . "Aie, aie, aie!" was all that Grandad could cry as he ran as fast as he could; and it was not till he reached the priest's vegetable garden that he paused for breath.

"Where can Grandad be gone?" we wondered, waiting three hours for him. Mother had come from the farm long ago and brought a pot of hot dumplings. Still no sign of Grandad! Again we had supper without him. After supper Mother washed the pot and was looking for a spot to throw the dishwater because there were melon beds all around, when she saw a barrel rolling straight toward her! It was quite dark. She felt sure one of the boys was hiding behind it in mischief and shoving it toward her. "That's right, I'll throw the water at him," she said, and flung the hot dishwater at the barrel.

"Aie!" shouted a bass voice. Imagine that: Grandad! Well, who would have known him! I swear we thought it was a barrel coming up! I must admit, though it was a sin, we really thought it funny when Grandad's gray head was all drenched in the dishwater and decked with melon peelings.

"Oh, you devil of a woman!" said Grandad, wiping his head with the skirt of his coat. "What a hot bath she has given me, as though I were a pig before Christmas! Well, boys, now you will have something for pretzels! You'll go about dressed in gold jackets, you puppies! Look what I have brought you!" said Grandad, and opened the cauldron.

What do you suppose there was in it? Come, think, make a guess! Eh? Gold? Well now, it wasn't gold—it was filth, slop, I am ashamed to say what it was. Grandad spat, dropped the cauldron, and washed his hands.

And from that time forward Grandad made us two swear never to trust the devil. "Don't you believe it!" he would often say to us. "Whatever the foe of our Lord Christ says, he is always lying, the son of a bitch! There isn't a kopek's worth of truth in him!" And if ever the old man heard that things were not right in some place: "Come, boys, let's cross ourselves! That's it! That's it! Properly!" and he would begin making the sign of the cross. And that accursed place where he couldn't finish the dance he fenced in, and he asked that we fling all the garbage there, all the weeds and litter which he raked off the melon patch.

So you see how the devil fools a man. I know that bit of ground well; later on some neighboring Cossacks hired it from Dad for a melon patch. It's marvelous ground and there is always a wonderful crop on it; but there has never been anything good on that bewitched place. They may sow it properly, but there's no saying what it is that comes up: not a melon—not a pumpkin—not a cucumber, the devil only knows what to make of it.

ARABESQUES

NEVSKY PROSPEKT[1]

There is nothing finer than Nevsky Prospekt, not in Petersburg anyway: it is the making of the city. What splendor does it lack, that fairest of our city thoroughfares? I know that not one of the poor clerks that live there would trade Nevsky Prospekt for all the blessings of the world. Not only the young man of twenty-five summers with a fine mustache and a splendidly cut coat, but even the veteran with white hairs sprouting on his chin and a head as smooth as a silver dish is enthusiastic over Nevsky Prospekt. And the ladies! Nevsky Prospekt is even more attractive to the ladies. And indeed, to whom is it not attractive? As soon as you step into Nevsky Prospekt you are in an atmosphere of gaiety. Though you may have some necessary and important business, yet as soon as you are there you forget all about it. This is the one place where people put in an appearance without being forced to, without being driven there by the needs and commercial interests that swallow up all Petersburg. A man met on Nevsky Prospekt seems

---

[1] Nevsky Avenue. (ed.)

less of an egoist than in the other streets where greed, selfishness, and covetousness are apparent in all who walk or drive along them. Nevsky Prospekt is the general channel of communication in Petersburg. The man who lives on the Petersburg or Viborg Side who hasn't seen his friend at Peski[2] or at the Moscow Gate for years may be sure to meet him on Nevsky Prospekt. No directory list at an information bureau supplies such accurate information as Nevsky Prospekt. All-powerful Nevsky Prospekt! Sole place of entertainment for the poor man in Petersburg! How wonderfully clean are its surfaces, and, my God, how many feet leave their traces on it! The clumsy, dirty boots of the ex-soldier, under whose weight the very granite seems to crack, and the miniature, ethereal little shoes of the young lady who turns her head toward the glittering shop windows as the sunflower turns to the sun, and the rattling saber of the ambitious lieutenant which marks a sharp scratch along it—all print the scars of strength or weakness on it! What changes pass over it in a single day! What transformations it goes through between one dawn and the next!

Let us begin with earliest morning, when all Petersburg smells of hot, freshly baked bread and is filled with old women in ragged clothes who are making their raids on the churches and on compassionate passers-by. At such a time, Nevsky Prospekt is empty: the stout shopkeepers and their assistants are still asleep in their linen shirts or soaping their noble cheeks and drinking their coffee; beggars gather near the doors of the cafe where the drowsy Ganymede,[3] who the day before flew around with the cups of chocolate like a fly, crawls out with no necktie on, broom in hand, and throws stale pies and scraps at them. Working people move through the streets: sometimes peasants cross the avenue, hurrying to their work, in high boots caked with mortar which even the Ekaterieninsky Canal, famous for its cleanness, could not wash off. At this hour it is not proper for ladies to walk out, because Russian people like to explain their meaning in rude expressions such as they would not hear even in a theater. Sometimes a drowsy government clerk trudges along with a portfolio under his arm, if the way to his department lies through Nevsky Prospekt. It may be confidently stated that at this period, that is, up to twelve o'clock,

---

[2] A St. Petersburg district. (ed.)

[3] Mythological figure: a beautiful boy carried to Olympus by the eagle of Zeus to be cupbearer of the gods. (ed.)

Nevsky Prospekt is not the goal for any man, but simply the means of reaching it: it is filled with people who have their occupations, their anxieties, and their annoyances, and are not thinking about the avenue. Peasants talk about ten kopeks or seven coppers; old men and women wave their hands or talk to themselves, sometimes with very striking gesticulations, but no one listens to them or laughs at them with the exception perhaps of street boys in homespun smocks, streaking like lightning along Nevsky Prospekt with empty bottles or pairs of boots from the cobblers in their arms. At that hour you may put on what you like, and even if you wear a cap instead of a hat, or the ends of your collar stick out too far from your necktie, no one notices it.

At twelve o'clock tutors of all nationalities descend upon Nevsky Prospekt with their young charges in fine cambric collars. English Joneses and French Cocos walk arm in arm with the nurslings entrusted to their parental care, and with becoming dignity explain to them that the signboards over the shops are put there so that people may know what is to be found within. Governesses, pale Misses, and rosy Mademoiselles walk majestically behind their light and nimble charges, telling them to hold themselves more upright or not to drop their left shoulder; in short, at this hour Nevsky Prospekt plays its pedagogic part. But as two o'clock approaches, the governesses, tutors, and children are fewer; and finally are crowded out by their tender papas walking arm in arm with their highstrung wives in gaudy dresses of every possible color. Gradually these are joined by all who have finished their rather important domestic duties, such as talking to the doctor about the weather and the pimple that has come out on their nose, inquiring after the health of their horses and their promising and gifted children, reading in the newspaper a leading article and the announcements of the arrivals and departures, and finally drinking a cup of tea or coffee. They are joined, too, by those whose enviable destiny has called them to the blessed vocation of clerks on special duties, and by those who serve in the Department of Foreign Affairs and are distinguished by the dignity of their pursuits and their habits. My God! What splendid positions and duties there are! How they elevate and sweeten the soul! But, alas, I am not in the service and am denied the pleasure of watching the refined behavior of my superiors. Everything you meet on the Nevsky Prospekt is brimming over with propriety: the men in long jackets with their hands in their pockets, the ladies in pink, white, or pale blue satin coats and stylish hats. Here you meet unique whiskers, drooping with extraordinary and amazing elegance below the necktie, velvety, satiny whiskers, as black as sable or as coal, but alas! invariably the property of members of the Department of Foreign Affairs. Providence has denied black whiskers to clerks in other departments; they are forced, to their great disgust, to wear red ones. Here you meet marvelous mustaches that no pen, no brush could do justice to, mustaches to which the better part of a life has been devoted, the objects of prolonged care by day and by night; mustaches upon which enchanting perfumes are sprinkled and on which the rarest and most expensive kinds of pomade are lavished; mustaches which are wrapped up at night in the most expensive vellum; mustaches to which their possessors display the most touching devotion and which are the envy of passers-by. Thousands of varieties of hats, dresses, and kerchiefs, flimsy and bright-colored, for which their owners feel sometimes an adoration that lasts two whole days, dazzle everyone on Nevsky Prospect. A whole sea of butterflies seem to have flown up from their flower stalks and to be floating in a glittering cloud above the beetles of the male sex. Here you meet waists of a slim delicacy beyond dreams of elegance, no thicker than the neck of a bottle, and respectfully step aside for fear of a careless nudge with a discourteous elbow; your heart beats with apprehension lest an incautious breath snap in two the exquisite products of art and nature. And the ladies' sleeves that you meet on Nevsky Prospekt! Ah, how exquisite! They are like two balloons and the lady might suddenly float up into the air, were she not held down by the gentleman accompanying her; for it would be as easy and agreeable for a lady to be lifted into the air as for a glass of champagne to be lifted to the lips. Nowhere do people bow with such dignity and ease as on Nevsky Prospekt. Here you meet with a unique smile, a smile that is the acme of art, that will sometimes melt you with pleasure, sometimes make you bow your head and feel lower than the grass, sometimes make you hold it high and feel loftier than the Admiralty spire.[4] Here you meet people conversing about a concert or the weather with extraordinary dignity and sense of their own importance. Here you meet a thousand incredible types

---

[4] At that time, the tallest building in St. Petersburg. (ed.)

and figures. Good heavens! what strange characters are met on Nevsky Prospekt! There are numbers of people who, when they meet you, invariably stare at your boots, and when they have passed, turn around to have a look at the skirts of your coat. I have never been able to discover the reason for it. At first I thought they were bootmakers, but they're not: they are for the most part clerks in various departments and many of them are very good at referring a case from one department to another; or they are people who spend their time walking about or reading the paper in restaurants—in fact they are usually very respectable people. In this blessed period between two and three o'clock in the afternoon, when everyone seems to be walking on Nevsky Prospekt, there is a display of all the finest things the genius of man has produced. One displays a smart overcoat with the best beaver on it, the second —a lovely Greek nose, the third—superb whiskers, the fourth—a pair of pretty eyes and a marvelous hat, the fifth—a signet ring on a jaunty forefinger, the sixth—a foot in a bewitching shoe, the seventh—a necktie that excites wonder, and the eighth—a mustache that reduces one to stupefaction. But three o'clock strikes and the display is over, the crowd grows less thick . . . At three o'clock there is a fresh change. Suddenly it is like spring on Nevsky Prospekt; it is covered with government clerks in green uniforms. Hungry titular, lower court, and other councilors do their best to quicken their pace. Young collegiate registrars and provincial and collegiate secretaries are in haste to be in time to parade on Nevsky Prospekt with a dignified air, trying to look as if they had not been sitting in an office for the last six hours. But the elderly collegiate secretaries and titular and lower court councilors walk quickly with bowed heads: they are not disposed to amuse themselves by looking at the passers-by; they have not yet completely torn themselves away from their office cares; in their heads is a full list of work begun and not yet finished; for a long time, instead of the signboards, they seem to see a cardboard rack of papers or the full face of the head of their office.

From four o'clock Nevsky Prospekt is empty, and you hardly meet a single government clerk. Some seamstress from a shop runs across Nevsky Prospekt with a box in her hands. Some pathetic victim of a benevolent attorney, cast adrift in a frieze overcoat; some eccentric visitor to whom all hours are alike; a tall, lanky Englishwoman with a handbag and a book in her hand; a foreman in a high-waisted coat of cotton with a narrow beard, a ramshackle figure, back, arms, head, and legs all twisting and turning as he walks deferentially along the pavement; sometimes a humble crafts-man . . . those are the only people that we meet at that hour on Nevsky Prospekt.

But as soon as dusk descends upon the houses and streets and the policeman covered with a piece of coarse material climbs up his ladder to light the lamp, and engravings which do not venture to show themselves by day peep out of the lower windows of the shops, Nevsky Prospekt revives again and begins to stir. Then comes that mysterious time when the street lamps throw a marvel-ous alluring light upon everything. You meet a great number of young men, for the most part bachelors, in warm frock coats and overcoats. There is a suggestion at this time of some aim, or rather something like an aim, something extremely unaccountable; the steps of all are more rapid and altogether very uneven; long shad-ows flit over the walls and pavement and their heads almost reach the Police Bridge. Young collegiate registrars, provincial and col-legiate secretaries walk up and down for hours, but the elderly collegiate registrars, the titular and lower court secretaries are for the most part at home, either because they are married, or because the German cook living in their house gives them a very good din-ner. Here you may meet some of the respectable-looking old gen-tlemen who with such dignity and propriety walked on Nevsky Prospekt at two o'clock. You may see them now racing along like the young government clerks to peep under the hat of some lady spotted in the distance, whose thick lips and fat cheeks plastered with rouge are so attractive to many, and above all to the shopmen, workmen, and shopkeepers, who promenade in crowds, always in coats of German cut and usually arm in arm.

"Hey!" cried Lieutenant Pirogov on such an evening, nudging a young man who walked beside him in a dress coat and cloak. "Did you see her?"

"I did; lovely, a perfect Bianca of Perugino." [5]

"But which do you mean?"

"The lady with the dark hair . . . And what eyes! Good God, what eyes! Her attitude and stunning figure and the lines of the face . . . exquisite!"

---

[5] Umbrian painter (1445-1523?) whose real name was Pietro di Cristoforo Vannuccio. Pupil of da Vinci. "Bianca" is his most famous painting. (ed.)

"I am talking of the blonde who passed after her on the other side. Why don't you go after the brunette if you find her so attractive?"

"Oh, how can you!" cried the young man in the dress coat, turning crimson. "As though she were one of the women who walk on Nevsky Prospekt at night. She must be a very distinguished lady," he went on with a sigh. "Why, her cloak alone is worth eighty rubles."

"You fool!" cried Pirogov, giving him a violent shove in the direction in which the brilliant cloak was fluttering. "Move on, you idiot, don't waste time. I'll follow the blonde."

"We know what you all are," Pirogov thought to himself, with a self-satisfied and confident smile, convinced that no beauty could withstand him.

The young man in the dress coat and cloak with timid and tremulous step walked in the direction in which the bright-colored cloak was fluttering, at one moment shining brilliantly as it approached a street lamp, at the next shrouded in darkness as it moved further away. His heart throbbed and he unconsciously quickened his pace. He dared not even imagine that he could have a claim on the attention of the beauty who was retreating into the distance, and still less could he admit the evil thought suggested by Lieutenant Pirogov. All he wanted was to see the house, to discover where this exquisite creature lived who seemed to have flown straight down from heaven onto the Nevsky Prospekt, and who would probably fly away, no one could tell where. He darted along so fast that he was continually jostling dignified, gray-whiskered gentlemen off the pavement. This young man belonged to a class which is a great exception among us, and he no more belonged to the common run of Petersburg citizens than a face that appears to us in a dream belongs to the world of actual fact. This exceptional class is very rare in the town where all are officials, shopkeepers, or German craftsmen. He was an artist. A strange phenomenon, is it not? A Petersburg artist. An artist in the land of snows. An artist in the land of the Finns where everything is wet, flat, pale, gray, foggy. These artists are utterly unlike the Italian artists, proud and ardent as Italy and her skies. The Russian artist on the contrary is, as a rule, mild, gentle, retiring, carefree, and quietly devoted to his art; he drinks tea with a couple of friends in his little room, modestly discusses his favorite subjects, and does not trouble his head at all about anything superfluous. He frequently employs some old beggar woman, and makes her sit for six hours on end in order to transfer to canvas her pitiful, almost inanimate countenance. He draws a sketch in perspective of his studio with all sorts of artistic litter lying about, copies plaster-of-Paris hands and feet, turned coffee-colored by time and dust, a broken easel, a palette lying upside down, a friend playing the guitar, walls smeared with paint, with an open window through which there is a glimpse of the pale Neva and poor fishermen in red shirts. Almost all these artists paint in gray, muddy colors that bear the unmistakable imprint of the north. For all that, they all work with instinctive enjoyment. They are often endowed with real talent, and if only they were breathing the fresh air of Italy, they would no doubt develop as freely, broadly, and brilliantly as a plant at last brought from indoors into the open air. They are, as a rule, very timid; stars and thick epaulets reduce them to such a confused state that they ask less for their pictures than they had intended. They are sometimes fond of dressing smartly, but anything smart they wear always looks too startling and rather like a patch. You sometimes meet them in an excellent coat and a muddy cloak, an expensive velvet vest and a coat covered with paint, just as on one of their unfinished landscapes you sometimes see the head of a nymph, for which the artist could find no other place, sketched on the background of an earlier work which he had once painted with pleasure. Such an artist never looks you straight in the face; or, if he does look at you, it is with a vague, indefinite expression. He does not transfix you with the vulturelike eye of an observer or the hawklike glance of a cavalry officer. This is because he sees at the same time your features and the features of some plaster-of-Paris Hercules standing in his room, or because he is imagining a picture which he dreams of producing later on. This makes him often answer incoherently, sometimes quite incomprehensibly, and the muddle in his head increases his shyness. To this class belonged the young man we have described, an artist called Piskarev, retiring, shy, but carrying in his soul sparks of feeling, ready at a fitting opportunity to burst into flame. With secret dread he hastened after the lady who had made so strong an impression on him, and he seemed to be surprised at his audacity. The unknown girl who had so captured his eyes, his thoughts, and his feelings suddenly turned her head and glanced at him.

Good God, what divine features! The dazzling whiteness of the exquisite brow was framed by hair lovely as an agate. They curled, those marvelous tresses, and some of them strayed below the hat and caressed the cheek, flushed by the chill of evening with a delicate fresh color. A swarm of exquisite visions hovered about her lips. All the memories of childhood, all the visions that rise from dreaming and quiet inspiration in the lamplight—all seemed to be blended, mingled, and reflected on her delightful lips. She glanced at Piskarev and his heart quivered at that glance; her glance was severe, a look of anger came into her face at the sight of this impudent pursuit; but on that lovely face even anger was bewitching. Overcome by shame and timidity he stood still, dropping his eyes; but how could he lose this divine being without discovering the sanctuary in which she was enshrined? Such was the thought in the mind of the young dreamer, and he resolved to follow her. But, to avoid her notice, he fell back a good distance, looked aimlessly from side to side, and examined the signboards on the shops, yet he did not lose sight of a single step the unknown lady took. Passers-by were less frequent; the street became quieter. The beauty looked around and he fancied that her lips were curved in a faint smile. He trembled all over and could not believe his eyes. No, it was the deceptive light of the street lamp which had thrown that trace of a smile upon her lips; no his own imagination was mocking him. But he held his breath and everything in him quivered, all his feelings were ablaze and everything before him was lost in a sort of mist; the pavement seemed to be moving under his feet, carriages drawn by trotting horses seemed to stand still, the bridge stretched out and seemed broken in the center, the houses were upside down, a sentry box seemed to be reeling toward him, and the sentry's halberd, and the gilt letters of the signboard and the scissors painted on it, all seemed to be flashing across his very eyelash. And all this was produced by one glance, by one turn of a pretty head. Hearing nothing, seeing nothing, understanding nothing, he followed the light traces of the lovely feet, trying to moderate the swiftness of his own steps which moved in time with the throbbing of his heart. At moments he was overcome with doubt whether the look on her face was really so gracious; and then for an instant he stood still; but the beating of his heart, the irresistible violence and turmoil of his feelings drove him forward. He did not even notice a four-storied house that loomed before him; four rows of windows, all lighted up, burst upon him all at once, and he was brought to a sudden stop by striking against the iron railing of the entrance. He saw the lovely stranger fly up the stairs, look around, lay a finger on her lips, and make a sign for him to follow her. His knees trembled, his feelings, his thoughts were aflame. A thrill of joy, unbearably acute, flashed like lightning through his heart. No, it was not a dream! Good God, what happiness in one instant! What a lifetime's rapture in two minutes!

But was it not all a dream? Could it be true that this girl for whom he would gladly have given his life for one heavenly glance, that she who made him feel such bliss just to be near the house where she lived, could she really have been so kind and attentive to him? He flew up the stairs. He was conscious of no earthly thought; he was not aflame with earthly passion. No, at that moment he was pure and chaste as a virginal youth burning with the vague spiritual craving for love. And what would have awakened base thoughts in a dissolute man, in him made them still holier. This confidence, shown him by a weak and lovely creature, laid upon him the sacred duty of chivalrous austerity, the sacred duty to carry out all her commands. All that he desired was that those commands should be as difficult, as hard to carry out as possible, so that more effort be required to overcome all obstacles. He did not doubt that some mysterious and at the same time important circumstance compelled the unknown lady to confide in him; that she would certainly require some important service from him, and he felt in himself enough strength and resolution for anything.

The staircase went around and around, and his thoughts whirled around and around with it. "Be careful!" a voice rang out like a harpstring, sending a fresh thrill through him. On the dark landing of the fourth floor the blonde stranger knocked at a door; it was opened and they went in together. A woman of rather attractive appearance met them with a candle in her hand, but she looked so strangely and impudently at Piskarev that he dropped his eyes. They went into the room. Three female figures in different corners of the room met his eye. One was laying out cards; another was sitting at the piano and with two fingers strumming out a pitiful travesty of an old polonaise; the third was sitting before a mirror combing her long hair, and had apparently no intention of discontinuing her toilette because of the arrival of an unknown visitor. An unpleasant untidiness, usually only seen in the neglected rooms of bachelors, was everywhere apparent. The furniture, which was fairly good, was covered with dust. Spiders' webs stretched over the carved cornice; through the open door of another room he caught the gleam of a spurred boot and the red edging of a uniform; a man's loud voice and a woman's laugh rang out without restraint.

Good God, where had he come! At first he would not believe it, and began looking more attentively at the objects that filled the room; but the bare walls and uncurtained windows betrayed the absence of a careful housewife; the faded faces of these pitiful creatures, one of whom was sitting just under his nose and staring at him as coolly as though he were a spot on someone's dress—all convinced him that he had come into one of those revolting places in which the pitiful vice that springs from a poor education and the terrible overpopulation of a great town finds shelter, one of those places in which man sacrilegiously tramples and derides all that is pure and holy, all that makes life beautiful, where woman, the beauty of the world, the crown of creation, is transformed into a strange, equivocal creature, where she loses with her purity of her heart all that is womanly, revoltingly adopts the swagger and impudence of man, and ceases to be the delicate, the lovely creature, so different from us. Piskarev looked at her from head to foot with troubled eyes, as though trying to make sure whether this was really she who had so enchanted him and had brought him flying from Nevsky Prospekt. But she stood before him lovely as ever; her eyes were even more heavenly. She was fresh, not more than seventeen; it could be seen that she had not long been in the grip of vice; it had as yet left no trace upon her cheeks, they were fresh and faintly flushed with color; she was lovely.

He stood motionless before her and was ready to allow himself to be once again deceived. But the beautiful girl was tired of this long silence and gave a meaning smile, looking straight into his eyes. That smile was full of a sort of pitiful insolence; it was so strange and as incongruous with her face as a sanctimonious air with the brutal face of a bribetaker or a manual of bookkeeping with a poet. He shuddered. She opened her lovely lips and began saying something, but all that she said was so stupid, so vulgar . . . As though intelligence were lost with innocence! He wanted to hear no more. He was absurd! Simple as a child! Instead of taking advantage of such graciousness, instead of rejoicing at such an opportunity, as anyone else in his place would probably have done, he dashed away like a wild antelope and ran out into the street.

He sat in his room with his head bowed and his hands hanging loose, like a poor man who has found a precious pearl and at once dropped it into the sea. "Such a beauty, such divine features! And where? In such a place . . ." That was all that he could say.

Nothing, indeed, moves us to such pity as the sight of beauty touched by the putrid breath of vice. Ugliness may go with it, but beauty, tender beauty . . . In our thoughts it blends with nothing but purity and innocence. The beauty who had so enchanted poor Piskarev really was a rare and extraordinary exception. Her presence in those vile surroundings seemed even more incredible. All her features were so purely molded, the whole expression of her lovely face wore the stamp of such nobility, that it was impossible to think that vice already held her in its grip. She should have been the priceless pearl, the whole world, the paradise, the wealth of a devoted husband; she should have been the lovely, gentle star of some quiet family circle, and with the faintest movement of her lovely lips should have given her sweet commands there. She would have been a divinity in the crowded ballroom, on the glistening parquet, in the glow of candles surrounded by the silent adoration of a crowd of admirers; but, alas! by some terrible machination of the fiendish spirit, eager to destroy the harmony of life, she had been flung with satanic laughter into this horrible swamp.

Exhausted by heartbreaking pity, he sat before a candle that was burned low in the socket. Midnight was long past, the belfry chime rang out half-past twelve, and still he sat without stirring, neither asleep nor fully awake. Sleep, abetted by his stillness, was beginning to steal over him, and already the room was beginning to disappear, and only the light of the candle still shone through the dreams that were overpowering him, when all at once a knock at the door made him start and wake up. The door opened and a footman in gorgeous livery walked in. Never had a gorgeous livery peeped into his lonely room. At such an hour of the night! . . . He was amazed, and with impatient curiosity looked intently at the footman who entered.

"The lady," the footman pronounced with a deferential bow, "whom you visited some hours ago bade me invite you and sent the carriage to fetch you."

Piskarev was speechless with amazement: the carriage, a footman in livery! . . . No, there must be some mistake. . . . .

"My good man," he said timidly, "you must have come to the wrong door. Your mistress must have sent you for someone else and not for me."

"No, sir, I am not mistaken. Did you not accompany my mistress home? It's in Liteyny Street, on the fourth floor."

"I did."

"Then, if so, please make haste; my mistress is very anxious to see you, and begs you come straight to her house."

Piskarev ran down the stairs. A carriage was, in fact, standing in the courtyard. He got into it, the door was slammed, the cobbles of the pavement resounded under the wheels and the hoofs, and the illuminated panorama of houses and lamps and signboards passed by the carriage windows. Piskarev pondered all the way and could not explain this adventure. A house of her own, a carriage, a footman in gorgeous livery . . . He could not reconcile all this with the room on the fourth floor, the dusty windows, and the jangling piano. The carriage stopped before a brightly lighted entrance, and he was at once struck by the procession of carriages, the talk of the coachmen, the brilliantly lighted windows, and the strains of music. The footman in gorgeous livery helped him out of the carriage and respectfully led him into a hall`with marble columns, with a porter in gold lace, with cloaks and fur coats flung here and there, and a brilliant lamp. An airy staircase with shining banisters, fragrant with perfume, led upward. He was already mounting it; hesitating at the first step and panic-stricken at the crowds of people, he went into the first room. The extraordinary brightness and variety of the scene completely staggered him; it seemed to him as though some demon had crumbled the whole world into bits and mixed all these bits indiscriminately together. The gleaming shoulders of the ladies and the black tailcoats, the chandeliers, the lamps, the ethereal floating gauze, the filmy ribbons, and the fat bass looking out from behind the railing of the orchestra—everything was dazzling. He saw at the same instant such numbers of respectable old or middle-aged men with stars on their evening coats and ladies sitting in rows or stepping so lightly, proudly, and graciously over the parquet floor; he heard so many French and English words; moreover, the young men in black evening clothes were filled with such dignity, spoke or kept silence

with such gentlemanly decorum, were so incapable of saying anything inappropriate, made jokes so majestically, smiled so politely,
wore such superb whiskers, so skillfully displayed their elegant
hands as they straightened their neckties; the ladies were so ethereal, so steeped in perfect self-satisfaction and rapture, so enchant-
ingly cast down their eyes, that . . . but Piskarev's subdued air,
as he leaned timidly against a column, was enough to show that he
was completely overwhelmed. At that moment the crowd stood
around a group of dancers. They whirled around, draped in the
transparent creations of Paris, in garments woven of air itself;
effortlessly they touched the parquet floor with their lovely feet,
as ethereal as though they walked on air. But one among them was
lovelier, more splendid, and more brilliantly dressed than the rest.
An indescribable, subtle perfection of taste was apparent in all her
attire, and at the same time it seemed as though she cared nothing
for it, as though it had come unconsciously, of itself. She looked
and did not look at the crowd of spectators crowding around her,
she cast down her lovely long eyelashes indifferently, and the
gleaming whiteness of her face was still more dazzling when she
bent her head and a light shadow lay on her enchanting brow.

Piskarev did his utmost to make his way through the crowd and
get a better look at her; but to his intense annoyance a huge head
of curly black hair was continually screening her from him; moreover, the crush was so great that he did not dare to press forward
or to step back, for fear of jostling against some privy councilor.
But at last he squeezed his way to the front and glanced at his
clothes, anxious that everything should be neat. Heavenly Creator!
What was his horror! he had on his everyday coat, and it was all
smeared with paint; in his haste to leave he had actually forgotten
to change into suitable clothes. He blushed up to his ears and,
dropping his eyes in confusion, would have gone away, but there
was absolutely nowhere he could go; court chamberlains in brilliant uniforms formed an inexorable compact wall behind him. By
now his desire was to be as far away as possible from the beauty of
the lovely brows and eyelashes. In terror he raised his eyes to see
whether she were looking at him. Good God! she stood facing
him. . . . What did it mean? "It is she!" he cried almost at the top
of his voice. It was really she—the one he had met on Nevsky
Prospekt and had escorted home.

Meanwhile she raised her eyelashes and looked at all with her bright eyes. "Aie, aie, aie, how beautiful! . . ." was all he could say with bated breath. She scanned the faces around her, all eager to catch her attention, but with an air of weariness and indifference she looked away and met Piskarev's eyes. Oh heavens! What paradise! Oh God, for strength to bear this! Life cannot contain it, such rapture tears it asunder and bears away the soul! She made a sign to him, but not by hand nor by inclination of the head; no, it was in her ravishing eyes, so subtle, so imperceptible that no one else could see it, but he saw it! He understood it! The dance lasted a long time; the languorous music seemed to flag and die away and again it broke out, shrill and thunderous; at last the dance was over. She sat down. Her bosom heaved under the light cloud of gossamer, her hand (Oh, heavens! what a wonderful hand!) dropped on her knee, rested on her filmy gown which seemed to be breathing music under her hand, and its delicate lilac hue made that lovely hand look more dazzlingly white than ever. Just to touch it and nothing more! No other desires—they would be insolence. . . . He stood behind her chair, not daring to speak, not daring to breathe. "Have you been bored?" she asked. "I have been bored too. I see that you hate me. . . ." she added, lowering her long eyelashes.

"Hate you? I? . . . I? . . . ?" Piskarev, completely overwhelmed, tried to say something, and he would probably have poured out a stream of incoherent words, but at that moment a court chamberlain with a magnificently curled shock of hair came up making witty and polite remarks. He agreeably displayed a row of rather good teeth, and at every jest his wit drove a sharp nail into Piskarev's heart. At last someone fortunately addressed the court chamberlain with a question.

"How unbearable it is!" she said, lifting her heavenly eyes to him. "I will sit at the other end of the room; be there!" She glided through the crowd and vanished. He pushed his way through the crowd like one possessed, and in a flash was there.

Yes, it was she! She sat like a queen, finer than all, lovelier than all, and her eyes sought him.

"Are you here?" she asked softly. "I will be frank with you: no doubt you think the circumstances of our meeting strange. Can you imagine that I belong to the degraded class of beings among

whom you met me? You think my conduct strange, but I will reveal a secret to you. Can you promise never to betray it?" she asked,
fixing her eyes upon him.

"Oh I will, I will, I will! . . ."

But at that moment an elderly man shook hands with her and
began speaking in a language Piskarev did not understand. She
looked at the artist with an imploring gaze, and gestured to him to
remain where he was and await her return; but much too impatient, he could not obey a command even from her lips. He followed her, but the crowd parted them. He could no longer see
the lilac dress; in consternation he forced his way from room to
room and elbowed all he met mercilessly, but in all the rooms
gentlemen were sitting at whist plunged in dead silence. In a corner of the room some elderly people were arguing about the su-
periority of military to civil service; in another some young men
in superb dress coats were making a few light remarks about the
voluminous works of a poet. Piskarev felt that a gentleman of venerable appearance had taken him by the button of his coat and was
submitting some very just observation to his criticism, but he
rudely thrust him aside without even noticing that he had a very
distinguished order on his breast. He ran into another room—she
was not there; into a third—she was not there either. "Where is
she? Give her to me! Oh, I cannot live without another look at her!
I want to hear what she meant to tell me!" But his search was in
vain. Anxious and exhausted, he huddled in a corner and looked at
the crowd. But everything seemed blurred to his strained eyes. At
last the walls of his own room began to grow distinct. He raised
his eyes: before him stood a candlestick with the light flickering
in the socket; the whole candle had burned away and the melted
wax lay on his table.

So he had been asleep! My God, what a splendid dream! And
why had he awakened? Why had it not lasted one minute longer?
She would no doubt have appeared again! The unwelcome dawn
was peeping in at his window with its unpleasant, dingy light. The
room was in such a gray, untidy muddle . . . Oh, how revolting
was reality! What was it compared to dreams? He undressed
quickly and got into bed, wrapping himself up in a blanket, anxious
to recapture the dream that had flown. Sleep certainly did not take
long to come, but it presented him with something quite different
from what he desired: at one moment Lieutenant Pirogov with his

pipe, then the porter of the Academy, then an actual civil coun-cilor, then the head of a Finnish woman who had sat for him for a portrait, and such absurd things.

He lay in bed till the middle of the day, longing to dream again, but she did not appear. If only she had shown her lovely features for one minute, if only her light step had rustled, if only her hand, shining white as driven snow, had for one instant appeared before him.

Dismissing everything, forgetting everything, he sat with a crushed and hopeless expression, full of nothing but his dream. He never thought of touching anything; his eyes were fixed in a va-cant, lifeless stare upon the windows that looked into the yard, where a dirty watercarrier was pouring water that froze in the air, and the cracked voice of a peddler bleated like a goat, "Old clothes for sale." The sounds of everyday reality rung strangely in his ears. He sat on till evening in this manner, and then flung himself eagerly into bed. For hours he struggled with sleeplessness; at last he overcame it. Again a dream, a vulgar, horrid dream. "God, have mercy! For one minute, just for one minute, let me see her!"

Again he waited for the evening, again he fell asleep. He dreamed of a government clerk who was at the same time a government clerk and a bassoon. Oh, this was intolerable! At last she appeared! Her head and her curls . . . she gazed at him . . . for—oh, how brief a moment, and then again mist, again some stupid dream.

At last, dreaming became his life and from that time his life was strangely turned upside down; he might be said to sleep when he was awake and to come to life when he was asleep. Anyone seeing him sitting dumbly before his empty table or walking along the street would certainly have taken him for a lunatic or a man de-ranged by drink: his eyes had a perfectly vacant look, his natural absent-mindedness increased and drove every sign of feeling and emotion out of his face. He only revived at the approach of night.

Such a condition destroyed his health, and the worst torture for him was the fact that sleep began to desert him altogether. Anxious to save the only treasure left him, he used every means to regain it. He had heard that there were means of inducing sleep—one need only take opium. But where could he get opium? He thought of a Persian who sold shawls and, whenever he saw Piskarev, asked him to paint a beautiful woman for him. He decided to go to him, assuming that he would be sure to have the drug he wanted.

The Persian received him, sitting on a sofa with his legs crossed under him. "What do you want opium for?" he asked.

Piskarev told him about his sleeplessness.

"Very well, you must paint me a beautiful woman, and I will give you opium. She must be a real beauty: let her eyebrows be black and her eyes be as big as olives; and let me be lying near her smoking my pipe. Do you hear, she must be beautiful! She must be beautiful!"

Piskarev promised everything. The Persian went out for a minute and came back with a little jar filled with a dark liquid; he carefully poured some of it into another jar and gave it to Piskarev, telling him to take not more than seven drops in water. Piskarev greedily clutched the precious little jar, with which he would not have parted for a pile of gold, and dashed home.

When he got home he poured several drops into a glass of water and, swallowing it, lay down to sleep.

Oh God, what joy! She! She again, but now in quite a different world! Oh, how charmingly she sat at the window of a bright little country house! In her dress was the simplicity in which the poet's thought is clothed. And her hair! Merciful heavens! how simple it was and how it suited her. A short shawl was thrown lightly around her graceful throat; everything about her was modest, everything about her showed a mysterious, inexplicable sense of taste. How charming her graceful carriage! How musical the sound of her steps and the rustle of her simple gown! How lovely her arm encircled by a bracelet of hair! She said to him with a tear in her eye: "Don't look down upon me; I am not at all what you take me for. Look at me, look at me more carefully and tell me: am I capable of what you imagine?" "Oh no, no! May he who should dare to think it, may he . . ."

But he awoke, deeply moved, harassed, with tears in his eyes. "Better that you had not existed! had not lived in this world, but had been an artist's creation! I would never have left the canvas, I would have gazed at you forever and kissed you! I would have lived and breathed in you, as in the loveliest of dreams, and then I should have been happy. I should have desired nothing more; I would have called upon you as my guardian angel at sleeping and at waking, and I would have gazed upon you if ever I had to paint the divine and holy. But as it is . . . how terrible life is! What good is it that she lives? Is a madman's life a source of joy to his friends and family who once loved him? My God! what is our life! An eternal battle between dream and reality!" Such ideas absorbed him continually. He thought of nothing, he almost gave up eating, and with the impatience and passion of a lover waited for the evening and his coveted dreams. The continual concentration of his thoughts on one subject at last so completely mastered his whole being and imagination that the coveted image appeared before him almost every day, always in positions that were the very opposite of reality, for his thoughts were as pure as a child's. Through these dreams, the subject of them became in his imagination purer and was completely transformed.

The opium inflamed his thoughts more than ever, and if there ever was a man passionately, terribly, and ruinously in love to the utmost pitch of madness, he was that luckless man.

Of all his dreams one delighted him more than any: he saw himself in his studio. He was in good spirits and sitting happily with the palette in his hand! And she was there. She was his wife. She sat beside him, leaning her lovely elbow on the back of his chair and looking at his work. Her eyes were languid and weary with excess of bliss; everything in his room breathed of paradise; it was so bright, so neat. Good God! she leaned her lovely head on his bosom . . . He had never had a better dream than that. He got up after it fresher, less absent-minded than before. A strange idea came into his mind. "Perhaps," he thought, "she has been drawn into vice by some terrible misfortune, through no will of her own; perhaps her soul is disposed to penitence; perhaps she herself is longing to escape from her awful position. And am I to stand aside indifferently and let her ruin herself when I have only to hold out a hand to save her from drowning?" His thoughts carried him further. "No one knows me," he said to himself, "and no one cares what I do, and I have nothing to do with anyone either. If she shows herself genuinely penitent and changes her mode of life, I will marry her. I ought to marry her, and no doubt will do much better than many who marry their housekeepers or sometimes the most contemptible creatures. My action will be disinterested and very likely a good deed. I shall restore to the world the loveliest of its ornaments!"

Making this reckless plan, he felt the color flushing in his cheek; he went up to the mirror and was frightened at his hollow cheeks and the paleness of his face. He began carefully dressing; he washed, smoothed his hair, put on a new coat, a smart vest, flung on his cloak, and went out into the street. He breathed the fresh air and had a feeling of freshness in his heart, like a convalescent who has gone out for the first time after a long illness. His heart throbbed when he turned into the street which he had not passed through again since that fatal meeting.

He was a long time looking for the house. He walked up and down the street twice, uncertain before which to stop. At last one of them seemed to him to be the one. He ran quickly up the stairs and knocked at the door: the door opened and who came out to meet him? His ideal, his mysterious divinity, the original of his dream pictures—she who was his life, in whom he lived so terribly, so agonizingly, so blissfully—she, she herself, stood before him! He trembled; he could hardly stand on his feet for weakness, overcome by the rush of joy. She stood before him as lovely as ever, though her eyes looked sleepy, though a pallor had crept over her face, no longer quite so fresh; but still she was lovely.

"Ah!" she cried on seeing Piskarev and rubbing her eyes (it was two o'clock in the afternoon); "why did you run away from us that day?"

He sat down in a chair, feeling faint, and looked at her.

"And I am only just awake; I was brought home at seven in the morning. I was quite drunk," she added with a smile.

Oh, better you had been dumb and could not speak at all than uttering such words! She had shown him in a flash the whole panorama of her life. But, in spite of that, struggling with his feelings, he made up his mind to try whether his admonitions would have any effect on her. Pulling himself together, he began in a trembling but ardent voice depicting her awful position. She listened to him with a look of attention and with the feeling of wonder which we display at the insight of something strange and unexpected. She looked with a faint smile toward her friend who was sitting in a corner, and who stopped cleaning a comb and also listened with attention to this new preacher.

"It is true that I am poor," said Piskarev, at last, after a prolonged and persuasive appeal, "but we will work, we will do our best, side by side, to improve our position. Yes, nothing is sweeter than to owe everything to one's own work. I will sit at my pictures, you shall sit by me and inspire my work, while you are busy with sewing or some other handicraft, and we shall not want anything."

"Indeed!" she interrupted his speech with an expression of scorn. "I am not a washerwoman or a seamstress who has to work!"

Oh God! In those words the whole of an ugly, degraded life was portrayed, the life of the true followers of vice, full of emptiness and idleness!

"Marry me!" her friend who had till then sat silent in the corner put in, with a saucy air. "When I am your wife I will sit like this!" As she spoke she pursed up her pitiful face and assumed a silly expression, which greatly amused the beauty.

Oh, that was too much! That was more than he could bear! He rushed away with every thought and feeling in a turmoil. His mind was clouded: stupidly, aimlessly, he wandered about all day, seeing nothing, hearing nothing, feeling nothing. No one could say whether he slept anywhere or not; only next day, by some blind instinct, he found his way to his room, pale and looking terrible, with his hair disheveled and signs of madness in his face. He locked himself in his room and admitted no one, asked for nothing. Four days passed and his door was not once opened; at last a week had passed, and still the door was locked. People went to the door and began calling him, but there was no answer; at last the door was broken open and his corpse was found with the throat cut. A bloodstained razor lay on the floor. From his arms flung out convulsively and his terribly distorted face, it might be concluded that his hand had faltered and that he had suffered in agony before his soul left his sinful body.

So perished the victim of a frantic passion, poor Piskarev, the gentle, timid, modest, childishly simple-hearted artist whose spark of talent might with time have glowed into the full bright flame of genius. No one wept for him; no one was seen beside his dead body except the police inspector and the indifferent face of the town doctor. His coffin was taken to Okhta quickly, without even religious rites; only a soldier who followed it wept, and that only because he had had a glass too many of vodka. Even Lieutenant Pirogov did not come to look at the dead body of the poor luckless artist to whom he had extended his exalted patronage. He had no thoughts to spare for him; indeed, he was absorbed in a very exciting adventure. But let us turn to him. I do not like corpses, and it is always disagreeable to me when a long funeral procession crosses my path and some veteran dressed like a Capuchin monk takes a pinch of snuff with his left hand because he has a torch in his right. I always feel annoyed at the sight of a magnificent catafalque with a velvet pall; but my annoyance is mingled with sadness when I see a cart dragging the red, uncovered coffin of some poor fellow and only some old beggar woman who has met it at the crossways follows it weeping, because she has nothing else to do.

I believe we left Lieutenant Pirogov at the moment when he parted with Piskarev and went in pursuit of the blonde charmer. The latter was a lively, rather attractive little creature. She stopped before every shop and gazed at the sashes, kerchiefs, earrings, gloves, and other trifles in the shop windows, was continually twisting and turning and gazing about her in all directions and looking behind her. "You'll be mine, you darling!" Pirogov said confidently, as he pursued her, turning up the collar of his coat for fear of meeting someone of his acquaintance. We should, however, let the reader know what sort of person Lieutenant Pirogov was.

But before we describe Lieutenant Pirogov, we should say something of the circle to which Lieutenant Pirogov belonged. There are officers who form a kind of middle class in Petersburg. You will always find one of them at every evening party, at every dinner given by a civil councilor or an actual civil councilor who has risen to that grade through forty years of service. A couple of pale daughters, as colorless as Petersburg, some of them already gone to seed, the tea table, the piano, the impromptu dance, are all inseparable from the gay epaulet which gleams in the lamplight between the virtuous young lady and the black coat of her brother or of some old friend of the family. It is extremely difficult to arouse and divert these phlegmatic misses. To do so requires a great deal of skill, or rather perhaps the absence of all skill. One has to say what is not too clever or too amusing and to talk of the trivialities that women love. One must give credit for that to the gentlemen we are discussing. They have a special gift for making these drab beauties laugh and listen. Exclamations, smothered in laughter, of "Oh, do stop! Aren't you ashamed to be so absurd!" are often their highest reward. They rarely, one may say never, get into higher circles: from those regions they are completely crowded out by the so-called aristocrats. At the same time, they pass for well-bred, highly educated men. They are fond of talking about literature;

praise Bulgarin, Pushkin, and Gretch,[6] and speak with contempt and witty sarcasm of A. A. Orlov.[7] They never miss a public lecture, though it may be on bookkeeping or even forestry. You will always find one of them at the theater, whatever the play, unless, indeed, it be one of the farces of the "Filatka" class,[8] which greatly offend their fastidious taste. They are priceless at the theater and the greatest asset to managers. They are particularly fond of fine verses in a play, and they are greatly given to calling loudly for the actors; many of them, by teaching in government establishments or preparing pupils for them, arrive at the moment when they can afford a carriage and a pair of horses. Then their circle becomes wider and in the end they succeed in marrying a merchant's daughter who can play the piano, with a dowry of a hundred thousand, or something near it, in cash, and a lot of bearded relations. They can never achieve this honor, however, till they have reached the rank of colonel at least, for Russian merchants, though there may still be a smell of cabbage about them, will never consent to see their daughters married to any but generals or at least colonels. Such are the leading characteristics of this class of young men. But Lieutenant Pirogov had a number of talents belonging to him individually. He recited verses from *Dimitry Donsky*[9] and *Woe from Wit*[10] with great effect, and had a talent for blowing smoke out of a pipe in rings so successfully that he could string a dozen of them together in a chain; he could tell a very good story to the effect that a cannon was one thing and a unicorn was another. It is difficult to enumerate all the qualities with which fate had endowed Pirogov. He was fond of talking about actresses and dancers, but not quite in such a crude way as young lieutenants commonly hold forth on that subject. He was very much pleased with his rank in the service, to which he had only lately been promoted, and although he did occasionally say as he lay on the sofa: "O dear, vanity, all is vanity. What if I am a lieutenant?" yet his vanity was

---

[6] Russia's greatest poet, Pushkin, is here satirically sandwiched between two relative mediocrities: F. V. Bulgarin (1789-1859) and N. I. Gretch (1787-1867), Gogol's contemporaries, who were journalists and editors of *The Northern Bee*, a St. Petersburg magazine. (ed.)

[7] (1791-1840), author of moralistic tracts for half-literate masses. (ed.)

[8] *Filatka and Miroshka,* popular vaudeville show by P. Grigoriev, performed in 1831. (ed.)

[9] Tragedy by V. A. Ozerov (1770-1816). (ed.)

[10] Comedy by A. S. Griboedov (1795-1829). (ed.)

secretly much flattered by his new dignity; he often tried in conversation to allude to it in a roundabout way, and on one occasion
when he jostled against a copying clerk in the street who struck
him as uncivil he promptly stopped him and, in a few but vigorous words, pointed out to him that there was a lieutenant standing
before him and not any other kind of officer. He was especially
eloquent in his observations because two very nice-looking ladies
were passing at the moment. Pirogov displayed a passion for everything artistic in general and encouraged the artist Piskarev; this
may have been partly due to a desire to see his manly face portrayed
on canvas. But enough of Pirogov's good qualities. Man is such a
strange creature that one can never enumerate all his good points,
and the more we look into him the more new characteristics we
discover and the description of them would be endless. And so
Pirogov continued to pursue the unknown blonde, and from time
to time he addressed her with questions to which she responded in-
frequently with abrupt and incoherent sounds. They passed by the
dark Kazansky gate into Meshchansky Street—a street of tobacco-
nists and little shops, of German artisans and Finnish nymphs. The
fair lady ran faster than ever, and scurried in at the gate of a rather
dirty-looking house. Pirogov followed her. She ran up a narrow,
dark staircase and went in at a door through which Pirogov boldly
followed her. He found himself in a big room with black walls and
a grimy ceiling. A heap of iron screws, locksmith's tools, shining
tin coffeepots, and candlesticks lay on the table; the floor was lit-
tered with brass and iron filings. Pirogov saw at once that this was
a workman's lodging. The unknown charmer darted away through
a side door. He hesitated for a minute, but, following the Russian
rule,[11] decided to push forward. He went into the other room,
which was quite unlike the first and very neatly furnished, showing
that it was inhabited by a German. He was struck by an extremely
strange sight: before him sat Schiller. Not the Schiller who wrote
William Tell and the *History of the Thirty Years' War*, but the
famous Schiller, the ironmonger and tinsmith of Meshchansky
Street. Beside Schiller stood Hoffmann—not the writer Hoffmann,
but a rather high-class bootmaker who lived in Ofitsersky Street
and was a great friend of Schiller's. Schiller was drunk and was
sitting on a chair, stamping and saying something excitedly. All

---

[11] When in doubt, plunge ahead. (ed.)

this would not have surprised Pirogov, but what did surprise him was the extraordinary attitude of the two figures. Schiller was sitting with his head upraised and his rather thick nose in the air, while Hoffmann was holding this nose between his finger and thumb and was flourishing the blade of his cobbler's knife over its surface. Both men were talking in German, and so Lieutenant Pirogov, whose knowledge of German was confined to "*Gut Morgen*," could not make out what was going on. However, what Schiller said amounted to this: "I don't want it, I have no need of a nose!" he said, waving his hands, "I use three pounds of snuff a month on my nose alone. And I pay in a dirty Russian shop, for a German shop does not keep Russian snuff. I pay in a dirty Russian shop forty kopeks a pound—that makes one ruble twenty kopeks, twelve times one ruble twenty kopeks—that makes fourteen rubles forty kopeks. Do you hear, friend Hoffmann? Fourteen rubles forty kopeks on my nose alone! And on holidays I take a pinch of rappee, for I don't care to use that rotten Russian snuff on a holiday. In a year I use two pounds of rappee at two rubles a pound. Six and fourteen makes twenty rubles forty kopeks on snuff alone. It's robbery! I ask you, my friend Hoffmann, isn't it?" Hoffmann, who was drunk himself, answered in the affirmative. "Twenty rubles and forty kopeks! Damn it, I am a Swabian! I have a king in Germany. I don't want a nose! Cut off my nose! Here is my nose."

And had it not been for Lieutenant Pirogov's suddenly appearing, Hoffmann would certainly, for no rhyme or reason, have cut off Schiller's nose, for he already had his knife in position, as though he were going to cut a sole.

Schiller seemed very much annoyed that an unknown and uninvited person should so inopportunely interrupt him. Although he was in a state of intoxication, he felt that it was rather improper to be seen in the presence of an outsider in such a state and engaged in such proceedings. Meanwhile Pirogov made a slight bow and, with his characteristic agreeableness, said: "Excuse me . . . !"

"Get out!" Schiller responded emphatically.

Lieutenant Pirogov was taken aback at this. Such treatment was absolutely new to him. A smile which had begun faintly to appear on his face vanished at once. With a feeling of wounded dignity he said: "I am surprised, sir . . . I suppose you have—not observed . . . I am an officer . . ."

"And what's an officer? I'm a Swabian." (At this Schiller banged the table with his fist.) "I can be an officer; a year and half a cadet, two years a lieutenant, and tomorrow an officer. But I don't want to serve. This is what I'd do to officers: phoo!" Schiller held his open hand before him and spat into it.

Lieutenant Pirogov saw that there was nothing for him to do but withdraw. Such a proceeding, however, was quite out of keeping with his rank, and was disagreeable to him. He stopped several times on the stairs as though trying to rally his forces and to think how to make Schiller feel his impudence. At last he decided that Schiller might be excused because his head was full of beer; besides, he recalled the image of the charming blonde, and he made up his mind to consign the incident to oblivion.

Early next morning Lieutenant Pirogov appeared at the tinsmith's workshop. In the outer room he was met by the blonde charmer, who asked him in a rather severe voice, which went admirably with her little face: "What do you want?"

"Oh, good morning, my cutie! Don't you recognize me? You little rogue, what delicious eyes!"

As he said this Lieutenant Pirogov tried very charmingly to chuck her under the chin; but the lady uttered a frightened exclamation and with the same severity asked: "What do you want?"

"To see you, that's all that I want," answered Lieutenant Pirogov, smiling rather agreeably and going nearer; but noticing that the timid beauty was about to slip through the door, he added: "I want to order some spurs, my dear. Can you make me some spurs? Though indeed no spur is needed to make me love you; a bridle is what one needs, not a spur. What charming little hands!"

Lieutenant Pirogov was particularly agreeable in declarations of this kind.

"I will call my husband at once," cried the German, and went out, and within a few minutes Pirogov saw Schiller come in with sleepy-looking eyes; he had only just waked up after the drunkenness of the previous day. As he looked at the officer he remembered as though in a confused dream what had happened the previous day. He could recall nothing exactly as it was, but felt that he had done something stupid and so received the officer with a very sullen face. "I can't ask less than fifteen rubles[12] for a pair of

---

[12] In nineteenth-century Russia the ruble was worth about fifty-one cents, but, like the nineteenth-century dollar, it bought approximately six or seven times more than it buys today. (ed.)

spurs," he said, hoping to get rid of Pirogov, for as a respectable German he was ashamed to look at anyone who had seen him in an undignified condition. Schiller liked to drink without witnesses, in company with two or three friends, and at such times locked himself in and would not admit even his own workmen.

"Why are they so expensive?" asked Pirogov genially.

"German work," Schiller pronounced coolly, stroking his chin. "A Russian will undertake to make them for two rubles."

"Well, to show you that I like you and should be glad to make your acquaintance, I will pay fifteen rubles."

Schiller pondered for a minute; as a respectable German he felt a little ashamed. Hoping to put him off, he declared that he could not undertake it for a fortnight. But Pirogov, without making any objections, readily agreed to this.

The German mused and began wondering how he could best do the work so as to make it really worth fifteen rubles.

At this moment the blonde charmer came into the room and began looking for something on the table, which was covered with coffeepots. The lieutenant took advantage of Schiller's deep thought, stepped up to her, and pressed her arm, which was bare to the shoulder.

This was very distasteful to Schiller. *"Meine Frau!"* [13]

"Was wollen Sie doch?" [14] said the blonde to her husband.

"Gehn Sie[15] to the kitchen!" The blonde withdrew.

"In two weeks then?" said Pirogov.

"Yes, in two weeks," replied Schiller, still pondering. "I have a lot of work now."

"Goodbye for now, I will call again."

"Goodbye," said Schiller, closing the door after him.

Lieutenant Pirogov made up his mind not to relinquish his pursuit, though the blonde had so plainly rebuffed him. He could not conceive that anyone could resist him, especially as his politeness and the brilliant rank of a lieutenant gave him a full claim to attention. It must be mentioned also that despite her attractiveness Schiller's wife was extremely stupid. Stupidity, however, adds a special charm to a pretty wife. I have known several husbands, anyway, who were enraptured by the stupidity of their wives and

---

[13] "My wife!" (ed.)
[14] "But what do you want?" (ed.)
[15] "You go . . ." (ed.)

saw in it evidence of childlike innocence. Beauty works perfect miracles. All spiritual defects in a beauty, far from exciting revulsion, become somehow wonderfully attractive; even vice adds an aura of charm to the beautiful; but when beauty disappears, a woman needs to be twenty times as intelligent as a man merely to inspire respect, to say nothing of love. Schiller's wife, however, for all her stupidity was always faithful to her duties, and consequently it was no easy task for Pirogov to succeed in his bold enterprise. But there is always a pleasure in overcoming difficulties, and the blonde became more and more attractive to him every day. He began inquiring pretty frequently about the progress of the spurs, so that at last Schiller was weary of it. He did his utmost to finish the spurs quickly; at last they were done.

"Oh, what splendid workmanship," cried Lieutenant Pirogov on seeing the spurs. "Good Heavens, how well they're made! Our general hasn't spurs like that."

A feeling of self-complacency filled Schiller's soul. His eyes began to sparkle, and he felt inwardly reconciled to Pirogov. "The Russian officer is an intelligent man," he thought to himself.

"So, then, you could make a sheath for a dagger or for anything else?"

"Indeed I can," said Schiller with a smile.

"Then make me a sheath for a dagger. I will bring it you. I have a very fine Turkish dagger, but I want to have another sheath for it."

This was like a bomb dropped upon Schiller. His brows suddenly knitted.

"So that's what you are after," he thought to himself, inwardly swearing at himself for having praised his own work. To refuse it now he felt would be dishonest; besides, the Russian officer had praised his workmanship. Slightly shaking his head, he gave his consent; but the kiss which Pirogov impudently printed on the lips of the pretty wife as he went out reduced the tinsmith to stupefaction.

I think it will not be superfluous to make the reader better acquainted with Schiller himself. Schiller was a real German in the full sense of the word. From the age of twenty, that happy time when the Russian lives without a thought of the next day, Schiller had already mapped out his whole life and did not deviate from his plan under any circumstances. He made it a rule to get up at seven, to dine at two, to be punctual in everything, and to get drunk every Sunday. He set, as a goal, saving fifty thousand in the course of ten years, and all this was as certain and as unalterable as fate, for sooner would a government clerk forget to look in at the porter's lodge of his chief than a German would bring himself to break his word. Never under any circumstances did he increase his expenses, and if the price of potatoes went up much above the ordinary he did not spend one copper more on them but simply diminished the amount he bought, and although he was left sometimes feeling rather hungry, he soon got used to it. His exactitude was such that he made it his rule to kiss his wife twice in twenty-four hours but not more, and that he might not exceed the number he never put more than one small teaspoonful of pepper in his soup; on Sunday, however, this rule was not so strictly kept, for then Schiller used to drink two bottles of beer and one bottle of herb-flavored vodka which, however, he always abused. He did not drink like an Englishman, who locks his doors directly after dinner and gets drunk in solitude. On the contrary, like a German he always drank with inspiration either in the company of Hoffmann the bootmaker or with Kuntz the carpenter, who was also a German and a great drunkard. Such was the disposition of the worthy Schiller, who was indeed placed in a very difficult position. Though he was phlegmatic and a German, Pirogov's behavior excited in him a feeling resembling jealousy. He racked his brains and could not think of how to get rid of this Russian officer. Meanwhile Pirogov, smoking a pipe in the company of his fellow officers— since Providence has ordained that wherever there is an officer there is a pipe—alluded significantly and with an agreeable smile on his lips to his little intrigue with the pretty German, with whom he was, according to his account, already on the best of terms, though as a matter of fact he had almost lost all hope of winning her favor.

One day he was walking along Meshchansky Street looking at the house adorned by Schiller's signboard with coffeepots and samovars on it; to his great joy he caught sight of the blonde charmer's head thrust out of the window watching the passers-by. He stopped, blew her a kiss, and said: "*Gut Morgen.*"

The fair lady bowed to him as to an acquaintance.

"Is your husband at home?"

"Yes," she answered.

"And when is he out?"

"He is not at home on Sundays," said the foolish little German.

"That's not bad," Pirogov thought to himself. "I must take advantage of that."

And the following Sunday he suddenly and unexpectedly stood facing the blonde German. Schiller really was not at home. The pretty wife was frightened; but Pirogov on this occasion behaved rather warily, he was very respectful in his manner, and, making his bows, displayed all the elegance of his supple figure in his close-fitting uniform. He made polite and agreeable jests, but the foolish little German responded with nothing but monosyllables. At last, having made his attack from all sides and seeing that nothing would entertain her, he suggested that they dance. The German agreed immediately, for all German girls are passionately fond of dancing. Pirogov rested great hopes upon this: in the first place it gave her pleasure, in the second place it displayed his figure and dexterity; and thirdly he could get so much closer to her in dancing and put his arm around the pretty German and lay the foundation for everything else; in short, he reckoned on complete success resulting from it. He began humming a gavotte, knowing that Germans must have something sedate. The pretty German walked into the middle of the room and lifted her shapely foot. This attitude so enchanted Pirogov that he flew to kiss her. The lady began to scream, and this only enhanced her charm in Pirogov's eyes. He was showering kisses on her when the door suddenly opened and Schiller walked in, with Hoffmann and Kuntz the carpenter. All these worthy persons were as drunk as cobblers.

But . . . I leave the reader to imagine the wrath and indignation of Schiller.

"Ruffian!" he shouted in the utmost indignation. "How dare you kiss my wife? You are a son of a bitch and not a Russian officer. Go to hell! That's right, isn't it, friend Hoffmann? I am a German and not a Russian swine." (Hoffmann gave him an affirmative answer.) "Oh, I don't want to wear horns! [16] Take him by the collar, friend Hoffmann; I won't have it," he went on, brandishing his arms violently, while his whole face was the color of his red vest. "I have been living in Petersburg for eight years, I have a mother in Swabia and an uncle in Nuremburg. I am a German and

---

[16] I.e., have an unfaithful wife. Reference is to horns worn by a cuckold. (ed.)

not a horned ox. Undress him, my friend Hoffmann. Hold him by his arms and his legs, comrade Kuntz!"

And the Germans seized Pirogov by his arms and his legs.

He tried in vain to get away; these three tradesmen were among the sturdiest people in Petersburg, and they treated him so roughly and disrespectfully that I cannot find words to do justice to this unfortunate incident.

I am sure that next day Schiller was in a high fever, that he was trembling like a leaf, expecting from moment to moment the arrival of the police, that he would have given anything in the world for what had happened on the previous day to be a dream. But what has been cannot be changed. No comparison could do justice to Pirogov's anger and indignation. The very thought of such an insult drove him to fury. He thought Siberia and the lash too slight a punishment for Schiller. He flew home to dress himself and go at once straight to the general to paint for him in the most vivid colors the seditious insolence of the Germans. He meant to lodge a complaint in writing with the general staff; and, if the punishment meted out to the offenders was not satisfactory, to carry the matter to higher authorities.

But all this ended rather strangely; on the way to the general he went into a cafe, ate two cream puffs, read something out of *The Northern Bee* and left the cafe with his wrath somewhat cooled. Then a pleasant fresh evening led him to take a few turns along Nevsky Prospekt; by nine o'clock he had recovered his serenity and decided that he had better not disturb the general on Sunday; especially as he would be sure to be away somewhere. And so he went to spend the evening with one of the directors of the control committee, where he met a very agreeable party of government officials and officers of his regiment. There he spent a very pleasant evening, and so distinguished himself in the mazurka that not only the ladies but even their partners were moved to admiration.

"Marvelously is our world arranged," I thought as I walked two days later along Nevsky Prospekt, and mused over these two incidents. "How strangely, how unaccountably Fate plays with us! Do we ever get what we desire? Do we ever attain what our powers seem specially fitted for? Everything goes contrary to what we expect. Fate gives splendid horses to one man and he drives in his carriage without noticing their beauty, while another who is consumed by a passion for horses has to go on foot, and all the satisfaction he gets is clicking with his tongue when trotting horses are led past him. One has an excellent cook, but unluckily so small a mouth that he cannot take more than two pecks; another has a mouth as big as the arch of the Staff headquarters, but alas, has to be content with a German dinner of potatoes. What strange pranks Fate plays with us!"

But strangest of all are the incidents that take place on Nevsky Prospekt. Oh, do not trust that Nevsky Prospekt! I always wrap myself more closely in my cloak when I pass along it and try not to look at the objects which meet me. Everything is a cheat, everything is a dream, everything is other than it seems! You think that the gentleman who walks along in a splendidly cut coat is very wealthy?—not at all. All his wealth lies in his coat. You think that those two stout men who stand facing the church that is being built are criticizing its architecture?—not at all: they are talking about how peculiarly two crows are sitting facing each other. You think that that enthusiast waving his arms about is describing how his wife was playing ball out of window with an officer who was a complete stranger to him?—not so at all, he is talking of Lafayette. You imagine those ladies . . . but ladies are least of all to be trusted. Do not look into the shop windows; the trifles exhibited in them are delightful but they have an odor of money about them. But God save you from peeping under the ladies' hats! However attractively in the evening a fair lady's cloak may flutter in the distance, nothing would induce me to follow her and try to get a closer view. Keep your distance, for God's sake, keep your distance from the street lamp! and pass by it quickly, as quickly as you can! It is a happy escape if you get off with nothing worse than some of its stinking oil on your foppish coat. But even apart from the street lamp, everything breathes deception. It deceives at all hours, the Nevsky Prospekt does, but most of all when night falls in masses of shadow on it, throwing into relief the white and dun-colored walls of the houses, when all the town is transformed into noise and brilliance, when myriads of carriages roll off bridges, postilions shout and jump up on their horses, and when the devil himself lights the street lamps to show everything in false colors.

DIARY OF A MADMAN

October 3

Today an extraordinary event occurred. I got up rather late in the morning, and when Mavra brought me my cleaned boots I asked her the time. Hearing that it was long past ten I dressed quickly. I admit I wouldn't have gone to the department at all, knowing the sour face the chief of our section will make at me. For a long time past he has been saying to me: "How is it, my man, your head always seems in a muddle? Sometimes you rush about as though you were crazy and do your work so that the devil himself could not make head or tail of it, you write the heading with a small letter, and you don't put in the date or the number." The damned heron! He must be jealous because I sit in the director's room and sharpen quills for his Excellency. In short I wouldn't have gone to the department if I had not hoped to see the cashier and to find out whether maybe I could not get something of my month's salary in advance out of that wretched Jew. That's another creature! Do you suppose he would ever let one have a month's pay in advance? Good gracious! the Last Judgment will come before he'd do it! You may ask till you burst, you may be in your final misery, but the gray-headed devil won't let you have it—and when he is at home his own cook slaps him in the face; everybody knows it. I can't see the advantage of serving in a department; there are absolutely no possibilities in it. In the provincial government, or in the civil and crown offices, it's quite a different matter: there you may see some wretched man squeezed into the corner, copying away, with a

disgusting old coat on and such a face that it nearly makes you sick,
but look what a villa he rents! It's no use offering him a gilt china
cup: "That's a doctor's present," he will say. You must give him a
pair of trotting horses or a carriage or a beaver fur coat worth
three hundred rubles. He is such a quiet fellow to look at, and says
in such a refined way: "Oblige me with a penknife just to sharpen
a quill," but he fleeces the petitioners so that he scarcely leaves
them a shirt to their backs. It is true that ours is a gentlemanly
office; there is a cleanliness in everything such as is never seen in
provincial offices, the tables are mahogany, and all our superiors
address you formally. . . . I must confess that if it were not for
the prestige of the service I should have left the department long
ago.

I put on my old overcoat and took my umbrella, because it was
pouring buckets. There was no one in the streets; some peasant
women pulling their skirts over their heads to cover themselves and
some Russian merchants under umbrellas and some messengers met
my eye. I saw none of the better class except a fellow clerk. I saw
him at the intersection. As soon as I saw him I said to myself: "No,
my dear fellow, you are not on your way to the department; you
are running after that girl who is racing ahead and you're looking
at her legs." What rogues clerks are! I swear, they are as bad as
any officer: if any female goes by in a hat they are bound to be
after her. While I was making this reflection I saw a carriage driving up to the shop which I was passing. I recognized it at once. It
was our director's carriage. "But he can have nothing to go to the
shop for," I thought; "I suppose it must be his daughter." I flattened
myself against the wall. The footman opened the carriage door and
she darted out like a bird. How she glanced from right to left, how
her eyes and eyebrows gleamed . . . Good God, I am done for,
completely lost! And why does she drive out in such rain! Don't
tell me that women have not a passion for these rags. She didn't
know me, and, indeed, I tried to muffle myself up all I could, because I had on a very muddy old-fashioned overcoat. Now people
wear cloaks with long collars, while I had short collars one above
the other, and, indeed, the cloth was not at all rainproof. Her little
dog, which had been too slow to dash in at the door, was left in the
street. I know the dog—her name is Madgie. I had hardly been
there a minute when I heard a thin little voice: "Good morning,

Madgie." "Well, I'll be damned! Who's that speaking?" I looked around me and saw two ladies walking along under an umbrella: one old and the other young; but they had passed already and again I heard beside me: "Shame on you, Madgie!" What the hell! I saw that Madgie was sniffing at a dog that was following the ladies. "Aha," I said to myself, "but come, surely I am drunk! Only I imagine that very rarely happens to me." "No, Fido, you are wrong there," said Madgie—I saw her say it with my own eyes. "I have been, wow, wow, I have been very ill, wow, wow, wow!" "Oh, so it's you, you little dog! Goodness me!" I must confess I was very much surprised to hear her speaking like a human being; but afterward, when I thought it all over, I was no longer surprised. A number of similar instances have as a fact occurred. They say that in England a fish popped up and uttered two words in such a strange language that the learned men have been for three years trying to interpret them and have not succeeded yet. I have also read in the papers of two cows who went into a shop and asked for a pound of tea. But I must admit I was much more surprised when Madgie said: "I did write to you, Fido; Polkan probably didn't bring you the letter." Damn it all! I never in all my life heard of a dog being able to write. No one but a gentleman by birth can write correctly. It's true, of course, that some shopmen and even serfs can sometimes write a little; but their writing is for the most part mechanical: they have no commas, no stops, no style.

It amazed me. I must confess that of late I have begun seeing and hearing things such as no one has ever seen or heard before. "I'll follow that dog," I said to myself, "and find out what she is like and what she thinks." I opened my umbrella and set off after the two ladies. They passed into Gorokhovaya Street, turned into Meshchanskaya and from there into Stolyarnya Street; at last they reached Kokushkin Bridge and stopped in front of a big house. "I know that house," I said to myself. "That's Zverkov's Buildings. What a huge place! All sorts of people live in it: so many cooks, so many visitors from all parts! and our friends the clerks, one on the top of another, with a third trying to squeeze in, like dogs. I have a friend living there, who plays beautifully on the trombone." The ladies went up to the fifth floor. "Good," I thought, "I won't go in now, but I will note the place and I will certainly take advantage of the first opportunity."

October 4

Today is Wednesday, and so I was in our chief's study. I came a little early on purpose and, sitting down, began sharpening quills. Our director must be a very clever man. His whole study is lined with bookshelves. I have read the titles of some of them: they are all learned, so learned that they are really beyond anyone like me— they are all either in French or in German. And just look into his face! Aie! what importance in his eyes! I have never heard him say a word too much. Sometimes when one hands him the papers he'll ask: "What's it like out of doors?" "Damp, your Excellency." Yes, he is a cut above anyone like me! He's a statesman. I notice, however, he is particularly fond of me. If his daughter, too, were . . . Damn it! . . . Never mind, never mind, silence! I read *The Bee*. They are stupid people, the French! What do they want? I'd take the bunch of them, I swear I would, and thrash them all soundly with birch rods! In it I read a very pleasant description of a ball written by a country gentleman of Kursk. The country gentlemen of Kursk write well. Then I noticed it was half-past twelve and that our chief had not come out of his bedroom. But about half-past one an event occurred which no pen could describe. The door opened; I thought it was the director and jumped up from my chair with my papers, but it was she, in person! Holy fathers, how she was dressed! Her dress was white as a swan—aie, how sumptuous! And the look in her eye—like sunshine, I swear, like sunshine. She bowed and said: "Hasn't Papa been here?" Aie, aie, aie, what a voice! A canary, a regular canary. "Your Excellency," I was on the point of saying, "do not ask them to punish me, but if you want to punish, then punish with your own noble hand." But damn it all, my tongue would not obey me, and all I said was: "No, madam." She looked at me, looked at the books, and dropped her handkerchief. I dashed forward, slipped on the damned parquet, and almost smashed my nose but recovered myself and picked up the handkerchief. Holy fathers, what a handkerchief! The most delicate batiste—amber, perfect amber! you would know from the very scent that it belonged to a general's daughter. She thanked me and gave me a faint smile, so that her sugary lips scarcely moved, and after that went away. I stayed on another hour, when the footman came in and said: "You can go home, Aksenty Ivanovich; the master has gone out." I cannot endure the flunkey set: they are always lolling about in the hall and don't even take the trouble to nod to me. That's nothing: once one of these animals had the gall to offer me his snuffbox without even getting up from his seat. Doesn't the fellow know I am a government clerk, that I am a gentleman by birth? However, I took my hat and put on my overcoat myself, for these people never help me on with it, and went off. At home I spent most of the time lying on my bed. Then I copied out some very good verses:

> My love for one hour I did not see,
> And a whole year it seemed to me.

> "My life is now a hated task,
> How can I live this life," I ask.

It must have been written by Pushkin.[1] In the evening, wrapping myself up in my overcoat, I went to the front door of her Excellency's house and waited about for a long time on the chance of her coming out to get into her carriage, so that I might snatch another glimpse of her.

November 6

The head of our section was in a fury today. When I came into the department he called me into his room and began like this: "Come, kindly tell me what you are doing?" "How do you mean?" I said. "I am doing nothing." "Come, think what you are up to!" Why, you are over forty. It's time you had a little sense. What do you imagine yourself to be? Do you suppose I don't know all the tricks you are up to? Why, you are philandering after the director's daughter! Come, look at yourself; just think what you are! Why, you are a nonentity and nothing else! Why, you haven't a copper to bless yourself with. And just look at yourself in the mirror—how could you think of such a thing!" Damn him! Because his face is like a druggist's bottle and he has a shock of hair on his head curled in a tuft, and pomades it into a kind of rosette, and holds his head in the air, he imagines he is the only one who may do anything. I understand, I understand why he is so angry with me. He is envious: he has perhaps seen signs of preference shown to me. But I spit on him! As though a court councilor were of so much importance! He hangs a gold chain on his watch and orders boots at thirty rubles—but to hell with him! Am I a tailor or a son of a

---

[1] Not quite. It was written by N. P. Nikolev (1758-1815). (ed.)

noncommissioned officer? I am a gentleman. Why, I may rise in the service too. I am only forty-two, a time of life in which a career in the service is really only just beginning. Just wait, my friend! I'll be a colonel and perhaps, please God, something better. I will have a reputation, and better maybe than yours. A peculiar notion you have got into your head that no one is a gentleman but yourself. Give me a fashionably cut coat and let me put on a necktie like yours—and then you wouldn't hold a candle to me. I haven't the means, that's the only trouble.

November 8

I have been to the theater. It was a performance of the Russian fool Filatka.[2] I laughed very much. There was vaudeville too, with some amusing verses about lawyers, and especially about a collegiate registrar, so outspoken that I was surprised that the censor had passed it; and about the merchants they openly said that they cheat the people and that their sons are debauched and ape the gentry. There was a very amusing couplet about the journalists too: saying that they abused everyone and that an author begged the public to defend him against them. The authors do write amusing plays nowadays. I love being at the theater. As soon as I have a coin in my pocket I can't resist going. And among our fellow clerks there are such pigs that they positively won't go to the theater, the peasants; unless perhaps you give them a free ticket. One actress sang very nicely. I thought of the other girl . . . ah, damn it! . . . Never mind, never mind . . . silence!

November 9

At eight o'clock I went to the department. The head of our section put on a look as though he did not see me come in. I, too, behaved as though nothing had passed between us. I looked through and checked some papers. I went out at four o'clock. I walked by the director's house, but no one was to be seen. After dinner, for the most part, I lay on my bed.

November 11

Today I sat in our director's study. I sharpened twenty-three quills for him and for her . . . aie, aie! for her Excellency four

---

[2] See p. 229, n. 8. (ed.)

quills. He likes to have a lot of quills. Oo, he must have a head! He always sits silent, and I expect he is turning over everything in his head. I should like to know what he thinks most about. What is going on in that head? I should like to get a close view of the life of these gentlemen, of all these *équivoques* and court ways. How they go on and what they do in their circle—that's what I should like to find out! I have several times thought of beginning a conversation on the subject with his Excellency, but, damn it all, I couldn't bring my tongue to it; one says it's cold or warm today and can't utter another word. I should like to look into the drawing room, of which one only sees the open door and another room beyond it. Ah, what sumptuous furniture! What mirrors and china! I long to have a look in there, into the part of the house where her Excellency is, that's where I should like to go! Into her boudoir where there are all sorts of little jars, little bottles, and such flowers that one is frightened even to breathe on them, to see her dresses lying scattered about, more like ethereal gossamer than dresses. I long to glance into her bedroom; there I imagine there must be marvels . . . a paradise, such as is not to be found in the heavens. To look at the little stool on which she puts her little foot when she gets out of bed and the way she puts a little snow-white stocking on that little foot . . . Aie, aie, aie! never mind, never mind . . . silence!

But today a light dawned upon me. I remembered the conversation between the two dogs that I heard on Nevsky Prospekt. "Good," I thought to myself, "now I will learn all. I must get hold of the correspondence that these wretched dogs have been carrying on. Then I shall certainly learn something." I must admit I once called Madgie to me and said to her: "Listen, Madgie; here we are alone. If you like I will shut the door too, so that no one shall see you; tell me all you know about your young lady: what she is like and how she behaves. I swear I won't tell anyone." But the sly little dog put her tail between her legs, doubled herself up, and went quickly to the door as though she hadn't heard. I have long suspected that dogs are far more intelligent than men; I am even convinced that they can speak, only there is a certain doggedness about them. They are extremely diplomatic: they notice everything, every step a man takes. Yes, regardless of what happens I will go tomorrow to Zverkov's Buildings. I will question

Fido, and if I am successful I will seize all the letters Madgie has
written her.

November 12

At two o'clock in the afternoon I set out determined to see Fido
and question her. I can't endure cabbage, the smell of which floats
from all the little shops in Meshchanskaya Street; moreover, such
a hellish reek rises from under every gate that I raced along at full
speed holding my nose. And the nasty workmen let off such a lot
of soot and smoke from their workshops that a gentleman cannot
stroll there. When I climbed up to the sixth floor and rang the bell,
a girl who was not at all bad-looking, with little freckles, came to
the door. I recognized her: it was the girl who was with the old
lady. She turned a little red, and I said to myself at once: "You
are looking for a bridegroom, my dear." "What do you want?"
she asked. "I want to have a few words with your dog." The girl
was stupid. I saw at once that she was stupid. At that moment the
dog ran out barking; I tried to catch hold of her, but the nasty
wretch almost snapped at my nose. However, I saw her bed in the
corner. Ah, that was just what I wanted. I went up to it, rummaged
in the straw in the wooden box, and to my indescribable delight
pulled out a packet of little slips of paper. The wretched dog,
seeing this, first bit my calf, and then, when she perceived that I
had taken her letters, began to whine and fawn on me, but I said:
"No, my dear, goodbye," and took to my heels. I believe the girl
thought I was a madman, as she was very much frightened. When
I got home I wanted to begin at once to decipher the letters, for I
don't see very well by candlelight; but Mavra had taken it into her
head to wash the floor. These stupid Finnish women always clean
at the wrong moment. And so I went out to walk about and think
over the incident. Now I shall find out all their doings and ways of
thinking, all the hidden springs, and shall get to the bottom of it
all. These letters will reveal everything. Dogs are clever creatures,
they understand all the diplomatic relations, and so no doubt I shall
find there everything about our gentleman: all about his character
and behavior. There will be something in them too about her who
. . . never mind, silence! Toward evening I came home. For the
most part I lay on my bed.

November 13

Well, we shall see! The writing is fairly distinct; at the same time there is something doggy about the handwriting. Let us read:

DEAR FIDO,

I never can get used to your common name. As though they could not have given you a better one? Fido, Rose—what vulgarity! No more about that, however. I am very glad we thought of writing to each other.

The letter is very well written. The punctuation and even the spelling is quite correct. Even the chief of our section could not write like this, though he does talk of having studied at some university. Let us see what comes next.

It seems to me that to share one's ideas, one's feelings, and one's impressions with others is one of the greatest blessings on earth.

H'm! . . . an idea taken from a work translated from the German. I don't remember the name of it.

I say this from experience, though I have not been about the world, beyond the gates of our house. Is not my life spent in comfort? My young lady, whom her papa calls Sophie, loves me passionately.

Aie, aie! never mind, never mind! Silence!

Papa, too, often caresses me. I drink tea and coffee with cream. Ah, *ma chère*, I ought to tell you that I see nothing agreeable at all in big, gnawed bones such as our Polkan crunches in the kitchen. The only bones that are nice are those of game, and then only when the marrow hasn't been sucked out of them by someone. What is very good is several sauces mixed together, only they must be free from capers and green stuff; but I know nothing worse than giving dogs little balls of bread. A gentleman sitting at the table who has been touching all sorts of dirty things with his hands begins with those hands rolling up bread, calls you up, and thrusts the ball upon you. To refuse seems somehow discourteous—well, you eat it— with revulsion, but you eat it. . . .

What the devil's this! What nonsense! As though there were nothing better to write about. Let us look at another page and see if there is nothing more sensible.

I shall be delighted to let you know about everything that happens here. I have already told you something about the chief gentleman, whom Sophie calls Papa. He is a very strange man.

Ah, here we are at last! Yes, I knew it; they have a very political view of everything. Let us see what Papa is like.

> . . . a very strange man. For the most part he says nothing; he very rarely speaks. But about a week ago he was continually talking to himself: "Shall I get it or shall I not?" He would take a paper in one hand and close the other empty hand and say: "Shall I get it or shall I not?" Once he turned to me with the question: "What do you think, Madgie, shall I get it or not?" I certainly couldn't understand a word of it; I sniffed at his boots and walked away. A week later, *ma chère*, he came in in high glee. All the morning gentlemen in uniform were coming to see him and were congratulating him on something. At the table he was merrier than I have ever seen him; he kept telling stories. And after dinner he lifted me up to his neck and said: "Look, Madgie, what's this?" I saw a little ribbon. I sniffed it, but could discover no aroma whatever; at last I licked it on the sly: it was a little bit salty.

H'm! This dog seems to me to be really too . . . she ought to be beaten! And so he is ambitious! One must take that into consideration.

> Farewell, *ma chère!* I fly, and so on . . . and so on . . . I will finish my letter tomorrow. Well, good day, I am with you again. Today my young lady Sophie . . .

Oh come, let us see about Sophie. Damn it! . . . Never mind, never mind . . . let us go on.

> My young lady Sophie was in a great fluster. She was getting ready to go to a ball, and I was delighted that in her absence I could write to you. My Sophie is always very glad to go to a ball, though she always gets almost angry when she is being dressed. I can't understand, *ma chère*, what pleasure there is in going to balls. Sophie always comes home from balls at six o'clock in the morning, and I can almost always guess from her pale and exhausted face that they had given the poor thing nothing to eat. I must confess I couldn't live like that. If I didn't get grouse and gravy or the roast wing of a chicken, I don't know what would become of me. Gravy is nice too with grain in it, but with carrots, turnips, or artichokes it is never good.

What an uneven style! You can see at once that it is not a man writing; it begins as it should and ends with dogginess. Let us look at one more letter. It's rather long. H'm! and there's no date on it.

Ah, my dear, how one feels the approach of spring! My heart beats as though I were expecting someone. There is always a noise in my ears so that I often stand for some minutes with my foot in the air listening at doors. I must confide to you that I have a number of suitors. I often sit at the window and look at them. Oh, if only you knew what ugly creatures there are among them. One is a very clumsy mongrel, fearfully stupid, stupidity is painted on his face; he walks about the street with an air of importance and imagines that he is a distinguished person and thinks that everybody is looking at him. Don't you believe it! I don't take any notice of him—I behave exactly as though I didn't see him. And what a terrifying Great Dane stops before my window! If he were to stand on his hind legs, which I expect the clod could not do, he would be a whole head taller than my Sophie's papa, who is fairly tall and fat, too. That blockhead must be a terribly insolent fellow. I growled at him, but much he cared; he hardly frowned, he put out his tongue, dangled his huge ears and looked up at the window—such a country bumpkin! But can you suppose, *ma chère*, that my heart makes no response to any overture? Ah no . . . If only you could see one of my suitors climbing over the fence next door, by name Trésor. . . . Ah, *ma chère*, what a face he has! . . .

Pfoo, the devil! . . . What rubbish! How can anyone fill a letter with foolishness! Give me a man! I want to see a man. I want spiritual sustenance—in which my soul might find food and enjoyment; and instead of that I have this nonsense. . . . Let us turn over the page and see whether it gets better!

Sophie was sitting at the table sewing something, I was looking out of the window because I am fond of watching passers-by, when all at once the footman came in and said "Teplov!" "Ask him in," cried Sophie, and rushed to embrace me. "Ah, Madgie, Madgie! If only you knew who that is: a dark young man, a court chamberlain, and eyes black as agates!" And Sophie ran off to her room. A minute later a court chamberlain with black whiskers came in, walked up to the mirror, smoothed his hair, and looked about the room. I growled and sat in my place. Sophie soon came in and bowed gaily in response to his shuffling; and I just went on looking out of the window as though I were noticing nothing. However, I bent my head a little on one side and tried to hear what they were saying. Oh, *ma chère*, the nonsense they talked! They talked about a lady who had mistaken one dance movement for another; and said that someone called Bobov with a ruffle on his shirt looked just like a stork and had almost fallen down on the floor, and that a girl called Lidina thought that her eyes were blue when they were really green—and that sort of thing. "Well," I thought to myself, "if one were to compare that court chamberlain to Trésor, heavens, what a difference!" In the first place, the court chamberlain has a perfectly flat face with whiskers all around as though he had tied it up in a black handkerchief; while Trésor has a delicate little countenance with a white patch on the forehead. It's impossible to compare the court chamberlain's figure with Trésor's. And his eyes, his ways, his manners are all quite different. Oh, what a difference! I don't know, *ma chère*, what she sees in her Teplov. Why she is so enthusiastic about him. . . .

Well, I think myself that there is something wrong about it. It's impossible that she can be fascinated by Teplov. Let us see what next.

It seems to me that if she is attracted by that court chamberlain she will soon be attracted by that clerk that sits in Papa's study. Oh, *ma chère*, if you knew what an ugly fellow that is! He looks like a turtle in a bag. . . .

What clerk is this? . . .

He has a very queer surname. He always sits sharpening the quills. The hair on his head is very much like hay. Papa sometimes sends him out instead of a servant. . . .

I do believe the nasty little dog is alluding to me. But my hair isn't like hay!

Sophie can never help laughing when she sees him.

That's a lie, you damned little dog! What an evil tongue! As though I didn't know that that is the result of jealousy! As though I didn't know whose tricks were at the bottom of that! This is all the doing of the chief of my section. The man has sworn eternal hatred, and here he tries to injure me again and again, at every turn. Let us look at one more letter, though. Perhaps the thing will explain itself.

MY DEAR FIDO,

Forgive me for not writing for so long. I have been in a perfect ecstasy. How truly has some writer said that love is a second life. Moreover, there are great changes in the house here. The court chamberlain is here every day. Sophie is frantically in love with him. Papa is very happy. I have even heard from our Grigory, who sweeps the floor and almost always talks to himself, that there will

soon be a wedding because Papa is determined to see Sophie married to a general or a court chamberlain or to a colonel in the
army. . . .

Damn it! I can't read any more. . . . It's always a court chamberlain or a general. Everything that's best in the world falls to the
court chamberlains or the generals. If you find some poor treasure
and think it is almost within your grasp, a court chamberlain or a
general will snatch it from you. God damn it! I'd like to become
a general myself, not in order to receive her hand and all the rest
of it; no, I should like to be a general only to see how they would
wriggle and display all their court manners and *équivoques* and
then to say to them: I spit on you both. Oh, damn it! I tore the
stupid dog's letters to bits.

December 3

It cannot be. It's idle talk! There won't be a wedding! What if he
is a court chamberlain? Why, that is nothing but a rank; it's not a
visible thing that one could pick up in one's hands. You don't get a
third eye in your head because you are a court chamberlain. Why,
his nose is not made of gold but is just like mine and everyone
else's; he sniffs with it and doesn't eat with it, he sneezes with it
and doesn't cough with it. I have often tried to discover what all
these differences come from. Why am I a titular councilor and on
what grounds am I a titular councilor? Perhaps I am not a titular
councilor at all? Perhaps I am a count or a general, and only somehow appear to be a titular councilor. Perhaps I don't know myself
who I am. How many instances there have been in history: some
simple, humble tradesman or peasant, not even a nobleman, is suddenly discovered to be a great gentleman or a baron, or what do
you call it. . . . If a peasant can sometimes turn into something
like that, what may not a nobleman turn into? I shall suddenly, for
instance, go to see our chief in a general's uniform: with an
epaulet on my right shoulder and an epaulet on my left shoulder,
and a blue ribbon across my chest; well, my charmer will sing a
different tune then, and what will her papa, our director, himself
say? Ah, he is very ambitious! He is a Mason, he is certainly a
Mason; though he does pretend to be this and that, but I noticed at
once that he was a Mason: if he shakes hands with anyone, he only
offers him two fingers. Might I not be appointed a governor or a
general this very minute or a superintendent, or something of that

sort? I should like to know why I am a titular councilor. Why precisely a titular councilor?

December 5

I spent the whole morning reading the newspaper. Strange things are going on in Spain. In fact, I can't really understand it. They write that the throne is vacant, and that they are in a difficult position about choosing an heir, and that, as a consequence, there are insurrections. It seems to me that it is extremely peculiar. How can the throne be vacant? They say that some Donna[3] ought to ascend the throne. A Donna cannot ascend the throne, she cannot possibly. There ought to be a king on the throne. "But," they say, "there is not a king." It cannot be that there is no king. A kingdom can't exist without a king. There is a king, only probably he is in hiding somewhere. He may be there, but either family reasons or danger from some neighboring state, such as France or some other country, may compel him to remain in hiding, or there may be some other reasons.

December 8

I quite wanted to go to the department, but various reasons and considerations detained me. I cannot get the affairs of Spain out of my head. How can it be that a Donna should be made queen? They won't allow it. England in the first place won't allow it. And besides, the politics of all Europe, the Emperor of Austria and our Czar . . . I must admit these events have so overwhelmed and shaken me that I haven't been able to do anything all day. Mavra remarked that I was extremely absent-minded at the table. And I believe I did accidentally throw two plates on the floor, which smashed immediately. After dinner I went for a walk down the hill: nothing edifying. For the most part I lay on my bed and reflected on the affairs of Spain.

2000 A.D., *April 43*

This is the day of the greatest public rejoicing! There is a king of Spain! He has been discovered. I am that king. I only heard of it this morning. I must confess it burst upon me like a flash of lightning. I can't imagine how I could believe and imagine myself to be

---

3 I.e., "woman." (ed.)

a titular councilor. How could that crazy, mad idea ever have
entered my head? It's a good thing that no one thought of putting
me in a madhouse. Now everything has been revealed to me. Now
it is all as clear as can be. But until now I did not understand; everything was in a sort of mist. And I believe it all arose from believing
that the brain is in the head. It's not so at all; it comes with the
wind from the direction of the Caspian Sea. First of all, I told
Mavra who I am. When she heard that the King of Spain was standing before her, she clasped her hands and almost died of horror; the
ignorant woman had never seen a King of Spain before. I tried to
reassure her, however, and in gracious words tried to convince
her of my benevolent feelings toward her, saying that I was not
angry with her for having sometimes cleaned my boots so badly.
Of course they are uncultured people; it is no good talking of
elevated subjects to them. She is frightened because she is convinced that all kings of Spain are like Philip II.[4] But I assured her
that there was no resemblance between me and Philip II and that I
have not even one Capuchin monk. I didn't go to the department
. . . the hell with it! No, my friends, you won't entice me there
again; I am not going to copy your horrible papers!

Martober 86 between
day and night

Our office messenger arrived today to tell me to go to the department, and to say that I had not been there for more than three
weeks. However, I did go to the department just for the fun of it.
The head of our section thought that I should bow to him and
apologize, but I looked at him indifferently, not too angrily and not
too graciously, and sat down in my place as though I did not notice anything. I looked at all the scum of the office and thought:
"If only you knew who is sitting among you!" Good gracious!
wouldn't there be a commotion! And the head of our section would
bow to me as he bows now to the director. They put a paper before me to make some sort of an extract from it. But I didn't touch
it. A few minutes later everyone was in an uproar. They said the
director was coming. A number of the clerks ran forward to show
off for him, but I didn't stir. When he walked through our room
they all buttoned up their coats, but I didn't do anything at all.

---

[4] (1527-98), the king under whom the Spanish Inquisition reached its infamous peak. (ed.)

What's a director? Am I going to tremble before him—never! He's a fine director! He is a cork, he is not a director. An ordinary cork, a plain cork and nothing else—such as you cork a bottle with. What amused me most of all was when they put a paper before me to sign. They thought I should write at the bottom of the paper, So-and-so, head clerk of the table—how else should it be! But in the most important place, where the director of the department signs his name, I wrote "Ferdinand VIII." You should have seen the awe-struck silence that followed; but I only waved my hand and said: "I don't insist on any signs of allegiance!" and walked out. From there I walked straight to the director's. He was not at home. The footman did not want to let me in, but I spoke to him in such a way that his hands fell to his sides. I went straight to her bedroom. She was sitting before the mirror; she jumped up and stepped back when she saw me. I did not tell her that I was the King of Spain, however; I only told her that there was a happiness awaiting her such as she could not imagine, and that in spite of the wiles of our enemies we should be together. I didn't care to say more and walked out. Oh, woman is a treacherous creature! I have discovered now what women are. So far no one has found out with whom Woman is in love: I have been the first to discover it. Woman is in love with the devil. Yes, joking apart. Scientific men write nonsense saying that she is this or that—she cares for nothing but the devil. You will see her from a box in the first tier fixing her *lorgnette*. You imagine she is looking at the fat man with decorations. No, she is looking at the devil who is standing behind his back. There he is, hidden in his coat. There he is, beckoning to her! And she will marry him, she will marry him. And all these people, their dignified fathers who fawn on everybody and push their way to court and say that they are patriots and one thing and another: profit, profit is all that these patriots want! They would sell their father and their mother and God for money, ambitious creatures, Judases! All this is ambition, and the ambition is because of a little pimple under the tongue and in it a little worm no bigger than a pin's head, and it's all the doing of a barber who lives in Gorokhovaya Street, I don't remember his name; but I know for a fact that, in collusion with a midwife, he is trying to spread Mohammedanism all over the world, and that is why, I am told, that the majority of people in France profess the Mohammedan faith.

No date. The day
had no date

I walked incognito along Nevsky Prospekt. His Majesty the Czar drove by. All the people took off their caps and I did the same, but I made no sign that I was the King of Spain. I thought it improper to reveal myself so suddenly before everyone, because I ought first to be presented at court. The only thing that has prevented my doing so is the lack of a Spanish uniform. If only I could get hold of a royal mantle. I should have liked to order it from a tailor, but they are perfect asses; besides they neglect their work so, they have given themselves up to speculating and usually end up being employed in laying pavement. I determined to make the mantle out of my new uniform, which I had only worn twice. And so that the scoundrels should not ruin it I decided to make it myself, shutting the door so that no one might see me at it. I ripped it all up with the scissors because the style has to be completely different.

I don't remember the date
There was no month either
The devil knows what to make of it

The mantle is completely finished. Mavra shrieked when she saw me in it. However, I can't make up my mind to present myself at court, for so far the delegation hasn't arrived from Spain. It wouldn't be proper to go without my delegation; there would be nothing to lend weight to my dignity. I expect them any hour.

The 1st

I am extremely surprised at the lateness of the delegation. What can be detaining them? Can it be the machinations of France? Yes, that is the most malignant of states. I went to inquire at the post office whether the Spanish delegates had not arrived; but the postmaster was excessively stupid and knew nothing. "No," he said, "there are no delegates here, but if you care to write a letter I will send it off in accordance with the regulations." Damn it all, what's the use of a letter? A letter is nonsense. Letters are even written by pharmacists. . . .

Madrid, February
thirtieth

And so here I am in Spain, and it happened so quickly that I can
hardly believe it. This morning the Spanish delegates arrived and I
got into a carriage with them. The extraordinary rapidity of our
journey struck me as strange. We went at such a rate that within
half an hour we had reached the frontiers of Spain. But of course
now there are railroads all over Europe, and ships go very rapidly.
Spain is a strange land! When we went into the first room I saw a
number of people with shaven heads. I guessed at once that these
were either grandees or soldiers because they do shave their heads.
I thought the behavior of the High Chancellor, who led me by
the hand, extremely strange. He thrust me into a little room and
said: "Sit there, and if you persist in calling yourself King Ferdinand, I'll knock the inclination out of you." But knowing that this
was only to try me I answered in the negative, whereupon the
Chancellor hit me twice on the back with a stick, and it hurt so
that I almost cried out, but I restrained myself, remembering that
this is the custom of chivalry on receiving any exalted dignity, for
customs of chivalry persist in Spain to this day. When I was alone
I decided to occupy myself with the affairs of state. I discovered
that Spain and China are one and the same country, and it is only
through ignorance that they are considered to be different king-
doms. I recommend everyone to try to write Spain on a bit of paper and it will always turn out China. But I was particularly dis-
tressed by an event which will take place tomorrow. Tomorrow at
seven o'clock a strange phenomenon will occur: the earth will sit
on the moon. The celebrated English chemist Wellington has written about it. I must confess that I experience a tremor at my heart
when I reflect on the extreme softness and fragility of the moon.
You see the moon is usually made in Hamburg, and very badly made
too. I am surprised that England hasn't taken notice of it. It was
made by a lame barrel maker, and it is evident that the fool had no
idea what a moon should be. He put in tarred cord and one part of
lamp oil; and that is why there is such a fearful stench all over the
world that one has to stop up one's nose. And that's how it is that
the moon is such a soft globe that man cannot live on it and that
nothing lives there but noses. And it is for that very reason that we
can't see our noses, because they are all in the moon. And when I
reflected that the earth is a heavy body and when it falls may grind

our noses to powder, I was overcome by such uneasiness that, putting on my shoes and stockings, I hastened to the hall of the Imperial Council to give orders to the police not to allow the earth to sit on the moon. The grandees with shaven heads whom I found in great numbers in the hall of the Imperial Council were very intelligent people, and when I said: "Gentlemen, let us save the moon, for the earth is trying to sit upon it!" they all rushed to carry out my sovereign wishes, and several climbed up the walls to try and get at the moon; but at that moment the High Chancellor walked in. Seeing him they all ran in different directions. I as King remained alone. But, to my amazement, the Chancellor struck me with his stick and drove me back to my room! How great is the power of national tradition in Spain!

January of the same year
which came after February

So far I have not been able to understand what sort of a country Spain is. The national traditions and the customs of the court are quite extraordinary. I can't understand it, I can't understand it, I absolutely can't understand it. Today they shaved my head, although I shouted at the top of my voice that I didn't want to become a monk. But I can't even remember what happened afterward when they poured cold water on my head. I have never endured such hell. I was almost going frantic, so that they had difficulty in holding me. I cannot understand the meaning of this strange custom. It's a stupid, senseless practice! The lack of good sense in the kings who have not abolished it to this day is beyond my comprehension. Judging from all the circumstances, I wonder whether I have not fallen into the hands of the Inquisition, and whether the man I took to be the Grand Chancellor isn't the Grand Inquisitor. But I cannot understand how a king can be subject to the Inquisition. It can only be through the influence of France, especially of Polignac.[5] Oh, that beast of a Polignac! He has sworn to harm me to the death. And he pursues me and pursues me; but I know, my friend, that you are the tool of England. The English are great politicians. They poke their noses into everything. All the world knows that when England takes a pinch of snuff, France sneezes.

---

[5] (1780-1847), reactionary prime minister of France in 1830. (ed.)

The twenty-fifth

Today the Grand Inquisitor came into my room again, but hearing his steps in the distance I hid under a chair. Seeing I wasn't there, he began calling me. At first he shouted "Poprischin!" I didn't say a word. Then: "Aksenty Ivanov! Titular councilor! Nobleman!" I still remained silent. "Ferdinand VIII, King of Spain!" I was on the point of sticking out my head, but then I thought: "No, my friend, you won't fool me, I know you: you will be pouring cold water on my head again." However, he caught sight of me and drove me from under the chair with a stick. That damned stick does hurt. However, I was rewarded for all this by the discovery I made today. I found out that every cock has a Spain, that it is under his wings [not far from his tail].[6]

The Grand Inquisitor went away, however, very angry, threatening me with some punishment. But I disdain his impotent malice, knowing that he is simply an instrument, a tool of England.

34 ꓒꓱqɯnʌ⅄ Yrae 349

No, I haven't the strength to endure more. My God! the things they are doing to me! They pour cold water on my head! They won't listen to me, they won't see me, they won't hear me. What have I done to them? Why do they torture me? What do they want of a poor creature like me? What can I give them? I have nothing. It's too much for me, I can't endure these agonies, my head is burning and everything is going around. Save me, take me away! Give me a troika and horses swift as a whirlwind! Take your seat, my driver, ring out, my bells, fly upward, my steeds, and bear me away from this world! Far away, far away, so that nothing can be seen, nothing. Yonder the sky whirls before me, a star sparkles in the distance; the forest floats by with dark trees and the moon; blue-gray mist lies stretched under my feet; a chord resounds in the mist; on one side the sea, on the other Italy; yonder the huts of Russia can be seen. Is that my home in the distance? Is it my mother sitting before the window? Mother, save your poor son! Drop a tear on his sick head! See how they torment him! Press your poor orphan to your bosom! There is nowhere in the world

---

[6] This phrase does not appear in the Academy edition of Gogol's works. Whether or not it belongs to Gogol at all is moot. (ed.)

for him! he is persecuted! Mother, have pity on your sick
child! . . .

And do you know that the Dey of Algiers has a boil just under
his nose? [7]

---

[7] This line originally read: "The French king has a boil just under his nose."
Since the word for boil in Russian, *shishka*, is a colloquialism for "trouble,"
the sentence could easily have been interpreted as an irreverent poke at
Charles X, who had abdicated in August of 1830, and it is highly probable that
Gogol was less than eager to become involved in a postrevolution imbroglio.
In its present form, the line refers to the deposal of the last Dey of Algiers,
Hussein Pasha, by the French, in 1830. (ed.)

ABOUT THE AUTHOR

NIKOLAI GOGOL was born in the province of Poltava, in southern Russia, on April 1, 1809. He was educated at the gymnasium at Niezhin, where he began writing as an adolescent. In 1828 he went to St. Petersburg, where he made an unsuccessful attempt at a career on the stage. In 1830 he published the first of the stories which subsequently appeared under the title of *Evenings on a Farm near Dikanka.* This work immediately obtained a great success. Gogol was appointed to a professorship in the University of St. Petersburg, where he taught history with no distinction and for a very short time. In 1835 he resigned and subsequently traveled to Western Europe, where he resided, especially in Rome, while working on essays, stories, and novellas. The first part of his novel *Dead Souls* appeared in 1842. In 1848 he made a pilgrimage to Jerusalem, and on his return, settled at Moscow, where he died on March 4, 1852. (See the critical-biographical introduction to this volume by Leonard J. Kent.)

ABOUT THE EDITOR

LEONARD J. KENT was born in Brooklyn, New York, in 1930. He took a bachelor's degree from Long Island University, a master's degree from New York University, and a doctorate in comparative literature from Yale University. He has taught on all levels in public and private institutions, was a professor of English and Dean of the Graduate School at California State University, in Chico, and is currently professor of English at Quinnipiac College, Hamden, Connecticut, where he also served as President from 1971 to 1977. Among other works, he has edited and revised (with Nina Berberova) the translation of *Anna Karenina*, edited and translated (with Elizabeth C. Knight) *The Selected Writings of E. T. A. Hoffmann*, written *The Subconscious in Gogol and Dostoevskij, and its Antecedents*, and authored some two dozen articles and reviews.